To Santa with Love

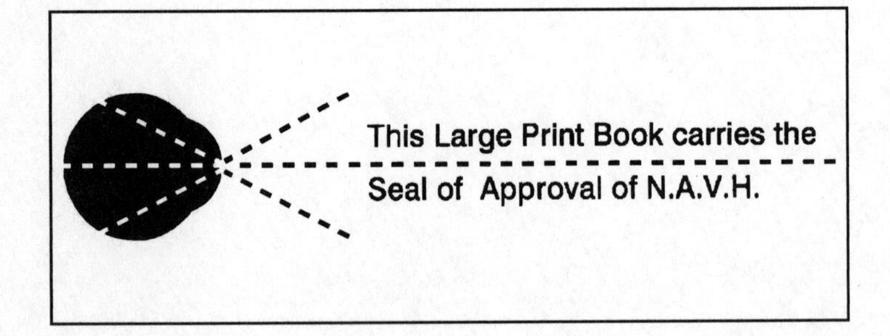
This Large Print Book carries the
Seal of Approval of N.A.V.H.

To Santa with Love

Janet Dailey

WHEELER PUBLISHING
A part of Gale, Cengage Learning

Detroit • New York • San Francisco • New Haven, Conn • Waterville, Maine • London

GALE
CENGAGE Learning™

Wheeler Publishing, a part of Gale, Cengage Learning.

Wheeler Publishing Large Print Hardcover.
The text of this Large Print edition is unabridged.
Other aspects of the book may vary from the original edition.
Set in 16 pt. Plantin.

LIBRARY OF CONGRESS CATALOGING-IN-PUBLICATION DATA

Dailey, Janet.
To Santa with love / by Janet Dailey. — Large print ed.
p. cm. — (Wheeler Publishing large print hardcover)
ISBN-13: 978-1-4104-4212-3 (hardcover)
ISBN-10: 1-4104-4212-8 (hardcover)
1. Christmas stories. 2. Large type books. I. Title.
PS3554.A29T57 2011
813'.54—dc22 2011030185

Published in 2011 by arrangement with Zebra Books, an imprint of Kensington Publishing Corp.

Printed in the United States of America
1 2 3 4 5 6 7 15 14 13 12 11

To Santa with Love

Chapter 1

After traveling westward from Dallas for what seemed like forever, the unending desert scenery had begun to bore Jacqueline Grey. The cloudless sky was bleached of blue, arching over a vast landscape of jumbled rocks and arid soil. The gnarled shrubs that survived here were more gray than green beneath the late November sun.

Jacquie raised a hand and let her gold bracelets jangle away from her wristwatch. It was almost noon. She'd gotten a late start out of Bisbee, Arizona, but considering that she hadn't gone to bed until after midnight, she figured she deserved credit for being behind the wheel and well on her way.

A wry smile curved her full lips. No one using a computer program to map out a trip from Dallas to Los Angeles would ever be routed through Bisbee, Arizona. The detour had been her idea. Her girlfriend Tammy had recently moved there with her husband.

The old mining town definitely had charm, bustling with visitors admiring its Victorian houses and climbing its hilly streets. But something about it had unsettled Jacquie. Maybe it was seeing Christmas decorations going up in the shops and boutiques — everything from strings of chili-pepper lights to a cowboy Santa with eight tiny coyotes pulling his sleigh. It just seemed too early for the seasonal displays, no matter what the calendar said. All the same, she'd been grateful for Tammy's hospitality, though she had been eager to get going again. Until she'd hit this unvarying stretch of road.

The sun glared on the asphalt ahead. A dull pain throbbed at Jacquie's temples, an unpleasant reminder of too many margaritas last night. With one hand on the steering wheel, she fumbled through her leather purse for sunglasses.

Once in place on the bridge of her nose, the lightly tinted lenses shaded her eyes, hiding their unusual turquoise-green color without concealing the curling length of her thick lashes. A raking movement of her long fingernails flipped the hair that had fallen across her cheek back over her shoulder. Sleek as cornsilk, her hair was a mix of pale gold and fine silver, an unusual but completely natural hue.

She glanced at her reflection in the rear-view mirror without really seeing it, feeling the headache begin to fade away.

Jacquie was aware of her looks without being conceited about them — since she'd hit her teens, she got noticed a lot and she didn't mind. As a child she was told often enough that she was going to grow up to be a beautiful young woman, and she still got more than her fair share of compliments, which she didn't dismiss. But she had her parents to thank for good genes, healthy habits, and an excellent dentist.

As for faults, Jacquie would readily admit to having her share of those too. For starters, she was too much her father's daughter — headstrong, independent, and proud. Secondly, she was spoiled. As an only child of relatively well-off parents, she'd been, to a certain extent, pampered and indulged. Naturally, she had a temper, a very human trait. And a few other shortcomings, just like everyone else.

Miles and miles of driving down lonely roads were making her cranky and self-absorbed, Jacquie thought irritably. The radio wasn't pulling in any stations and she'd switched it off. She'd tried singing to herself but the songs she could remember only echoed the restless mood that had bugged her for the last several months — and brought her here to southern Arizona en route to California.

When she'd finally made it to Tammy's house, she'd tried to make her road trip sound like a fabulous adventure. She'd struck out on her own for the first time, stopping only occasionally on the fifteen-hour drive from Dallas to Bisbee. The argument she'd had with her dad, Cameron Grey, before she'd left home had been laughingly related for Tammy's benefit.

But in reality it hadn't been funny at all. Remembering it, Jacquie wished she could take back some of the bitter words she'd hurled. Since she hadn't understood the reason for her restlessness, she hadn't been able to explain it to her father or, later, her mother.

Looking to the horizon for oncoming trucks on the road — there were none and no cars either — she mentally replayed the fight. Round One: her announcement that she hadn't taken her midterm exams. Without telling her parents in advance, Jacquie had filed to withdraw from all her courses, essentially putting her university education on hold. She wasn't sure she wanted to continue. She hadn't known why. But maybe, in retrospect, she'd waited a little too long to 'fess up to what she'd done.

"What do you mean?" her father had demanded, an incredulous frown wrinkling his forehead. "You only have two years before you get your degree."

"My degree in what, Dad?" Jacquie had replied somewhat cynically. "I'm a liberal arts major, which means I'm just getting an education in a little bit of everything because I don't know what I want."

"College is your best chance to figure that out," he'd retorted. "At least you're getting an education."

He just didn't want to understand. "I told you — it's not as if I'm flunking everything," she'd said heatedly. "Students in good standing are allowed to withdraw if they file in time. There's no penalty."

"Maybe so. But there are a lot of people in this world who'd love to trade places with you."

"You're so right." Jacquie had seized on her father's attempt to remind her of her good fortune. "And one of them can take my place. The university admits less than one-tenth of applicants. I'm making room for someone out there on the waiting list."

"My, my. How magnanimous of you," her father had mocked. "And just what do you plan to do instead of attending college?"

"The very same thing I would do after I graduate." She'd been on shaky ground and she'd known it, but she was unable to keep the sarcasm out of her voice. "Get a job."

Frustrated, her father ran a hand through his silver-gray hair. "Really. Good luck. Without an education, what kind of job do you think you'll get? In this economy —"

"I don't even know what kind of job I want," she interrupted him, adding quickly, "and sitting in a classroom isn't going to tell me." She'd steered clear of the subject of the economy, not wanting her dad, a devotee of financial news and online money blogs, to go off on a tangent.

"A degree is worth more than you seem to think. A lot more. Let me give you an idea of jobs that don't require one. Waitress. Sales associate. Hairdresser. Office go-fer. Housekeeper."

"Excuse me?" Jacquie hadn't liked the condescending tone of his voice. "Those happen to be honest jobs."

"I never said they weren't," he answered defensively. "But is it wrong to want something more for my daughter?"

"Like what?"

"A career," he retorted. "Do I have to spell it out?" He didn't wait for an answer, forging on. "Don't you want to find challenging work that you love? Would it be so bad if it paid well? And someday," he added, going for broke, "how about you find yourself a husband with smarts and ambition? I don't see you marrying a truck driver, if you really want to know."

"Don't be a snob," she said scornfully. "Truck drivers make pretty good money, from what I hear."

"You're not planning —"

"To drive a semi? No, Dad. But I'm keeping an open mind. Besides, you aren't paying fifty thousand a year in tuition just so I can meet Mr. Right. Believe me, he hasn't showed and besides, I want to be on my own for a while."

He'd glared at her. "What do you know about earning your own living, Jacquie? You haven't done a day's work in your life!" he snapped. "It's rare to even see you helping your mother around the house!"

That was the point when really angry words had flown back and forth. Her father's angry accusations, mostly to the effect that Jacquie was expecting a free ride, financed by him, forced her to insist on her right to live the way she wanted — and she backed it up by vowing that she wanted nothing from him. Her mother, wiser than both of them, had stayed out of it completely. Thinking of her, Jacquie felt a pang of guilt.

The fight had concluded with slammed doors and mutual antagonism. She'd known her father would simmer down eventually. Whether he would ever understand her point of view was an open question. But no matter what, she'd had to leave, if only to see if she really could make it on her own, at least for a while.

The end result of the argument: she was on her way to Los Angeles to start a whole new life. Why there? No particular reason. It'd been the first big city that came to mind when her dad demanded to know where she was going.

Before she had answered his question, he'd bitterly added that he was sure she would stay close enough to run home when the world got too rough — and just like that, Los Angeles had popped into her head. It was as far west as she could go, that was all, and not the city she would have chosen if she'd given it more thought. But once the answer was out of her mouth, Jacquie was too stubborn to be talked out of her choice.

A glance at the speedometer of her foreign economy car made her ease up on the accelerator with a rueful sigh. So far she'd gotten a speeding ticket in Texas, another in

New Mexico, and a hangover in Bisbee. Not an auspicious beginning for her whole new life.

She was still trying to ignore the niggling feeling that her dad might be right. Once out of the pleasant neighborhood she'd grown up in and heading down the highway, she had realized it would take weeks to get settled elsewhere, even temporarily, and find work. And there were other things to consider.

Like the holidays.

When she and her father had retreated to their corners, he'd seemed to assume that she'd given up or given in, but she hadn't. Jacquie startled him into speechlessness with her second announcement: she was going to get a head start on her plans by leaving home before Thanksgiving. Her mother still hadn't wanted to get between her stiff-necked husband and just-as-stubborn daughter. Maureen Grey had said with a sigh that there were a million turkeys in the world and one would now be spared, and added that there would be other Thanksgivings in the future. But Jacquie still felt bad about taking off the way she had.

Christmas was five weeks away. Even if she could land a job in California, she knew that time off wouldn't be automatic for a new hire. It looked like she wouldn't be going home for the holidays. This little rattletrap wasn't built for thousand-mile commutes and her pride wouldn't let her accept airfare from her parents.

Never in her life had Jacquie imagined a Thanksgiving without family, but by that Thursday morning, she'd arrived at Tammy's. Later in the day, the three of them had gone to a good restaurant in Bisbee for a fixed-price, home-style feast featuring chestnut stuffing, cream gravy, cranberry sauce, and a gigantic roast turkey, sliced to order, that made the rounds of the dining room on a clanking cart. Not quite like home.

But there'd been no cooking to do and no cleanup — Tammy disliked both and her husband was fine with whatever she wanted. Secretly, Jacquie found her girlfriend's solution a little depressing. She'd managed to be a good sport, but she'd learned her lesson. Spending Christmas on her own with casual pals and no family at all wasn't going to be wonderful.

Jacquie sighed. She would just have to think about how she'd handle that when the time came. Not now.

She jabbed a manicured finger at the radio buttons again, picking up a country music station playing a vaguely familiar melody. When she realized she was listening to an instrumental arrangement of a Christmas carol, she frowned and switched the radio off. She must be nearing civilization, she thought, looking for a radio or microwave tower, not seeing either. But the desert wasn't as empty as it appeared.

Before long the roofs of a small town appeared ahead of her. Jacquie had had only coffee for breakfast, her stomach not up for anything more substantial in the morning, even with her late start. She realized that the hollow, queasy feeling was linked to her persistent headache.

She felt no curiosity as to what small town it might be. Other than verifying which highway would take her into Tucson, Jacquie hadn't paid much attention to the route she'd picked out that morning on a gas station map. The car didn't have GPS, and her smartphone had chirped its last and died in Bisbee. Somewhere along the way she'd realized that the charger for it was back in Dallas and it wasn't the kind you could pick up just anywhere. Especially not in . . . she squinted at the sign that announced the town limits of Tombstone, Arizona.

Driving on, she caught her first glimpses of the place. It wasn't very big. Colorful signs done up in old-timey lettering adorned storefronts and other enterprises. The covered sidewalks made of planks provided shade for a few aimless tourists in neatly pressed chinos and fanny packs, and jeans-clad locals going about their business.

Turning the car into the driveway of a service station, Jacquie entertained an idle thought of having lunch somewhere around here, then wandering through the historic western town. It wasn't totally decked out with holiday stuff yet, though she caught a few glimpses of red and green.

She spoke to the station attendant, a young guy in coveralls, who gave her directions to the restaurants located on the main street of the town, two short blocks from the highway.

More concerned with her destination than oncoming traffic, Jacquie started to accelerate across the road. A horn blared. Her startled gaze swung toward the sound, seeing the jeep an instant before it crunched and bounced off the front side of her car. Neither vehicle had been traveling very fast, but the collision gave her a heavy-duty jolt.

Shaken but unhurt, Jacquie tried to open her car door. The glimpse just before the impact of a little blond boy sitting in the passenger seat of the jeep filled her mind with terrifying thoughts. Her door was jammed. Her frightened attempts to open it failed until a superior force from outside yanked it open.

Jacquie stared into the tanned, lean face bending toward her. The man's cheekbones and jawline could have been sculptured out of granite, relentlessly hard and grim. His mouth was thinned into a forbidding line — she couldn't see much more of his face. A dusty brown Stetson was pulled low on his forehead. The sunglasses he wore revealed only the silvery, slightly distorted reflection of her own image.

She was clutching the wheel for dear life even though the car had come to a halt, looking up at him, stunned and shocked. Not liking what she could see of herself, Jacquie turned her head away from him.

"Are you all right?" his growling voice demanded.

Her heart seemed to be lodged in her throat, choking off any words she might have wanted to speak. Jacquie was reduced to nodding numbly to let him know that she was okay. There was an ominous tightening of the man's jawline before he straightened and moved away.

On wobbly legs, Jacquie forced herself to step out of the car. Her heart raced at a crazy pace and her breathing was much too shallow — both aftereffects of the collision, she told herself unsteadily. She pressed fingertips to her temples, which were throbbing again, harder, wondering if she'd blacked out for a second or two at impact, or worse, suffered a concussion. Then she raised her head to gaze at the man standing tall in front of her.

Five foot six in socks, Jacquie wasn't short by normal standards, but the man was a lot taller than she was, easily over six foot with broad shoulders, taut abs and not an ounce of spare flesh. His hands rested on a concho belt slung through the fraying loops of well-worn jeans. She moved her gaze to the stern face.

"You didn't even look when you pulled out," the man accused her. His low voice reminded her of thunder rolling to a crescendo. "Of all the empty-headed, feather-brained —"

The rest was bit off in midsentence as a barely perceptible movement of his head indicated a shift in his attention. Jacquie glanced hesitantly over her shoulder. The little blond boy she'd glimpsed in the jeep was hobbling toward them on crutches, his right leg in a bright blue fiberglass cast decorated with stickers.

Her heart sank, until she realized that he didn't seem at all fazed. His rounded eyes were riveted on her.

"Are you really all right?" the boy asked anxiously.

Her voice returned in a sighing laugh as her mouth curved into a tremulous smile. "Yes, thank you. I mean, I'm scared out of my wits," she admitted, "but I'm not hurt."

"I thought I told you to stay in the jeep, Robbie."

The boy's eyes flickered to the man beside Jacquie, then skittered to the rocky ground near his feet, his chin tucked against his chest. "Yessir," he said.

The boy's concern was genuine and Jacquie couldn't stop herself from trying to soften his father's rather harsh attitude. The return of her voice brought a return of her poise and strength. Ignoring the man beside her, she walked the few steps to Robbie.

"How about you?" she asked gently, pushing her sunglasses on top of her silver blond head and bending toward him. "Are you okay?"

He peered at her through stubby brown lashes, his gaze locking with fascination on the long hair that swung forward over her cheeks. "Yes ma'am."

"I'm glad to hear that." Jacquie smiled.

"Your hair is pretty," he said absently.

Her eyes darted to his tousled head. "Yours is almost the same color," she pointed out.

The small, thin fingers of his right hand, the arm resting on the crook of his crutch, moved forward as if to touch the spun silver gold of her hair, but the man's voice put a stop to that.

"Wait for me at the station with the attendant, Robbie," the man ordered crisply.

The small chin lowered again. "Yessir," the boy mumbled. His hands tightened on the crutches to propel himself forward, offering a tentative smile to Jacquie. "I'm happy you didn't get hurt."

"So am I." Jacquie straightened and watched his awkward progress toward the service station.

The man's broad shoulders blocked her vision after the boy had gone farther. Oh well. She supposed the time had come to trade insurance information and contact numbers and get that hassle out of the way.

The set line of his mouth told her that he wasn't looking forward to it either. He didn't say his name or reach into the jeep for the necessary papers. She would take the initiative. Recovering some of her usual aplomb, Jacquie smiled warmly.

"I know an apology isn't enough, but I really am sorry about the accident. I'm not usually so careless," she offered.

The mirroring sunglasses prevented her from seeing his eyes, yet she couldn't shake the sensation that his gaze had just raked her curving figure, taking note of the snug fit of her jeans and the bare skin of her middle revealed by a crop top of clinging knit. Not exactly the right weather, now that she was out of her car, for such revealing clothes, but so what. She didn't care and he didn't seem to either. Not one flicker of admiration appeared on the man's carved features.

Even under the circumstances, Jacquie's female instincts kicked in and summed him up. Verdict: he was all man, the traditional type, although he probably wasn't more than ten years older than she was. Strong and silent. Evidently her apology wasn't going to be enough. He stood his ground, as though he was waiting for her to say something else. She found it vaguely irritating that he didn't seem to respond to the warmness of her smile.

"At least you recognize you were careless," he muttered, a faint curl to his upper lip.

Counting to ten, Jacquie turned away from him. It was never wise to lose your temper when you were in the wrong. "How much damage did I do to your jeep?" she asked instead.

"A dented bumper, no worse than that," the man answered, a mocking inflection in his tone. "It's made to take punishment. Can't say the same for yours."

A glance at the banged-up bumper of the jeep affirmed his words a second before he mentioned her car. Jacquie pivoted around, dismay pulling down the corners of her mouth when she saw the crumpled front end of her little car.

"The engine block could be cracked," the man muttered.

"Oh gosh. I hope not."

He gave a shrug, indicating that it wasn't his problem. His tone didn't soften when he added, "The police will be here shortly to write up a report. There were witnesses."

She looked around. The people she'd noticed on the streets were keeping their distance and trying not to stare, but it was obvious that the sound of crunching metal had gotten everyone's attention. The fender bender was probably the most excitement the town had seen for days, she thought rue-fully.

The man nodded the crown of his Stetson toward the service station. "Brad's in today.

He can give you some idea of the extent of the repair work."

"Um, what were you saying about the police?" Jacquie asked weakly, thinking with dread of the two speeding tickets she'd already received, and the citation she was about to get as the erring driver in this accident.

What with fines and the repairs to the car, her supply of cash wasn't going to be as large as she thought by the time she reached Los Angeles. And it wasn't like her father had handed over his platinum card for her to have fun with — she had a debit card for an account that he refilled to a set amount each month and that was it.

"I said they'd be here shortly," he spoke the words again with biting conciseness.

"There . . . there really isn't any need to involve them in this," she began hopefully, blinking her eyes at him and getting no outward reaction to her appeal. "I mean, after all, the damage was mostly to my car. No one was hurt, so why bother them?"

"There was an accident, the damage wasn't minor. It has to be reported." His commanding voice left no room for argument.

"I see." Jacquie nodded, pretending her previous request had been made in ignorance of the law.

At that moment, a patrol car pulled into the service station behind them. It was just as well that Jacquie hadn't argued the point.

The officer greeted Robbie's father with easy friendliness, but not by name. It bothered her that she still didn't know it. The actual questioning period was brief, due mainly to the straightforward account the tall man provided. The officer took one look at Jacquie, who could practically hear his mental assessment of her. Clueless tourist and blond to boot. He surveyed the damage and looked down at her dangling license plate.

"Texas, huh? You're a long way from home. Gotta run the number. It'll be a few minutes."

Jacquie nodded.

Her bad luck that Mr. Stetson had been involved in the accident and not some other man who might be more susceptible to her charms — Jacquie believed she could have avoided the citation for reckless driving if so. But the man's presence seemed to demand that she get what was coming to her.

Within seconds after the police form was in her hand, another was thrust at her by sun-browned fingers. Before she got a chance to read the writing scrawled on the plain paper, the man finally informed her that it was the name and address of his insurance company and asked for hers — a command phrased in a politely worded request that somehow still grated.

Rummaging through her oversized purse, Jacquie found a slip of paper and a pencil and quickly wrote down her information. He shoved it into his shirt pocket after a verifying glance at what she'd written.

"Good enough," the man said coldly, more to the officer than to Jacquie.

Without a backward glance, he strode toward the jeep where he climbed in, sliding his long legs under the wheel. She watched with simmering anger while he pulled into the nearby service station to collect Robbie, wishing that she'd given in to the sarcastic impulse to tell him it'd been nice to run into him.

From the passenger seat of the open-sided jeep, a small hand waved good-bye. Jacquie returned the gesture with a determined flourish of her arm, wondering how such a sensitive little boy could have such an insensitive father. In another second, she squelched the thought, reminding herself that her momentary carelessness had put a child, already injured, at risk. His father had every right to be angry.

With the assistance of the officer and the service station attendant, her car, no longer able to move under its own power, was towed the few yards to the garage. She heaved a sigh, trying not to think about the size of the repair bill. Or the time involved.

"How long do you think it will take?" Bracelets jingled as she tucked silken hair behind her ear, anxiously studying the mechanic's face after his initial inspection of the damage. That had taken a good half hour and he hadn't said a word during it, leaving her to fret in silence.

"Can't tell," he shrugged. "A while, I expect. Providing I can get the parts I need. That's a foreign-made car you got."

Jacquie feared the worst.

"You want me to give you an estimate before I get started fixin' it, right?" He tilted a cap back on his receding hairline and wiped the grease from his hands with a rag.

"Of course." She nodded, but she knew it was only a business formality. She really had no choice but to let him fix it, regardless of how badly it depleted her cash reserve. Glancing down at her hands, she saw the piece of paper she held and unfolded it. For a moment or two, she studied the precise handwriting and spoke the name out loud.

"Choya Barnett." A frown creased her forehead. "What kind of a name is that?"

The mechanic looked at her blankly. "What?"

"Choya." Jacquie tried again. "The man in the jeep — that's his name."

A chuckle of understanding broke through the confusion as the mechanic spoke.

"It's a cactus that grows around here. Cholla cactus. Prickly as all get out," the mechanic explained with a smile. "You don't want to mess with it."

"I got that feeling," she said with a sigh. "Is it his nickname?" She tilted her head to one side.

"No, it's his real name," he told her. "Choya Barnett got called that because old man Barnett found him in a bed of cholla when he was a baby. Barnett spelled it the way it sounded."

She wanted to laugh. Jacquie bit hard on her lower lip, reducing the impulse to a silent giggle. So he had been named for a thorny cactus — it described his attitude perfectly. Then she collected herself, taking in the interesting detail of his being abandoned as a baby. That seemed odd, more like a tall tale than anything, but the mechanic had mentioned it as though it was a plain fact. She nodded at him, not about to ask for more information. Choya Barnett wasn't someone she was going to get to know.

"If you want to go eat, miss, while I get an estimate written up, feel free," the mechanic suggested. "I'm going to have to do an online search for a few parts I need."

"Yes, I think I will," Jacquie agreed. Food would do her good — she was still a bit jumpy and probably not thinking straight.

She moved the sunglasses resting on top of her head back down onto her nose as she gathered up her purse and walked out the station door.

Crossing the highway as fast as she safely could, Jacquie paused for a moment on the opposite side, where she decided to walk in the shade, seeking relief from the blazing sun overhead. Its brilliance made her eyes hurt but it really wasn't all that warm. On Allen Street, she quickly sought the nearest restaurant, hoping it had muted lighting. It did but the place wasn't exactly quiet. A busboy was tacking foil garlands to the wall with a staple gun. *Bang. Bang.* The sound made her jump, but no one else seemed bothered by it. Welcome to the wild west, she thought wryly.

The lunch hour crowd had pretty much filled the available seats, and there was only one remaining booth and one table in the place. She decided on the booth and slid into it, accepting the menu that the busy waitress offered before walking away. Studying the specials, she paid no attention to the opening of the restaurant door until she heard the clumping sound of crutches.

A glance in the general direction of the door and she saw Robbie Barnett, a shy smile on his face. He made his way determinedly through the crowded room, heading for the empty table diagonally across from her.

"Hello," the boy said cheerfully.

"Hello again," Jacquie responded. Her wide smile made his brown eyes glow with pleasure. The look she darted behind the boy told her that Choya Barnett had been detained near the door by another customer who looked like a regular, just as he did. The hostess seemed to know both of them. She was relieved that Choya didn't seem to have noticed her. "Are you here to have lunch?"

"Yes, ma'am." Robbie looked with longing at the vacant booth seat opposite Jacquie. It was on the tip of her tongue to invite him to sit with her, but she knew it would probably infuriate his father if she did.

In silence, she let him continue on his way

to the empty table. Yet her gaze remained on the small, blond-haired boy, irresistibly drawn to him. She felt renewed guilt over the accident and something else she couldn't quite define. Misplaced maternal instinct, maybe. But why? This sweet kid had to have a loving mother and undoubtedly took after her. He wasn't at all like his dad in terms of personality.

This isn't all about you, Jacquie. You slammed into the man's jeep. You spoke to him for less than a minute. Don't judge him so harshly. The little voice in her head sounded like her own mother. Jacquie told herself to give Choya Barnett the benefit of the doubt.

Balanced on his crutches, Robbie pulled out a chair and maneuvered himself and the unwieldy cast on his right leg in front of it. The boy was small and the chair was large. He sat on the edge of the chair seat, legs dangling, looking awkward as he wriggled back.

"Wearing a cast is no fun," she said sympathetically. "But I like the bright blue."

"The doctor let me pick the color. I put the stickers on."

She looked more closely. The stickers were mostly of animals and superheroes, but someone had added *Get Well Soon* and *Big*

Hugs ones in several places. Probably his mother.

Absently, he tried to cross his legs and couldn't do it. He gave Jacquie a sheepish look and let the casted leg hang again. Rising to her feet, she crossed the short space to the table. Her fingers closed over the back of the chair next to Robbie Barnett and slid it closer to him.

"I think you would be more comfortable if we rested your leg on the seat of this chair," she suggested brightly. Maybe she shouldn't get involved, but she was concerned for him.

Helping him to slide back, she positioned the second chair to serve as a leg rest and lifted his cast onto it.

"How's that, Robbie?" she asked.

"Fine." A shy smile curved his mouth as he again peered up at her through his spiky lashes.

"My name is Jacquie," she said, bending a little to offer her hand as she introduced herself.

"That's a boy's name." He frowned while he very seriously shook her hand.

"It's short for Jacqueline," she explained.

"Like mine is long for Rob, I guess." He nodded with understanding. "I'm seven, almost."

"Oh, I'm a lot older than that. I'm twenty-one." Jacquie smiled, remaining in a slightly bent position.

"That's nothing. My dad is thirty-three," Robbie replied with a faint shrug of his small shoulders, as if that was practically ancient.

"Excuse me," a cool voice said behind Jacquie. Its low, controlled tone left her in no doubt that Choya Barnett was speaking, even before she turned. "I didn't give my son permission to eat with you."

Jacquie turned her head and straightened, bringing the full brilliance of her blue-green eyes to bear on him. He wasn't wearing the dusty Stetson and mirrored sunglasses. His dark brown hair was thick and well-groomed, framing a wide, tanned forehead.

But his eyes were a surprise. They were a strange, tawny shade with gold flecks that reminded her of a predatory animal — a big cat like a mountain lion. They were watching her now with the suggestion of coiled alertness, as if he were ready to spring without warning. An antagonistic feeling stirred within Jacquie and her chin came up as she spoke.

"We were just chatting," she said in an icily composed tone. "I was over here in the booth." She indicated it with a curt gesture.

The strong male mouth quirked at her statement. His eyes flicked downward to his son, who got busy unrolling the fork in a paper napkin on his placemat, obviously aware of his father's displeasure.

And too intimidated to talk back, Jacquie thought angrily.

"I asked Robbie to wait for me at this table by himself," he replied, his gaze holding hers. "I didn't realize you were in the booth next to it."

He was being deliberately insulting. Her blood heated to a slow boil. Jacquie sensed that he resented her inadvertent intrusion into his life and was determined that she should be aware of it. She was grateful for the country music that started up over the sound system, loud enough for Robbie not to hear her reply to his father.

"Well, I am," she murmured. "Do you mind? I don't think you own this place."

"Right on both counts," he said smoothly. "I do mind, because I intended to have a quiet lunch with my son. However, I don't own it and I guess you get to sit wherever you want." He stepped around her, dismissing her as effectively as if he had told her to get lost.

Short of standing there looking lost and snubbed, she had little choice but to return to her booth seat. Choya, a cactus, she thought to cool her growing temper. Prickly on the outside to keep anyone from coming too close. Protective of his son.

She realized that she wanted him to like her for some inexplicable reason, and felt even angrier about that.

So much for good manners, Jacquie told herself as she picked up the menu again. They were obviously wasted on Choya Barnett. He had made himself clear: she was not forgiven and he didn't trust her.

If that was the way he wanted it, then she would simply ignore him.

CHAPTER 2

Unfortunately, Choya Barnett was not a man who was easy to ignore. He exuded a presence that could be felt even when Jacquie wasn't looking at him. No matter how she tried not to let him dominate her consciousness during lunch, he did. She could feel the vibration of his low voice despite the clatter and conversation in the restaurant as he responded now and then to his son's higher-pitched talk.

And there was something else — both Barnetts looked slightly different somehow since she'd last seen them. Jacquie wasn't about to stare openly and it took her a while to figure out why. Then she finally got it. Their freshly groomed hair showed they'd both had haircuts. She started to wonder if he was waiting for his wife, but the waitress didn't bring an extra place setting. Shortly after Jacquie had been served, two blue-rimmed oval plates for father and son sailed by on a tray, each topped with a juicy hamburger and bristling with french fries. A glass of soda over ice and a glass of milk took up the rest of the tray.

"Can I get you boys anything else?" the waitress asked, setting down the plates and filled glasses.

"No thanks. We're fine with this," Choya said.

"Looks awesome!" That was Robbie.

"Enjoy your lunch." The waitress left them to it.

"Son, go easy on the ketch —" she heard Choya say, advice that was interrupted by several noisy squirts from a squeeze bottle.

"Oops." Robbie giggled.

Choya gave a low chuckle, which surprised her. Out of the corner of her eye she caught the flash of white napkins he pulled from the dispenser to deal with the mess. Jacquie picked at her grilled chicken salad, forcing herself not to glance their way too often as they ate.

Unsuccessfully.

Masculine and virile, he was handsomer than she'd thought at first. Sharing a meal with his son seemed to relax him, but he just didn't have that average-dad look, even when he was chowing down on burgers and fries. Choya Barnett was definitely intriguing. Jacquie looked around the room. She wasn't the only woman who seemed to think so.

The waitress, a plump but shapely older lady, had a ready smile for him when he asked for refills on their drinks and came right over. A few of the female customers looked on approvingly at the two of them, but Choya was focused on Robbie for the most part, looking at his surroundings only occasionally. The tawny gold eyes seemed never to reveal anything of what he was thinking. Eyes were supposed to be mirrors of the soul. Didn't he have a soul?

Jacquie chided herself for that ridiculous thought. She was well aware that she was piqued because he never, not once, looked her way. He took the waitress up on her offer of two slices of pie. Apple for him, cherry for his son.

She ordered coffee and sipped at it, thinking. When Choya made a half-turn, still seated, to signal for the check, Robbie took a chance and gave her a conspiratorial grin.

Jacquie couldn't help but smile back. But she shook her head in warning just before Choya turned around again. The Barnetts, father and son, discussed the merits of their different kinds of pie while they waited for the check.

Robbie had to take after his mother, she decided. His brown eyes were a somewhat changeable color, about all that was reminiscent of his father. Jacquie found herself wondering what kind of a woman his wife was. Choya Barnett would intimidate anyone who didn't have a will of iron.

Maybe that was why he didn't like Jacquie. She had stood up to him, even though she'd made sure his son hadn't heard her. Not that it mattered, she reminded herself, when the Barnetts finally left. She dawdled over a second cup of coffee. The waitresses didn't seem to mind, as the lunch crowd had thinned out quickly. The busboy had finished hanging the Christmas garlands and the place had quieted.

Jacquie was grateful for that. As soon as her car was repaired, she would be leaving town. She vowed silently not to spend the Tombstone-to-Tucson leg of her journey obsessing over what had happened with Choya. As far as the accident was concerned, it wasn't like it was going to be reported to her parents or anything. But she ought to touch base. She made a mental note to call them so they wouldn't worry — there had to be a pay phone somewhere in town, since hers was dead until she could buy a charger for it. Jacquie started looking in her purse for quarters. No luck. However, she did have singles. She left a couple of them for a tip under the salt shaker, then rose and went to the register.

A woman with a nameplate pinned to her blouse was taking pint-size elves out of a box and curling the toes on their red felt shoes around a pencil.

"Those little guys are cute," Jacquie offered.

The cashier beamed. "They sure are. I just love Christmas, don't you? I can hardly wait to get started on the decorations each year."

"Oh — yes. I know what you mean," Jacquie said quickly. She cleared her throat and changed the subject. "Would you mind exchanging a few dollars for quarters?"

"Sure thing, honey," the woman said, setting the elves aside. She opened the cash drawer and found a roll of quarters, cracking it open. "How many do you need?"

"I'm not sure. I guess three dollars' worth. No, make it four."

Transaction completed, she went outside, using the jingling handful of coins to reach her parents' number in Dallas. It rang six times before their voicemail picked up. To her relief. She didn't want to bawl about the accident or get into her second thoughts about her big plan or apologize again for skipping out on Thanksgiving. She settled for an upbeat message, saying only that she'd taken a side trip to Tombstone as a lark, and explaining about her phone not working. Then she promised to call again as soon as she could.

She hung up and blew out a breath. She hadn't lied, just left a few things out. Jacquie sincerely didn't want her father and mother to worry, and she really was all right.

The mechanic gave her the unpromising advice — when she returned to the station after making the call — that she should take a walk around town and see some of the sights. He informed her that for sure her car wouldn't be repaired before five that afternoon. Since it was Saturday, he warned her it was more than likely that he wouldn't be able to obtain the needed parts for at least two more days.

Jacquie refused to think about the possibility of being stuck in this town over the weekend. Who would have thought that a visit to Bisbee would have landed her in this mess with her car broken down? She should have driven straight through to Los Angeles and not stopped to see Tammy. Hindsight always was a wiser view.

Luckily there were plenty of places to visit in the old historic town, pocket-size museums with relics of the town's Wild West past and gift shops. There was an interesting old theater that had once done double duty as a bordello and a grand old saloon. There was even a barbershop with a rotating red-and-white pole in a steel support outside. The door was open and a bracing whiff of shaving soap and clean-smelling cologne drifted to her.

Remembering her father's crack about her becoming a hairdresser, Jacquie suppressed a smile and peeked in the plate-glass window, spying a middle-aged man mostly covered by a snow-white cloth. He'd just had a haircut and was getting a shave. His heavy legs were clad in faded jeans and his roping boots were propped comfortably on the adjustable footrest of the barber's chair.

She noted the Stetson hung up on a hat rack near the door. It was undoubtedly his. Belatedly, she realized that Choya and Robbie must have come in here for their haircuts. There couldn't be more than one barbershop in a town this small. And the barber was smiling jovially at her, as if he knew exactly who she was. Choya probably gave him and his customers an earful about the blonde who'd smashed into his jeep. Feeling embarrassed but not wanting to cut and run, Jacquie could swear that the barber was mentioning her name to his current client. The middle-aged cowboy turned his foamy face in her direction and gave her a wink before the razor descended. Startled, Jacquie managed a small smile and withdrew, reminding herself that she had other things to do besides explore this little town.

She considered booking a room in one of the motels just in case, but she was afraid it might be a jinx. She didn't want negative thinking to automatically keep her in Tombstone over the weekend.

So she toyed with the idea of phoning Tammy in Bisbee if the worst should occur and she had to stay until Monday or even Tuesday. But she decided against backtracking and not only because she didn't want to wear out her welcome at her girlfriend's place. Just why she wasn't sure. Maybe she subconsciously wanted the solitude of a couple of days spent alone in a relatively peaceful place. She needed to formulate more definite plans for her future.

The thought — and the sheer size — of Los Angeles seemed suddenly daunting. Even though she'd grown up in a big city, they'd lived in a neighborhood of Dallas that was essentially suburban, a half hour's drive from its gleaming new skyscrapers.

It all seemed far away now. On impulse —

and an angry impulse at that — she was headed for a huge, sprawling, fast-paced metropolis she'd never been to, where she knew no one. Jacquie had no idea of what she would do when she finally got there.

Along about four o'clock, she wandered slowly through the streets, making her way in the general direction of the service station. A cool breeze rustled through the remaining leaves of the trees in the small town park and they swayed gently, as if beckoning her to sit on one of the benches beneath them.

There was no official Christmas display in the park, but she guessed there would be one and soon. If not for tourists, Tombstone wouldn't exist.

Preoccupied by her tangled thoughts, Jacquie didn't see the small blond boy in the far section of the park. In fact, she didn't even notice him until he came toward her bench. He moved awfully fast for a kid on crutches.

"Robbie!" she said with genuine surprise. "Hello there. I didn't expect to see you again. I thought you'd probably gone home."

"Not yet. I was at the library." He shook his head, a pleased grin splitting his thin face at her immediately welcoming smile.

"My dad will be coming to get me pretty soon, though."

Just when she'd succeeded in pushing Choya Barnett to the back of her mind, his image cropped up again. She inwardly shrugged it away.

Robbie waved to a thickset man in jeans across the way whom she recognized as the customer at the barbershop. "Hi, Mr. Lewis!"

"Hey there, Robbie!" The man waved back to him and tipped his hat to her, going into the saloon. It must be nice, she thought, for a kid to grow up in a friendly little town where everybody knew everyone else — so long as you weren't a stranger there yourself and the story of the day, like her. She distracted herself from that with the thought that it was possible that the Barnetts lived elsewhere. She might as well ask.

"Where do you live? Here in Tombstone?" she asked.

"Nope. On a ranch in the Dragoon Mountains." His tongue drawled out the word *dragoon* with slight difficulty.

"I see. I guess your father had business in town today," Jacquie said thoughtfully.

Robbie nodded. "He brings me with him sometimes if it's not a school day. It's fun to see all the people. My dad says he'll take me to Tucson soon. I've never been. He has, lots of times. There's even more people there, 'specially before Christmas."

"I haven't been there myself but I'm sure you're right." Jacquie smiled at his eagerness. "So, do you like living on a ranch?"

"Most of the time it's a lot of fun," he informed her earnestly. " 'Cept now, since I broke my leg. I can't do much, so I read. I got out two books on animals." He patted the flat canvas sack hanging over his shoulder.

She was about to say that the town didn't look big enough to have a library, but caught herself in time. "Well, reading is a great way to pass the time." Another question occurred to her. "Do you have any brothers or sisters?"

"No, there's just me and Gramps and Dad," Robbie answered simply.

"And your mother, of course." Jacquie was suddenly aware that she was trying to get information out of him, but she was too curious to stop herself.

The small face suddenly became masked and uncommunicative. "No."

Jacquie hesitated, her mind racing with possibilities. If his mother wasn't around, had she separated from Choya Barnett or had they divorced? Why had she left her child?

The shuffling of the boy's crutches brought her attention swiftly back to him. His chin was downcast and his face was hidden by a shock of straight blond hair. As if feeling her gaze, Robbie Barnett slowly raised his head, giving her a long, considering look.

"My mother died when I was little," he said, putting an end to her unanswered questions. "I don't remember her."

Jacquie winced. She hadn't even thought of that possibility and she regretted being so nosy. For all the calmness of his voice, there was a touching wistfulness in his eyes. Jacquie didn't miss the underlying sadness. Instinctively, it occurred to her that it wasn't his mother's death the boy mourned as much as the fact that he didn't remember her.

Reaching out, her fingers touched the smoothness of his cheek.

"I'm sorry, Robbie," she murmured, and she meant it.

He stared at her for a long moment, not moving. When she withdrew her hand from his cheek, his gaze shifted to her fingers. Jacquie wanted to say something, to ask what was wrong, but she couldn't.

Finally Robbie broke the silence, turning his earnest brown eyes to her face. "Daddy lets me keep her picture in my room. She was really pretty."

Jacquie nodded quietly. "I'm sure she was."

"You look a lot like her. Your hair is the same color and everything," he declared fervently.

Smiling, Jacquie understood now why the boy seemed to have been drawn to her almost from the beginning. He'd seemed fascinated by her hair when he'd first seen her after the accident. So much so that his father had intervened to keep his son from touching it.

"That's a nice compliment, Robbie," she responded, "especially when you've already told me that your mother was a very pretty woman. Thank you."

His statement brought up another interesting possibility. If she did resemble his mother, could that be the reason Choya Barnett had been so abrupt with her? Some unknown tragedy had taken his wife and the mother of his only child from him, and suddenly, there was Jacquie, an unwitting, innocent, but very much alive reminder of all he'd lost. That would certainly explain his chilly attitude toward her.

Light brown brows were drawn together as Robbie studied her again. "Are you married, Jacquie?" he asked.

"No, not me," she laughed gently, glad that he'd changed the subject. "I'm not ready to be tied down yet."

"Oh. Well, are you staying in Tombstone?" He tipped his head to one side in confusion.

"Only as long as it takes to have my car fixed," she told him. Adopting a teasing western drawl, she added, "Just passin' through, pardner. Which reminds me." Jacquie glanced at her wristwatch, surprised to discover it was nearly five o'clock. "I'm supposed to be at the service station by five. It's nearly that now."

"I wish you didn't have to go," Robbie mumbled, the corners of his mouth drooping.

In a way, Jacquie wished she didn't have to go either. Then she scolded herself for being sentimental. Robbie had a dad who loved him, and a grandpa, and what seemed to be a happy life, despite the loss of his mother. His little-boy interest in her was fleeting, which was as it should be. She shouldn't let herself get emotional over him when, once her car was repaired, she would never see him again.

She quickly gathered her bag from the bench and stood up. Robbie stood in silence, watching her every motion yet not looking up into her face.

Solemnly, Jacquie offered him her hand in farewell. "Good-bye, Robbie. Your dad will be here in a little while to take you home, right?"

"Yeah. Bye," he answered gruffly, briefly touching her hand before he used his crutches to turn himself around to retreat the way he'd come.

Jacquie stared at the crestfallen figure hopping away, a ridiculous lump rising in her throat. A strong impulse took hold of her to forget about the time and her car and wait with the little boy until his father showed up.

But a few more minutes together wouldn't make the parting any easier.

Resolutely squaring her shoulders, Jacquie turned away toward the sidewalk — and drew in a sharp breath when she saw Choya Barnett standing in her way, his expression impassive. How long had he been there? Jacquie could only guess. Something inside said that it couldn't have been long or she would have sensed his presence even if she hadn't seen him.

"Hello." She spoke quickly, trying to shake

the feeling that she had been caught doing something she shouldn't.

The only acknowledgment of her greeting was a curt nod of the dusty-brimmed Stetson. The mirrorlike sunglasses were again shading his eyes, but Jacquie knew the cat-gold gaze was studying her relentlessly. He started forward, long legs carrying him with supple ease.

Jacquie turned her head in the direction that Robbie had taken, but her gaze never strayed from Choya Barnett.

"Robbie," she called smoothly, but with every nerve tensely alert, "your dad's here. I told you he wouldn't be long."

A whispering breeze stirred her hair and she brushed a hand across her cheek as if pushing away an imaginary lock of hair, taking a few seconds to find her composure. For some unknown reason, she felt she needed to explain why she'd been with Robbie.

"I was on my way to the garage to see if my car had been repaired. I stopped in the park here for a while and Robbie came over," she offered.

"Your car isn't fixed yet?" Choya had reached her side, or as close as he was going to come, stopping a good five feet from her to wait for the slower approach of his son.

"I'm hoping it is." Jacquie smiled, trying to deny the tingling sensation of unease. "But the mechanic warned me that getting the right parts was going to be a problem. Unfortunately, my car is an import and an economy model —"

"So I noticed." The expression on his face, that part that wasn't concealed by dark sunglasses, didn't register much interest in her explanation. As soon as she had finished speaking, the strong chin tilted downward toward the boy pausing in front of him, closer to Jacquie than to his father.

"Are you ready to leave, son? Gramps will probably be waiting dinner." It was hardly a question. The man had worded it as such, but it was clear he expected no other answer except agreement.

"Yes, sir." Robbie voiced the anticipated agreement, but without enthusiasm. The light brown eyes swept upward to Jacquie's face. He was clearly reluctant to leave her.

"Good-bye again, Robbie." She intended the words to sound cheerful, but they were oddly taut.

"Ah — not just yet." Choya Barnett's voice was brisk to the point of sharpness, cutting away the vague sense of intimacy that Robbie's yearning gaze had enveloped her in. Her gaze swung to his father's carved features, imposingly rugged and powerful. "The garage is on the way to my ranch. Catch a ride with us."

She was taken aback. The distance to the garage was a little over two blocks. Choya's command — it certainly wasn't an invitation — didn't seem to make much sense until she noticed the beaming smile of gratitude and adoration that Robbie gave his father.

The man's heart wasn't totally made of stone, she decided. Not if he was willing to put up with her obviously unwelcome company for two whole blocks in order to please his son. And she had to admit, if reluctantly, that everyone in town seemed to know him and like him.

A speculating light entered her eyes. "That's thoughtful of you. Thanks." She wondered why that sardonic line had tilted the firm male mouth. He might be a friend to all, but she couldn't get him to smile at her, not even once.

"My jeep is parked at the curb," he said.

Falling into step with Robbie, Jacquie followed the wide shoulders of Choya Barnett to the street, his long strides leading the way.

There was a suggestion of impatience in his pace, as if he'd had second thoughts about giving in. Well, too bad. He had offered and she certainly hadn't asked for a lift, because she didn't need one.

But here you are, about to get in. Jacquie dismissed the little voice as Choya paused beside the passenger side of the jeep, glancing inside.

He turned to watch their progress through the concealing lenses of his sunglasses. "The back is filled with stuff and it's dusty," he stated crisply. "The two of you should be able to share the front seat well enough. It's not a very long trip."

"I'm sure we can," Jacquie agreed, glancing down at the boy hesitating beside her.

"Hand me your crutches, Robbie." Choya reached out for the first crutch, shifting it to his other hand while he waited for Robbie to balance himself against the jeep before giving up the second. With the crutches stowed in back, Choya picked up his son, carefully lifting him onto the front seat. As Jacquie moved to join Robbie, a strong hand took her elbow and gave her a boost onto the shared seat.

Her thanks for his help was spoken into empty air and cut off by the slammed door.

"It doesn't close good unless you slam it,"

Robbie explained. Jacquie wasn't so sure of that, watching Choya walk around the front bumper without looking at either of them. She pulled out the seat belt on her side and put it around herself and the boy.

With an economy of movement, Choya opened the driver's side door and swung himself behind the wheel, long legs smoothly fitting in the confined area. He turned the key in the ignition and they were driving away.

His face seemed even more masculine in profile. He looked straight ahead, concentrating on his driving. Feeling ignored, Jacquie turned her attention to the child nestled against her shoulder. His expression was one of complete contentment.

"You never did tell me how you broke your leg, Robbie," she said as the increasing speed of the jeep tangled her cornsilk hair around her face. She couldn't see the window button, if there was one. She felt around for something to roll up the window and gave up. It seemed more important to hold on to Robbie.

"I got bucked off a bull." His mouth twisted into a reluctant grimace, followed by a self-conscious glance at his father.

"A bull?" Jacquie repeated in disbelief.

"I'm going to ride in the rodeo when I

grow up," he informed her importantly. "Gramps said you should start learning when you're young."

A frown furrowed her forehead as she studied the blond head tucked under her own. "You don't mean you actually tried to ride a full-grown bull?"

"Robbie." The male voice was low and carried a vague warning in its tone, although Choya's attention didn't leave the road.

There was an instant of silence. Then small shoulders moved in an eloquent shrug. "Well, it was really a bull calf," Robbie admitted. "I'm not big enough to ride a real bull yet."

"I should hope not!" Jacquie laughed. Then she glanced curiously at the driver. "Do you ride in the rodeo?" she asked Choya.

"No," he replied with no further elaboration. He didn't seem to want to make small talk.

"I see," she responded, refusing to give up. "I thought maybe Robbie was copying you — like father, like son."

"It was entirely his idea." This time the strong jaw turned, tilting downward toward the boy. "Wasn't it, Robbie?"

"Yes, sir," Robbie murmured guiltily. "And I won't try it again unless you or

Gramps are there."

That revealing statement completed the sketchy description of the accident for Jacquie. She'd wondered right away why Choya Barnett had been so determined not to allow the boy to brag about his injury. Robbie was too young to realize the danger in his obviously unsupervised attempt to ride a calf. The broken leg hadn't seemed to instill any sense of caution either, she decided thoughtfully.

The jeep was slowed and turned into the driveway of the service station where the car had been left. The mechanic was standing in the open arch of the overhead garage doors. He walked forward at the jeep's approach.

"Hey, Choya. Miss Grey, I'm really sorry," he said before Jacquie could slip from the passenger seat, "but I wasn't able to get those parts I needed from Tucson. I can't have your car repaired now — but I might could sometime before Monday afternoon. Can't promise that for sure, though."

"Oh, no!" Even though he'd warned her of the likely outcome, her grumbling protest came automatically in a sigh.

"I'm sorry," the mechanic repeated with a philosophical smile.

"I understand. It's not your fault." She

frowned not at him but out at the highway where she noticed a motel in the near distance. "I'll just have to find somewhere to spend the night, that's all."

"There are a couple of nice places right in Tombstone. That motel down the road still has a vacancy sign," the man behind the wheel suggested.

It didn't really matter where she ended up, Jacquie decided. "That'll do, then. Thanks for the lift, Mr. Barnett," she said as she stepped out of the jeep.

"Jacquie —" Robbie began eagerly.

But his father interrupted whatever it was his son was going to say. "If you want to get your things from your car, I'll take you on to the motel."

The offer surprised her, more so than the lift to the garage. Her eyebrows raised just a fraction before she nodded a yes.

"Thank you. I appreciate that."

Her car was parked inside the garage's service bay, well within view of the jeep outside. As she gathered her overnight bag and cosmetic case from the rear of her car, Jacquie glimpsed the somewhat intense discussion going on between father and son. Judging by the faintly sulky expression on Robbie's face when she returned, the conclusion hadn't been in his favor.

"Do you have everything you need?" Choya inquired, but his tone was indifferent.

"Yes, thank you." Jacquie nodded, feeling somehow that she shouldn't have accepted his offer.

The man was a definite puzzle, offering her two rides when he so obviously wanted to be rid of her. There was little doubt that she'd been the subject under discussion. Why, she didn't know.

If Choya Barnett wanted to separate her from his son, then why was he prolonging the time she spent with them? Or had the offer been a means of interrupting Robbie before he said something his father wouldn't approve of? That seemed likely.

Sliding onto the seat with Robbie, Jacquie balanced her bags on her lap, taking care they didn't bump the cast on his leg as Choya Barnett shifted the jeep into forward gear. A covert sideways glance studied the carved profile, the lean angular jaw and the firm mouth. He was good at keeping his emotions, if he had any, out of his expression.

Jacquie smiled wryly to herself. *Face it. You're fascinated with the man. He's unlike anyone you've ever met and you'd like to know what makes him tick.* The very fact that he wasn't overwhelmed by her looks made him all the more intriguing. It would be less than honest not to admit she found him something of a challenge.

When Choya stopped the jeep in front of the motel, Jacquie fully expected him to let her out and leave immediately. Before she could thank him again, he was switching off the engine and swinging his long legs out to walk around to her side. Her eyes widened, watching him. He glanced at her, undoubtedly guessing that she was surprised.

Nothing in his face told her anything. The impassive features made it impossible for her to determine whether he was doing it out of politeness or a desire to make sure he was definitely rid of her.

He took the overnight bag from her. "I'll carry this in for you," he stated in a tone that didn't allow any argument. "Robbie, move over a bit."

Jacquie straightened away from the boy's warm little body and gave Choya the bag, easing her feet to the ground to stand beside him. Curiosity overpowered her as she stared into the blankness of his sunglasses.

"Why are you doing this?"

"Doing what?" His head drew back slightly, arrogance in the set of his jaw. He seemed surprised himself, but only because his action had been questioned. "I'm merely trying to be hospitable to a stranger who's found herself stranded in our town."

"Really?" The single word was edged with doubt.

"What other reason would I have?" He stepped to the side, indicating the tinted-glass walls of the motel's front office with a nod and gesturing for her to precede him.

"I'm not sure," she murmured as she started toward the door.

He ignored that. "Robbie, stay here where Mrs. Chase can see you," he said to his son. "You can listen to the radio if you want. I'll be right back."

Inside the motel office, Choya introduced her to the owner. Mrs. Chase was a motherly woman and very friendly, who greeted Choya with genuine warmth. It was obvious that they'd known each other forever — she seemed to be more to him than another member of his unofficial fan club, Jacquie thought. And the same was true for Robbie. Mrs. Chase waved through the glass at the little boy in the jeep, peering at him through a wreath of faded artificial greenery trimmed with red lights. Robbie beeped the horn once in reply and grinned at her.

"Can't he come in and have a lollipop?" she asked his father.

"If you're not too busy, it's all right with me," Choya replied.

"Of course I'm not," she said indignantly. "Go tell him to get in here and keep me company."

"In a minute." His father explained the circumstances leading to Jacquie's need for a room, but omitted the fact that he'd been involved in the accident. The woman showed no surprise whatever that Choya Barnett had assigned himself the task of finding Jacquie accommodation for the weekend.

While he was outside again helping his son from the jeep, she got through the obligatory business of showing her ID and paying for the room with her debit card, silently thanking her father for that. Mrs. Chase asked the usual questions and Jacquie answered politely, not really minding the older woman's curiosity about her. The debit card payment went through and she accepted the keycard to her motel room. She turned to watch Robbie scoot by his father, who held the door for him, and then past her.

Having already been snubbed once for asking Choya the reason for his seeming solicitude, Jacquie didn't risk it again as she walked through the open door in the opposite direction.

"Be right there," she heard him call after her. She heard the front office door close and open once more, but didn't turn around until she realized the next sounds — thunks and scuffles — were made by Robbie. She looked over her shoulder to see him clamber into the jeep again, a lollipop in his mouth.

Apparently Choya and Mrs. Chase had a few things to talk about. She kept on walking to the open staircase at the end, sitting down about halfway up it, letting her mind wander as she waited for him, not wanting to enter her room just yet. The staircase was sheltered and warmer than the breezeway.

Mrs. Chase peered through the wreath again, first to check on Robbie, and then, craning her neck, looking in Jacquie's direction.

"No need to fill me in. I already heard the whole story about how you and that young lady ran into each other. Brad's mother is quite the chatterbox," she laughed, turning to Choya.

"Strictly speaking, the young lady ran into me," he pointed out.

"Oh, a few dents and dings won't show on that old jeep of yours. Weren't you planning to buy a new car anyway? High time

you did."

"If you say so." Choya waved to his son when he heard him beep. "And thank you for not asking that question in front of Robbie. You two always gang up on me."

"Do we?" Mrs. Chase asked innocently.

"Lulu, you know damn well you do." There was a smile on Choya's face. "But I don't mind. And you're right about the jeep not looking any worse than it usually does. Her car was damn near totaled. She was all right, though, once she got her breath back."

"I'm glad no one was hurt. Jacquie Grey seems like a lovely girl."

Choya inclined his head in agreement with that. He kept his gaze on Mrs. Chase, as though he were anticipating her next words.

"So, have you had a chance to talk to her? Not about the accident — I mean *personal* conversation." She emphasized the next-to-last word with a smile.

He blinked. "Nope."

Mrs. Chase flipped through some paperwork as if she hadn't even heard his response. "You should. She's smart too — a university student."

"Did she tell you that?"

"I saw her college ID next to her driver's license when she signed in. I used to have a friend on the street where she lives in

Dallas, though Louise moved away years ago. But I remembered the name of the street. It's a very pleasant neighborhood. I'm sure she comes from a nice family."

"Are you matchmaking, Lulu?"

Mrs. Chase slid the papers she'd been pretending to peruse into a folder and put it into a drawer. "Who, me? She just seems so sweet. I also heard that Robbie's taken quite a shine to her."

"The town grapevine never quits, does it?" Choya thrust his hands into the pockets of his jeans. "Yes, he has. I'm not sure that's a good thing."

"Well, I'm not surprised that he likes her," the older woman said reassuringly. "He's a very affectionate kid."

"True enough."

Mrs. Chase studied his closed expression for a moment. "Think of it as a point in her favor, Choya."

"In a way I guess it is," he admitted. "But she's only passing through. That's what she told Robbie."

"Hmm." Mrs. Chase shrugged delicately. "The way she looks at you makes me think you could persuade her to stay if you wanted to. At least for a little while," she amended.

"You're wrong about that. She doesn't

much like me." He avoided her inquiring gaze. He'd known Lulu Chase all his life, but he wasn't going to share every detail of his encounter with Jacqueline Grey.

"She's still shook up from that accident. Give her a chance to calm down and rest."

"That's exactly what I'm doing," he pointed out. "And after that she'll most likely be on her way. It'll be good-bye and good luck."

"You can do better than that," the older woman chided him.

"I don't want to."

Mrs. Chase put her hands on her hips and fixed him with a stern look. "Are you really going to pass up a golden opportunity like this? You two ran into each other for a reason. The universe is sending you a sign."

He grinned at her. "And an insurance adjuster."

"Be serious. You certainly don't seem interested in anyone from around here. Choya, take it from me — you've been alone too long."

He scowled, looking at his faint reflection in the window glass and not at his interrogator. Then he sighed and said in a low voice, "Maybe so. I've been busy. What with taking care of the ranch and Robbie, and my dad getting on in years, I have my hands full."

"He's such a good boy," Mrs. Chase said thoughtfully. "You and Sam have done a fine job raising him. But it would be nice if —"

"Not going to happen." Choya shook his head firmly. "Not with her."

"Why not?"

He searched his mind for a solid reason that would satisfy Mrs. Chase and came up with a sketchy one. "She doesn't look where she's going, for one thing. And furthermore —"

"Choya! Anybody can have an accident and that jeep of yours is irrefutable proof."

He gave her a half smile, beginning to enjoy the verbal sparring match. "And isn't that all the more reason I need a woman with a good head on her shoulders? When I get around to dating again, I'll let you know. It's not a priority."

"Oh, please," Mrs. Chase scoffed. "You sound older than Sam sometimes. How can you let a girl like that get away?"

Choya gave a slight cough. "What do you want me to do, hold her prisoner? I will admit I like looking at Jacquie Grey but I don't need any more aggravation in my life."

"You're awfully judgmental. I have half a

mind to fix you up with my cousin's niece. Bertha is as sensible as they come and not too much older than you —"

He held up a hand to stop her from saying more. "Thanks but no thanks."

"But — well, you know best, Choya." Mrs. Chase gave a resigned shrug and peered out the window again. "Look at her, sitting on the stairs waiting for you. She's alone too." She shook her head sadly. "What a shame."

Choya only shrugged, to her evident dismay.

Mrs. Chase fixed him with a steely look. "You can't just drop her off here and head back to the ranch. Do the right thing in every situation. I always told you that," Mrs. Chase said firmly.

"And I always tried to live up to it. But this situation is — kind of sudden. I'm doing what I can."

"Hm. We'll see about that. First things first: you stay on Brad about fixing that car. Once he gets to tinkering with those old engines, he forgets everything else."

"Yes, ma'am."

"Okay, go holler at Robbie to get back in here," she sighed. "And when you get back home, tell Sam I said hello, y'hear?"

"I will." Choya pushed the door open and gestured to Robbie to come inside again.

His son didn't need any persuading. The door of the jeep swung open and the little boy half-swung, half-scooted back toward the motel's front office, an old Ranger Rick magazine curled around the side bar of one crutch.

"I gotta show this to Mrs. Chase," he said to his father. "It has a picture of baby armadillos!"

"You do that. Sorry, Jacquie," Choya called to her. "I'm coming."

Jacquie stretched and stood up, feeling a little stiff from sitting on the concrete stairs. She looked Choya's way to make sure he hadn't forgotten her overnight bag. The sunglasses had been removed in the relative dimness of the front office after the glare of outside and were tucked in his shirt pocket. But the tawny cat eyes told her no more of the reason he'd stopped to talk to the motel owner than his expression did.

She assumed they'd known each other for years, like everyone else in Tombstone. Absently, she wondered how long a person had to live here to not be thought of as an outsider. Decades, most likely.

Unlocking the motel room door, she swung it open to let him enter first. Without a word he stepped by her into the room, flicking on the switch for the overhead light and setting her bag in an armchair. Jacquie started to follow him into the room. She bent her head to hide the smile that swept across her face as she suddenly wondered what he would do if she handed him a tip for carrying the bag. He wouldn't find it amusing, that was for sure.

The open toe of her sandal hooked the edge of the throw rug inside the door. She was thrown forward, handbag and cosmetic bag dropped as her arms reached out to break her fall.

But the expected sprawl onto the floor never happened. With the reflex action of someone accustomed to reacting swiftly, Choya Barnett stepped forward, catching her before she ended up in a heap. One minute Jacquie was falling forward and in the next an iron band was around her waist, abruptly checking her movement and drawing her upright in one motion. He held her as if she weighed nothing, easily but with strength.

"Oof!" Gasping her surprise at the tumble she hadn't taken, she felt her heart start beating again. Her hands were resting weakly against a hard wall. With difficulty she focused her eyes on it and discovered the white collar of his shirt opened at the throat to reveal the deep tan of his chest. Then she became aware of the powerful arms that held her. She liked the feeling. She liked it a lot.

Tipping back her head, pale gold hair cascading over her shoulders, she gazed into the rugged face only inches from her own. The amber flame in his eyes seemed to catch at her breath as it burned over her features. The impulse to kiss him was too strong to resist.

Willingly, she let her lips move closer to his. She could have sworn she felt him tremble under her hands for a fraction of a second — but that couldn't be. When their bodies met, he was hard all over, tense and ready. His head dipped toward her in response to her invitation and the fiery warmth of his mouth closed over hers, about to deepen the unexpected kiss. But before another second passed, she was thrust away and held firmly at arm's length before she was released completely from his touch.

Her lips were still parted in anticipation of the scorching kiss that had been doused before it had ignited. She blinked in disbelief at the unemotional gold-flecked eyes that gazed at her so coolly now — and asked him a question that was meant to be just as cold.

"You aren't as indifferent to me as you'd like to pretend, are you?" Her voice was low and breathless.

"I'm a man," he stated as if at this moment she had any doubt about it. "You got a little too close. I don't think you meant to, but it happened. Physical reaction. Couldn't help it."

"That wasn't what I meant, Choya."

He dismissed that with a shake of his head. "I don't have any ulterior motives, if that's what you're getting at. Just trying to do the right thing."

"Really? Is that all?"

"Yes," he said dryly. "But I promise not to make that mistake again."

She shook her head, unable to understand what she was hearing. "Why . . . why don't you like me? What have I done?" She raised a hand to her forehead, fingers nervously smoothing the hair away from her face. "It can't be because of the accident. Your jeep barely got scratched but I may not even be able to pay for my car —"

His mouth thinned with amusement. "It wasn't the accident," Choya Barnett said quietly. "Do you really want to know?"

"Yes."

"My guess, Jacquie, is that you have a talent for trouble. And I mean trouble with a capital T. I don't know what to do with you."

"What — what kind of an answer is that?" Indignation made color rise into her face. Was he joking? She couldn't be sure. Bewildered and even more annoyed, she wondered why she'd been willing to give him the benefit of the doubt for one single second. "I really don't see why you bothered to give me a ride to the garage and brought me to the motel," she demanded, faint anger growing that she should be so unjustly labeled. "Next question. Why did I say yes?"

"You tell me. But when I sense trouble, I keep it where I can see it. Does that make sense to you?" A dark eyebrow arched in inquiry.

Jacquie averted her head. "Not really. I'm not sure who you think you are, Choya Barnett. I hope you understand if I don't thank you for all you've done," she snapped.

She was losing her temper, and fast. Invariably when she became angrily emotional, tears would start to fall. She wanted Choya Barnett gone before she lost control of her temper.

"I do understand," he replied with dry cynicism.

Her hands doubled into fists as the motel door closed behind him. She picked up the cosmetic bag and handbag she had tossed onto the floor before her near-fall, and in a fit of rage, hurled them onto the bed, wishing she'd thrown them at him instead. How he must be laughing at the way she'd invited him to kiss her. She had never been rejected like that in all her life. Trouble! He didn't know the meaning of the word!

A few hours later, Choya stopped by the service station to check on Jacquie's car.

"Hey, Brad."

The mechanic looked up from the engine he'd hauled out of an old car to rebuild and waved a wrench at him, his hands too greasy to offer one to shake. "Hi, Choya — what's up? Did you get Miss Grey settled at the motel?"

"Yup." Choya looked around the garage nonchalantly, spotting her badly damaged car in a dark corner.

"Good thing there was a vacancy," Brad said. "The parts place in Tucson just called me back. Nothing's going to get there until Tuesday and I told her Monday."

"Can you give me an idea of the cost?"

The mechanic set down the wrench and scrubbed up with gooey soap at a blackened sink. "Did your insurance guy ask for details?"

"Uh, yeah."

"Let me check my notes." He whistled as he finished up at the sink. "I was kinda surprised to see you drive up with her this afternoon. You two on speaking terms now?"

Choya gave a low chuckle. "You could say that. She's really something."

"That's for sure. Hell of a way to meet, though. But if you ask me, I'd say a fender bender is easier than online dating."

Choya showed only mild interest. "Never tried that. Guess you have."

Brad rolled his eyes. "Count yourself lucky. It's crazy. But here's a hot tip. Don't say you work in a garage. They tag you with an invisible sticker that says Grease Monkey."

"Yeah? What should I say? Not that I'm going to go online."

The mechanic dried his hands with a clean rag. "You have to say what women want to hear. Give them the idea that you got it goin' on. You could mention that you're a rancher with a five-thousand acre spread, but don't act like you never go into town. Put in that you love to dance and stuff like that, and post a recent photo — stand tall and smile for real. Say that you're looking for a real lady and you want to treat her right."

"Got it. But I learned to dance from a

book. You know, with diagrams. Tripped over my own feet and pretty much gave up." Choya laughed again.

"Same here." Brad went over to a three-ring binder on the shop counter, flipping the pages until he got to the estimate for Jacquie's car. "Okay, like I said, I told her maybe Monday but it's going to be Tuesday."

"Can you make it longer?" Choya asked.

"Huh? I can't do that, Choya."

Choya laughed. "Yeah, I know. I was kidding. So how much is it going to be?" He took a piece of scrap paper and a stubby pencil from a box to jot down Brad's response.

The mechanic read the itemized estimate aloud line by line. "Got all that?"

"Yes. Thanks." Choya folded the paper and tucked it in his shirt pocket. Brad didn't have to know that he was thinking of paying Jacquie's repair bill just in case her insurance company didn't respond promptly. Choya wasn't sure if it was because he felt a gentlemanly obligation to help her or a self-protective instinct to get her the hell on her way to wherever she'd been going. Probably a little of both.

Chapter 3

The sharp rocks seemed to penetrate the thin soles of her sandals, jabbing the sensitive bottoms of her feet until Jacquie was reduced to picking her way alongside of the road. Although it wasn't yet midmorning, the sun was already beginning to make its strength felt.

When she had started out a few minutes before, it had seemed logical to walk the short distance to the famous cemetery just outside of town. She'd read about it in the stack of brochures on the night table — it was something to do and none of its inhabitants was going to bother her with small talk. But not daring to walk on the busy highway, Jacquie had been forced to walk on the uneven gravel of the road's shoulder. After the first few jagged edges of the sharp gravel had dug into her soles, she kept her attention on the ground. A horn blared behind her, signaling an approaching vehicle.

"Oh, knock it off!" she grumbled, exclaiming sharply as she hopped away, nearly turning her ankle on an oversized chunk of stone.

But the vehicle that honked didn't whizz by as others had done. Instead it pulled to a stop beside her. The cutting words that had been forming to check any proposition from a stranger died in her throat as Jacquie recognized the jeep beside her and the man driving it.

"Good morning, Miss Grey. Are you leaving town?" Choya Barnett inquired mockingly. He wasn't wearing sunglasses and the lazy, tawny-colored eyes seemed to find her discomfort amusing.

"Not on foot," she retorted. She hadn't slept well last night, tossing and turning until well after midnight, and she blamed her sleeplessness more on the man she faced now than on the fact she had been trying to sleep in a cheap motel bed. "What are you doing in town this morning? Checking to see where 'trouble' was?" Her voice was sarcastic.

He ignored that. "If you intend to walk far, you really should have more substantial shoes, not those paper-thin pieces of leather."

"Thanks for the advice. I just came to the

same conclusion, but I didn't happen to pack hiking boots. Go away." Jacquie started walking again, determined to treat Choya the way he'd treated her.

"Maybe you should ask Santa for a pair for Christmas." The jeep rolled slowly along, keeping pace with her.

"I was planning to ask him for cash," she retorted. "It goes with everything, you know."

"Oh, shut up and get in," he requested with an impatient sigh when she grimaced unwillingly at the rocks beneath her feet.

"No," she snapped.

"I said get in," Choya Barnett said again. "You might as well. A few yards down the road you'll probably end up with a twisted ankle or cut foot and you'll have to accept the offer anyway. Get in now and save yourself some pain. Besides, I'm driving in your direction."

She'd heard those words before. Twice. And taken him up on both offers, which she deeply regretted. Jacquie came to a dead stop. "You don't even know where I'm going," she accused.

"There's only one place you could possibly be going," he replied with thinning patience.

"Oh?" Her hands slipped challengingly to

her hips. “And what is that?”

“Boothill Cemetery. Every tourist goes there.”

He sounded so insufferably certain that Jacquie hated to admit he was right. The problem was, looking down the road, there was no alternative destination she could point to except rocks and shrubs. Which were probably infested with snakes and scorpions and other critters almost as obnoxious as he was. She couldn’t very well go off the road to prove him wrong.

“You don’t expect me to think you’re merely walking for exercise, do you?” Choya asked pleasantly.

“Just because you made a good guess,” Jacquie muttered, “you don’t have to be so smug when you happen to be right.”

“Then stop arguing and get in.” The clipped order was followed by a single word she’d never heard from him. “Please,” he added.

If it hadn’t been for that — and mean little rocks biting through the soles of her sandals — she would have refused. Quite truthfully, she wanted the ride even if she questioned his motives for offering it.

“Where’s Robbie?” she asked coldly as she made her way across the gravel to slide onto the passenger seat of the open jeep. In the short time she'd known him, she'd gotten used to seeing father and son together. It seemed odd to see Choya alone. "Did you leave him home today?"

Gold eyes bored into her for an instant before the jeep surged forward onto the highway. "Actually, he happens to be in Sunday school."

Jacquie stared straight ahead. "Did you ever go?"

He waited for a beat before he responded. "You mean when I was a kid? Sometimes. Why do you want to know?"

"Just wondering. You seem to follow your own rules and no one else's."

He only grinned in reply, which irked her to no end.

"Let me rephrase that, Choya," she said crossly. "You make up your rules as you go along and change them whenever you want to."

Her remark was barbed, but her basic opinion of the man hadn't really changed. It was just too bad that she still found him incredibly attractive, even after his refusal to follow through on what had promised to be a spectacular kiss. And she still didn't understand why he'd stopped.

With a flash of insight, Jacquie figured out the key to his attraction — and her own weakness. Choya Barnett was flagrantly male, more virile and masculine than anyone she had ever dated in college. His body radiated it from head to toe. Or, she thought miserably, toe to head. Those long, muscular legs, for starters. Lean abs. Solid chest and massive shoulders. Dark good looks and great hair she was dying to get her fingers into. And — damn it — those eyes. Mountain cat eyes. Aloof. Spellbinding. Revealing nothing.

"I usually had other things I wanted to do," Choya stated. "Even when I was a kid."

Jacquie looked at him blankly, so lost in her contemplation of him that she had forgotten her previous comment. When his gaze swung back to her, she felt the force of his male vitality.

"What?" She fought against the electrifying sensation that raced through her veins.

"I said," he repeated dryly, "that I usually had other things to do besides go to church. And I still do."

The indifference in his look cut her. It was easy to return a caustic reply when his brief glance swept over her and back to the road.

"Very important things like keeping track of my whereabouts." The cool toss of her head was at odds with the green-blue glitter of battle in her eyes.

The jeep slowed and bounced into the graveled parking lot, stopping in front of the stick fence protecting the cemetery. Weathered markers were visible beyond it. Against the skyline were rising mountains, barren and grim. At their base were undulating plains of sand and sage and cactus.

Without a thank-you or good-bye, Jacquie slid out of the passenger seat, wincing as her thin soles pressed into sharp gravel again. There was a fine film of dust on her light-colored jeans. She slapped it off, wishing perversely it was Choya's face she was hitting instead of her legs. Refusing to look at the jeep, she stalked toward the gift shop that housed the entrance to the cemetery.

"Just so you know, one of the things I wanted to do today," Choya's low voice came from directly behind her, stopping her short, "was talk to you."

Pivoting, Jacquie tilted her head to challenge him. "I can't think of a thing you could possibly want to discuss with me. I know you don't intend to apologize for your rudeness yesterday." But there was a questioning lift to her voice on the last statement.

"No, I'm not going to apologize," he answered smoothly.

Her lips tightened and she spun toward

the door. "Then we don't have anything to talk about."

Remote as the possibility of him apologizing had been, she'd felt compelled to ask. Now, if he had said he was sorry . . . well, she didn't know. She had no idea of what she should do. The man was an enigma and impossible to pin down. Thinking how likely she was to surrender to his next move, whatever it might be, made her uneasy.

The gift-shop door she yanked open wouldn't slam shut. It was held by his strong hand. She might not want to hear what Choya Barnett wanted to say to her, but he was definitely following her with the intention that she should.

In the shop, she stopped, searching impatiently for the exit door to the cemetery. His hand took hold of her elbow and guided her to the right.

"This way," he told her calmly.

Aware of the interested looks from the clerk, who greeted Choya by his first name, and the handful of tourists pretending to examine knickknacks, they made their way to the exit door, Jacquie tried to ease the look of displeasure from her face. Outside, they walked several paces before his hand fell away.

Taking deep, relaxing breaths, Jacquie

resolved to stay as composed and controlled as he was — and as blasé about his presence as he was to hers. At a strolling pace, she started wandering among the tombstone markers, the wind-and-sand-smoothed rocks making an uneven path for her feet. Sage and cactus and twisting, gnarled bushes grew rampant in the graveyard, nearly obscuring some markers.

The emptiness surrounding the rocky hill where the remains of western frontiersmen lay was overwhelming. It was barren country, virtually unmarked by the passage of time and civilization. In this lonely land, it was easy to believe the legends of Apache warrior ghosts, hidden in the distant mountains that rose into the blue sky.

Shielding her eyes with a hand against the climbing angle of the morning sun, Jacquie studied the mountain-crested horizon. Choya Barnett was standing behind her and slightly to her right. An inner radar seemed to pinpoint his location when her peripheral vision failed to see him.

"Those are the Dragoon Mountains," he informed her, obviously following the direction of her gaze.

"That's where your ranch is, isn't it?" Her gaze ran the length of the mountains, her interest increased in spite of a silent effort to deny it.

"Robbie told you?"

"Yes." Jacquie glanced over her shoulder to bring the impassive face into her line of vision. His measured look was difficult to hold. She turned the rest of the way around, pretending an interest in a plain wooden cross at the head of a rocky grave. "He didn't say much. What of it?"

"It's Robbie I wanted to talk to you about."

"Oh?" She darted him a cautious look. "What about him?"

"He's going to be spending time in town this afternoon. Tombstone is too small for the two of you not to meet sometime."

"And?" Jacquie prodded, feeling her irritation beginning to build.

"I have to be blunt. And I'm not going to apologize for that either. I would prefer that you don't encourage him to become more friendly," he stated.

"What am I supposed to do?" she asked him icily. "Tell him to get lost?"

"I'm sure someone like you can get a kid to leave you alone without breaking his heart."

She heard multiple accusations in his words. Where to begin? Should she even respond? He'd fallen silent.

"Someone like me?" Jacquie said at last. "What's that supposed to mean?"

"You're a beautiful girl and that alone gets you more attention than you know what to do with." He held up a hand when she began to protest. "Don't argue the point." There was a definite edge to his low voice. "So you've undoubtedly had plenty of experience telling admirers to get lost. A little boy should be easy to handle."

"I like Robbie. And he's not an 'admirer.' He's a friendly, openhearted kid who likes a lot of people." Troubled, she moved on to the next rock-mounded grave. What a place to have a conversation like this. "And you don't." She couldn't resist the jab. "You especially don't like me."

"That's neither here nor there." His jaw tightened. "Listen to me, Jacquie. My son sometimes forms intense attachments to people and he expects them to feel the same way. When it's someone like Mrs. Chase or Edwina —"

"Who on earth is Edwina?" she asked, puzzled.

"She's a waitress at the restaurant where we all ate."

"Oh. The one in the pink uniform who brought your food?" Jacquie remembered her now.

"That's her. He's known and loved both of them since he was a baby."

"Mrs. Chase seemed very nice," she said acidly. "And so did Edwina. They both certainly seem to think the world of you too."

"Yeah, well — that's neither here nor there. They're friends of the family and they live around here and probably always will. But you're just passing through" — he hesitated — "at least I think you are. You haven't said."

"Correct. Good guess. Like you care one way or the other."

"Never mind that. Robbie is another story. I've never seen him light up the way he does around you."

She knew what he was talking about, but dismissed it instantly. "What of it?" she said casually. "Little boys have crushes on girls and grown women all the time. Anyway, he hardly knows me. He'll forget about me in less than a day after I go."

"I don't think so. You remind him too much of his mother." Choya stopped, looking at her.

Jacquie wasn't quite so quick to reply to that. She had thought of that possibility herself. But she shook her head. "He told me he doesn't remember her."

"Not consciously. But it's just that — look, Jacquie, for some reason he just keeps talking about you. And you're leaving tomorrow or the day after at the latest. He's not going to understand that — or why he's been rejected."

Jacquie hesitated. Only Choya could answer her next question but she wasn't sure she wanted to ask it. "Do I really resemble his mother that much?" Her questioning eyes met the piercing alertness of his without flinching.

Surprisingly Choya was the first to look away. His profile was sharply defined by the blueness of the sky. Yet he didn't seem disturbed or disconcerted by her guess.

"I suppose Robbie told you about Rosemary too," he said quietly.

"He didn't mention his mother's name." An intense curiosity seized Jacquie. "Am I very much like her?" she repeated.

His topaz-bright gaze focused on her again, moving over her features in quick assessment. Jacquie discovered she was holding her breath. A protest welled inside that she could look like anyone but herself.

"No," he said in a quiet but emphatic voice. His attention shifted to a strand of pale golden hair that had fallen over her shoulder, and which contrasted with the lightweight blouse that was the same brilliant turquoise color as her eyes. "Your hair is the same color. Moonbeams trapped in a mountain pool," he murmured almost absently.

Jacquie didn't take those poetic words as a compliment. He wasn't really talking about her.

His gaze was hard when it slashed back to her face. "But the comparison ends there. My wife had brown eyes and freckles sprinkled across her nose. She was small and delicately built but every inch a tomboy. None of those descriptions would fit you."

"No, they don't. And I get the point," Jacquie answered, taking a deep breath and turning away. She had always been proud of her just-right height and definitely curvy figure. He made both sound like drawbacks. As far as being a tomboy, she had never caught frogs or climbed trees. As a very little girl, she'd gone for plush toys in pastel colors that matched her canopy bed and frilled curtains. However, she'd never been a goody-goody. In time, she'd had adventures of her own — the suburban kind. She'd scared her parents half to death the night she'd decided to sleep under the stars by herself. In a deep vee of the roof, where they couldn't find her. And that wasn't the only thing that got her grounded, sometimes for weeks.

She'd outgrown all that years ago. Kids outgrew everything. She didn't understand why Choya was so worried about his son.

He interrupted her thoughts in the same controlled tone. "I don't know if I'm explaining this right."

"Keep trying."

"It's just that Robbie was too young when Rosemary was killed for him to have any memories of her. To him she's a beautiful blond woman in a photograph."

"Killed?" The word startled her. "How?" The second question was blurted out before Jacquie considered the wisdom of probing deeper into his personal life.

"A car accident — not that it really concerns you."

There was a slight shake of her head in apology. "I'm sorry."

"For prying, or that my wife is dead?"

Jacquie tensed, put off by his tough tone and the words he chose to use. But she knew she'd crossed a line with her blunt query, though she had not meant to trigger what had to be extremely painful memories. She wouldn't escalate the situation by responding impulsively again. "Hey," she said softly, "I didn't mean to pry. And I am genuinely sorry for what happened to you — and to Robbie."

Choya gave her an odd look. "Are you?"

She didn't need to prove anything to him. The apology had been instinctive and from her heart. To say so might only prompt another dig from him. Still, she had to be tactful.

Jacquie considered her next words as she spoke them slowly. "I think you're afraid that Robbie is looking for — I don't know exactly how to say it, but —"

"Mother love." Choya said the words dryly and without a trace of sentiment. "The real deal. Is that what you're getting at?"

Jacquie flushed. "That sums it up, yes. And he can't be blamed for that. And neither can I. If you remember, I just happened to get stuck in Tombstone."

"I don't blame you." Choya stood before her, his bland expression unchanging as if carved in granite. "I'm merely asking you not to encourage him."

"I haven't. But I have been nice to him. There's nothing wrong with that." She forced a confidence she didn't feel into her voice. "Look at it from his point of view, Choya. With only you and his grandfather, he's surrounded by men. The solution is simple enough — why don't you just get married again? He does need a mother. A photograph of the one he had isn't enough. No matter how much he loved her, he doesn't remember her. And she's gone forever."

Jacquie stopped, aware that she'd undoubtedly said too much. He was likely to guess that she'd been thinking about him most of the night. At least she hadn't mentioned the obvious fact that Choya Barnett had loved Rosemary too. Maybe he still did.

A hard sound almost like laughter came from his throat. "Are you saying I should marry just for my son's sake?"

"No. Of course not." Jacquie's reply was subdued.

"You're awfully young to be giving advice on the subject. What do you know about it?" Choya countered with a watchful narrowing of his gaze.

"Nothing. I've never been married. Or engaged."

"Do you want to be?"

"Some day." In her mind, Jacquie pictured her parents' marriage, an unusual combination of endearing friendship, combustible personalities and ready laughter. They were lucky to have found each other and created a lasting love, and they both knew it.

"Any likely candidates?"

She glared at him. "Not a one. And that's fine with me. Can we talk about something else?"

He didn't answer right away and she turned her back on him, unsettled by his request that she leave his son alone and the emotions behind it. Jacquie picked her way along the eroded rocks that formed the path at the foot of the graves, concentrating on details of what she saw to distract herself. She noted several Chinese names on the headstones. Others were marked with a name and a date and a few starkly simple words: *Killed by Indians.* One epitaph drew a shudder from Jacquie. It was the grave of an unfortunate man who'd fallen afoul of the swift and not always sure justice of the frontier west: *Hanged by Mistake.*

She could empathize.

At the tombstones of the Clantons and the McLaurys, Jacquie read the inscription with surprise, then instinctively turned to the man who silently followed her.

She asked him for an explanation.

"It says they were murdered. Weren't they killed in a gunfight at the OK Corral?" she questioned.

"Yes." His sun-browned hand cupped a

match flame to a cigarette, protecting the fire from the teasing breeze. "But the Clantons were very popular in Tombstone. The same can't be said for Wyatt Earp and his brothers. For a while there was considerable question as to whether it was a fair fight."

"Was it?" Jacquie tipped her head to the side curiously.

"It depends on whether you were talking to one of the Clantons' friends or an Earp supporter." Choya exhaled a cloud of smoke, pinching the match between his fingers. "The general consensus now seems to be that it was."

As she digested the information, Jacquie moved toward the entrance to the gift shop. The long cylindrical stalks of an unfamiliar type of cactus caught her attention. Its wayward growth resembled a pincushion, minus the cushion. She paused beside it.

"What kind of cactus is this?"

"An ocotillo," Choya answered.

"Got it." She'd picked up on the *y* sound and mentally spelled it with a double *l*.

The faint narrowing of his eyes revealed that he'd guessed she was wondering if it was the cactus he'd been named for. Jacquie only shrugged and didn't ask. She didn't feel like baiting him. And fences were a safe subject. He seemed to think so too.

"As you can see," he went on, "the fence separating the parking lot from the cemetery is made from the stalks of the ocotillo. It was a common practice years ago to make solid stick corrals from the ocotillo because there wasn't much lumber around here."

"It doesn't look all that strong." Jacquie studied it.

"The thorns are just about as effective as barbed wire."

"I'll take your word for it." She walked on.

He shrugged and reached around her and opened the door to the gift shop. "By the way, you still haven't given me your answer."

For an instant, the carved male features were close to her own face and Jacquie's heart turned over. A searing fire flashed through her veins. The impulse again returned with impulsive sweetness to feel the hard pressure of his mouth against her own. This time she didn't give in to the desire as she had done before. They were in a public place and that helped. The totally elemental reaction she had to him whenever he was near was controllable. It took a lot of effort, but she could do it.

"What answer?" Her blankness was not deliberate. Jacquie was concentrating on letting her senses recover so she could think clearly.

The clerk in the gift shop glanced up when they entered. Choya smiled slightly and nodded, a flicker of impatience in his tawny gaze. There was no one else in the shop by now and Jacquie guessed by his silence that he didn't want the clerk overhearing their conversation.

His hand firmly grasped her elbow and escorted her out the door to the parking lot, releasing her immediately. Her skin tingled where his fingers had made their imprint.

"I asked that you wouldn't encourage my son, and I want your answer that you won't," Choya demanded calmly as they paused beside the jeep. His gaze flickered with buried flame, but there was no other outward display of emotion.

"If I see Robbie, I'll be polite and friendly," she declared. She looked back at Choya's face, irritated that she could still be so attracted to the man. "But I'll make it clear that I'm leaving tomorrow — very clear. Does that satisfy you?"

There was relief in his eyes. "Yes, it does. Would you like a lift back to your motel?"

Jacquie passionately wished she could tell him no, but the memory of the painful gravel on the roadside deterred her.

"If it wouldn't be taking you out of your way," she agreed with a saccharine smile.

Now that Choya Barnett had received the answer he wanted, he didn't appear to think it was necessary to maintain a conversation. The ride was short and Jacquie kept her attention diverted from his strong hands on the wheel — and all the rest of his manly charms — by staring at the unrolling asphalt of the road ahead. Only when he had let her out in front of her motel room did she allow herself to watch him, and then it was from the window of her room as he drove off.

For nearly two hours, she alternately paced the confines of the small room and lounged on the bed. Her restlessness increased with each ticking second until she felt she would scream if she stayed in the room another minute.

Her first plan, which was not to appear in town at all, was cast aside. So Choya Barnett wouldn't like it if she ran into his son in town — so what? She hadn't promised that she wouldn't see Robbie, only that she wouldn't encourage his friendship. There was no need to voluntarily condemn herself into making a prison out of her motel room.

Sliding her rose-shaded sunglasses onto her nose, she picked up her oversized leather bag and walked out, locking the door behind her. With a map from the motel front office pointing out the buildings of historical significance, she wandered along the old streets for the second time, pausing in front of some buildings and entering others that were open. She avoided the barbershop, where she was sure she'd been the subject of conversation.

Once she saw Robbie aimlessly hobbling along the board sidewalk and she darted into a doorway before he saw her. Truthfully she would have welcomed the company of the small boy — they had some things in common. The wild, impetuous streak in Robbie that had prompted him to ride a bull calf was a trait she shared with him — that and the occasional loneliness of being an only child.

Late in the afternoon the rumblings of her stomach reminded Jacquie that she hadn't eaten since breakfast. The painted sign of a restaurant lured her down Allen Street and she was nearly at the door when she heard the thumping of a pair of crutches behind her.

"Jacquie!" Robbie's voice called her name eagerly. "Wait!"

Biting her lip, she started to ignore him, then realized it was useless. He was too close. Fixing a bland smile on her face, she stopped and turned around.

"Hello, Robbie," she greeted him politely, but took care not to sound too warm. "How are you this afternoon?"

"Fine. I was beginning to think I wouldn't see you today. Where have you been?"

"Mostly in my motel room," Jacquie lied.

"What were you doing there?" His eyes rounded curiously.

"Resting. I have a long drive ahead of me tomorrow." She was keeping to her promise to make it clear to the boy that she was leaving.

He gave her a wistful look. "Do you have to go?"

"Of course," Jacquie laughed, trying to sound nonchalant despite the twinge of guilt she felt at the dullness that clouded his face. "I wouldn't have been here at all if it wasn't for the damage to my car. I have to go to Los Angeles."

"Why?"

It was a good question. Jacquie simply shrugged indifferently. "Because I do, that's all." The subject needed changing. "Where's your father?"

"At a meeting. It's just for ranchers." Robbie leaned on his crutches and swung the blue cast back and forth.

"I didn't know ranchers had meetings," she said lightly.

"He had to be there," Robbie said importantly. "They're talking about minerals. And rights. Things like that. And leases," he added. "Whatever they are."

"Oh." She didn't really understand what the boy was getting at and she suspected he didn't either.

"But he'll be coming pretty soon, I guess."

"Well, you'd better wait here for him," she said with false brightness, and started to turn away.

"Where are you going?" The aluminum crutches were quickly shifted to follow her.

"Into the restaurant to have something to eat." Her hunger was growing with each minute. She didn't intend to deny herself food just to avoid Robbie.

"Can I come with you?" he asked eagerly.

"Um, I don't think that's a good idea," Jacquie said quickly. "How will your dad know where you are?"

"He'll find me," Robbie replied with certainty. Then there was a flash of hesitancy. "Am I bothering you? Dad says I bother people sometimes when they really don't want me around."

Jacquie could see that Robbie was mentally bracing himself for a rejection. He had obviously sensed her attempts to ease away and wasn't happy with the painful truth. She couldn't blame him. Damn Choya Barnett, she raged silently. What harm could it possibly do to spend a few minutes with his son?

"Heavens no, you don't bother me!" She flashed him a brilliant smile. "I like you, Robbie. I just don't want to get into any trouble with your dad if he finds you in the restaurant with me. But if you don't think he'll mind, come on in and have a milkshake while I eat." Silently, Jacquie added that his father could get just as angry as he liked at her for breaking her promise. She didn't have to pay attention.

"Okay! Can I have a banana milkshake?" Robbie asked with a wide grin.

"You bet."

CHAPTER 4

Robbie slurped noisily on his straw, sucking up the last drop of milkshake from his glass. Jacquie smiled inwardly at the sound and sipped at her iced tea. Without thinking, he wiped his sticky hand on his jeans and came up with a stray sticker that had come loose from his cast.

With a proud smile, he showed her the scaly creature depicted on it. "That's a Gila monster."

"Wow. He looks tough."

Robbie nodded. "They live in the desert. My dad says anyone that does has to be tougher than tough."

That motto was another tall order for a small boy. But she wasn't going to say anything that would sound like criticism of his dad. "I'm sure he's right," she replied.

They both leaned back in their chairs and sighed with contentment. The bell above the restaurant door jingled, signaling the entrance of a customer. She didn't turn around and Robbie didn't seem to hear it. His eyes were fixed on her face.

"What's your favorite animal?" he asked unexpectedly.

Jacquie thought for a second. "Hm. I really don't have one. But I do have a favorite zoo. It's in Dallas. That's where I come from."

"That's in Texas, right?"

"Yes. It's a big city. And the zoo is in a big building. It has birds that fly through a jungle that grows inside and monkeys and other animals and a beautiful aquarium. There's even a river on the first floor with otters in it."

His eyes were wide with interest. "A river in a building? Awesome. How did they do that?"

Jacquie laughed. "I really don't know. But it's a wonderful place. You would enjoy it."

"I bet I would," he said eagerly. "It sounds really cool."

Robbie played with the straw, then looked up. He put it back in his mouth, his hands around the glass, looking straight down into it. Spiky lashes quickly veiled his guarded eyes.

Jacquie straightened in her chair, her chin jerking slightly upward an instant before footsteps stopped at their table. There was a blaze of gold over her features, the eyes of a mountain cat that had found its prey.

"Hello, Choya." She gave him a dazzling smile of feigned surprise.

"Hello." He returned the greeting without enthusiasm.

"Hi, Dad," Robbie piped up. "I was just keeping Jacquie company while she ate her dinner."

"So I see." He remained standing, towering above them both as if contemplating which of them to pounce on first. Robbie squirmed uncomfortably and it took all of Jacquie's willpower not to do the same. Choya picked up the crutches leaning against a chair and pointedly handed them to Robbie. "You can go out to the jeep. I'll be there in a few minutes."

"Yessir." Robbie didn't even glance at Jacquie as he balanced himself on the crutches and proceeded from the restaurant.

Resentment flashed in her eyes, but she concealed it by making a show of searching through her bag for her wallet. With the wallet and the check for the meal in her hand, she rose from the table, brushing past Choya as if he wasn't even there.

"Do you always break your promises so quickly, Jacquie?" he said accusingly.

"I thought about it first, believe me. I made that damn promise too fast and I made it on your terms," she hissed. "You pressured me into it."

She waited impatiently at the cash register while the waitress rang up the amount and gave her the correct change. When they stepped outside, Jacquie finished speaking the heated words she'd held back. Fortunately there was no one else outside to hear them but Choya.

"I broke my promise for a very good reason — because a little boy felt he had to ask if he's bothering me because he's lonely. And for your information, I met him by chance just as I was going into the restaurant. I haven't been with him all afternoon."

Choya nodded, but he didn't look like he believed her. "Nice of you tell him about that zoo. Now he's going to badger me to go there."

"It's a big world, Choya. Robbie is curious and he's smart. You should take him there. I can't."

"Don't tell me what to do." His tone was level but the curt remark startled her all the same.

"My guess is that you tell other people what to do all the time. Especially me. It's not just your prerogative," she retorted.

"Robbie is my child, not yours, and he's not going to get attached to you. I thought I got that across," Choya snapped.

"You did. Ten times over." She was breathing heavily now, with anger. "Why don't you just lock him up? He'd be really safe then."

Her free hand clenched into a fist and she forced it open, reaching up to clutch the strap of her bag to her shoulder, ready to storm off. His reaction was pure instinct: his hand snaked out to seize her wrist and keep her from slapping him.

Which happened to be something she dearly wanted to do. But she controlled the impulse. Barely.

"Let go!" She yanked herself free but the action knocked the large bag from her hand. She hadn't bothered to fasten the clasp and its contents spilled over the boardwalk and into the street.

"Look what you've done!" she snapped. She rubbed her wrist where he'd held it, uncaring that the accident had broken the tension to some degree.

As she stooped to begin gathering the scattered things, Robbie came hobbling from the jeep parked in front of the restaurant. "I'll help, Jacquie."

He maneuvered himself into a sitting position on the board sidewalk and began picking up the items that had rolled into the street.

Picking up a tube of lipstick near the pointed toe of Choya Barnett's boot, Jacquie glared up. "You could help," she accused.

Then she wished she'd said nothing as he bent down beside her, dark brown hair waving thickly beneath the brim of his Stetson. Unceremoniously he began dumping items back in her handbag with no regard for neatness or order. With her heartbeat quickening at the sight of the rippling muscles beneath his shirt, Jacquie soon didn't care either, anxious only to be out of range of his animal attraction.

When Robbie had gathered everything he could reach, Jacquie moved swiftly to the edge of the sidewalk, holding the large bag open for his handful. This time she closed it securely and stayed well away from Choya.

"Would you like a ride back to your motel?" Robbie asked.

Smiling tightly, Jacquie shook her head, refusing to even glance at his father. "No, thank you. I'm not going back right now."

The real truth was she didn't want to be with Choya, ever again, under any circumstances.

All the same, at this hour, there were very few places she could go, except to a saloon.

She might have a wild streak, but it wasn't so strong that she would venture into a strange bar alone. She would walk slowly back to the motel but she wouldn't accept the offer of a ride.

"Good-bye, Robbie." She bent down and offered her hand to the boy. "You take care of yourself."

He shook it solemnly, a glimmer of apprehension in his eyes but no tears. "Good-bye, Jacquie."

She straightened, meeting the impenetrable expression of his father. "Good-bye, Choya." She didn't offer him her hand, letting her fingers curl around the strap of her handbag. "It's been quite an experience running into you. From first to last."

His alert gaze ran over the taunting smile on her face, his mouth quirking at one corner. But he didn't respond to her play on words. "Good-bye," he said with finality.

As Choya moved away to help Robbie into the jeep, Jacquie turned away and began walking down the street in the opposite direction from her motel. She pretended an interest in the contents of a shop window until she heard the jeep start and pull away from the curb. She glanced over her shoulder and waved once more to Robbie.

When they were out of sight, she felt

crazily alone. The sun was touching the roofs on its downward slide. Sighing unconsciously, she turned and started walking toward her motel. Tomorrow she would be gone and all that had happened to her here would become a tale she would relate at some party or other. In a way, it hardly seemed right.

That night Jacquie slept soundly, not waking until well after eight in the morning. She showered quickly and packed what she'd brought to the motel, setting the overnight case beside the door so she could pick it up when she came back with her car.

With the strap of her handbag slung over one shoulder, she tucked one side of her blond hair behind an ear and started for the garage. Snug jeans in a faded blue molded the long length of her legs. The navy blue top with the stitched-on star in the center left little to the imagination.

As she was crossing the nearly empty highway to the garage, she saw the mechanic standing beside the gas pumps.

"Hi there. Is my car fixed?" she called to him.

He nodded and waited until she was closer to answer. "I didn't think the parts would get here so soon, but they did. I got started on it first thing. It's all ready for you, just like new."

"I don't think that car ever was new," Jacquie laughed as she followed him into the small office. "What did it come to? I hope I can afford it."

The man laughed briefly in return and picked up an itemized bill from a cluttered desktop. "I tried to be as fair as I could," he replied, handing it to her.

The curved brim of the man's cap was pulled low over his receding hairline, hiding his eyes. Yet Jacquie could feel the slow appraisal of his gaze moving over her while she studied the bill. She was too accustomed to such looks to be insulted. She really did believe there was no harm in looking or thinking. And Choya had been right when he'd said she knew how to handle those who weren't satisfied with that.

"It all seems to be in order." She breathed in deeply, glancing from the paper to give the mechanic a bright smile. The total was lower than his estimate.

"I overestimated the labor cost a bit," the mechanic explained, returning her smile. "I never worked on that model of car before and I wasn't sure how long it would take."

"I appreciate your honesty."

Sliding the strap from her shoulder, she set her bag on a relatively empty corner of the desk and unfastened the clasp. She hadn't bothered to put the contents in order after they'd spilled in the street the afternoon before. She began sifting through the oversized bag, searching for her wallet.

"That's the trouble with big bags." She smiled ruefully. "They hold so much that you never can find anything when you want it."

There was an understanding gleam in the man's eyes that said he could patiently wait all day. A twinge of fear raced through her when her rummaging search didn't turn up the wallet. Smiling nervously, she began taking the larger items out and placing them on the desk beside her bag. Soon the bottom of the bag was in sight and still no wallet.

"It can't be gone!" she breathed with a touch of panic, and began going through the articles she'd laid on the desk. The wallet wasn't among them. Raking her fingernails through the waving thickness of her white-gold hair, she paused in her search, troubled eyes meeting the questioning glance of the mechanic. "My wallet's gone. It has all my money and my debit cards and my identification . . . everything was in it."

"Are you sure you didn't leave it somewhere?" he suggested.

"No, I didn't." She shook her head, then hesitated. "At least — may I use your phone? And do you have a list of local businesses?"

"Of course." He turned the black phone on his desk toward her and pointed to a printout of phone numbers under the glass top. He had a computer to order parts, but the garage phone was an old, heavy model that looked like it had been used every day for the last fifty years. He picked up a clean rag and swiped a streak of lube from its side. "Be my guest."

Jacquie didn't care if it was covered in axle grease. She scooped up the receiver and looked for the right number on the list. The rotating dial was agonizingly slow. The line she wanted rang twice and someone at the restaurant where she had eaten the previous afternoon answered with a drawled but cheerful hello. Quickly she asked if her wallet had been found or turned in. At the negative answer, she explained that she'd dropped her handbag outside the door and everything had spilled out of it. She asked if someone would check to see if her wallet had landed under the board sidewalk.

After waiting for heart-pounding seconds, the answer was still no. A phone call to the police got the same answer: it hadn't been turned in. Whoever found it had obviously kept it or emptied it and thrown it away where no one else would find it.

When she hung up, her mind was frantically searching for a solution. What was she going to do without money or a debit card? It would take several more calls to obtain the number to cancel it. And the bank wouldn't send a new one right away. Especially not to an address in the middle of nowhere for a customer with no ID.

"Maybe you left it at the motel," the mechanic said.

"I don't think so." She nibbled thoughtfully at her lower lip. "I packed everything before I came here. If it was there, I would have found it."

"I wish there was something I could do," the man murmured sympathetically.

Hope glimmered. "Well, maybe there is." It was one thing to be flat broke, another to be broke and on foot. "I need my car."

"Yeah. But . . ." the mechanic faltered, glancing at the itemized bill lying on his desk.

"I'll pay you back, I promise," Jacquie rushed, "every dime of it — just as soon as I find a job."

The man readjusted the cap on his head, plainly reluctant to agree. Jacquie's father had once accused her of depending more on her feminine allure than her intelligence. He wasn't entirely wrong. It had often proved the easiest means of getting her way.

"Honestly!" Her brilliantly expressive eyes darted to the name stitched above the pocket of his coveralls. "Brad, I absolutely have to have my car and you really can trust me to pay up."

"Um, Jacquie, I . . ." He shifted uncomfortably, looking awkward as a coaxing smile curved her mouth. "I don't really see how I could. This is just a small garage and the repair costs added up to more than I can carry."

"I know," she agreed, moving toward him. "But I really need my car," she pleaded earnestly. She wanted to reach out and clutch his arm, even if it would make her seem desperate, as if he was the only person in the world she could turn to for help.

He swallowed nervously, his gaze focused on her moist, slightly parted lips. She could sense that he was weakening and felt a rush of power. Some men were so easily maneuvered.

"I'd do anything." She added the breathy promise with suggestive emphasis on the last word.

A redness began creeping up from the

neckline of his shirt. His gaze fell away, hesitating for a second on the rounded swell of her breasts, then refocusing on the desktop. Nervously he cleared his throat and Jacquie knew victory was within her grasp.

Until a low voice pulled it out of reach. "That's an all-inclusive statement. What's the problem here?"

At the sound of Choya Barnett's voice, Jacquie's lashes closed, but she didn't turn around. The mechanic took a quick, embarrassed step away from her, a dull red spreading across his face.

"Choya," the man said with a nervous half-grin. "I didn't expect to see you in town today."

"I had to take Robbie to the doctor, then on to school," he explained, but Jacquie could tell that his piercing gaze hadn't left her back. "And no one answered my question."

"Well, um, it seems that Jacquie" — the mechanic darted her an anxious look — "lost her wallet or it got stolen. She, uh, doesn't have any money."

"You had it yesterday at the restaurant," Choya stated flatly.

Jacquie breathed in deeply. How did he manage, in the space of their remarkably short acquaintance, to always find her in the worst possible situation? With a defiant toss of her head, she glanced over her shoulder, her cool gaze meeting the metallic hardness of his.

"Yes, I did," she said with forced calm. "But if you remember, everything in my handbag got spilled out as I was leaving. More than likely my wallet didn't make it back in. I'm thinking someone came along, found it, and didn't return it."

"Did you make the usual calls?"

"Of course. To the restaurant and the cops."

"Did you leave it at your motel?" His implication was fairly obvious. He probably believed she'd conveniently forgotten the wallet in the hopes of getting out of paying the repair bill for her car.

"No. I thought of that."

"It's easy to overlook something you're trying too hard to find. Maybe we should go and check together," Choya suggested with a flick of a dark eyebrow.

That was the last thing she wanted to do. But she would have to. He'd been there when it happened. And he was unbelievably observant.

"By all means. Let's do that." With suppressed fury, Jacquie began stuffing the small heap of what she'd dumped out back into the handbag.

How dare he, even indirectly, accuse her of lying? Her smile to the mechanic was determinedly sweet. There was some measure of satisfaction in seeing Choya's mouth tighten with disgust at the smile. If he thought she was some kind of con artist, she might as well act like one. After all, she thought sarcastically as she swept through the door ahead of him, she didn't want to disappoint the high and mighty Choya Barnett.

"My wallet won't be at the motel," she declared, sliding into the passenger seat of the jeep.

"Why? Did you hide it somewhere along the road on the way here?"

Was that another lame attempt at a joke or an accusation? Either way, he could have kept it to himself. "No, I didn't!" Her temper flared. "It is missing, damn it!"

There was no doubt as to his reaction in the tawny cat eyes. He didn't believe her. Trembling with anger, Jacquie folded her arms around her bulky handbag and stared straight ahead. Tears welled in her eyes, a result of the ferocity of her emotion.

With the engine growling steadily, Choya turned the jeep onto the main highway. "Skip the tears," he told her. "I don't buy the helpless female act."

"I always cry when I lose my temper!" Jacquie retorted in a choked voice. "I wouldn't waste tears trying to appeal to you."

"As long as we understand each other," he said indifferently.

"I understand you very well. You're as stubborn as a mule once you make up your mind about something or someone," she accused angrily. "But I didn't do anything wrong."

"There is a possibility that your wallet is lost," he conceded dryly, "but I wasn't wrong either. You do seem to have a way of attracting trouble, just like I said."

A thousand insulting retorts sprang to mind, but Jacquie doubted that any of them would penetrate his thorny exterior. He was a cactus by name and a cactus by nature — she would be a fool to keep getting herself pricked.

Keeping her mouth shut, she tossed him the keycard to her motel door when he stopped the jeep. She took a firm hold on her temper and blinked away the few hot tears before following him to the door. With her gaze focused on a point between the wide shoulders, it was difficult not to remember the last time he'd been in her room and the searing briefness of his kiss.

His aggressively masculine presence dominated the small room. The unmade bed suddenly seemed to suggest an intimacy that disturbed Jacquie's senses. She paused inside the doorway and leaned against the wall, folding her arms in front of her.

"Search away, Choya," she invited. "I would help, but I wouldn't want you to accuse me later on of hiding the wallet somewhere."

His gaze flicked sharply to her, then scanned the room. She watched his methodical search. The motel room was sparsely furnished and it didn't take much time for him to finish.

"Maybe you should go through my stuff," Jacquie suggested caustically. "I might have concealed it under the contraband."

Choya glanced at the overnight case near her feet. "Okay. I accept that your wallet is actually missing. Let me guess. So is all your money."

"Every cent of it, except three pennies that were loose in the bottom of my handbag. Plus my debit card and all my ID, not to mention old snapshots and some other little mementoes that can't be replaced." Her chin was thrust forward at a rebellious angle. "I am totally, one hundred percent broke, with the exception of my clothes and my car, which is technically the property of the garage, considering I can't pay that huge repair bill."

"The accident was your fault." He stood in the center of the room, tall and decidedly in command. "You can't blame me for the damage to your car."

"I don't." She released an angry breath and straightened away from the wall.

"You must have family or friends who'll help you out."

"Yes, I do." But she would almost rather starve than call home. Begging her parents for help when she'd been on her own for less than a week was the last thing she wanted to do. She assumed they'd picked up her message on their voicemail. She would have to fill in the blanks if she reached them in person — and tell them all about this infuriating new situation.

"I suggest you call them," Choya said briskly, his tone bordering on an order.

Jacquie slid a hand through her hair, shaking its length down her back. As much as she resented his suggestion and dreaded making the phone call, it was the only logical solution now. Without money, how could she find a place to sleep or buy food or anything?

Sighing, she walked to the phone beside the bed and placed a collect call to home. She crossed her fingers, feeling stupidly suspicious, and offered a silent prayer that her mother would answer.

"Collect?" her father's voice boomed at the other end of the line. "From who?"

"Dad, it's me, Jacquie," she rushed, but the operator broke in, asking if he would accept the reversed charges.

"No, I won't, by God!" he declared.

Jacquie's mouth opened in a silent gasp. He was still angry, apparently. Very angry.

"She wanted to be on her own and if she wants to talk to me badly enough, she'll pay for the phone call herself." And the receiver was slammed down.

Jacquie thanked the operator and hung up. Her teeth sank into her lower lip. Considering how vehemently she'd declared her independence, she could hardly blame her father. Proudly she lifted her head and met Choya's speculating gaze.

"Nothing doing," she informed him, faking an air of unconcern. The truth was that her father's hot-tempered reply hurt, probably as much as she had hurt both her parents.

"There's no one else you can call?"

Jacquie considered her girlfriend Tammy

in Bisbee. Newly married and starting a new job, her friend didn't have the wherewithal to cover the amount Jacquie needed. And Jacquie wouldn't dream of asking Tammy's husband. She barely knew him and had shown up unannounced on Thanksgiving as it was. He'd undoubtedly refuse. So be it. She'd had it up to here with male self-righteousness anyway.

She shook her head. "No. It's all right," she shrugged nonchalantly. "I'll get by."

"How?" he challenged.

"I'll find a way," she declared.

"Oh, right. Like today," Choya said in a measured voice. It aggravated her beyond belief that he was able to be so calm. "Don't forget that I got to watch you trying to persuade Brad to let you have your car back without paying. Good luck with that."

"I would've paid him!" Jacquie flashed.

"Yeah." His mouth quirked sardonically. "I'd forgotten you vowed you would do anything." His dark head was tilted to one side, his carved features set. "What would you have done if he'd taken you up on that?"

"Oh, I'd think of something," she answered after a beat. At his skeptical look, she added somewhat desperately, "I started filling out my jeans when I was twelve. I know a little about men and how to make them think the way I want them to."

Amusement teased the corners of his mouth. "Do you now." His gold gaze moved insolently over her.

One of her finely arched brows shot up. Jacquie wasn't going to be dismissed by him.

"Do you know what you sound like?" She hooked her thumbs in the belt loops of her jeans and walked the way she did in clubs to get guys to look at her when her ego needed stroking. She and her posse of girlfriends would dissolve in giggles when they did. But now she was serious. Her head was tipped back, her silver-gold hair streaming down her back. "You sound as though you're sorry I didn't come to you for help. Do you want me to ask you for money?"

Something harsh flickered across his chiseled features, a suggestion of strong emotion that was quickly gone. Jacquie had seen it, but she kept the knowledge from being revealed in her eyes as she returned his speculating study.

"Would you make me the same promise of 'anything' as an incentive?" His hard mouth tightened. "And forget to keep it?"

"I wouldn't forget." She moistened her lips, her gaze running provocatively over his wide shoulders, then to his compelling features. "In fact, keeping a promise like that might even be fun."

A muscle twitched along his powerful jawline. "Do you think so?"

"I know so," Jacquie replied with an almost kittenish purr. "Don't you?"

"No."

"You still don't trust me, do you?" She laughed throatily. This was crazy. But she couldn't seem to stop. "You still think that I might cheat you in some way. I wouldn't, though. I always pay my debts in full."

In a fluid movement, she eliminated the distance that separated them. Her hands spread over his chest to the width of his shoulders, then circled them while she pressed her soft curves against his granite length. He gripped her just above her hips, tightening as if to shove her away, then hesitated.

Jacquie smiled slowly, certain now that she hadn't made a mistake. She could guess what was going on in his mind. Unfortunately, she couldn't get a grip on hers. She felt like a trapped animal. Between her own mistakes and bad luck, she was.

"Are you beginning to see how much fun it could be, Choya?" She said his name with a seductively husky pitch to her voice.

She heard the hiss of his sharply indrawn breath. Her fingers slid into the thick brown locks of the hair at the back of his neck. Rising on tiptoes, she touched her lips against the firm line of his mouth. Persuasively she began kissing him, lightly, tantalizingly, until his mouth was not quite so stiff against hers.

The musky scent of aftershave clung to the sun-browned skin of his smooth cheeks, a heady combination with the warm, male scent of his body. Her heart began to race in an instinctive response.

Pliantly she molded her body more firmly against him, letting him take her weight. The stamp of his virility was marked in every muscled inch of him, proof that he couldn't resist her indefinitely.

Her kiss deepened with unforced passion and his hard mouth answered the pressure, although the initiative remained hers. With a shuddering sigh tinged with regret, Jacquie took her lips from his, sliding her hands from the muscled column of his neck to his shoulders.

Through the curling sweep of her lashes, she looked into the tawny gold of his eyes. They revealed nothing, nor did the bold, almost severe lines of his face.

"Now do you see?" she purred. He held still. Very still.

With the swiftness of a striking serpent,

her hand lashed out at his cheek, a satisfying sting in her palm. Her eyes blazed with the fire of revenge as she twisted free of the large hands on her hips.

"But I would never come to you!" she hissed as his cold surprise turned to icy fury. "I would never ask you for money! I don't need your help! I don't need anybody's help!"

"Don't you?" Choya countered in a voice that was low and controlled.

Her lips parted slightly in surprise. She had expected retaliation — verbal abuse, a barrage of insults, but not a leading question like that. Her anger evaporated with chilling swiftness as he turned away.

Stunned, she watched him, unable to believe that she could assault his ego with no payback. She'd felt safe pretending to seduce him because she'd known he didn't want her. He'd only played along to see how far she would go in her irrational state.

What a sport.

But now — now, she didn't feel safe. His reaction hadn't followed the pattern she'd expected. Choya wasn't even making an outraged exit. He was walking toward the unmade bed.

Chapter 5

His objective wasn't the bed. It was the phone. Without a glance at Jacquie, he picked up the receiver and dialed a number. She was still staring at him in shock when he turned around to hold her gaze.

"Brad?" he said into the receiver. "This is Choya. How much was Jacquie Grey's repair bill again?" He paused, listening to what must have been a breakdown. "I'm going to pay it — never mind about the insurance for now. Yes, you heard me right. Just give me the total one more time."

Her mouth opened to protest, but nothing came out. Her gaze followed the black receiver as it was returned to its cradle. She trembled. The storm inside her had broken and she could think again. But she wondered why she felt so numb.

"You're expensive, Jacquie." His low voice said her name with insulting emphasis. "It's going to take some time to get my money's worth."

Her gaze flew to his face. "I wasn't serious and you know it," she breathed.

A dark eyebrow arched with amusement. "No? You made me an interesting proposition. I think I'll take you up on it."

"I didn't proposition you!" Jacquie protested in shocked astonishment.

"What would you like to call it? Bribery?"

"I . . ." She faltered, the words stammering off the end of her flustered tongue. "I was jerking your chain."

"Good and hard," he pointed out.

"But I told you I would never c-come to you."

"Suit yourself." The wide shoulders shrugged with his even reply. "But it's the only way you'll get your car."

"You can't keep it. It's mine," she declared frantically. "The title's in my name. I'm not going to sign it over to you."

"Oh well. I don't have to drive it." There was a wicked glint in his eyes. "The way I see it, the car is mine until the debt against it is paid in full. Either pay me the money or we'll revert to the old system of bartering goods and services for payment."

Jacquie swallowed. "Very funny. I'll send you the money, I swear I will."

The grooves on either side of his mouth

deepened. “As you pointed out, I don’t trust you. Payment in advance is the only thing I’ll accept.”

Appealing to him was useless. Jacquie reached down into her shaken soul for a bit of bravado. She slid her trembling hands into the pockets of her jeans and boldly met his look.

“All right, I’ll pay you,” she agreed. “I’ll get a job and earn the money.”

Her assertion only seemed to amuse him more. “Doing what, and where? Not here in Tombstone. The tourist season is just about over and we’re not exactly a Christmas destination. There aren’t any jobs to be had. What would you do for a place to sleep and food to eat in the meantime? I’m offering you both for the same price you’d have to pay to any other man.”

“There are people other than men on this earth!” Jacquie fired back, his logic cornering her.

“But your feminine wiles wouldn’t work very well on a woman,” Choya reminded her. “What do you intend to do about your motel bill? The manager is a woman, remember? I don’t think Mrs. Chase would take it kindly if you tried to skip out without paying. In the eyes of the law, you’re a vagrant with no visible means of support and no money and no possessions of any value."

"Mrs. Chase is very nice and she just happens to like me —"

He interrupted her heated reply. "Maybe so but she has bills to pay too. Of course, you could get a lawyer and plead your case in small claims court to get your car back. It's every other Thursday during the tourist season if you can get a slot. After that, it's once a month. The circuit judge gets here when he can."

"I'm sure he's another friend of yours. Choya, you can't expect me to agree to let you —" Jacquie couldn't even get the words out. Her head drew back in negative denial. "You know how I feel about you. How unwilling I would be to have you —" Again the words lodged.

"Unwilling?" A chuckle sounded deep in his throat. "Really? You?"

"Stop it!" She was furious again but no longer irrational. "You're just trying to scare me. You wouldn't dare touch me."

The tawny yellow eyes never left her face as he moved lazily toward her. Jacquie's first impulse was to retreat, but that was what he wanted her to do. She stood her ground, refusing to give him the satisfaction he sought and not believing for an instant that he meant one word he'd said.

When he stopped in front of her, Choya reached out and caught a handful of hair. It shimmered white-gold against his sun-browned fingers. Jacquie didn't move. She wouldn't struggle like a mouse under a cat's paw.

His other hand came up to cup the back of her head. Its warmth lulled her for a fraction of a second. And Choya kissed her again. It was the gentlest possible kiss but her senses were on fire as the strong band of his arm encircled her. An ounce more of pressure and she was sure she'd lose her mind.

A hot sensation began to lick through her where his muscled thighs warmed hers. The power of his kiss and his strong hold was draining her resistance. The hands that she'd kept rigidly at her sides were now raised to rest on his biceps. She gasped softly, needing air to keep the whirling sensuality from taking over.

Choya allowed her a few seconds to breathe as he freed her lips and began to explore the sensitive cord in her neck and the hollow of her throat. Involuntary shivers of excitement tingled down her spine. Her breasts swelled against the knit material of her top.

He must have felt or sensed the betraying response of her flesh, for his mouth returned to her lips with a demanding expertise that parted them with consummate ease. Suddenly his virility and her sexual attraction to him became more than Jacquie could resist. With a shuddering moan, she surrendered to the pleasure of his embrace, forgetting all about the crazy fight.

With a sweeping motion, she was lifted off her feet and cradled effortlessly in his arms.

Automatically her hands wrapped themselves around his neck as his hard male lips maintained their ownership of hers. Lost in the feeling of sensual abandonment, Jacquie felt as if she was floating on a cloud. A very strong, safe cloud. She wasn't going to fall to earth. She didn't want to come down.

Then, beneath her, was the firmness of a mattress and the white crispness of a bed sheet. Her arms were still around his neck, her fingers locked. And then . . .

Choya's mouth left hers and didn't return.

"Unwilling really isn't the right word," he whispered. "Tell me what you want."

Reality came back with a rush. What on earth was she doing? And how had he undermined her defenses? She'd been kissed before, held before . . . *but never like this,* she told herself. Scorching heat flamed through her face and neck. His hand slid along her thigh in a last caress as he straightened away from the bed.

Sliding awkwardly from the bed, Jacquie spoke first, oh so casually. "Nothing from you. But thanks for asking." She straightened her clothes, wishing she didn't feel so dazed, desperate to take back control of the situation. "There is one thing you could tell me. Why did you stop so soon?"

"Maybe I enjoy the anticipation," Choya responded evenly, watching her move away from him. "There's plenty of time."

There was an empty feeling in her heart. Faking boredom didn't make her feel better. She secretly craved more of what he could do. Never in her life had she been handled so expertly — and set aside so easily, she reminded herself.

"No, there isn't," Jacquie snapped, "We're right back to square one. I'm going to pay you for the repair bill on my car as soon as I can. I'll go to Tucson — I'll find a job there."

He studied her with renewed amusement. "The long-distance bus stops in Tombstone on Mondays. It's not free."

"It can't be that expensive. I'll wash dishes at the restaurant or make beds at the motel."

"But I pay more."

"What the hell are you talking about, Choya?"

"You're not the only one who's in a fix." His words had a measured tone. She was suddenly sure he'd planned every second of this encounter — and she, like a fool, hadn't seen it coming.

"My father is getting old and it's becoming difficult for him to get around anymore," he said calmly. "It's common knowledge that I've been considering hiring a housekeeper. Maybe someone mentioned it to you —"

"No. They didn't."

"Well, no one will be surprised by your presence in my home," Choya replied without any hesitation. "In fact, it's only a matter of time before the story of you losing your wallet will circulate. A lot of people will probably think I'm doing you a good turn by hiring you."

Was that all he wanted? A *housekeeper?* She found that very hard to believe. An incredulous laugh slipped out of her throat. "First you tell me not to talk to your son, and now you want me around the house? That doesn't make sense."

"Well, maybe I overreacted. I know my son and I didn't know you."

Jacquie snorted. "And you still don't. So

is that your way of saying that you made a mistake? Can I get it in writing?"

"Sure."

She crossed her arms over her chest, watching him warily.

"Look, Jacquie, we both know I'm not talking about anything permanent. But Robbie would be happy for as long as it lasts. And you'll be free to come and go."

"In your jeep?"

"Ah" — he thought that over — "I have a truck too. It's old but it runs great."

"How old?"

Choya grinned. "Older than you and me put together. The clutch is a real challenge. But you'll have to learn to drive it, because I use the jeep so much."

"While my car sits in Brad's garage. No deal."

"A job is a job, and you need one."

He was right about that. But working for *him* was something else again. It didn't matter that the entire population of Tombstone, including the motherly Mrs. Chase, thought Choya Barnett was a great guy and would undoubtedly vouch for him. But she and Choya really didn't like each other — hot kisses notwithstanding. On the other hand, what choice did she have? It wouldn't be easy to find another way to earn the money she owed.

Maybe she should take the damn job he was offering. It seemed like the only way out of her predicament. But even so.

"Do you honestly think people are going to believe I'm only your housekeeper?"

"It doesn't matter to me what they think." He grabbed a pad of paper and a pencil with the motel's logo on it from the table in the room. "Let's do the arithmetic. This is what you owe Brad" — he jotted down the figure — "divided by — how many weeks is it until Christmas?"

"Five."

He noted that, calculated the dividend and showed it to her. "That would be your weekly pay."

She almost smiled. "Really? Then I'd be out of here before Christmas."

He tapped the eraser end of the pencil on the paper. "Not so fast. I didn't subtract your room and board."

"Wait a minute. You're not going to nickel-and-dime me for every can of beans I eat —" She stopped, wondering how he'd gotten her to take him seriously. This was beginning to sound like a negotiation.

"Of course not. But money's tight," he said, shaking his head and giving her a sad look. "The ranch breaks even most years, what with taxes and, um, the occasional tornado. You know how it is," he added vaguely. "Anyway, the adjustment will bring your weekly pay down a little." He showed her the revised figure.

"That's a big bite!"

He grinned. "You'll be on that bus by New Year's Eve." He had the nerve to chuckle. "Sorry. I meant you'll be in your car."

Jacquie spun away from him, her mind reeling. She took the pad of paper he silently proffered and studied the jotted numbers. It was this — or deal with her father's wrath. She didn't want to accept defeat. More than that, she didn't want to go back home. Yet.

"Okay. I'll try it," she said suddenly. "One week at a time. No, make that one day at a time."

"Whatever you say." His eyes lit up with surprise. "Are you sure?"

"No guarantees, Choya. All I said was that I would try. But we're going to draw up a list of rules for both of us and we're going to stick to them."

He handed over the pencil. "Get started."

"Don't you want some input?"

Choya towered over her, but she no longer felt intimidated. "You go ahead and write down what you want first."

She wavered. If they came up with a workable way to cohabit — and didn't that sound dry and dull, she thought with an inward sigh — what about Robbie? Jacquie consoled herself by thinking how happy he would be if she was there for Christmas. That alone was worth sticking with the arrangement Choya proposed.

Then, thinking of her mom, Jacquie stopped short. She would have to rely on her mother's understanding nature when she explained why she wouldn't be coming home for Christmas. Her dad's tendency to fly off the handle was nothing new. But Jacquie standing her ground was unprecedented. Her mother might even approve.

Oh, how she hoped so. Jacquie distracted herself by remembering Robbie's sweet little face. She'd bet the bank that Robbie enjoyed everything about the holiday. She was going to make it super-special just for him.

And then, she told herself with a flash of guilt, she would be on her way come New Year's Eve, just like Choya said.

Jacquie pressed her lips together and tried to think of rules and regulations instead of the little boy with the shy smile. Eventually she succeeded and wrote down Rule One. It was only two words long.

No kissing.

■ ■ ■ ■

They'd gone miles down the highway before they turned onto a rutted gravel road winding into the mountains.

Jacquie stared at the desolate scenery through the dust cloud kicked up by the jeep. The landscape didn't seem real somehow — if she'd known it looked like this or that his ranch was this isolated she might not have agreed to come here, even temporarily. But it wasn't as if Choya had lied to her, and she hadn't thought to ask.

The jeep bounced over the little-traveled road. The bone-jarring ride would have wakened her if she'd been asleep. The road twisted and curved along the foot of the mountains. Here and there along a mountain slope was the telltale scar of an abandoned mine.

Occasionally Jacquie glimpsed a derelict building, long deserted, or a barely visible track leading away from the main road. Sometimes there was a small sign on a fence post, giving the name of a ranch. Mainly it was an endless landscape of sage and cactus and sunbaked rocks.

And dust. Swirling dust entered the open sides of the jeep and covered everything.

The gritty particles powdered her face and skin and drifted over her clothes. Jacquie longed to ask how far they still had to go, certain the dust would suffocate her if she had to endure the ride much longer. But the silence was not one she wanted to break.

When she had viewed the Dragoon Mountains from Boothill Cemetery, the deceiving distances of the desert had made them seem so close. Now Jacquie realized that Choya's ranch was miles from civilization, surrounded by undulating, arid land.

The jeep bounced off the road onto a rutted track seemingly leading to nowhere. Her heart sank.

When there seemed to be nothing on the horizon but desert scrub, unexpectedly large, light shapes took form. One was a stucco-walled house, low and sprawling with a half-story added on under the wide, overhanging roof. The other was a similarly constructed building with a fenced enclosure extending from it.

Two large cottonwood trees shaded the west side of the house. That was a touch of home — cottonwoods grew here and there by the river that wound through Dallas. Somewhere underground there must be water. The thought gave her a little comfort. Only cactus decorated the front yard. It couldn't be called a lawn since there was no grass, only more desert sand and rock.

Coming closer, Jacquie decided she liked the look of it after all. Green grass and flowering shrubs would have been incongruous against the barren landscape beyond. The native plants seemed to be right at home and thriving. Tougher than tough — she remembered Robbie repeating Choya's words and wondered if she had what it took to live up to them.

The jeep braked to a stop in front of the house and the dust cloud caught up with it, blowing in the open sides. Jacquie choked and began coughing.

Maybe she didn't.

"Does it ever rain here?" she asked hoarsely.

Choya cast a sliding glance in her direction. "Sure. Once or twice a year." He nodded toward the mountains, so much closer now. "Sometimes we get a dusting of snow on the Dragoons, but that's rare. Nothing you could ski on, of course."

Stepping out of the jeep, he reached in back for her suitcases and handbag, tossing the latter to Jacquie. She barely caught it before the contents spilled.

"Here we are," he said cheerfully.

"Give me a minute." She was still wheezing. Jacquie didn't want to walk in with tearing eyes and a barking cough. "I can't catch my breath."

Disconcerting laughter glinted in his eyes. "Think you can walk? I could carry you over the threshold."

"No way," Jacquie retorted. "Robbie would get the wrong idea. And so would your father."

"Robbie's in school," Choya pointed out, "but my dad's around here somewhere." No one opened the front door or looked out a window. There was no sound but the whistling of the wind. "Maybe he's taking a nap."

She straightened in the seat and swung her legs out, sliding her feet down to the ground. The action triggered a few more coughs. She reached into her bag for a tissue to wipe her eyes, then crumpled it and tucked it in her pocket.

"Seriously, I could carry you and the suitcases."

"Oh, quit showing off. There's no one here to see." He only shrugged and led the way to the front door. Jacquie followed him, glaring at his back and keeping her grip on her bag. She stumbled on the flagstone path but didn't fall. Choya turned around.

"Don't worry. I can walk," she snapped. "Even though I'm from Dallas." She caught up to him.

"Very good," he said patronizingly, "you'll have to, until you learn to drive that." He nodded toward an ancient Ford pickup painted an odd shade of red. Jacquie stopped and took a few steps to the side to get a better view of it. It wasn't so much red as it was rusty. The high, rounded front grille and curved fenders told her it had rolled off the assembly line sometime in the 1930s.

"Was that the truck you were talking about? You mean it actually runs?"

"Yup."

She looked at it dubiously. "You're kidding."

"No, I'm not. They don't make them like that anymore. It was Sam's first truck and he bought it used."

"But —"

"He'd love to teach you how to drive it, but using the clutch is hard on his knees. Maybe I will. If you don't mind me telling you what to do, that is."

He chucked her under the chin and Jacquie lifted her head in indignation, about to say something cutting. He'd said the truck would be her transportation, but that didn't seem likely now. She didn't like the feeling that she'd been tricked.

"I hope you're planning to buy another car. As in today," she said crossly. "There's no way in hell I'm driving that monster."

"I am, actually. Believe it or not, I was thinking about it before you slammed into my jeep."

"Oh, sure you were," she retorted with obvious indignation, glaring up at him. "Don't lie to —"

He took the opportunity to shut up her up with a quick kiss on her parted lips.

"Mrmmf!" She pressed them together and twisted her head away. In another second, he was opening the unlocked front door with no show of concern. Furious, she wiped her mouth with the back of her hand, even as her senses flamed to life. "The first rule was no kissing!"

"You looked like you wanted one."

"I didn't."

Choya studied her face for a brief second while she gathered her wits. It wasn't that she didn't like his kisses. She did. Too much. They kept her from thinking straight, though. If this arrangement was going to work, they had to keep a certain distance. To her annoyance, he smiled in satisfaction.

Someone inside had heard the front door open and was coming to it. A tall, gaunt man stepped out into the shadow of the building's overhang. His angular features had a rough-cut look that not even the weight of years on his shoulders had blunted, with a leathery face crisscrossed with wrinkles. His eyes were a piercing pale blue.

Choya turned to look his way, but the older man's gaze didn't move to him until he'd made a thorough study of Jacquie. Choya stayed where he stood near the cement slab in front of the door.

"Sam, this is Jacqueline Grey," Choya spoke clearly and distinctly. "She's going to keep house for us for a while." His tawny eyes shifted to her wary expression. "Jacquie, this is my father, Sam Barnett."

Except for his ruggedness, there was nothing about the older man that reminded Jacquie of his autocratic son. With a rush, she remembered the service station mechanic explaining that Sam Barnett had found Choya as a baby abandoned in a cactus patch, had reared him and later legally adopted him.

There was something forthright about the older man that appealed to Jacquie. Despite his cragginess, he had an open face and a direct gaze. Good. She would need an ally if she was going to pull this off. Her lips relaxed their tight line as she searched the lined face.

"Hello, Mr. Barnett," she said. "I know you weren't expecting me, but here I am."

"How about that." Sam Barnett looked her up and down, a twinkle suddenly brightening his blue eyes. "Ain't you a pretty gal. Son, you just made my day." He grinned at Choya. "Where'd you find her?"

Choya grinned back, like he was about to say something like oh, by the side of the road. Jacquie visibly braced herself. Now that she'd arrived in the back of nowhere, she realized that she hadn't given any thought to the reality of living in an all-male household. The inevitable comments and jokes were going to wear thin fast.

Sam, who didn't seem to miss much, noticed her silent discomfort.

"Oh, Lord," he said, abashed. "What did I just say?"

"Start over. With hello." Choya shot him a warning look.

"Well, then — hello. And pardon me, miss," Sam began hesitantly. "I'm just not used to having ladies around. I do try to watch my language around the boy, though." His eyes crinkled as they took her in from head to toe. "You ain't from around here, are you?"

"No." She shook her head, feeling truly

defeated.

"Jacquie is from Texas," Choya inserted. "Dallas, to be exact."

"I went there once. Big cars and bigger buildings. I couldn't wait to get back here where a man can breathe. So what brought you to Tombstone, Miss Grey?"

"You can call me Jacquie," she said as politely as she could.

Choya took over from there. "She was just passing through but she had to stop. Car trouble. Turned out to be a major repair job too. And then her wallet with all her money was lost. She's here temporarily until she can earn enough to pay that bill and put by some traveling cash."

Sam Barnett nodded sagely. "I see. But can't her folks help?"

"Ah — Jacquie's the independent type. She doesn't want to ask her folks for a penny if she can possibly help it."

Jacquie nodded. If that was going to be the official story, she'd stick to it. At some point she would be alone with Sam Barnett and he would want to know all about her over a friendly cup of coffee. It was just as well that the introduction was simple and straightforward and easy to remember.

"I see," his father said approvingly.

Inwardly she sighed. The way her dad had

refused to talk to her still stung. She'd been casual about it at the time, preferring to keep Choya in the dark. But now, picking up on the easy camaraderie and trust between Choya and his father, she felt a little envious.

That — and homesick. The green-shaded neighborhood where she'd grown up seemed very far away. And so did all its conveniences. She shifted her bag to the other shoulder and surveyed the landscape again. It occurred to her that it was actually a good thing that her car was safely parked in back of the service station in Tombstone. The deep ruts on these backcountry roads and cow tracks would have jolted the axles apart in less than a mile.

"Now, we're forgettin' our manners," Sam said to his son with joking sternness. "No more jawin'." The old man turned his attention to her. "Miss Jacquie, you come on in." He waved her inside with a gallant gesture. "We got a nice little room for ya behind the kitchen, but I gotta sweep it out. Let's see, there's some clean sheets in the linen closet — and I have to take a pillow from Robbie's bed —"

The last statements were mumbled to himself as he made a verbal list of the things that needed to be done. He pivoted with difficulty, leaning heavily on a cane that Jacquie just noticed in his right hand. Awkwardly he hobbled into the house, depending on the cane for support.

Choya stepped aside to follow her into the house. Jacquie walked into an austerely furnished living room. A blackened fireplace of natural stone was on the far outside wall. The long sofa was covered with a Navajo blanket, the only vivid color in the room. Two large chairs sat opposite it, one with a footstool and reading lamp beside it. An antique rolltop desk was against one wall where rows of shelves were lined with books. Oak floors gleamed satin smooth. For a male household, everything was surprisingly clean and tidy.

A long, white-walled hallway branched off to the left from the living room, but Choya indicated the direction his father had gone. The short hallway he took led into the kitchen.

The room was dominated by a large, painted wood table in the center with a red-checked vinyl tablecloth on its top. The wood cupboards were old and painted white, and a large porcelain sink gaped in a yellowing countertop. The refrigerator was modern, and she noticed a microwave, but the gas stove looked like an antique. The floor was tiled and continued in a short stretch to an outside door.

In between the back of the kitchen and the outside door was a second door. It was this door that was Sam Barnett's destination. Leaning on his cane, he pushed it open and waited for Jacquie.

"It's not much," he said, "but it gives you some privacy from the rest of the house."

By that, Jacquie guessed that he meant the other rooms on the first floor didn't lead into it or to it. The bedrooms had to be upstairs in the half-story she'd noticed. She darted a sideways glance at Choya, wondering if he minded that she wasn't close to whatever room it was that he slept in.

Tough luck if he did. Rule Two was that she got her own room and no one came in without knocking. She was half-tempted to post the written-out list of rules they'd both agreed to on her door. It was short and to the point.

Rule Three: she got paid in cash at the end of every week. Rule Four: she got to make up any other rules she thought were necessary and he had to say yes to them.

Posting the list seemed like the wrong move, though she suspected Choya was going to need some reminding now and then. But if they were on her door, Sam would peruse them and so would Robbie. One look at it and shrewd old Mr. Barnett was likely to guess more than she wanted him to know.

Choya gave her a bland smile. Jacquie shot him a warning look, thinking that the room's distance from the others could be a disadvantage as well. If he wandered into the kitchen for a late-night cup of cocoa, he might try to strike up a conversation that could lead to another violation of Rule One. She swept past him to where his father was standing and looked in.

The room was small. A double bed sat in one corner, taking up most of the floor space not occupied by a chest of drawers, metal shelves and a straight-backed chair. A plain braided rug was on the floor in front of the bed. It was a starkly simple room, serving its purpose without any attempt to please the eye.

Choya walked in and set her suitcases on the bed. "You can unpack," he said. "I think I'll pick up Robbie at school so he doesn't have to take the bus. He'll want to see you right away." Then, turning to the tall, gaunt man looking in, he said, "I won't be home for lunch, Sam."

A silent message must have accompanied his statement, because the older man nodded and limped away from the doorway. Jacquie tensed, wary now that Choya apparently wanted to see her alone. She decided it was better to ask questions than wait for orders.

"Is your father expecting a hot meal or is a sandwich okay?"

"Whoa." He held up a hand. "You're not on duty yet. I'm sure he'd rather see you settled in than anything else."

"Just thought I'd get started. I want to work off my debt as fast as possible, so I may be putting in overtime."

"Doing what?" he smirked. "We go to bed by ten around here."

Jacquie understood. "Don't be disgusting." Too bad he'd insisted on adding Rule Five, his sole contribution to the list. No slapping.

"Sorry." His mouth straightened. "I'll try to behave. Make yourself at home while I'm gone."

"Okay," Jacquie muttered, wondering why she'd ever thought this was a good idea. Choya's golden gaze moving over her made her feel warm all over. She knew only too well how dangerously attractive he was to her.

He gave a resigned sigh. "Need anything from town?"

"No." She pushed her hair back over her shoulders. She could feel the grit in it. What she wanted more than anything right now was a long, hot shower.

Choya stopped at the motel first to tell Mrs. Chase he'd hired Jacquie as a temporary housekeeper and that she would be staying at the ranch. Lulu hadn't seen them leave — Jacquie had left the keycard in the box provided for that purpose and a note on the counter because the motel owner had stepped out of the office.

Which meant that the rest of Tombstone wouldn't know they'd left either. Fine with Choya.

Mrs. Chase gave him a big hug and congratulated him on not being a total fool. Then she wished him the best of luck and sent him out with a white-chocolate snowman for Robbie.

A few minutes later, he pulled his jeep into the school parking lot and waited in the area set aside for parents picking up kids. Robbie wasn't used to seeing him there, so Choya claimed a spot in front where he'd be fully visible to the kids pouring out the doors when the final bell rang. Robbie went a lot slower than they did lately, what with the crutches. But a couple of his pals always stayed with him and made sure he got out okay.

He heard the ringing inside the low brick building and waited. One minute later, a school aide came out the door and stood to one side, clutching the metal handle. A herd of youngsters stampeded out, ignoring her admonitions to walk, not run, and shouting over her requests that they pipe down. In a flash they scattered to waiting cars or joined little groups of kids hoofing it home. The children who lived farther out headed for the two school buses outside the parking lot.

He wanted to head off Robbie before he did the same. Choya caught a glimpse of the bright blue cast just before his son swung out the doors, his school backpack over one shoulder. He got out of the jeep and called to him. Robbie looked his way with surprise, then came over on the double.

"Dad! Why are you here?"

Choya ruffled his hair. "I was in town. Just thought you and I could drive home together for a change."

"Didja have another rancher meeting?"

"Nope. I was running errands."

Robbie let his father pick him up and deposit him on the passenger seat, then slid his backpack into the footwell.

"How was school?" Choya asked as he got in around the other side.

"It was okay," Robbie said. "I got an A on my science test. It was easy."

"Good. I'm proud of you. How about we get some ice cream to celebrate?"

"Sure!"

Choya waited until after they'd polished off two cones between them and gotten back in the jeep to tell Robbie that Jacquie was at the house. The boy looked at him with joyous disbelief. "She is? How come?"

"Well, that car of hers is going to take longer to fix than we all thought, for one thing. So she's going to stay with us for a while. Help fix lunch for your gramps, maybe do a little housework."

"Really?" Robbie's tone was quiet but he was clearly thrilled. "For how long?"

"I'm not sure. But probably for several weeks. Maybe longer. And you're not to give her any trouble."

"I wouldn't! Not ever! I promise to pick up my clothes and stuff. Every day."

"Well, that's a first," his father said wryly, pulling out of the parking space and heading for the road that led out of Tombstone. "Hey, I have something for you from Mrs. Chase. Go ahead and eat it now. What's the difference?"

"Thanks!" Robbie leaned back and unwrapped the foil from the snowman. He picked off the sugar carrot nose and the dark chocolate buttons, eating those before the body. All of a sudden he sat up straight, resting his hands on the dashboard. "Dad . . . wait. Pull over. Right here."

"Why?" Choya looked through the windshield. Either Robbie had spotted an armadillo in danger of becoming roadkill or there was a golden eagle in the sky. He didn't see anything ahead of the jeep or above it. But he did what Robbie requested and pulled over in back of the sign that welcomed visitors to Tombstone.

Robbie had lifted up his backpack and unzipped it, looking for something.

"What's up, son?"

"You'll see." His fingers curled around something small as he unlatched the door with his other hand. "Can you put me on your shoulders?"

"Huh?" Choya gave the boy a baffled look. "What for?"

"Please," Robbie begged. "Please just do it."

Choya shrugged and got out, lifting Robbie with ease from the passenger side. Getting a kid with a cast on his leg onto his shoulders was harder, but they managed it.

"You're a little old for this," Choya pointed out. "And quit kicking me. How's the view?"

"Great," Robbie said with satisfaction. "Now go to the front of the sign."

His father complied, pausing in front of it. The sign said what it always did.

WELCOME TO TOMBSTONE, ARIZONA
THE TOWN TOO TOUGH TO DIE
POPULATION: 1,060

"So what's this all about? Is this a school assignment?" he asked Robbie.

"Nope. Can you get closer?"

"Okay. How's that?"

"A little more closer. Good. Thanks, Dad."

Choya looked up and saw his son reach out with the stub of an old crayon. So that's what he'd had in his hand. Robbie crossed out the final zero in the population number and wrote in a one above it.

"Population one thousand and sixty-one. For Jacquie."

Choya chuckled and the boy on his shoulders wobbled, unbalanced by the leg in the cast. "Stop it, Dad!"

"I sure hope the sheriff doesn't drive by and see us," Choya said, surveying the empty road.

"You can explain," Robbie said seriously.

"Wait. Don't move." He reached out again and wrote something in straggling capital letters next to the changed number.

Choya peered at the letters: **J.A.K.K.Y.** He shook with laughter and Robbie dropped the crayon.

"So she'll know it's for her," Robbie explained. "Is that how you spell her name?"

"Close enough. Let's get out of here."

"Do you think she'll like it that I did that, Dad?"

Choya paused to adjust the boy on his shoulders. "I hope so," he said in a gruff voice.

CHAPTER 6

Jacquie turned toward the suitcases, resting her hands on top of one. What had she let herself in for? She honestly hadn't realized until her arrival just how far away and lonesome the Barnett ranch was. Choya had said there might not be much to do for someone who was used to city living. But he'd added that the rugged land and the constantly changing sky above it had a way of captivating the imagination. His brief description made it sound almost romantic. So far . . . it wasn't. Too eager to find a solution that didn't involve money from home, she hadn't asked enough questions about where he lived. Or anything else.

The small window in the room offered a view of the mountains, no longer remote but broodingly close. For a few seconds she entertained the wild idea of just running away, then shook her head, sitting down disconsolately on the bed.

Once again she'd made a rash decision without thinking it through. She'd landed herself in the middle of nowhere without a way to call home, if it came to that. On her first tour of the house, she hadn't seen a landline phone in the living room or one on the kitchen wall. Choya probably relied on a cell phone and as for Sam — who knew? Jacquie hadn't seen a satellite dish attached to the house either, so there probably wasn't TV service or an internet connection.

There were books to read. There was Sam. She could talk to him. And there was Robbie. She could talk to him too. He'd probably be very happy to introduce her to Gila monsters and other interesting wildlife. She shuddered. But she would shake claws with one for his sake.

She told herself she couldn't give up this quickly, not without a cent to her name and no way to skedaddle out of here. Then Jacquie heard a shuffling noise and stood up.

Sam Barnett limped to the doorway of her room. Instead of his cane, he was using a straw broom for support. Fighting to get a grip on her composure, Jacquie could only manage a sideways glance at him as he began awkwardly pushing the broom around on the tiled floor.

"I'll do that," she said quickly, unable to be idle while an elderly man, practically crippled with arthritis, cleaned her room.

He hesitated, then handed her the broom. "I been doin' all this for so many years, it's going to seem strange havin' someone else do the work." He didn't hurry out of the room. "Fact is, Choya's wife — she died several years ago — well, she left most of the housework to me. And my own Gladys has been gone for over thirty-six years. This house hasn't known a woman to take care of it. I guess it don't look like much."

"It's a very nice home." It was on the tip of Jacquie's tongue to ask whether there was a phone or a satellite dish, but she decided against it. He probably wanted to chat.

"I'll go fetch the sheets." Sam Barnett turned, keeping a balancing hand on the wall, and limped from the room.

Maybe not.

Jacquie stood for silent seconds, then began sweeping the room. She had completed that and was stoically unpacking when Sam returned with the clean bedsheets. He stayed this time, keeping up a steady monologue of his first years on the ranch. At appropriate spots, Jacquie made suitable responses, wondering with an inward smile if he would ever run out of anecdotes.

When she was finished, he showed her the parts of the house she hadn't seen. She found nothing unexpected. All the rooms were plain and serviceable. Then it was back to the kitchen where he suggested a late lunch. Sandwiches would be fine, he said, explaining that his appetite wasn't what it used to be.

Jacquie was relieved. She was hungry but doubted that the nervous churning of her stomach would let a heavy meal stay down.

He gave her the cook's tour, pointing out the pantry, which was well-stocked with staples, and where they kept utensils, cutlery, and dishes.

They worked together to prepare sandwiches, in sync, as if they'd done it for years, which amused her. She put a half-sandwich on her plate and wrapped up the other one, then sat down.

The meal was over with soon enough. Sam offered to help with the washing up, but Jacquie declined — not out of any belief that it wasn't a man's place, but because she hoped he would leave the kitchen and allow her a chance to think in peace. He stayed right where he was, but stopped talking. To digest, she supposed.

She hung up the damp dishtowel and

rinsed out the sink. That took all of ten seconds. Now what? Ask Sam to show her how to shift the clutch in the venerable pickup? She doubted Choya was really planning to buy a new car. She was stuck. His nice old dad looked like he was ready for a nap and any driving lessons would have to wait.

Just then, Sam perked up again. He took it upon himself to explain the household schedule: when the meals were eaten, the shopping was done, the clothes washed and a rough-and-ready cleaning schedule. Jacquie paid little attention to any of it, although she pretended to listen.

Her nerves were taut, as finely drawn as a bowstring. The sound of a vehicle pulling to a stop outside the house sent her heart leaping. Her gaze flew to the wall clock above the refrigerator. It couldn't possibly be late afternoon already!

"That must be Choya," Sam commented, turning toward the archway to the living room.

At the opening of the front door, Jacquie half rose out of the kitchen chair, wanting to see him and not knowing why. There was the rapid thumping of crutches on the polished wood floor of the living room before Robbie burst into the kitchen, his face aglow with excitement.

"Jacquie!" He rushed forward almost faster than his crutches could propel him. "Dad said you were here, but I couldn't hardly believe him. Jacquie, I'm so glad you didn't leave!"

Positive that any second Robbie would pitch headlong to the floor, Jacquie stepped away from the chair, reaching out with her arms to catch him. He practically threw himself into them, discarding the crutches with a crash to wrap his arms around her middle in a fierce hug.

It was such a completely uninhibited and genuine embrace that Jacquie couldn't help responding to it. She returned his hug, the boy's warmth easing the inner agitation that gripped her.

Robbie tipped his head back, his brown eyes earnestly studying her. "Are you really going to stay? Dad said you were."

The smile on her lips became hesitant as she loosened his grip and bent down to his level. Her hands trembled on his shoulders. How could she possibly tell this little boy that his home wasn't good enough for her?

"Yes — but only for a while," she answered.

He must have sensed her reluctance. He wrapped his small arms around her neck, clinging to her in desperation as he buried his head against her shoulder.

"I hope you stay forever and ever," Robbie declared in a throbbing voice.

Instinctively, Jacquie smoothed the silken top of his head, brushing a light kiss on the area. A tightness gripped her throat.

Out of the corner of her eye, she glimpsed a slight movement near the entrance to the living room. Her gaze swerved to investigate, encountering the muscled frame of Choya. Even in stillness, he possessed a vitality, a charged aura that seemed to crackle about him.

Tawny eyes held hers, impassively studying her and the boy clutching her so possessively. Nothing in the chiseled granite features revealed any trace of his thoughts. There was no indication of how long he had been standing there or how much he had overheard.

Shaken by the discovery of his presence, Jacquie slowly untangled Robbie's arms from around her neck, keeping a supporting hand at his waist while she retrieved his crutches. Ignoring Choya wasn't easy as she smiled at the boy.

"Have you seen my room?" Robbie asked eagerly. "I have a whole bunch of Indian arrowheads. Gramps and me, we go looking for them. Now you can come along too."

"Of course," Jacquie agreed weakly.

"And I want to show you my horse. I have one of my very own," he declared proudly, again brimming with excitement. "No one else can ride him except me — Dad said so. I'll let you ride him, though. I can't ride him until I get my cast off. Can you ride a horse, Jacquie?"

"Not very well," she admitted, since her horseback riding had been limited to an occasional outing with a group at a suburban stable.

"I'll teach you." He shifted his crutches. "Come on, I'll show you my horse. His name is Apache. This all used to be Apache land, did you know that?"

"Yes, I did."

"Save your tour for later, Robbie," Choya ordered. "You have to change out of your school clothes and do your chores first."

Robbie gave his father an impatient glance and turned back to Jacquie. "We're going to have a lot of fun together. After I get my cast off, we can go riding together over some of the same trails that Cochise and Geronimo rode. And there's this place by a waterhole where Gramps and I find our arrowheads. When it's warm we can swim there, too, and have picnics and —"

"Robbie," Choya's low voice firmly interrupted his son, "Jacquie's not here to be your playmate."

The boy swallowed the rest of what he was about to say and nodded. Jacquie straightened, the fiery sparkle of battle in her eyes as she met the gold mask of his gaze.

"Don't speak for me, Choya. I'd love to spend some time with Robbie. And you don't have to worry that his homework won't get done."

The line of Choya's mouth tightened. Robbie glanced bewilderedly from her to his father. The charged silence was broken by the soft chuckle of Sam Barnett.

"I was beginning to think that girl had no spirit at all." His blue eyes twinkled as he glanced at Choya. "She's barely said one sentence since you left."

There was a visible relaxing of the hard set of Choya's features, and even amusement in the eyes that swept over Jacquie before moving to his son.

"Go and change your school clothes, Robbie," Choya repeated in a calmly chiding tone.

Robbie hesitated. "I don't want to get Jacquie in trouble."

"Seems to me that Jacquie can look out for herself," was the even reply.

The answer apparently satisfied the boy. With an I'll-see-you-later smile to Jacquie, he thumped out of the kitchen in the direction of his bedroom. Sam Barnett gripped his cane and pushed himself from the chair.

"I didn't get my afternoon nap," he announced. "I think I'll lay down for an hour before dinner."

Stubbornly, Jacquie maintained her challenging stance, refusing to relent an inch although she had been left alone with Choya. If anything her annoyance increased. She held his gaze with unwavering defiance.

"If I'm going to live here, Robbie can't go around thinking you'll be mad if he wants to be with me," she said in a low voice. "You agreed to drop all that." He had, back at the motel, but it wasn't something she felt like putting into the rules. Robbie's feelings were a lot more important than her relationship, such as it was, with Choya. "Remember?"

"Yes." He moved leisurely into the kitchen. "But for a second, I forgot. He can be a little too eager sometimes. And if you're living here, it's not so easy to put him off."

She hesitated. "Oh. Well, maybe you have a point."

"So how did it go with my dad?" Choya inquired.

She got the feeling he was asking the question mostly to distract her. "He certainly was happy to have someone to chat with. He didn't leave me alone for a second," she said ruefully.

"Sorry about that."

"I didn't mind. Not much, anyway," she added honestly.

Choya shook his head. "Want me to talk to him?"

"No!"

"Okay. Just asking. Did you get unpacked and settled in?"

"I unpacked."

Choya stopped and gave her a long look. "Think you'll last the week out here? You can tell me. If it's not going to work, I'd rather hear it sooner than later."

He didn't add *when Robbie gets more attached,* but she could finish the sentence for him.

The grooves deepened around his mouth as he studied her face. Jacquie felt suddenly cold. She folded her arms over her chest and just stood there, afraid he would take her hand. "I don't know, Choya. I've never been anywhere so lonely. Tombstone was tiny, but there were shops — and sidewalks — and people around. Out here it's just the four of us. Do you understand?" She didn't add that she was worried about how she could keep him at a distance when there were so few distractions.

"I think so."

She wanted to ask him if his late wife had liked such a solitary existence, but it seemed completely inappropriate. Jacquie fell silent, looking away from him.

"We usually eat around six and I have chores to do. But I can cook if you'd rather not —"

"No, no. I can do it. I need to do it," she corrected. "Otherwise I'll just sit and stare out that little window in the back room." Before Choya could try to change her mind, Jacquie ordered her weak legs to carry her from the kitchen. He didn't stop her. He must have guessed that she was only running from his presence and not picking a fight.

She suddenly wanted to be by herself and there was nowhere to do that but in the small bedroom off the kitchen. She closed the door behind her. As she moved away, there was a knock on the door and she hesitated.

"Like I said, I'm going to do chores," Choya stated. "See you at dinner. You really don't have to cook. We'll just open a couple of cans of stew. Wouldn't be the first time."

She didn't answer.

"And, uh," he went on, "I guess we'll boil some frozen green beans too. With a little butter. We could squeeze lemon juice on them too, so we don't die of scurvy."

Despite her nervousness, she smiled. But she still didn't answer. How was she ever going to manage her attraction to him now that they would be living in the same house for the next five weeks?

Striding footsteps carried him away, followed by the slam of the outside door. She waited for a few minutes to make sure he was gone, then emerged herself.

There was a laundry room and small bathroom across from her bedroom. Jacquie used it to splash cold water on her face. The reviving chill was just what she needed to bolster her resolve as she entered the kitchen. It would probably cure her jitters if she stopped obsessing and just did something with her hands. After all, cooking and cleaning were supposedly the reasons for her being here.

She banished all thought of her mixed emotions as she concentrated on the menu for the evening meal. Never much of a cook, she kept it simple — fried chops, potatoes, a vegetable, and coleslaw. The stove proved to be a worthy opponent to her effort, cantankerously refusing to light, then stubbornly resisting her attempts to regulate the flame.

Finally the potatoes were boiling and the chops were in the iron skillet and a half-bag of frozen vegetables got dumped into a saucepan to simmer with a pat of butter. Jacquie felt secure that she could leave all that to cook while she fixed coleslaw.

As she was nearly finished mixing dollops of mayo, salt, and a touch of sugar with fresh slivered cabbage from another bag, she heard a sizzling hiss from the stove. A quick glance saw the lid of the potato pan bouncing while boiling water bubbled down the side. At the same instant, she noticed smoke rising from the skillet.

Grabbing a pot holder from a drawer, she dashed to the old black-and-white stove, hesitating over which to rescue first. Deciding on the potatoes, she leaned forward to reach the pan on the rear burner. Her long hair fell forward. The outside door slammed, followed by footsteps. "What are you doing?" Choya demanded.

Jacquie checked her movement to dart him a quick glance, then reverted her attention to the pan. "What does it look like? The potatoes are boiling over!"

Her breath whooshed out as his arms

circled her waist, lifting her off her feet and simultaneously pushing her away from the stove. She staggered backward at his abrupt release as he took the pot holder from her hand and set the pan aside.

"Don't you know you can catch your hair on fire leaning across a stove like that?" he glowered. "Especially when it's as long as yours!"

"I didn't think," Jacquie breathed, then glanced at the stove. The smoke was really billowing from the skillet now. "The meat!" she exclaimed.

Choya turned, wrapping the pot holder around the handle and lifting the skillet from the fire. Quickly he shut off the burner before setting it back down. With a fork, he turned over the chops, revealing the charred sides. His quizzical glance at Jacquie really annoyed her.

"I said I would cook. I didn't say I could cook," she said defensively.

He lifted the lid on the pan of potatoes and a scorched smell filled the air. She brushed a hand across her forehead.

"All you had to do was turn the heat down," Choya said dryly.

"That's easy to say," she protested, feeling his criticism was unwarranted. "That stove is an antique. Only my grandmother would know how it works."

"Sam doesn't have any trouble with it."

"Which proves he's as old as my grandmother!" Jacquie retorted.

There was a glint of laughter in Choya's eyes, then he turned toward the stove. "Come here. Let me show you how it works."

Ignoring the tingle that danced down her spine at standing so close to him, Jacquie listened attentively to his instructions. He spoke clearly and concisely, sliding a mocking glance at her only when he had finished.

"Now see what you can do about salvaging the meal while I wash up," he ordered.

"I'll try," she sighed, and poked a fork into the pork chops to see how badly they were ruined.

As Choya started to walk away, a faint smile curving his hard mouth, Robbie hobbled into the kitchen. He halted just inside the room and sniffed the air, wrinkling his nose in distaste.

"What's that?" He frowned warily.

"Dinner," Choya replied with a meaningful look at Jacquie. "Or perhaps it's a burnt offering." Her cheeks flamed at his laughing taunt.

"Come on, son," he said. "Let's wash our hands."

The meal was edible but barely. Okay, so she hadn't told Choya that her experience in the culinary arts was limited to watching chef shows. There was no law that said she had to practice what they preached.

It was food. It was hot. It was on the plates. She'd done her job. Choya and Robbie didn't comment or complain, but Sam had clicked his tongue in dismay at the sight of the blackened pork chops.

The minor disaster meant that Jacquie had to spend a lot of time cleaning up, since the stove had to be scoured where the potatoes had boiled over. Then Robbie had appeared in the kitchen when she'd finished. A checkerboard was in his hand and he challenged her to a game.

"I'm an expert," he declared, and proceeded to beat her soundly. When he proposed a second game, Jacquie suggested it was time for him to be in bed.

"Okay," Robbie agreed without argument. "We can play again tomorrow night. Don't feel bad that I beat you. I been playing checkers since I was three. Dad is teaching me chess, but I'm not very good at it yet."

Jacquie smiled and said that chess was complicated. Silently considering the way Choya had outmaneuvered her so many times, she was certain he was a master at that particular game.

At Robbie's request, she tucked him into bed, then left his room when Choya appeared to wish his son goodnight. She didn't beat a hasty retreat, just walked away, feeling somewhat more at peace, even after the not-great dinner. Cooking was soothing, even when you screwed it up. And all three Barnetts had been awfully nice about it.

As she entered her own bedroom, she congratulated herself on offering Choya such a calm goodnight when she'd walked past him. She had felt his tawny eyes narrow on her, no doubt measuring her mood.

Yawning, she didn't particularly care that it would undoubtedly change again. She was just plain bone tired. She undressed for bed, crawling beneath the covers.

Within minutes of her head touching the pillow, she was asleep. Mental exhaustion made it a dreamless state and nothing wakened her.

Until a hand gripped her shoulder, shaking it slightly.

Jacquie tried to shrug it away and snuggled deeper beneath the covers. The hand tightened.

"Rise and shine," the voice said.

"Go away," she mumbled sleepily without opening her eyes. Then memory returned as to where she was and who had just spoken. She rolled onto her back, automatically drawing the covers over her breasts. The gray light of dawn was peering through the window as she focused her somewhat bleary gaze on Choya.

She choked back the impulse to order him from her room and asked instead, "What do you want?" An equally foolish question, since she didn't really want to know the answer.

Still groggy from heavy sleep, her senses were slow to alertness. Every part of him that her guarded look saw indicated his freshness and overwhelming vitality. Half-closed eyes of shimmering sand-gold returned her study with disturbing results.

"How did you get in here?" she asked indignantly.

"I knocked. You told me to come in. Don't tell me you were talking in your sleep."

"I don't know. How would I know? I was sleeping!"

He sat back on the bed. "Do you know how beautiful you are? Your hair like that, all messed up, and that pouty mouth" — he stopped talking for a second or two — "I gotta get out of here. You're pure temptation."

Jacquie shook her head to clear it. Refreshed by her deep sleep, she was still drowsy but well aware that his sensual energy was having its usual, powerful effect on her.

"Where's Robbie?" she whispered.

"On the school bus."

"Where's Sam?"

"He got a ride with a friend. He likes to meet a lady friend for coffee in Tombstone. Early-bird senior A.M. special."

That meant they were alone. But she couldn't just . . . she just couldn't . . . She tried not to want him. It didn't work.

She reached out to him and he didn't draw away. In fact, his strong arms enfolded her and half lifted her out of the bed. When he stopped, she was drawn close to him, her feet and legs tangled in the bedsheets.

The strap of her pale blue shortie nightgown had slipped from her shoulder, revealing the rounded swell of one breast. The blocking grip of Choya's hand kept the strap from sliding farther and revealing more.

Deliberately he studied what the gown exposed, his gaze wandering to the pulsing vein in her neck, then on to the softness of her lips parted in surprise. His glittering eyes skimmed over the alluring disarray of her hair before he brushed a kiss on her temple.

Jacquie's hands rested on the solidness of his waist. Tangled as she was in the covers, she had no desire to struggle. The touch of her hands against him was more for support than any thought to resist him.

This wasn't the plan. It was against every one of the rules. She didn't care.

The male line of his mouth descended to play with her lips, teasing the way they trembled at his touch. It was an exquisite kind of torture for Jacquie, almost afraid to feel the branding hardness of a kiss of possession yet unable to make herself twist away to avoid it. The fresh-air scent of him enveloped her — he'd been outside to send off his son and come back in again to wake her up.

"If you don't get up and fix my breakfast," his warm breath flowed over her skin as he spoke against her lips, "I may decide to have it in bed. With you."

"I can't." Her lips quivered against his teasing mouth.

Motionless for an instant, Choya asked, "Why?"

"Because" — Jacquie breathed shakily, his intense attraction almost more than she could cope with in this semi-languourous state — "I can't get up until you let go of me."

Lazily he drew his head back, dark hair shining in the indoor light. Cat-soft eyes moved over her face, almost physically touching each feature before they glowed with a seductive light.

With deliberate slowness, he laid her back on the bed. Then he bent over her, a hand resting on the sheeted mattress on either side of her.

"You're free," he said. "You can get up and get dressed now."

She hesitated, uncertain that he meant what he said.

"Don't you want to . . ." Jacquie lifted her head from the pillow. Choya straightened and scooted back. He was fully clothed, she saw. No shirt buttons were being undone. Everything zipped. The triumphant look in his eyes was the last straw. "Oh. I guess not. Fooled again." Temper flashed in her eyes that he should toy with her so, but Jacquie kept it under control.

"Not yet," he murmured. "I don't want you saying I took advantage of you because you were half-asleep."

"You —" She grabbed a pillow and whacked him with it.

Choya grabbed it from her. A few tiny feathers floated free. "I do want to, Jacquie. You know that."

"Get out of here." She shoved past him and got up, moving swiftly from the bed, hurrying to her clothes on the straight chair. When she glanced over her shoulder, Choya was leaning against the door frame, his arms folded across his waist. He looked as though he planned to stay.

"Will you please leave my room so I can dress?" Jacquie made the demand in a wary tone.

"Don't mind me," Choya drawled. "Go right ahead."

Seething inwardly, she wanted to order him out at the top of her lungs, but something in the veiled alertness of his gaze said he was waiting for that. With a nonchalance she was far from feeling, she shrugged and turned her back to him.

Without removing her nightgown, she slipped on the faded jeans. The action gave him an unlimited view of naked thigh and leg, but that was all. Quickly zipping up the jeans, Jacquie pulled the nightgown over her head.

The cascading waves of her silvery blond hair covered her creamy shoulders as she kept her back squarely toward him. With an economy of movement she pulled on a strawberry-colored knit top and turned around.

There was an arrogant arch to one of her eyebrows. He didn't seem to notice it.

"What would you like for breakfast?" she inquired, playing nice.

There was a half smile on his mouth as he straightened away from the door. "Whatever you fix is fine." And he walked from the room.

At the breakfast table, a few soggy cornflakes in a kid-size bowl told her that Robbie had fueled up before school. She hoped Sam was enjoying his early-bird breakfast in town.

Choya was devouring the eggs she scrambled for him, dousing them with hot sauce and washing it down with black coffee that he'd made himself. Jacquie nibbled at a piece of toast.

"That was great. Thanks." He got up and carried his plate to the sink. "Need anything before I head out? I'm going to pick up Sam around noon, maybe run a few errands," he added.

"Have fun. I guess I'll get started on the cleaning."

Choya nodded and went to get his jacket, looking out the front window as he slid it on. "There's not too much to do," he said in a friendly voice. "Feel free to look around for whatever you need. There's an old sheet in the laundry room that you can use for rags. Sam's been saving it." He gave her a wink but she wasn't looking forward to an entire morning by herself on the isolated ranch.

He left, closing the door quietly behind him. Jacquie waited until she heard him drive off before she got up and went looking for a pair of scissors first and then the sheet. She found it folded neatly on a shelf over the washing machine and she took it down, shaking it out. Absently, she snipped at the edges, then tore it into sections.

If my friends could see me now, she thought, shaking her head. Jacquie was rather glad they couldn't. Armed with a few rags and other cleaning supplies she tossed into a plastic bucket, she headed for the main rooms of the house.

Bars of brilliant sunlight made the oak floors gleam, lending cozy warmth to the living room. The traces of frost in the corners of the windows were the only clue to how cold it was outside. For the moment, she was content to be indoors.

Jacquie set down the bucket and took a spray bottle of multipurpose cleaner from it, reading the label to make sure it was safe for woodwork. Then she wadded up a rag and spritzed it, prepared to dust the bookshelves. Her first swipe brought up almost invisible grit — the desert dust was going to be a constant enemy, that was clear.

But it wasn't hard work and the cleaner had a nice lemony smell. She did several shelves at random, trying to remember if you were supposed to start at the bottom or the top, and deciding it didn't matter. The bookcases weren't quite as neat as they'd seemed at first. Someone, probably Sam, had a habit of saving newspaper and magazine articles that interested him between books. She stopped when she saw a thin manila folder and drew it out, curious as to what it contained.

Jacquie put down the wadded rag and opened the folder to see clippings, mostly about Choya and all from a while ago — the kind of articles that every small-town newspaper ran about local kids. Awards for livestock raising, an appearance now and then on the honor roll. Junior rodeo competition and an award for a summer stint working for a wild-horse relocation program. He seemed to have been an all-around good kid. She touched a finger to Choya's smooth, unlined face in one newspaper photo, charmed by his boyish, gap-toothed grin at the age of nine.

The articles were in order by date. He'd grown into an "outstanding young fellow," as one reporter put it, by eighteen. Jacquie studied that photo, catching a glimpse of the man he would become in his stronger, more mature features and the gleam in those eyes. She thought with an inward smile that he must have done some hell-raising by then — and after. But it wasn't as if Sam would keep clippings from the Tombstone police blotter in his brag book.

She leafed through the rest and came to a wedding announcement with a photo of Choya and Rosemary. How young they looked — and how happy. They'd had everything to look forward to. After that, there was nothing. She realized she'd been expecting to find something about the accident that had claimed his first wife's life and she was relieved that she hadn't. Feeling a little sad, Jacquie closed the folder and tried to remember where it had been. She wanted to put it back exactly where she'd found it, just in case.

The shelf was obvious, just not the place.

Had it been next to the book on how to dance? She didn't think so but she was curious about the book — it wasn't new. Holding the folder under her arm, she took it from the shelf and examined the cover. The title was straightforward — *Western Swing and Two-Step for Beginners.* Jacquie opened it and saw a handwritten note on the flyleaf:

> To Choya from Dad on your twelfth birthday. Just to get you started.

She flipped through the pages, shaking her head at the confusing diagrams of footsteps and dotted lines. Choya must have been mystified. Had he learned? Every Texas guy she'd ever gone out two-steppin' with had told her that his momma taught him how. But Choya hadn't had that privilege. Still, Sam had obviously tried. She wondered if Choya ever went dancing now. Somehow he didn't seem like the type.

Jacquie put the book and folder back, and wandered into the small room that Choya had told her he used for a study. It was spare and utilitarian, with a masculine air, like the rest of the house. There was an old desk with deep drawers, a swivel chair made of oak, and a laptop. Closed.

She still hadn't seen a satellite dish anywhere outside. Maybe he relied on picking up a stray wi-fi signal or maybe he took it into town if he wanted to go online. The subject hadn't come up. She spotted the landline phone she'd been looking for on the desk, thinking that she would have found it sooner if it ever rang. There wasn't an answering machine.

So.

Choya hadn't told her where the phone was, but he hadn't *not* told her either. She supposed he would have if she'd asked.

She rested her palm on the back of the receiver without picking it up, feeling the curved black plastic grow warm against her skin. She wasn't ready to call home, though she couldn't put it off indefinitely. Jacquie knew she would quickly end the call without saying a word if her father picked up. And he usually did.

Jacquie hesitated, then lifted the receiver, pressing it to her ear to listen to the dial tone. She even dialed her parents' number — then pressed the button to disconnect the call before the first ring. Carefully, she put the receiver back in its cradle and went back to dusting.

Choya was right about there not being very much cleaning to do. She found a few small things, the kind that men tended to leave around — a bolt missing a nut, a matchbook from the restaurant in town — and pulled open a drawer on a side table to drop them into it.

The drawer was empty and the stray bolt

rattled around in it. She opened another drawer beneath it. Nothing in that either. Giving in to feminine curiosity, she poked around a little. There was no sign of Choya's social life outside of the matchbook and that didn't count. There were no souvenir coasters or ticket stubs or anything like that. But he had to have dated since his wife's death — it had been five years. She wondered about it but not for too long.

What he did and who he did it with was none of her business. She grabbed the handle of the bucket and straightened, heading for the bedrooms upstairs and telling herself not to snoop. Once there, Jacquie stuck to her task. But she couldn't help noticing that there were no signs that a woman had ever lived there, besides the photo of Robbie's mother in his room.

She dusted the windowsills, stopping halfway through when the spray bottle gave up on her. Nearly empty — it felt light when she shook it. Jacquie hesitated, then went to a narrow closet she'd spotted in the hall, figuring it had to hold linens and, she hoped, more cleaning supplies. Her guess was correct — the Barnetts believed in stocking up and no wonder, considering how far they lived from town.

Jacquie paused before picking up another

bottle of the same cleaner, her gaze fixed on the shelf above it, attracted by the bright colors of tablecloths and other household linens folded neatly and stacked. There was no musty smell, but she would guess they hadn't been used for years. She left them there, unwilling to disturb the memories of Rosemary they must hold. If she wanted to pretty up the place, she could buy something new in town for the kitchen table.

The checked vinyl cloth that decorated it was looking more than a little worn, though it was clean. She spotted something that looked like it under all the others and tugged it out. It was a tablecloth but it had been used to wrap something else. She felt around the corners of the folds, guessing that it was a photograph album. Taking it out would definitely count as snooping. Jacquie lifted the stack of tablecloths and put the wrapped album back underneath.

Chapter 7

The next day dawned bright and clear and even colder. After the Barnetts left and went about their daily lives, she thought of going into town or rather, she wished she could. She didn't even get as far as the ranch yard. The low temperature and strong wind kept her inside until early in the afternoon, dawdling through a couple of books she'd chosen at random from the shelves, then flipping through a magazine.

Bored, Jacquie stood at a window, studying the scenery. She'd learned plenty about the surrounding land, thanks to Sam. To the north was the virtually impregnable stronghold of Cochise. Beyond it was Apache Pass. To the southwest lay Tombstone. The nearest neighboring ranch was to the south. Everywhere Jacquie looked, she saw the savage beauty of the Sonoran Desert.

Left to her own devices for the third time

in two days — it wasn't as if Choya left her a list of things to do — she'd run out of housework. Her natural restlessness was surfacing and she asked herself wryly why it had taken this long. Going into town, she supposed, would alleviate it, but hitchhiking was not an option.

Sighing a second time, she hooked her thumbs into the belt loops of her black jeans. The metal of the silver concho belt she wore was warm against her fingers. A horse whinnied near the barn and she decided to brave the cold. Jacquie found her jacket and borrowed a scarf that she knew was Choya's, wrapping it thickly around her neck. It smelled like his after-shave. She buried her nose in it for a minute, then, without thinking, pressed it to her lips.

The horse whinnied again and she wandered toward the sound.

At the corral, she rested her forearms on the upper bar and the toe of her shoe on the lowest. Three horses were in the enclosure. At the sight of Jacquie, they snorted and trotted nervously to the far end.

"Don't worry," she said softly. "I'm not going to try and escape or anything."

As if. The first problem would be catching a horse; the second would be saddling it.

She didn't have the vaguest notion of how to go about doing either. At the riding stable in Dallas, the horses had always been saddled and tied to a post.

The horses pricked their ears and faced the rutted track leading to the ranch yard. Jacquie turned, stepping away from the corral when she recognized the school bus bringing Robbie home. It was later than she thought. She looked around for Sam Barnett — had he come back from town, dropped off by his friend? She hadn't heard the car if so. He'd told her that meeting his grandson every day was important to him. She hadn't accompanied him, remaining in the house but watching from a window yesterday. Their ritual was long-established and she saw no reason to intrude.

Well, if he was in the house, he wasn't aware of the bus's arrival and there was no time to go get him. She would have to do the honors. Feeling a little awkward, she walked forward to meet Robbie as the bus stopped.

When the doors swished open, Robbie greeted her silently with a wide grin. He paused at the steps to glance over his shoulder at the other children in the bus, school papers half-falling out of a folder tucked under his arm.

"See?" Jacquie heard him call. "I told you!"

Some childish argument had been won or lost. It sounded like he'd gotten in the last word.

He maneuvered down the bus steps, a little unsteady on his feet. The cast had been removed yesterday and the muscles of the leg he'd broken were not on a par with the healthy leg. Plus, his feet had grown, according to Choya, during the weeks the cast had been on. The new sneakers he'd bought his son didn't fit quite right and it occurred to her that they could trip him up. Either way, Robbie seemed more concerned that he would drop his school papers than that he might fall.

"Let me carry that stuff," Jacquie offered when he was safely on the ground.

As Robbie handed the folder to her, she noticed the bus driver give her a curious look and nod. Then the doors were closing and the bus was turning to leave. There had been something more than mere surprise in the driver's expression. Jacquie glanced warily at Robbie.

"What was all that about in the bus?" she asked.

"Nobody believed me when I told them you were living with us," he answered, starting toward the house.

"The school kids have never seen me, that's why." She ruffled his hair, then smoothed it. "Or the bus driver either. I came into Tombstone on a weekend, remember?"

"Yeah, kinda. Anyway, now they know I was telling the truth."

Oh, great, Jacquie thought to herself. The whole town would discover she'd moved out here within a few days of crashing into Choya and the gossip would start. She wished she had the nerve to call Mrs. Chase and ask her what people were saying.

Nothing doing. She barely knew the woman.

"What did you tell them about me?" she questioned.

Robbie seemed to hesitate. "Just that you were staying with us."

Her finger encountered the smooth finish of a stiff paper among the other plain papers in her hand. Curious, Jacquie separated it from the others and found herself looking at an enlarged photograph of a smiling young woman with short, cornsilk-colored hair — Robbie's mother. He must have taken it out of the frame that sat on a table by his bed.

"Why did you take this to school, Robbie?" Jacquie eyed him suspiciously.

He peered at her anxiously through his lashes, his pale golden hair gleaming brightly in the sun. "So I could show them what you looked like. You do look like her." He hastened to add, "And you're prettier than any of the other kids' mothers."

"But that's not a photo of me. And you didn't actually tell them I was your new mother or anything like that, did you?"

Robbie looked uncomfortable. "No."

Jacquie sensed it was a truthful answer and also that it wasn't the whole truth. "Do they think I'm your mother?"

"Well, maybe some of them do," he conceded.

"And you didn't tell them differently?" she said with a sigh. His chin dipped toward his chest. "Robbie, I am not your mother. I'm not even your stepmother. It wasn't right for you to let any of your classmates even think that I am."

"I know," he mumbled.

"Tomorrow you'll have to tell them the truth."

Large, luminous brown eyes turned toward her. "I wish you were my mother, though."

The yearning innocence in his words dissolved Jacquie's irritation — and made her feel deeply ashamed that she hadn't been more tactful. Kneeling beside him, she gazed into his wistful face.

"You know it's not possible," was her gentle reply.

"Why?" Robbie asked solemnly. "Why couldn't I pretend that you're my mom? There wouldn't be anything wrong with that."

"Oh, Robbie," Jacquie sighed again, wishing she were more immune to his charm.

"It would be just-pretend between you and me. I wouldn't tell anybody else," he persisted as he saw her waver. Choya had told her that Robbie formed intense attachments quickly. He hadn't been wrong.

"No. And I mean it." He looked hurt, but she couldn't give in. Jacquie shook her head. "I'm not your mom. I came here to help out around the house, so your dad and grandpa don't have to do everything. That's all there is to it."

He didn't hide his disappointed frown.

Jacqiue straightened, trailing a hand over his shoulders. "Come on. Let's go in the house. After you change clothes, want to help me make brownies? You can have one before dinner."

It was an obvious bribe. He looked up at her with troubled eyes, not ready to give up.

"No. I don't want a brownie."

She put a palm on his forehead to tease him. "Oh my. You must have a fever."

He batted her hand away and pushed ahead of her into the house. "No! I don't want to be sick for Christmas!"

Jacquie sighed and followed him.

Minutes later, Robbie headed out to play in the barn. She closed the front door of the house behind him. It would do him good to work off some steam. Besides, his parting comment had made her think of the upcoming holidays. Whether Choya had decorations and things like that stored somewhere, she didn't know. He might prefer an artificial tree, she supposed. The thought depressed her. Her parents had always set up a huge, freshly fragrant evergreen and her mother had done the decorating, letting Jacquie help as soon as she was old enough.

She heard the front door open and close again as Sam returned home and she reached for a magazine, opening it halfway through as though she'd been reading it.

"Hey there, Jacquie. What are you up to?"

"Nothing much." She set the magazine aside. "Sit down." She rose and turned his favorite chair toward the kitchen table. Sam eased his long body into it a little stiffly.

"Glad to hear it. Because I had something I wanted to ask you."

"Okay." Jacquie moved to the counter to brew a pot of coffee for both of them. "Ask away."

"I'm not sure where to start —"

"That's not like you, Sam," she interrupted him with a smile. They had become good friends fast. Jacquie suspected that the old man thought of her as a daughter — and liked the idea very much.

"Okay, Choya put me up to it," he confessed with a twinkle in his eye. "He wanted to know if there's anything special you like to do around Christmas. We never made much fuss about it out here, but we do celebrate it. I don't think Robbie broke all the ornaments last year," he joked. "There might even be a working string of lights left."

"I see," she laughed. "Should we sort through them?"

"If you could help me git the boxes, we could start to."

Several minutes later, they were going through the contents of a couple of large cardboard boxes she'd taken down from the hall closet. Sam handled the ornaments carefully, holding each bauble in a gnarled hand to admire it before setting it on the dishtowel she'd provided to keep them from rolling around on the table.

"Robbie picked out this striped snowball when he was three. Him and Choya started collecting ornaments every year after that."

She peered into the other box, which was filled to the flaps. "How many are there?"

"Never counted. But you name it — reindeer and Santas and colored balls and glass birds with feather tails — he wanted it. Choya let him buy every trinket and twinkly thing he saw. Robbie loves Christmas."

Jacquie understood what Sam didn't say directly: none of the ornaments had been chosen by Choya's first wife. She wondered briefly what Choya had done with those. Maybe they were stored away like the album she'd found hidden, in some other closet she hadn't opened.

Every Christmas had to have been painful for Choya, but he obviously hid his feelings too. The whimsical ornaments he let Robbie choose year after year was one way he could make sure that Robbie's memories were happy ones.

"It's a good time to buy more," Jacquie said. "A lot of the Christmas stuff goes on sale around now."

"Well, not in the Tombstone shops," Sam replied. "Mebbe in the malls out around Tucson — and Choya's been busy. But he'll get around to it. He always does."

Jacquie had reached into the bottom of the box and lifted out a garland of sparkling fake cranberries interspersed with plastic popcorn. "Wow. This has to be twenty feet long. You Barnetts must like big trees."

"Yes we do." Sam grinned with pride. "We use that every year. But the tree has to be the real deal."

She smiled, glad to hear that. "This is great," she said, coiling it on the table. "And it beats real popcorn and real cranberries. I stuck my finger with a needle a million times the year we made our own garlands. Never again."

She remembered to serve the coffee as they emptied the boxes and Sam talked about the past to his heart's content. The mellow mood and his eagerness to reminisce made her think of something that had been on her mind since she'd met Choya.

"Sam — is that a true story about you finding Choya as a baby in a cholla patch? I heard it the first day I came to Tombstone."

"Oh?" He straightened slightly in his chair, studying her a little warily. "From who?"

Jacquie took a deep breath and forged on. She did want to know. "Brad — you know, the garage mechanic who fixed my car after the accident."

"Is that the feller's name? Haven't been into that place for a while. But I think I knew his uncle back in the day."

She nodded. Sam seemed to be stalling for time by taking a slow sip from his cup, then draining it.

"Whatever Brad told you — that ain't the whole story, Jacquie."

"But is it true?" she persisted.

"He was a foundling, yes," the older man said slowly. "But the how and where of it — that part got a little embellished over time. Cholla isn't called jumping cactus for nothing. Those spines get under your skin and stay there. No one would leave a baby right smack in the middle of a cholla patch."

Her steady gaze was meant to encourage him but it seemed to be making him a trifle nervous. His gnarled hands encircled the warm cup. "Is there more of this or did we drink it all?"

"No, there's more." Jacquie got up to fix him a refill. "Two sugars?" she asked him.

"Make it three."

Sam stirred his cup vigorously when she set it on the table. "Bring on the half-and-half."

She'd put a splash of milk in his first cup. "It's bad for you," she remonstrated.

"Hasn't killed me yet," Sam reasoned.

Jacquie looked in the fridge and picked up a small square container, shaking it. "Almost gone."

Sam held out his cup and she dribbled in the last of it.

"Thanks," Sam sighed. "Sorry for the fussin' — I needed a little time to think. Where were we?"

Jacquie was gentle but direct. She was burning with curiosity by this point and Sam's uneasiness only made it worse. "Did you find Choya out here on the ranch?"

"It was on Barnett land, but not here. We owned a big section that was close to Tucson," Sam said with deliberate slowness. "There weren't all those subdivisions then. It was about as rugged and lonely as this."

She hadn't known they'd owned land near the sprawling desert city. From the way Sam spoke, it seemed safe to assume it had been sold.

"One track on it ended in a clearing in the desert — there were some chollas around it, sure. I used to drive there at the end of the day just to think, watch the sunset sometimes."

He took a sip of the thick sweet coffee, growing thoughtful. "It was right close to Christmas. Just two days before."

That was a detail no one had mentioned. Jacquie's eyes widened but she didn't interrupt him.

"It was cold as the dickens, too, what with the sun going down early and a norther on the way. I didn't plan on sticking around. But then I saw something.

"No particular color to it. At first I thought it was a boulder, but I didn't remember one being there. It moved a little and I went over to see what was doing that. It turned out to be a baby carrier — the kind with a big handle and a half-cover."

"I know the type you mean," Jacquie said.

"And there he was inside of it, bundled up in a fuzzy thing with a hood, eyes open and strong enough to rock himself. I looked around for whoever had left him, but I didn't see a soul and didn't hear a sound except the wind blowing."

"Who would abandon a baby in a place like that?" Jacquie whispered softly.

"I thought the same thing myself once I realized that someone had. But I knew he hadn't been there long. That fuzzy thing he was inside of was warm and so was he, because I put a hand on him right away to make sure. He smiled at me. I couldn't tell how old he was. Not newborn. Maybe five, six months old."

Jacquie sat back, speechless for a moment.

"I figured it was someone who'd seen me go there often, and she had to know the area well to leave the baby and get away quickly before I saw her."

"She? How did you know it was a woman if you didn't see anyone there?"

Sam cleared his throat. "The police thought the same thing, because of the way he was wrapped up nice and neat. When I brought him in, one of the lady officers made sure he wasn't wet before someone went out to get formula and a bottle. There were blankets under the fuzzy thing, fixed just so in layers, the way women know how to do."

Jacquie didn't.

"A man wouldn't have done it so particular," Sam said with conviction. "And I just had a feeling — I couldn't explain it then and I can't now — that a woman was watching me while I got him in the car and buckled that carrier thing down. It wasn't like I could go looking for her or shout out. I was afraid he would cry and it was nearly night and cold as hell. I turned on the engine to get the heat going and looked him and the carrier over real carefully. There wasn't a note.

"The lady officer didn't find one either.

But his little clothes were new and clean and his diaper had just been changed. So what I thought at the time was that he hadn't exactly been abandoned. He'd been left for me to find because she'd seen me coming." He paused for a beat. "And she saw me go. With her son."

Jacquie nodded. The old man spoke freely enough but there was a catch in his voice even now.

"Why she picked me, I never understood. I was considered the most confirmed bachelor in the county, though I did have the ranch and a respectable income. And the Barnett name stood for something." He hesitated. "Those were hard times then, like now. A lot of people out of work, houses foreclosed on, no jobs to be found."

"Did you try to find her?"

Sam nodded and put down the cup. "Of course. So did the police. I made discreet inquiries on my own, even hired a private investigator after a while — he was thorough and expensive. He checked hospitals and clinics all over the southwest."

"And?"

"The babies born around summertime of that year — Choya turned out to be about the age I'd thought — well, they all matched up with the records on file, and all were confirmed with their parents or other relatives. The doc who first examined him said it was possible the baby hadn't been born in a hospital — it happens all the time."

"So what did you do?"

"I gave up on the inquiries but I didn't give up on Choya. I went to family court and asked to be appointed temporary guardian. I'd had him for a while when a family court judge made a final ruling, based on — oh my, a lot of things. Character references and proof of income and residence, and last but not least, filed affidavits from folks who were willing and able to help me with little Choya. The court wasn't going to hand over a foundling just like that — they ain't supposed to rubber-stamp adoptions. But I suspected that the judge wasn't eager to put Choya into the foster care system either."

Jacquie raised an inquiring eyebrow. "Help? From who?"

"Among others, a lady friend I had at the time. Mrs. Chase. From the motel. Only she wasn't Mrs. Chase then, she was Lulu Williams. She was about your age then, the oldest of nine on a farm and she knew a thing or two about babies. I never coulda done it without her to teach me the basics of diaperin' and feedin' and bringin' up a baby that young."

Silently she remembered her feeling that Choya and the motel owner had known each other for a long time. Jacquie nodded, encouraging Sam to continue.

"Even with her help, I didn't get much sleep that first year, but then, neither did little Choya," he said philosophically. "After a year, I applied to adopt him and in another year he was legally my son and had my last name."

"And that nickname," she pointed out.

Sam shook his head. "It's not a nickname. That's his full legal name. I couldn't call a baby like that just plain Billy or Bo. No, he's Choya Barnett — it says so right on his adoption papers." He gave her a wink. "Fits him, don't it?"

"Yes. Especially the part about cholla getting under your skin. He's good at that."

Sam grinned. "The way I look at it, then and now, Choya was meant to be a Barnett. His momma picked me out to be his rightful dad even though I never saw her face or found out one thing about her."

"What if you had?" Jacquie wondered out loud.

Sam fell silent. "One time I thought I did."

"Really? Where?"

"I was in a department store in Tucson

with Choya when he wasn't more than five. He'd never been in a big place like that and he was crowing about everything he saw. Then he let go of my hand and disappeared into the displays. By the time I caught up with him, he was in the dress department and surrounded by women, making friends with them all. But one young gal was holding back — and damned if she didn't look like him, with dark hair and them golden eyes —"

He stopped short. The door seemed to blow open and a blast of frigid wind came through it, along with Robbie.

"Well, I guess I've gone on long enough," Sam said in a low voice. He watched his grandson come in and throw his arms around Jacquie.

"Hi! I'm back from the barn!" Robbie pressed his cold cheek against hers.

"I noticed," she said with a smile, returning his enthusiastic hug and letting him go. "Close the door and hang up your jacket."

"Okay!" He went to do both and came back. "Hi, Gramps," he said, then saw the ornaments and the boxes on the table. "Are we going to get a tree today?" he asked excitedly.

"Nope," said his grandfather. "It's not

time yet. Besides, you have homework to do."

Robbie looked pleadingly at Jacquie, who began to put the fragile ornaments back in the boxes as carefully as she and Sam had taken them out. "Don't look at me like that," she laughed. "You have five minutes to sit down and unzip that backpack you threw on the floor."

"But I don't want to sit down. You said we could make brownies."

"Ah, it's too late for that now." Truth be told, she wanted to think about all she'd just learned. Her mind was still going over everything Sam had said.

"Please — I don't want to do homework."

"How about if I read my book next to you while you do?"

Robbie lifted the cover of her thick novel and riffled through the first pages. "This has too many words. Bet I finish first."

She opened the spring catch of an old mason jar to get a couple of chocolate-chip cookies for him and put them on a plate. "Here's some fuel. Get started."

The evening meal could not have been classified as a success. Although Choya had shown her how to operate the stove, Jacquie still had difficulty judging the amount of heat for cooking. Tonight it had been the corn that was scorched.

Sam, probably out of self-preservation, had offered to take over or even to just help with the meals, but Jacquie had steadfastly refused. Stubbornly she had insisted on cooking everything herself. She was determined to master the stove, even though she knew it was irrational to want to get the better of an inanimate object. But she really did hate the damn thing. Despite her determination, she sometimes wondered if she would ever learn how to cook — she wasn't sure she would have the patience for it.

Except for Choya's comment about a "burnt offering" the first time she'd fixed a meal, he dropped the topic of her substandard cooking ability. Tonight he'd been even more silent than usual, but his tawny gaze had narrowed on her several times. Jacquie simply ignored him. She couldn't begin to guess the reason for his silence and she wasn't going to try.

After the dishes were washed and Robbie was tucked into bed, Jacquie avoided the living room where Choya and Sam were, in favor of her bedroom. She had decided that she had to make another attempt to appeal to her father. By now her mother would have softened him up, even though Jacquie hadn't gotten up the courage to call the Dallas number from the study phone. She was going to send a carefully worded letter that would explain the pickle she'd gotten herself into without alarming them.

When she sat down to write the first draft, she found it wasn't easy to strike just the right note. No matter what, her father tended to fly off the handle. If she were to say that Choya had made an offer she couldn't possibly refuse and they came out here to rescue her from his villainous clutches, Sam and Robbie would be confused and upset. And if they got the idea she couldn't be trusted with a car or a debit card or a handsome man with golden eyes, they'd never let her out of their sight again, even though she was over twenty-one.

The several sheets of crumpled stationery in the wastebasket revealed her number of failures. Finally Jacquie crinkled up the last partially written letter and threw it in the basket with the others. A letter was not the answer. Tomorrow while Sam was taking his afternoon nap, she would phone them again.

If her father answered, she would change her voice and say that Miss Jacqueline Grey was calling collect, just to test him. If her mother answered, she would be herself.

The house was silent as she stepped from

her room. She paused in the hall, glancing at her watch. As impossible as it seemed, it was after ten o'clock. The absence of any sound indicated that everyone else was in bed. She walked across the small hall to the laundry room and bathroom, piling her long hair on top of her head and fastening it with two bobby pins as she went.

A brisk shower chased away the tension and frustrations that had built when she'd been trying to compose the letter. She still had no idea what she would say when she talked to her parents on the phone.

With most of the water from the shower spray patted off, she wrapped the oversized bath towel around her and tucked the fold securely. The terry cloth material nearly reached the middle of her thighs, its soft roughness warm against her skin.

Her cosmetics were on the shelf above the sink. Reaching for a jar of moisturizing cream, she removed the lid and began creaming her face. Jacquie felt a large dab slide down her nose and splat into the sink. She swore under her breath — she'd used too much and she didn't want to wipe up the mess with a washcloth, not when she was the one who was doing the laundry. Tissues, tissues — there were never any around when you needed them. She went back into her bedroom, accidentally hitting the bathroom light switch with her elbow and turning it off.

It didn't matter. The lamp by her bed spilled its illumination into the hall and it was enough to see by.

She sat down on her bed and reached for her purse, looking through it for a packet of tissues. Good thing she'd brought her own. Beauty necessities weren't things that old Sam would ever think to provide.

There was a fresh pack and she took it with her on her way back to the bathroom. Jacquie stifled a scream when the light switched on — she hadn't touched it — and stumbled against Choya.

She stepped back, angry. "What are you doing in here?" she snapped.

"Looking for aspirin. We keep a bottle in the medicine cabinet down here." He opened it to show her. "And there it is. Sorry if I startled you."

She glared at him just the same. Her heart was racing. And she knew what she looked like with her face half-creamed: goofy as all get out.

He grinned. "The light was off. I really didn't think you'd be beautifying in the dark."

Jacquie took a hasty step in the direction

of her clothes, then stopped. "You still could have knocked," she said sharply. She wasn't going to flounce off and make him laugh. Clumsily, she dabbed more cream on her face.

"I could have," he agreed, walking over to the stand by the sink where Jacquie was.

Unwillingly her gaze slid to the male reflection joining hers in the mirror. The ruggedly hewn features were unreadable as he watched her intently.

"What are you looking at?" Jacquie asked with studied indifference. She wished for the robe that was in her room, although its short length would not have offered much more cover than the towel did.

"It's been a long time since I watched a woman getting ready for bed," Choya commented.

Interesting thing to say. His offhand tone didn't fool her. Her stomach began somersaulting nervously and she rubbed the cream more vigorously to give her cheeks some color. She didn't believe for one minute it was a casual remark and nothing more. She lowered her lashes, unwilling to reveal the feelings he'd stirred in her. Even without darkening mascara, they lay long and thick, a light brown against her skin.

"Really?" she said as casually as she could,

still rattled. She hadn't forgotten not being able to find a single clue as to his social life. Her curiosity had been put on hold. Choya came and went however and whenever he wanted to, and he had been away from the ranch for hours at a time more than once. But never at night.

So what? She hadn't been living with him long enough to draw conclusions.

She stared at herself in the mirror briefly, not liking the knowledge that she'd kept track without having a reason to. Why should she care when he didn't finish what he started with her?

Not for anything did she want him to know the way his nearness was disturbing her. The breadth of his shoulders silently intimidated; his height made her feel too short to challenge him.

Choya seemed to withdraw, watching her with an aloofness that was unnerving.

"What's on your mind, Choya?" she asked tartly. "I'm beginning to think that you didn't come in here for the aspirin. If you wanted to ambush me, you succeeded."

"I really didn't know you were in here and I actually do have a headache. A bad one."

She turned her gaze to him, handing him the small bottle at the same time. "Here you go. Take two and and don't call me in the morning. Now out. I'd like to get to bed."

He cleared his throat. "Don't you want to know why I have a headache?"

"Not really."

"Robbie's teacher stopped me today to see if congratulations were in order. It seems there's a rumor circulating that I've remarried."

"I certainly didn't start it," Jacquie said. A little too quickly.

"You wouldn't happen to know who did, would you?" His tawny gold eyes had narrowed on her.

"How could I?" she managed to laugh. "I haven't spoken to anyone in a fifty-mile radius except you, your father, and Robbie."

"I think we're straying off the subject," Choya reminded her. "Let's get back to that pesky rumor that you seem to be avoiding."

"I'm not."

"Do you think it's possible that my father or my son might have mentioned you?" Choya persisted.

The conversation with Robbie was fresh in her mind. The memory must have flickered across her face, because his expression hardened.

"Of course it's possible," Jacquie hedged, reluctant to admit that Robbie had let his classmates believe that she was his new mother.

"It's even possible that my son talked to his classmates and teacher about you in such a way that they might believe we're married, isn't it?"

"I really don't know," she lied, shrugging one bare shoulder.

"If you did, you certainly wouldn't condone or encourage Robbie, would you?" His jaw was set in a tense line.

Nervously, Jacquie moistened her lips, wondering how much Choya actually knew and how much he was only guessing.

"That's a silly question." Her tone made it clear that his question was ludicrous.

"Then answer it," he challenged.

"Robbie is not the type to lie or tell tales. He would never claim that I was his new mother when he knows I'm not," Jacquie stated in an attempt to avoid a direct answer.

"Robbie phrased it a little differently. He said you agreed to be his 'pretend' mother."

Jacquie took a slow, deep breath. So much for the ability of little boys to be truthful. "He did? That was wishful thinking. I didn't encourage him."

"I'd like to believe that. But I'm still not sure he's giving me the straight story. He kept changing the details until I confronted him with the questions his teacher asked me," Choya stated.

"You're taking this too seriously. To him it was probably a harmless game of pretend." She screwed the lid back on the jar of moisturizing cream. "Kids do it all the time."

"Yes, they do. Especially when they want something badly enough. If what they want is a new video game or dirt bike, then it's harmless," he said quietly. "But Robbie wants a mother. He seems to think you'll do just fine."

"I can't help what he thinks and I didn't put ideas in his head," Jacquie protested. "Robbie knows I'm not his mother and never will be."

"He might say that. He might even believe it right now, but you won't be pretending to leave when you go. You'll be gone." He put a definite emphasis on the last word.

Jacquie replaced the jar on the shelf and turned to face Choya. "Guess so. But that's not news to you. We've had this — discussion — before I agreed to move out here."

"I remember it."

She threw him an accusing look. "You're still afraid he'll become too attached to me. But you willingly took that risk when you proposed this arrangement." She was silent for a second, then added, "Which, by the way, is not working."

She had to say something to keep him at bay and the words just popped out. But there was truth in them.

He studied her for long, measuring seconds through half-closed eyes. "I take it that you mean it's not working for you," he said in a low voice. "What's wrong?"

She seized on the obvious. "There isn't much for me to do and there really isn't a reason for me to be here. You three can manage just fine. That's clear."

"What are you saying?" he asked uneasily. "That I lured you out here?"

Jacquie took a deep breath. "Look, I came of my own free will. I can't say I understood exactly why at the time —" She broke off. She did now, though she hadn't then. The man was irresistible, his son was adorable, and she'd had no alternative whatsoever.

"Well?"

"Choya, I didn't have much choice. My car —"

"Just take it and go, if that's what you want. You don't owe me anything."

"And you're going to drive me into Tombstone in the middle of night? The garage is closed. Brad is dreaming of carburetors jumping the fence."

"Right. What was I thinking?" He propped an arm against the doorjamb and rested his head against it.

She pushed a stray lock of hair out of her face and adjusted the towel. Then she jabbed a finger at him. "You're thinking that it's my fault Robbie said something at school that embarrassed you. It isn't — and it's not that big a deal. Go in and explain to the teacher and get it over with. Robbie's seven years old. He gets to make mistakes."

He straightened and folded his arms. "I can do that. But I still wish it hadn't happened," he said quietly.

"Choya, it seems to me that Robbie's doing fine."

"That's because you're here."

"For less than a week." She shook her head, a tiny movement. "He can't be that attached to me. He has you and he always will. And his grandfather."

Choya sighed from the bottom of his soul. "Something else is happening. You're the cause." His golden eyes moved over her thoughtfully. "I wanted you here and I was willing to take a chance if it were for a few weeks. But if he's thinking that you're about to become his mom — maybe you should go, if that's what you want to do."

The words felt almost like a blow. She

fended them off with coldness. "Not yet. It's not like I can call a taxi, right?"

A muscle was twitching uncontrollably along his cheek. Choya didn't seem to want to believe that she shared his concern for his son. Or that she wanted the best for the boy, just as he did.

They'd gotten distracted. The way they kept falling into each other's arms and breaking the rules hadn't helped at all. Robbie was vulnerable and he had to come first. She'd speak her mind one last time on that subject while she had the chance.

"Robbie doesn't have to get hurt, you know." She kept her eyes on Choya's impassive face. "The game of pretend only started today. Make it clear that it stops now. You can lay down the law with him in a way that I can't."

Choya didn't reply for several seconds. "I guess I'll have to. Damn it. I wanted this to work and it doesn't look like it's going to." He scowled fiercely as he added, "I could have done better by you and I didn't."

The remark didn't exactly constitute an apology but it was sincere. On impulse, she reached out and stroked his lean cheek with the tips of her fingers. "Don't think twice," she whispered. "We both tried. Maybe it's nobody's fault it didn't work out."

She had the sensation that he'd moved closer to her even though he hadn't taken a step. His voice was raw when he spoke in reply. "I think about you all the time, Jacquie. I'm not going to stop just because you're not here."

There was a second to blink at his unexpected declaration. In the next, she was being swept off her feet, an arm pinned between her body and his chest. The other was caught in his encircling grip. Blood hammered in her ears, her breath taken away.

"No. Don't. We shouldn't." Desire and reluctance mingled in her voice.

Choya shoved the bathroom door open wider with his shoulder. Jacquie twisted and strained against his hold as he carried her to the bedroom. Her blue-covered bed loomed in the dark. He settled her on it in one swift, sure move.

The center of the bed dipped beneath his joining weight. Jacquie opened her mouth, but her instinctive cry was silenced by his kiss. She was pinned beneath the hard length of his body. Dizzying waves of sensual response washed through her, but she fought them back.

When her long fingernails began to dig into his muscled shoulders, it seemed to excite him more. The heat and pressure of his body was irresistibly and deeply pleasurable.

Choya shifted slightly, using one large hand to caress her and the other to capture her chin. Once more his mouth closed over hers in frank possession.

He broke off the kiss but only for a second to brush his thumb over her lips, then tasted the honeyed sweetness of her mouth with renewed passion. His sensual expertise sparked an animal response within her, forcing her to struggle with herself as well as Choya.

With her efforts divided into two battlefronts, her strength weakened. Alternately she fought his kiss and returned its fire. His hand slid from her chin along her throat and over the nakedness of her golden tan shoulders. The rough, very masculine caress sent quivers down her spine.

Sensing it, Choya followed the trail of his hand, nibbling at the sensitive area below her earlobe and the hollow of her shoulder. A willing sigh of delight escaped her lips. While his mouth continued an exploration of her pleasure points, his hand moved downward, encountered the protective towel and pulled at the tuck that held it in place.

Jacquie hung on to it. "Stop — let me get

my breath," she begged, stalling for time.

In answer he lifted his head, studying her for a moment, then bent down to nuzzle her, rubbing his lean cheek against the flushed skin of her face. The seductive tickle of faint stubble made her arch in arousal until he stopped — she didn't want him to. He just looked at her. Desert starfire flickered through the window to bronze his features.

Never had he seemed so stunningly male or so disturbingly attractive as he did at that moment. He opened his hand to spread strong fingers through the molten silver of her hair.

"What do you want?" His lips quirked.

"You."

His mouth began its descent.

Capturing hers with persuasive ardor, he kissed her like she'd never been kissed before, not even by him. Jacquie's hands caressed his neck, tangled in his hair, then moved down to test the delicious strength of his muscled arms. Then — she couldn't help it — they slid to the solidness of his back. The wildfire racing through her veins burned the last bridge of inhibition. The searing longing inside her for his possession was transmitted in the hungry response to her lips.

His workshirt was rough-soft against her skin, stimulating her nerve ends to a fever pitch of awareness. She could feel his heart drumming in his chest, racing to the tempo of her own.

When he changed position slightly, trying not to crush her, Jacquie was still caught in the spell of his seductive touch. She was frozen, incapable of movement at the momentary withdrawal of his body heat. Every fiber pulsed with her need of him.

"Choya," she whispered in an aching plea for him to return.

An arm slipped beneath her and he half lifted her toward him. There was another movement, then she was being pressed back against the coolness of the sheets, the bedcovers cast aside. He was pulling off his shirt. Fast.

Afraid he would leave her again, she reached out to cling to him. Her hands slid around the rippling bareness of his shoulders, drawing him down. The fiery warmth of his skin melted away the last vestige of chill.

The hungry demand of his kiss removed the fear that he might stop. Jacquie gloried in the knowledge, her breasts swelling under his arousing touch. The world had spun away, leaving only the two of them in the universe.

His lips opened warmly over hers, then lifted. In the momentary lull of sensation, Jacquie floated slowly back to ordinary consciousness. The mindless bliss began drifting away. She closed her eyes tightly to shut out the reality — that she was actually inviting him to make love to her. She shivered against him when she failed to block out the knowledge. He gathered her more closely to him, brushing a gentle kiss on the silken mass of hair near her ear.

His tenderness was too much to take. She would never be able to leave if she gave in to it, no matter how much she wanted him. This time she would do the refusing.

Tentatively, her hands pushed him away. "We shouldn't be doing this. For a thousand reasons. Leave me alone. Go away." Her voice was strangely calm.

Choya tensed as if to employ his superior strength and Jacquie held her breath.

At the shifting movement of his weight off the bed, her heart cried out for him to stay and to hold her tightly in his arms. Stiffly she stayed where he had left her, listening to his nearly silent movements and holding back her pain until he had left the room.

One tear fell, then another. More and more flowed freely down her cheeks into the pillow beneath her head as she lay there, unmoving. She turned and buried her face in its dampness to muffle her sobs.

Chapter 8

Her eyes opened reluctantly. The full light of a morning sun streamed through the window. For an instant, she couldn't even remember where she was. Then it all came back to her.

Throwing back the covers, she slid from the bed. A corner post offered support — she was standing but still not quite awake. Her glance out the window focused on the shiny, spreading stalks of a cholla cactus.

Choya. He hadn't come back. She'd slept alone.

Memories assailed her — good and bad. How close they had come — the desire had been mutual, the attraction nearly too powerful to resist. Ultimately, she'd done the right thing by telling him to go, but she still wanted to crawl beneath the covers and hide from the bright light of day.

Jacquie walked to the closet and chest of drawers, dressing without any particular concern about her appearance. The lateness of the hour was sinking in. She figured that Choya didn't want to talk to her. That had to be why she had been allowed to sleep so late. He or Sam must have made breakfast and gotten Robbie onto the school bus.

She owed it to all of them to follow through and not let her emotions get in the way of doing what had to be done. Jacquie went back to the bed, shoving the blanket and bedspread to the foot, and began stripping the top sheet from the mattress.

Footsteps stopped outside her door. The knob turned and it swung open. Jacquie glanced over her shoulder, her blank gaze focusing on Choya framed by the doorway. Tall, vitally masculine, he paused there.

The light in his tawny eyes was one she had never seen before. Not that she cared. At this moment, she didn't care about anything.

"I thought I heard you moving around," he said quietly. "I guessed" — his alert gaze swept appraisingly over her — "you would sleep late."

Jacquie turned her head away. "I guess everyone had breakfast." Her voice was as flat as her spirit.

"Sam took care of it," Choya replied.

Shrugging her lack of interest, she started

tucking the ends of her shirt into her jeans. She was aware that he was still standing there watching her, and his presence disturbed her.

Her nerves still tingled in response to Choya's presence.

A stride or two and Choya was near her. Jacquie was aware of it, but focused doggedly on what she was doing. When he stopped behind her, she didn't acknowledge him with so much as a look.

His hands lightly gripped the sides of her waist, their touch unexpectedly paralyzing her for an instant. She didn't resist when he drew her back against the muscled hardness of his chest or when his arms crossed around the front of her. The lusty scent of his maleness, familiar and intoxicating, made her heart skip a beat.

Out of the corner of her eye, Jacquie saw the dark gleam of his brown hair. Then he buried his mouth along the side of her neck.

"Jacqueline." He said her name in a huskily caressing tone.

For an instant, she relaxed against him, finding solace and comfort after the sensual whirlwind of last night. But his tenderness was going to get them both in trouble again.

Last night they had gone too far, thinking only of themselves and no one else once they'd fallen into each other's arms. He couldn't come here this morning and expect her to surrender to the incredible sensations he caused again. She was fully awake, if not rested. Her exhaustion couldn't get in the way of her ability to reason.

Jacquie turned in his embrace. She wedged her arms against his chest, gaining distance from his bent head. The smoldering light of his gaze roamed possessively over her upturned face.

"Look, what I said last night still holds," she told him with chilling aloofness.

He drew back sharply, his gaze narrowing to a piercing intensity. The brilliant fire in her eyes left Choya in little doubt of her determination.

"Dammit, Jacquie, I —"

"What do you have to swear about?" she interrupted, twisting free of his arms to glare at him indignantly. "This isn't just about you and me. Think about that."

"Stop it." Choya caressed her shoulders.

A finely arched brow lifted as she freed herself from his hands. "That's exactly what I'm doing," she assured him.

He took a deep breath to control the emotions she'd aroused. "You know damn well that's not what I meant." His lips were compressed into a grim line and his whole body seemed tense. "And I'm not here to apologize for what I didn't do."

"If you didn't come here for that, then you must have had another reason." She began tucking in her shirt again.

"I do," Choya declared. "Want to hear it?" His gaze moved over her almost unwillingly, stopping at her face.

"As usual, I don't have a choice." Jacquie gave an exaggerated sigh and shook back her hair.

"Why do you insist on making this difficult for me?" he snapped.

"Difficult for you?" she taunted. "What's the matter, Choya? Are you feeling guilty for taking it that far last night? Let it go. I was more than willing. But not today. It's not all right and we both know it."

"I had no expectations," Choya replied tightly, a muscle twitching along his jaw. "I just wanted to see you."

"Why?" She rounded her eyes. "Are you planning to talk me out of going? You'd better not."

He glared at her. "You could do me the favor of listening. Is that too much to ask?"

"Right now, yes. Anyway, I take full responsibility for agreeing to stay on. It isn't good for Robbie —"

"We went over that. There's more to it."

His fingers encircled the soft flesh of her upper arm. He pulled her closer.

Jacquie didn't flinch from the emotion in his eyes or attempt to struggle out of his grip. She actually wasn't afraid of him. "Choya, you and I hardly know each other. We're not in love. We shouldn't be playing house —"

"Is that what you call it?"

She leveled a look at him. "It's accurate. I wouldn't call my responsibilities work, would you?"

"Jacquie, please shut up. Just listen without interrupting."

"Nice of you to throw in the 'please,' " she said sarcastically. "Choya, I can say whatever I want and I will. You really have no idea who I am and what I'm all about." She hated the nasty edge in her voice, but she had to do whatever it took to put him off.

"Give me a chance." He sounded almost desperate.

Jacquie tipped her head, the silken curtain of her hair swinging to the side. "That's not a good idea."

Choya reached out as if to touch it, but dropped his hand, as if the remembered softness of her hair against his skin would be too much for him. His jaw was clenched.

A fiery gleam was in his eyes. He pivoted sharply and walked from the room with long, impatient strides.

When the outside door slammed shut, Jacquie sank limply onto the bed. Her words had been self-protective — and meant to protect Robbie from further harm — but they left a bitter taste in her mouth. The throbbing ache in her heart hadn't eased. Trying to put an end to a relationship that never should have happened was much more complex than just taking off. The unexpected discovery confused her. At least the details — like getting her car back and letting her parents know — remained to be worked out. That was something else to focus on.

She headed for the kitchen. She would have to force herself to eat something. Jacquie paused on the threshold, looking around the room. The table had been cleared but there was something under the napkin holder, folded crookedly in half and decorated with stickers. Robbie had printed her name on it.

Oh no. She could keep his father at arm's length but not him. She couldn't pretend she'd never seen it, not if she was going to get it together and leave today or tomorrow. No, she would have to look at the card he'd made — and respond.

Slowly she unfolded it. Several unpasted stickers fell out and she scooped them up in her hand as she read the note. The printed words swam in front of her.

I am sory about what I did. I hope you ar not mad at me. Plese do not be mad. With lov from Robbie. P.S. the xtra stickers ar for you!

Had he decided to apologize on his own or had Choya asked him to do it? She brushed away her tears and swallowed hard. Either way, he was forgiven. But her resolve to leave was shattered.

No matter what Choya thought, she would do right by Robbie and that meant sticking around. If she took off now, so close to Christmas, the little boy would think that his minor mistake had been the cause.

It wasn't.

During the next few days, Choya was studiously polite. He had to have read Robbie's card to her but he chose not to mention it. Apparently he was waiting for her to make a move.

Let him wait. She was in no rush to answer questions he wasn't asking. He could see that she wasn't going to walk out on Robbie. Jacquie stuck to the established routine as far as the little boy was concerned. She had thanked him for the card, of course — and accepted his apology as sincerely as he had offered it. Robbie didn't seem to have an inkling of what had passed between her and his father, and that was exactly how it should be.

Choya was going to get tired of holding back, she knew that. Every time he was in a room with her or sat down at the table to share a meal, the conversation was limited to safe topics and didn't vary. She could sense that he was unable to figure her out and found that irritating. Tough luck.

When circumstances forced them to be together, his gaze rarely left her, but his self-control never allowed her to see what he was thinking. He didn't come near her or indicate the slightest desire to touch her again.

Her relief was genuine. Yet, maddeningly, there were times when she would glance at him and remember the exciting caress of his hands and the mastery of his kiss. Then she would grow hot all over and have to excuse herself from the table or the room to escape his alert gaze and rid her mind of its wayward thoughts.

Giving in to them or him wasn't an option. Neither was giving up on his kid.

On Saturday, Robbie claimed her company. He conducted Jacquie on a grand tour of the ranch yard and his favorite places to play. The last stop was the barn. The shadowy darkness was a welcome change from the glare of the sun.

"I come here a lot," he informed her, scuffling through the scattered pieces of old straw on the cement walkway. "There's a lot of neat places to play. I even have a secret hiding place in here." He darted her an uneasy sideways glance an instant after he said that. "I'd like to show it to you, but —" He frowned.

Jacquie guessed the reason for his obvious dilemma. "If you showed it to me, it wouldn't be a secret place anymore," she reasoned.

"You don't mind, then?" Robbie breathed anxiously.

She smiled. "Of course I don't."

"Come on." He started off again. "I'll show you my horse, Apache."

A gentle-eyed palomino leaned his head over a manger, whinnying at the small boy who approached. It was a small horse, a little over fourteen hands, the perfect size for a growing boy.

"You can ride him if you want," Robbie offered as he stroked the velvet nose thrust toward him. "He won't throw you or anything like that. Dad says he doesn't have any bad manners."

Jacquie stroked the sleek neck. "Thanks, Robbie, but I'm afraid I don't know anything about saddling a horse. Maybe another time."

"I can show you," he assured her hopefully.

"Ah, no. I don't think so," Jacquie said.

" 'Another time' will be too long from now," he protested. "And he won't stall like Gramps' old truck."

"Maybe so. But Apache could spook and throw me."

"Can you ride, Jacquie?"

At the sound of Choya's voice, Jacquie whirled around. Her sudden movement startled the palomino, his hooves scraping through the straw to the concrete floor as he backed hurriedly away from the manger.

With the same cat quietness that had enabled him to enter the barn unheard, Choya walked toward them. His tawny gaze inspected her expression of wary alarm.

"Yes, fairly well," she replied. She wondered why he wanted to know.

"I told her she could ride Apache," Robbie piped up.

Choya glanced down at the boy. “Why don’t we let her ride Johnnycake instead?”

“What’s that? The worst horse in the stable?” The cantankerous answer was softened with a smile for Robbie’s benefit. She didn’t have to let Choya Barnett bring out the worst in her.

“Johnnycake?” Robbie questioned with a hooting laugh, missing the edge in her tone of voice. Choya didn’t seem to think her comment was funny. He surveyed her coldly. “He’s real gentle, Jacquie.” He glanced at his father. “She doesn’t know how to saddle a horse, Dad. I was going to show her.”

“Would you like to learn?” he challenged.

Jacquie hesitated. She wanted to do nothing that would bring her into prolonged contact with Choya, but she did want to depart on good terms and leave Robbie with happy memories. If that meant getting on a horse, she would do it.

“I — I guess so.”

“I’ll get Johnny out of the corral, Rob.” Choya glanced briefly at his son. “You show her where the tack is.”

With the gear collected, they met Choya at the corral fence. He didn’t show her how it was done. He told her how to saddle and bridle a horse. His instructions were clear and concise and Jacquie discovered it wasn't as difficult as she had thought.

When the buckskin was saddled, Jacquie mounted and rode him around the yard. He was a lot more tractable than some of the stable horses she'd ridden in Dallas. The growing tension of the last several days vanished from her mind and body. She was brimming with confidence when she cantered him back to the barn.

Her smile faded as Choya caught at the bridle and stopped the buckskin beside him. "You're welcome to ride him whenever you like," he told her briskly. "But don't leave the yard unless someone is with you."

"Are you afraid I'll keep riding and forget to come back?" Jacquie asked in a low voice. Maybe she'd let him stew for too long if he really thought she couldn't be trusted not to cut and run.

"That would be a dangerous thing to do," he replied in a matter-of-fact voice. "Even Robbie knows that."

"Oh, I know you would come after me," she said lightly.

"The danger is being alone in the desert."

"Is it?" she mocked, and slid from the saddle.

"He's a good horse, isn't he?" Robbie came forward.

"Yes, he is." Jacquie directed her attention to unsaddling the horse.

Robbie swung himself up on a hay bale and watched her, beaming. "Aren't you glad you're staying here with us?"

She flashed a glittering look at Choya. "It's certainly been an experience."

The line of his jaw tightened at her innuendo. He shoved the reins into Robbie's hand and walked away with a muttered comment that he had other things to do. His abrupt departure seemed to take the sting out of her resentment. Her gaze followed the wide shoulders, a hint of melancholy in its jewel depths.

On Sunday, Jacquie rode again, keeping to Choya's edict to stay close to the house. Her ride on Monday was longer, a reconnaissance tour of the land surrounding the ranch yard. The following day her previously unused muscles began protesting the vigorous exercise.

A hot shower that night eased much of their stiffness, but they still ached with uncomfortable soreness. Sleep promised to be elusive and Jacquie tied the sash of her robe around her waist and walked into the kitchen. A cup of cocoa before going to bed might help.

The microwave beeped when the back

door slammed. Jacquie tensed, knowing it had to be Choya since he had been out earlier, checking on fences or something like that. She'd assumed he had come back already, but his appearance in the kitchen proved her wrong.

Her heart turned over at the sight of him, so tall and vital despite the lines of weary concern etched around his mouth. She turned quickly back to the microwave, trying to hide the clamoring reaction of her senses to his masculinity.

"I'm fixing myself some cocoa. Would you like a cup?" she offered.

"Yes." He walked to the cupboard, removed a mug and set it on the counter near Jacquie. His cool gaze raked her from head to toe. "Don't you ever wear anything under your robe? Or are your pajamas packed? Did you, uh, ever make a decision about what you plan to do? Keep me in the loop."

Jacquie colored. "Drop it." She took her cup out of the microwave and prepared his mug to replace it. "I just showered," she added defensively. The searing memories of their pleasurable encounters rushed forward in all vividness.

A chair leg scraped the floor as Choya yanked it away from the table. "Whatever. I'm not in the mood to argue."

"Really?"

"I've had a long day and I'm tired." He rubbed his forehead as he drew the words out through a tightly clenched jaw.

Jacquie assessed his weary face. He didn't look like he was lying. She didn't have to be on guard. "Do you have a headache? Go lie down on the couch. I'll bring this to you."

The microwave beeped again and she took out his mug, holding it close to her. The robe gaped open a little on the top, but she couldn't close it, not with hot cocoa in her hand. Choya was standing beside the chair, his hand gripping the back, a trace of white around his knuckles. Her breathing changed to a quick, uneven rate. She reached shakily for a chair.

"Are you trying to tempt me?" he accused in a voice that was soft but harsh.

"No!"

Frozen by the mesmerizing quality in his narrowed gaze, she didn't resist when he took the cup and set it safely down. His hands closed over her arms and drew her toward him. The descending mouth tipped back her head, automatically arching her body toward him. The warmth of his kiss melted her, making her pliant against his hard body.

It felt so good. It even felt . . . right. For

days on end, Jacquie had felt empty inside. Now that hunger was being fed by Choya's unexpected embrace. She parted her lips, craving more, and his kiss deepened with satisfying passion.

A tanned hand slid up her shoulder to push aside the collar of her robe. His mouth began a sensual exploration of the exposed hollow of her throat.

That was almost too much for her. Her hands lifted to strain against his chest, twisting her body to elude the searching caress of his lips. "Not again, Choya. Please let me go," she begged while she still had some self-control left.

Smoothly he swung her off her feet into the cradle of his arms. The smoldering gold of his eyes burned over her face. Her heart skipped a beat, then accelerated madly at the promise of possession in their depths.

"You can't seem to make up your mind, can you?" His voice was a husky murmur. "I'll help you decide."

And he carried her out of the kitchen to her opened bedroom door. For an instant she was too overwhelmed by his mastery to struggle. Then, at the sight of the turned-down covers of her bed, her resolve came back. "Put me down. I totally mean it."

Choya laughed and set her down without

releasing her. His gaze moved suggestively over her rigid body, almost physically touching her curves.

"You wish you did." He smiled sensually. "I'm not inclined to believe you."

"You'd better!" Jacquie tried to pull free of his grip. "Get your hands off me!"

"Whatever you want," Choya mocked. He obeyed. But the invisible connection between them seemed stronger than the physical one.

"Stop driving me crazy," she cried desperately.

"Isn't that your game, Jacquie?" he asked.

"I'm not playing any damn game!"

"Then what is it you're trying to prove?" The sardonic gleam left his gaze as he studied her intently. He seemed to hesitate, thinking over her words and studying her expression to see how much truth they contained.

"That — that I'm not going to leave. Not yet."

"Oh," he said in a mocking tone. "I guess we can all be grateful for that. Thanks for the update."

His reply stung. "I'm staying because of Robbie."

"Is that the only reason?"

The angry glitter of proud tears shimmered in her turquoise green eyes. "You read the card he left for me. He would have blamed himself if I'd left then."

Choya nodded, but his jaw was visibly tensed. "So how does this work? You decide completely on your own if and when you're going? Mind if I put in my two cents on the subject? This is my house and he is my son, you know."

"Go ahead. I'd love to hear what you have to say. Have you told him or Sam anything?" she said in a choked voice.

"No. You'll have to." Sadness shadowed his eyes. "Sounds like you want to."

He reached out and brushed cornsilk hair from her cheek. Jacquie drew back from his touch, leaving his hand suspended in midair.

"Just so you know, I'm not going to kick you out," he said quietly, letting his hand fall to his side.

"Why not? It would make it easier. On me," she added.

"Because I don't want you to go. Believe me, Jacquie, I never intended to back you into a corner with what I had to say about Robbie." One corner of his strong mouth lifted in a brief, self-deprecating smile. "You take everything so damn personally."

"Is that bad?"

"No. Look, I didn't know what to say or

do that night we talked. You're the first woman since —"

"We don't have to get into that, Choya."

His mouth quirked. "Don't flatter yourself. I'm not that virtuous. I was going to say that you're the first woman I've brought home to the ranch. I don't know why I expected it to be easy." He sighed.

"Let's call a truce."

He hesitated. "The second we get close, things started happening too fast."

"Good point," she said sarcastically, "and neither of us seems to be any good at stopping."

"If you do stay," he began, then paused. "How long do I have? Give me an exact date. So I can prepare Robbie."

"I was wondering when you were going to get around to him."

Choya frowned at her tone. "Were you?"

"Yes. I really care about him, no matter what you think."

He clamped his mouth tightly shut, paused for an instant, then spoke more calmly. "Jacquie, when you leave, it won't be the worst thing that ever happened to me. I'll get over it in good time. But my son" — he broke off briefly — "he's not that tough. Not that I'd expect him to be at his age."

"For God's sake, Choya, the last thing I want to do is hurt him! I'll stay until Christmas if you don't give me a reason to leave. There — that's your answer. Is that what you wanted to hear?"

Choya held her proudly demanding gaze for a long, hard moment, then, pivoting, he walked from the room without giving her an answer.

After a restless night's sleep, Jacquie awakened to the strident buzz of the alarm clock. She dressed swiftly, wondering all the while if Choya had accepted her terms. He might be ticked off enough to drive her into Tombstone this morning and tell her she was free to leave.

There was no sign of him in the kitchen. Jacquie hesitated at the hall leading to the living room. Perhaps she should find him to see if he'd had second thoughts or arrived at some other decision on his own.

In a few minutes, Robbie would be coming down for breakfast. She started to fix it, her thoughts in turmoil. One thing was clear, though: Jacquie was still sure that leaving immediately was the wrong thing to do.

The food was on the table. Jacquie, Robbie, and Sam were all sitting down and eating when Choya came in from morning chores. His encompassing good-morning nod told her nothing. She tried to ease the anxiety of waiting with the reminder that he would probably want to speak to her alone at some point today.

"Dad" — Robbie paused as he finished spreading peanut butter over his toast — "can we go to Fort Bowie this Saturday?"

"I don't think so," Choya replied.

Robbie grimaced. "But you promised to take Gramps and me way back in summer, and it's halfway into December."

"And it's cold out and could get worse. Winter's here." Choya didn't look at Jacquie.

"So?" Boyish brown eyes looked at Choya blankly.

"You could catch the sniffles. I don't want you to miss any more school this year. I had to keep you home or with me for nearly a month because of your broken leg," he explained patiently.

"It didn't matter," Robbie asserted. "I probably got more work done because I couldn't run around."

There was a dubious shake of the dark head. "I'm not even sure the fort's open this late in the year. And don't forget that we have to walk there once we park and it's over a mile. Your leg's not that strong and it's rough terrain for your grandfather."

"We can make it, can't we, Gramps?" Robbie turned to Sam for confirmation.

"Eventually," the older man agreed with wry humor, "if we had all day."

"So let's go." Robbie seized on his grandfather's words. "Jacquie could pack us a lunch and come along. We could all have a picnic together. Please, Dad?"

"We'll see." Choya lifted a coffee cup to his mouth, avoiding a direct answer.

"What's there to see about?" Robbie wanted to know.

"Where is this Fort Bowie?" Jacquie asked when Choya flashed his son an impatient glance.

"At Apache Pass," Robbie answered, forgetting his argument with his father for an instant.

"It's the ruins of the adobe fort built back when Cochise was making his raids," Sam explained. "It was to protect the settlers and traders going through Apache Pass. Later it was the main base during Geronimo's War. When he surrendered, the fort was abandoned. Now it's a National Historic Site."

"I bet there's lots of neat arrowheads and stuff," Robbie declared. "Can we go, Dad?"

"Don't keep pestering your father," Sam

warned. "He just might tell you that you can't go because you asked him so many times."

"But Jacquie wants to go, don't you, Jacquie?" The corners of his mouth sulked downward. "She's never been there before. Me neither. Not for years and years."

"You aren't that old," Choya answered dryly. "Between now and Saturday — well, who knows what might happen."

He avoided looking at Jacquie. Did he want to exclude her from a family excursion? Was that what he meant by preparing Robbie? She could almost answer both questions herself. Not in her favor.

"I'll think about it, son," he was saying. "But don't keep bugging me about it or I might do just what Gramps said." He stood up and moved away from the table.

"Ah, gee!" Robbie grumbled and dunked a corner of his cinnamon toast into a glass of milk.

"Where are you goin'?" Sam glanced up at Choya.

He didn't answer his father right away. The tawny gaze slid briefly to Jacquie. She held her breath, wondering if he intended on taking her into town and getting her on her way out of it.

"To check the north fence," he answered,

and set the empty cup back on the table.

She nodded in his direction, thinking unwillingly that the waiting and wondering was tough for him too. Confusion clouded her eyes as she watched him walk toward the small hallway that led to the back door.

Quickly, she pushed her chair away from the table and followed him. He was nearly at the screen door when she entered the hall, her lighter footsteps drowned by the firm tread of his.

"Choya?" she called.

He paused, one hand holding the screen door ajar as he waited for her to reach him. His aloof gaze read the unvoiced question in her eyes.

"We need to talk," he said. "Away from Robbie and Sam. How about we go for a long ride this afternoon — just the two of us?" With that he walked out the door.

Jacquie stared after him without another word.

CHAPTER 9

Perched on top of the corral fence, Jacquie munched an apple. The buckskin was waiting patiently for his share, nostrils flared, inhaling the scent in anticipation. Sighing, she handed him the core, absently ruffling his black mane.

Restless and uneasy, she hopped down from the fence into the corral, wiping her palms on her jeans. She grabbed hold of the buckskin's halter and led him through the door into the barn, then she saddled and bridled the docile horse and was ready to lead him outdoors to mount up.

Choya had said they would be going for a long ride, without Sam or Robbie coming along. She was sure Choya would bring up the subject of her departure once they were well away from the house and out in the wilderness. Good strategy. The balance of power would subtly shift, given what a novice she was as a rider.

Shrewdly, she guessed that had to have entered into his thinking before he made the offer. There would be no domestic distractions or business to concern him. Robbie would be cared for by his grandfather, and they would be alone. It was a very male strategy. He would literally lead the way, tall in the saddle, while she and her easygoing horse trailed him.

As far as the weather, the temperatures were going to plummet by sundown. If they couldn't get back before nightfall — she dismissed an instant fantasy of being cuddled and wrapped up in his big old blanket jacket by the campfire under a starry sky.

No matter the time of day, it would be too cold and too rocky to get physical. Her virtue — what was left of it — was safe. Of course, the end result would be the same after Christmas. Good-bye and good luck to him. He was tougher than tough, he'd survive.

How and when she would say essentially the same thing to his seven-year-old son was becoming more and more difficult to even imagine.

Impatient, wondering where the hell Choya was, Jacquie left the buckskin tied in the stall and hurried into the house.

No Choya. Had he phoned to say he'd be late?

Sam was dozing in an armchair. His gaunt frame looked relaxed and his face was peaceful. If Choya had called, his dad would have taken the message and left it where she could see it. Apparently the younger Barnett hadn't. There was no message.

It wouldn't hurt to practice her riding. She could even head out, stay within view of the house. The dust that the jeep raised on the roads would announce his return from miles away.

Hesitating in the kitchen, Jacquie considered packing a lunch. It seemed unnecessary. She'd be close enough on her practice ride to double back and slap some sandwiches together for both of them then.

She did grab a quilted down vest. As a last thought, she helped herself to leather riding gloves that were too big for her and a hat that was too big for Robbie.

Back astride the buckskin, clutching the reins inexpertly, she had to make another decision: which way to go. Reining the horse away from the lane, Jacquie touched a heel to its flank and set off. Once she was a fair distance from the lane, she would turn and ride so that the ranch house was in sight.

It was already cold and startlingly clear.

Deceptively so. Jacquie still marveled at the odd, almost magical way the clarity of the desert air could make objects seem closer than they were — or conversely, far away. Jacquie rode at a trot for a while before she wheeled her cooperative horse in a wide circle to align herself to look back at the ranch buildings. They were there, but tiny. How had she come so far in so short a time? She headed back toward them, going up and down the rises and hollows of the undulating land.

The ranch buildings shone white in the chilly sun, seeming larger, now off to her left. Jacquie halted the horse in a dry streambed that meandered in that direction. Maybe it was the stream that Choya had mentioned, the one which watered the cottonwoods by the house in spring. She would follow its course.

A few small hills and low valleys later, the ranch seemed to have disappeared. Her angle had taken her into the rocky beginnings of the Dragoons instead. Broken pillars of granite thrust up amid boulders and washes of small, tumbled rocks that looked treacherously unstable.

The buckskin picked his way through it, sure-footed as a mule. Weren't some horses able to find their way home? Hers certainly seemed to know the way. He must have been out here before. The ranch buildings could appear any minute in the near distance.

But they didn't. Disoriented, she told herself that she wasn't lost. Yet. A feeling of fear made her fingers curl tightly around the reins.

An animal trail branched off to the right and she decided to follow it for the time being. If the trail turned into the mountains, she would abandon it.

Although the trail wound and twisted, dipped and climbed, it maintained the general direction that Jacquie wanted to take. The problem was that time was going by and she wasn't covering as much ground as she'd thought she would. The rocky terrain and her limited horsemanship forced her to keep the buckskin at a walk.

Worried about where they were, she absently blamed the buckskin's uneven gait on the broken path. When they reached a smooth stretch of sand, it didn't alter. Glancing down, she saw he was favoring his right front leg. She stopped and dismounted, cursing her rotten luck.

With her hands on her hips, she studied the surrounding land. She had accomplished exactly nothing and was undoubtedly going in circles. She hadn't reached high enough ground to be able to see the ranch, let alone get back to it. Jacquie surmised that they had wandered into a shallow, irregularly shaped narrow valley beneath the mountains, sloping so gradually she hadn't been aware of descending into it. Which way was up? She didn't know. And now she was on foot with a lame horse.

"Come on, Johnny," Jacquie sighed heavily and took a short hold of the reins. "We can't stay here, that's for sure."

Leading the limping buckskin, she continued on the trail, which was becoming more difficult to see. A dry thirst parched her throat, and a hollowness of coming hunger tightened her stomach. She was beginning to realize just how foolish she'd been. She had packed no food and hadn't thought to bring water.

When she'd first arrived at the ranch, she'd listened with half an ear to Choya's warning that the mountain desert was unforgiving terrain, and no place for a novice. Since then, she had become familiar with the unending ruggedness of the landscape, but with that familiarity had come a subconscious disregard for its danger. She was up against it now and all alone.

The trail forked. The way to the left

wound around a hillock toward the mountains; to the right it continued in the direction that Jacquie thought she should take. But when she started that way, the buckskin balked.

Jacquie took a firmer grip on the reins and tugged. “Come on, feller,” she coaxed, but he refused.

The instant she stopped tugging, the horse shifted toward the left fork in the trail. Crooning to him softly, she tried to persuade him to change his mind without success.

Straightening his black forelock, she murmured, “Do you know something that I don’t know?” She tried again to lead him along the right fork and again the buckskin refused.

Giving up, she walked to the left and the horse willingly followed. The twisted, curving trail climbed up into the edges of the mountain. Rarely was Jacquie able to see beyond the next turn. She had no idea where she was going; she just hoped the horse did.

A large boulder forced the trail to bend around it, and on the other side, Jacquie stopped in surprise. Nestled in a pocket of the mountain slope was a sparkling pool of water, shaded on three sides by rising rock walls. The horse shouldered her forward.

There were animal tracks around the small pool. Tufts of grass grew near its edges. Jacquie watched the buckskin drink deeply from the water before she kneeled to scoop a small handful to her mouth. It was icy cold but sweet and wonderfully refreshing.

When she had slaked her thirst, she sat down by one of the walled sides, leaning against the rock face. The buckskin limped to the grass, his teeth tearing at the green blades. Now she at least had water.

But evening was nigh. She hummed the old song under her breath. It was hauntingly apt.

The western sky was on fire. The setting sun was crimsoning the sky with streaks of red and flame orange. Clouds purpled above its light while the desert reflected its burning glow. Jacquie had witnessed this sunset spectacle before. The cold stillness of approaching night had already invaded the land. Darkness would steal in quietly when the sun dipped below the horizon.

To leave the mountain pool when night was creeping in would be foolish. Here she had water and the horse had food even if she didn't. She concentrated on the beauty of the sunset and tried not to think about the growling in her empty stomach or the dropping temperature.

She knew instinctively that Choya was out looking for her. Possibly she had been missed before she'd even known she was lost. She wished he would find her, but there was little chance of that, at least not before nightfall. He would search the lane and road first, with no idea of which way she'd gone and no logical way to puzzle it out. Her wandering had been utterly random. Logic had had nothing to do with it.

Lavender hues began to dominate the sky. It was twilight. The evening star twinkled dimly. Jacquie shivered at the chill in the air and hugged her arms around her middle. It would be dangerously cold tonight and her blouse sleeves offered almost no protection. She would have to tuck her arms inside the armholes of the down vest — it was big enough.

The buckskin lifted its head, its ears pricked toward the trail. Jacquie looked and saw nothing, but she could hear movement. She tensed. This was probably the only watering hole for miles. Maybe it was a wild animal coming for a drink. The buckskin's sides heaved in a searching whinny.

His call was answered by the whicker of another horse, then Jacquie heard the creak of saddle leather. It had to be Choya. Hastily she scrambled to her feet, her heart thumping wildly against her ribs. Not more than five minutes ago she had been wishing he would find her. She knew he'd be angry and with good reason. Her carelessness could have gotten her badly injured or worse. The horse already was.

He rounded the boulder and heat flushed her cheeks. The sorrel horse halted and Choya sat silently in the saddle, his unwavering gaze locked on hers, his tawny eyes piercing like a golden arrow. Then his gaze shifted to the buckskin.

"Don't say it," Jacquie muttered angrily when its sharpness returned to her. "I know I did something stupid."

"Were you trying to commit suicide?" His voice rolled out low, like thunder. "No food, no water, and obviously no matches or you would have a fire."

She tossed her head back in a gesture of defiance. "I got tired of waiting for you. I decided to just ride around for a while. I wasn't that far from the house."

"Mind if I ask why?"

"I wanted to practice. It was clear and sunny when I started. But the land isn't as flat as it looks."

"No, it isn't. And the clearest air plays

tricks. The desert can fool you."

"I didn't realize that until I couldn't see the ranch buildings anymore."

"So you kept on going."

His flat tone was grating. The romantic fantasy she'd entertained of him playing hero seemed ludicrous. A hero didn't give lectures or point out how the heroine did everything wrong.

Even if she had. But it would be nice if he would just shut up — and hand over that warm jacket.

"Listen, Choya, I really didn't plan on spending a December night out here," she retorted. "I made a mistake. I know that's not allowed but —"

"Jacquie, give it a rest."

She shut up. What else could she do? She was still cold and miserable. "How did you find me?"

Choya swung effortlessly from the saddle. "A horse leaves tracks. I followed them."

"I'm impressed," Jacquie declared bitterly. "I might have made it back if Johnny hadn't gone lame."

Dropping the sorrel's reins to the ground, Choya walked over to the buckskin and ran an exploring hand over the right front leg. Lifting the hoof, he reached into his pocket and took out something that looked like a knife. There was a scraping sound, then he released the hoof and the buckskin stood squarely on all four feet.

"There was a stone in his shoe," he told Jacquie.

"That's all?" She stared at him in disbelief. "That's what made him limp? He isn't really hurt?"

"I imagine his foot is a little sore right now," Choya conceded. "Nothing worse than a slight bruise."

If only she had known what was wrong. She felt bad for the horse. Her ignorance had hurt him. The thought made her angry with herself, which was followed by self-pity.

She stared at her rescuer as he walked toward her, tall and dark. The half light of dusk threw his angular features into sharp relief, accenting their ruggedness and the strong line of his mouth. He walked past her to the sorrel and pulled a rifle from the saddle scabbard.

Her turquoise eyes widened. "What are you doing?"

Choya cocked the rifle and pointed it into the air. He fired two shots fairly close together, paused and fired a third, then he returned his rifle to the scabbard and glanced at Jacquie.

"I'm signaling Sam that I found you," he explained tersely.

"Can he hear that?" She frowned, wondering if she was closer to the house than she'd thought.

"Sound, especially a rifle shot, carries a long way in this country." He moved to the leather pouches tied behind the saddle.

She didn't know what he was doing. "Aren't we going to head back?" she asked stiffly.

Unfastening one side of the pouch, Choya glanced at the fading golden light of the western horizon. "Not now. The trail is too difficult to follow in the dark."

"Do you mean we have to stay here all night?" Jacquie breathed with alarm.

"That's exactly what I mean." He removed a packet of sandwiches from the saddlebag and tossed it to her. "You might as well eat while I start a fire."

His grimness as he began gathering sticks from the surrounding brush bordered on a kind of anger that Jacquie found difficult to fathom. It made her even more tense, although she was grateful he'd ridden out to rescue her. But each passing minute added to the electrically charged feeling that crackled between them.

Despite her hunger, she could only eat one

sandwich. She set the others aside for Choya. A small campfire was blazing as night drew its curtain over the sunset.

With that accomplished, he unsaddled the buckskin, setting the saddle and blanket near Jacquie. Taking the lariat from his saddle horn, he strung a picket line for both horses, then unsaddled his own.

His continued silence was unnerving. Teasing, even making fun of her multiple mistakes she could have handled, but not this. Her nerves were already frayed. When he set his saddle on the ground near hers, her control snapped.

"Well, here we are, Choya." Her voice trembled hoarsely. "What a fiasco. My first ride into your damn desert is going to be my last. I don't belong here. I should never have said yes to you."

His jaw tightened forbiddingly. "Maybe not. And you're right about not belonging here. You don't. I know this isn't the kind of place a woman can be happy. I went through something like this once before and I swore I never would again."

"What?" She was baffled by his words and his anger.

"I'm not going to get into it, Jacquie. Not now. Not ever. You don't need to know my whole damn life story. Let bygones be bygones." His voice was raw with bitterness.

He didn't look at her. The saddlebags were draped over his shoulder. He swung them down and opened one flap, towering above her, a dark silhouette against the campfire. He removed a small square object and held it out to her.

"This is yours," he said gruffly.

Fighting tears of frustration that he had failed again even to reply, Jacquie scrambled to her feet. Impatiently she took the object he held out to her. Her lips parted to forcefully repeat her demand, but words failed her for a few seconds as the familiar shape of the object got her attention.

She gazed at it in disbelief. "M-my wallet!"

"Yes, it is," was the low response.

Hurriedly she opened it. Nothing was missing, as far as she could tell. "My money — it's all here." She raised her head, trying to see his face in the flickering firelight. "Where did you get it?" Then a chilling thought struck her. "You had it all the time, didn't you?" she accused.

"No!" Choya snapped and breathed in deeply, almost angrily. "Of course I didn't," he added in a calmer voice.

Something in his expression made Jacquie doubt his answer. "Then where did it come from?" she challenged. "How did you get it?"

"From Robbie."

"Robbie?" She echoed the boy's name in shock. "How did he get it?"

"The day you spilled all that stuff in your purse on the sidewalk, he stuck the wallet inside his shirt," he said grimly. "He didn't want you to leave, remember?"

Jacquie nodded.

"He decided if he took your wallet you wouldn't have any money to buy gas for your car."

"Let alone pay for the repairs," she added with a short, ironic laugh. "So Robbie's had it all this time."

"He's been keeping it in his secret hiding place in the barn."

She raked a weary hand through her long hair, flipping it back to stream over her shoulders. "No wonder he didn't want to show me his hiding place," she murmured. Tears shimmered jewel bright in her eyes. "What made him decide to give it to you?"

"When I came back to the ranch this afternoon and discovered you and the horse were gone, Robbie was with me. He was half crazy with fear that you were hurt or lost. And for some crazy reason he thought that you might've run away," Choya stated.

"So, using kid logic, he decided that if he gave the wallet back, I would find you safe and sound, otherwise something terrible would happen to you."

She wanted to cry but she managed — just barely — not to. All of this had happened to her because a little boy hadn't wanted her to leave him. Hiding her wallet had triggered the entire chain of events that had brought her to the ranch, kept her there, and made her fall for Choya. Of course, she hadn't fallen in love. Her experience was more like jumping off an emotional cliff just to see what it felt like. Big thrill, bad result.

Dipping her chin, she closed her eyes briefly against the rush of pain. Then she raised her head to gaze into his shadowed face.

"I thought I would feel so happy if the wallet was returned. But I'm not."

"Don't tell Robbie that. The kid's confused enough as it is. And he's scared," Choya began in harsh quietness. "Damn it, Jacquie — why are you — don't cry, okay? Just don't."

"I can't help it!" Jacquie told him, swallowing a sob. "I don't want him to be scared and wondering if I still like him and if I'm going to stay when I'm not!"

The words brought a fresh flood of tears down her cheeks that stung in the freezing night air. Her shoulders shuddered with involuntary, silent sobs. Choya stood in front of her.

"At least you care — about him." The savageness in his tone wasn't directed at her. "Don't sweat it, Jacquie. And forget about Christmas. That was the biggest mistake of all. I wanted you here for Robbie's sake, but it's only one day out of the year, right?"

He took a hesitant step forward. His hands closed lightly over her shoulders to draw her against him. Jacquie tried weakly to push him away but racking sobs made her efforts puny. He gathered her close to his chest, rocking her gently in his arms.

Her cries were muffled by his shirt. Indifferently she was aware of the comforting hand stroking her silken hair. She clung to him, feeling like a lost lamb being welcomed back to the fold.

His dark head bent near hers, and gently he kissed her tear-drenched lashes and wet cheeks. When his mouth found hers, it carried the salty taste of her own tears.

His kiss breathed warmth and strength into her. Under its reviving spell, life flowed back into her. Jacquie's arms wrapped around his neck, but he disentangled them. His strong arms lowered her to the ground and a blanket was thrown over her. She shivered underneath it, wishing he would come to her. He wouldn't.

"Go to sleep," Choya ordered.

The buckskin stamped the ground restlessly, as Jacquie watched Choya walk to the opposite side of the campfire. He might as well have walked to the other side of the moon.

Her lashes fluttered. Something was wrong. There was no soft mattress beneath her. No pillow cushioned her head. There was only hard, uncomfortable ground beneath her and the frosty chill of a December dawn in the desert around her. The memory of her futile attempt to find her way back to the ranch put the strange surroundings in perspective.

Jacquie opened her eyes, propping herself up on one elbow to look for Choya. He was over by the horses. Her frightened expression softened, then her muscles protested stiffly as she forced herself to her feet.

The buckskin was saddled and Choya was tightening the cinch on his sorrel. At her movement, he flicked a brief glance in her direction. The touch of his gaze was like a splash of cold water and she froze. The metallic gold eyes had as much warmth in them as the ashes of the dead campfire. She shuddered uncontrollably.

"Good morning." His indifferent greeting pierced her heart.

"Looks like it's going to be a nice day," Jacquie said stiffly.

With the reins of both horses in his hand, he walked toward her. The boldly masculine features were drawn in an aloof expression.

He handed her the buckskin's reins. "It's a long ride back," he said briskly. "We'd better get started."

"Yes," she agreed, keeping her misery out of her voice. She mounted quickly before he saw the agonizing pain in her eyes.

As she pointed her horse toward the narrow trail, Choya called her name. She halted the buckskin and waited, her shoulders rigidly squared. He reined his sorrel even with her mount.

"Here." In his sun-browned hand was the metal ring with her car keys.

"How did you —"

"That's why I was late yesterday. I went to town to get your car. Brad and his buddy helped me out. One drove, one followed in his car, I drove the jeep. They went back together."

"Oh." In a stronger voice, she began to question his decision. "But why —"

"You know," he interrupted her, "the second you and I are alone, no matter where we are, we start fighting."

"That's not true," she protested weakly.

He shook his head in firm disagreement. "The right thing to do is not to drag this out. You shouldn't have tried to persuade yourself otherwise. I did some serious thinking last night, Jacquie. I didn't sleep. I'm exhausted. I've had it."

"I'm sorry," she said again. "Sorry about everything, I mean."

"Don't be. It just isn't going to work. We both know it."

Her wondering eyes asked the question she couldn't voice: *Are you sure?*

"I'm sure. Let's get it over with, Jacquie."

She shoved the keys in the pocket of her jeans and kicked the buckskin's flanks, moving him out ahead of Choya.

Not another word was exchanged during the entire ride. The crushing silence ripped at her heart until it was in shreds by the time they reached the ranch yard. Her chin was quivering traitorously as she dismounted beside the corral. Unable to risk a glance at Choya, she dropped the reins and started for the house, leaving him to take care of the horses.

Robbie was racing across the yard toward her at a reckless pace. A grin of eager welcome was splitting his face from ear to ear. Sam Barnett was hobbling after him with his cane.

Standing stock-still, Jacquie waited for Robbie to reach her. Her head pounded with dread, knowing that his happiness about her return wasn't going to last. Choya's long strides were carrying him toward her.

"Jacquie! Jacquie! You're back!" Robbie cried in delight. When he would have hurled himself at her, Choya intercepted him, swinging him off his feet and straddling him on one hip. The boy readily transferred his affectionate greeting from Jacquie to his father. "You found her and brought her back, Dad! I knew you would! I just knew it!"

"Why aren't you in school?" Choya cast a sideways frown at Sam.

"I was waiting for Jacquie." Robbie beamed at her.

Sam shuffled forward, leaning heavily on his cane. "He refused to go until he'd seen Jacquie for himself. He was darned near makin' himself sick over it. There wasn't much else I could do but let him see she was all right," he said, giving the explanation that Choya had silently demanded.

"I was afraid something would happen, and Jacquie and you wouldn't ever come back," Robbie added his fervent words to his grandfather's. His expression became suddenly apologetic. "I'm sorry about your wallet, Jacquie. I wasn't going to keep it. I was going to give it back to you. I only took it because I wanted you to stay."

"I know," she sighed, glancing helplessly at Choya's grim expression.

"Go up to the house, Jacquie," he ordered. His arm tightened around his son's waist. "I'll handle this."

Jacquie opened her mouth but nothing came out. She closed it, briefly meeting Sam's puzzled look, and darted for the house. From her room, she could hear Robbie protesting the news of her imminent departure, followed by his crying sobs. If only she could have told Robbie herself, found some way to ease his pain.

But it had to happen, sooner or later. Choya had ended the stalemate and done what needed to be done.

Without regard to neatness or order, she jammed her clothes and belongings into the suitcases. Inside, her heart was crying as tearfully as Robbie was. From her wallet, she took out enough money to cover the car repairs and the motel bill. She slipped it under the alarm clock on the nightstand. When the last suitcase was filled, Choya appeared in the doorway of her room.

"Are you ready?" he asked.

Jacquie nodded, passing a hand across her face as though making certain no tears were on her cheeks. Choya picked up the two largest suitcases and juggled a third, leaving her to carry two small bags.

As she walked out of the room, she didn't pause for a last look. Whatever she might have left was going to stay left, and she didn't need a last glance to be able to remember the room and this ranch in the months ahead.

When they walked outdoors, Robbie was huddled in a shadowy corner beneath the overhang. Jacquie looked at his bowed head with deep compassion and shared hurt. While Choya stowed her luggage in the back of her car, Sam limped forward. "I was just beginning to get used to having you around." He smiled wryly and held out his hand. "If you'd stayed a while longer, you mighta learned to cook."

Jacquie returned his smile weakly. "Thanks for everything, Sam."

The elderly man nodded his gray head

and stepped back. He glanced toward the house where Robbie was hunched in his ball of misery.

"Aren't you going to come and say good-bye to Jacquie?" his grandfather called. The amiable question was met with silence. "You don't want her to leave without saying that, do you, Robbie?" Sam asked again. Nothing. He glanced apologetically at Jacquie. "I'm sorry. I don't know what's wrong with that boy's manners. I'll go get him."

"No." She placed a hand on his arm to stop him. "I . . . I understand how Robbie feels. It's okay, really."

The last of her belongings were packed in the car. Choya stepped away from the open door. There was a lump in her throat as her gaze lingered on his impassive face.

The car keys were in her hand and the driver's door was open. But if Choya would say the right words, Jacquie knew she would never slide behind the wheel. He said nothing. Swallowing hard, she moved to get in.

"Jacquie!" It was Robbie who hurried toward her. "Jacquie, I don't want you to go!" He stopped in front of her, his face stained with tears and more were running down his cheeks. "I want you to stay!"

She knelt beside him. "I have to go, Robbie," she explained with a tight smile. "It's not your fault. Don't ever think that, okay?"

He hurled himself into her arms, wrapping his small hands around her neck to cling to her desperately. Jacquie hugged him, closing her eyes as the pain in her heart became unbearable.

"Please don't go," he sobbed into her blouse. "Please, Jacquie!"

"I'm sorry," she whispered. Her mouth formed the words against his silky, fine hair, almost the same shade of pale gold as her own.

"Please," he begged. "I love you. Please!"

A tear squeezed through her lashes, followed by another. "I love you too, Robbie," Jacquie murmured, "but I have to leave."

"Why?" he pleaded to understand and clutched her tighter.

Jacquie knew if she had a hundred years to explain, it wouldn't be enough. Her brief stay on the ranch had been mistaken from start to finish. She'd tried to do her best but expecting a motherless child to think of her as a pal was the biggest mistake of all. When it came right down to it, she had a lot of growing up to do and she was going to have to do it on her own.

Without Choya. He had a son to raise and better things to do with his life than chase her or argue with her or — love her.

But oh, it was hard to say good-bye to them all. So hard. Opening her eyes, she focused her blurred vision on Choya, mutely appealing to him for help.

His gaze narrowed. He seemed about to say something, then the line of his mouth thinned. Stepping forward, he gripped Robbie by the shoulders and drew him away from her.

"Good-bye," she whispered, but it was really said to Choya, not Robbie. She slid behind the wheel of the car before she completely lost control.

"You can't go!" Robbie started forward, partially checked by his father's hand on his shoulders. "We're supposed to go to Fort Bowie on Saturday, Jacquie. You can't leave until after that."

"I can't stay until Saturday," she said, forcing an artificially bright smile. "I guess I'll have to see it some other time."

"You'll never find it by yourself," Robbie argued. "You've got to look through this pipe to find it and everything." She closed the car door and slipped the key into the ignition. "Don't go, Jacquie! Please stay!"

There were too many unshed tears lodged in her throat for Jacquie to reply. Staring straight ahead, she started the engine. Robbie's cries were much too poignant for her to listen to many more without giving in. She didn't look back until she was driving down the lane. Then she glanced in her rearview mirror.

Robbie had broken free of Choya and was running after the car but not fast enough to have a prayer of catching up. She could see that he was calling to her. Thank God she couldn't hear him. Soon she couldn't see him either as her eyes blurred with tears and the dust cloud from her accelerating car obscured him from view.

Chapter 10

Too tired to think, Jacquie stepped from the car. Automatically, she walked to the side door of the two-story white house, stretching shoulder muscles cramped from the long drive from Tombstone. The door was locked to morning visitors, but the scent of bacon frying was drifting through an open kitchen window. Jacquie knocked and waited.

A woman with light brown hair peered cautiously through the door's window. Her blue eyes rounded in a mixture of disbelief and delight. There was a momentary fumbling with the lock, then the door was thrown open and the screen door unhooked to admit Jacquie.

"Hello, Mom," Jacquie managed before she was engulfed in her mother's embrace.

"Jacquie! Honey!" she exclaimed before she stepped back to look at her daughter. "We've missed you so much! Just that one voicemail message and you didn't say where you were, just that you were all right —"

Her mother was bubbling over with happiness. "And then that collect call — oh, my goodness, I've hardly been able to live with your father, he's been so upset about that ever since."

"I'm sorry, I —"

"Look at me," her mother declared with a laughing sigh. "You've barely walked in the door and I'm already scolding you like you were a child. I'm so happy you're back!"

"So am I." At this moment, Jacquie was just glad to be there, with her mother's arm curved warmly around her waist.

Which made her think of Choya, holding her — never again, she reminded herself. She was going to have to get used to that.

"You look exhausted. Why don't you come sit down? I was just fixing breakfast for your father. Would you like some? Did you drive all night?"

"Yes to everything," Jacquie laughed at her mother's tumbling words.

Her mother paused and sighed with happiness, her eyes twinkling brightly. "Good answer. I've forgotten the questions."

"What's all the commotion, Maureen?" Her father appeared in the doorway, tucking in his shirt, silver hair glinting in the light. Jacquie looked at him lovingly, wondering how she could have forgotten how very handsome he was.

The entire angry argument that had preceded her departure seemed as if it hadn't happened. "I'm back, Dad," she said softly.

His mouth curved faintly with a smile and he opened up his arms to her. "Welcome home, baby."

Jacquie flew into the bear hug of his arms with the same abandon Robbie had once shown to her. "I'm so sorry about everything," she declared with a tiny sob.

"So am I." He kissed her soundly on the cheek. "Let's just forget about it."

Her eyes sparkled with affection and a touch of mischief. "I bet I'm going to be surprised by how much you've learned since I've been away."

"Oh? You mean I got smarter?" he teased. "That's a sure sign that my little girl has done some growing up."

"Quite a bit." Jacquie nodded. She filled them both in on the ranch and the Barnetts, talking animatedly. She'd rehearsed most of it on the road, wanting to sound confident.

"Sit down, you two," her mother instructed. "Breakfast is ready." She started pouring the orange juice as father and daughter moved to the small dinette table.

"So, how was the weather on the way?"

"Getting chilly. It's really cold at night in the high desert."

"Why did you decide to stay on in Tombstone?" her mother asked blandly. Jacquie wasn't fooled. "Robbie sounds like an awfully nice little boy. And you must have gotten along well with his parents."

"It was just his dad," Jacquie said hastily. "Robbie's mother died several years ago."

Her mother's delicate eyebrows raised ever so slightly. "Oh. You didn't mention that just now."

"I thought I had." She met her father's inquiring look. "What?"

"Oh — nothing," he said.

"That's right, Dad," was her light reply. "Nothing to report. Mr. Barnett was very nice and I enjoyed being with his family, but he was looking for someone permanent."

She smiled up at her mother. "I can't believe I'm sitting here eating breakfast with you. This is delicious, by the way."

Her father sighed as he helped himself to more bacon. "Well, it sounds like your first foray into the real world went well. Maybe you'll make it to Los Angeles on your next go."

"I'd like to try." Jacquie sipped at her

orange juice and carefully avoided the curious glances of her parents. "It's a big world out there. I want to see more of it."

"So tell us about Tombstone. It's not very big, is it?" It was her father who asked.

"No, but they call themselves The Town Too Tough To Die." She made a joke out of it. "I hadn't been there more than a minute when I cracked up the car — oh, it wasn't that serious," she said hastily at her mother's indrawn breath. "But I had to have it repaired before I could go on. Then I lost my wallet with all my money, ID, et cetera, and couldn't pay to get my car out of the shop."

"Is that when you called me?" Cameron asked. At Jacquie's silent nod, he sighed. "I was angry when you did. Your mother and I had just been arguing about the way I'd lost my temper before you left. I kicked myself a thousand times after you phoned for not finding out where you were. Your cell phone went straight to voicemail, so we figured you'd lost the charger."

"I left it here," she said.

"I understand. I do that myself all the time," her father said. "Of course, I stick closer to home."

"We were glad to hear from you, though," her mother said, not looking at her husband but at Jacquie. "No matter what, you can always call home."

Her father echoed the statement. Jacquie understood that to mean he was sorry he'd lost his temper and refused her collect call to him. She really was happy to just let it go.

"It was strange not having you here," her father mused. He'd finished his breakfast and was leaning back in his chair.

She nodded. "I had second thoughts. I almost didn't realize it at the time — I was kind of overwhelmed at the beginning." Jacquie smiled faintly.

"I think you have a lot of spunk," her mother declared. "There you were stranded with no money and no car and what did you do but get yourself a job. I'm proud of you. I stopped being frantic with worry as soon as we got the message you left. Now tell me more — you were talking sort of fast."

Spreading jam on her buttered toast turned into a project for Jacquie. She went right to the edges, very carefully, then set her knife aside. "Well, being housekeeper and cook on a ranch was all right. Some days it seemed to never end and some days I had time on my hands."

"My little girl doing housework and cooking!" Her dad laughed incredulously. "We should have been there, Maureen. That would have been a sight worth seeing!"

"Cam!" her mother said warningly.

"Dad's right." Jacquie wanted to keep the conversation light and avoid any questions that might become too probing. "It was ridiculous. Ch — Mr. Barnett had this monster antique stove that I had to do the cooking on. He referred to my meals as 'burnt offerings.' "

"What about his wife? I mean his late wife. How long had he been married?" her mother asked.

"I never asked. He'd been a widower for a while. The strong and silent type." She shifted quickly away from his marital status. "His little boy, Robbie, wasn't much like him. I wish you could have met him, Mom. What a scamp. You would have fallen in love instantly."

"Sounds like you did," her father commented at the warmth in her voice.

"Yes," Jacquie admitted. She put the memory of their emotional parting firmly aside. She'd done a lot of crying on the lonely road home, and she'd do more — but not in front of her parents. She bit into the slice of toast and coughed a bit. "Crumbs," she explained. Jacquie put the toast down and wiped her eyes with a napkin.

"It must have paid well for you to earn enough to get the car fixed and have enough money to come home," her father observed.

Did she detect a note of suspicion in his voice? Or was it her own guilty conscience? Jacquie wasn't certain which it was.

"Actually my wallet was found with everything in it, money and all. But by that time I'd already decided that I wanted to come home," she explained, adding with a bright smile, "and here I am!"

"What are you going to do now?" Her father eyed her thoughtfully. "Do you plan on getting another job around here or what?"

"I know it's way too late to enroll for the next term at the university," Jacquie answered, "but I thought I'd talk to a couple of my professors and see if I can sit in on a few classes."

"I thought college was a waste of time," he mocked her gently.

"That was ages ago," she teased him back, "when I didn't know what I wanted to do with my life." She smiled, not offended or angered by his reminder of her past outburst. "I think I might like to teach elementary school. Maybe the first or second grade with children Robbie's age."

"My girl leaves a rebel and comes back a woman in less than a month." He shook his silvery head, marveling at the idea. "I don't know if it's the rancher I should thank for this change, but I'd certainly like to shake his hand someday."

Jacquie's face crimsoned. She couldn't help herself. His statement was the truth, but he had been speaking figuratively.

"I couldn't have been that bad when I left," she laughed self-consciously, hoping neither of her observant parents would guess the reason for her blush.

"You were a handful, but no, not that bad." Her father smiled.

"That's good to know." She breathed in deeply. "Well, what have you two been doing while I was gone?" she asked, diverting the conversation to a safer topic.

"The usual. Cam and I lead boring lives, don't we, honey?"

Her father parried with a compliment. "Life is never boring with you and Jacquie around, Maureen."

She laughed and then remembered something. "Jacquie, we got a wonderful invitation in the mail yesterday from Gale and Dudley. They wanted to know if we would join them in Galveston for Christmas. You were included, of course. Do you want to go?"

Jacquie forced a smile to her lips. "You mean skip decorating the tree and the party and everything we do here?" Spending the holiday with her father's second cousin and his screechy wife didn't sound magical.

"It would be a change, don't you think?"

Her father said something about not minding a trip to the beach in December, but Jacquie didn't really hear it.

Her father left for his office shortly after breakfast. He still did executive consulting in his field, too energetic to fully enjoy his early retirement from the insurance company. Jacquie helped her mother clear the table, letting her do most of the talking. Together they unloaded the car, carrying the luggage to Jacquie's bedroom.

"Is something wrong, Jacquie?" Maureen Grey tipped her head to one side and studied her daughter's face.

"Wrong?" Jacquie tensed, smiling nervously. "What do you mean?"

"You seem . . . well . . . preoccupied, I guess." Her mother frowned.

She gave a shrug. "I suppose I'm just tired from the long drive and lack of sleep."

"Of course — you need rest and I've been

chattering away like a magpie. We can finish unpacking later," her mother suggested. "Meanwhile, you climb into bed and get some sleep. We have plenty of time to talk."

"Sounds like a plan." Jacquie suddenly felt as tired as she had claimed to be. She gave her mother a quick hug. "It's good to be home."

Tears shimmered in her mother's warm blue eyes. "You have no idea how glad your father and I are to have you back. Now get some sleep."

"I will," Jacquie promised.

There was a cool nip in the air, although Dallas in December was nowhere near as cold as the mountain desert outside of Tombstone. Jacquie gathered books and papers from the passenger seat and stepped from the car. The university had allowed her to audit a few classes for no credit since the fall term was nearly over, but she was taking her studies seriously. Another night of analytical reading was ahead of her, making up for the times when she'd merely squeaked by with the minimum of effort.

Plus, it was the only certain way she had to block out her potent memories of Choya. With each passing day they became more vivid. So far she hadn't confided in her parents about him, although she thought her mother suspected there was more to her story than Jacquie had told.

She entered the house through the side door into the kitchen.

"Mom, I'm home!" Jacquie called.

Setting her books on the dinette table, she walked to the cupboard and removed a glass, then to the refrigerator where she filled it with cold milk. Her mother appeared in the doorway, a beaming smile on her attractive face.

"There's someone here to see you," she announced.

"Who?" Jacquie asked uninterestedly, raising the glass to her lips.

"Mr. Barnett from Arizona. Honey, what's his first name? I'm not sure I heard it right. It's very unusual."

Jacquie nearly choked on her milk. "Choya!"

"Yes, that's it." Her mother nodded.

"What's he doing here? How did he know where I was?" Liquid fire raced through her veins at the thought that he was in the next room. She panicked, knowing she didn't dare see him again.

"Didn't you give him your home address?" her mother said. "You must have — anyway, he's here."

"Tell him" — she rubbed her hand across her forehead, trying to force herself to think — "tell him that I'm sorry but I can't stay. I'm on my way to the library to do research. I've got to go — now." Setting the glass on the counter, she rushed for her books on the table.

"Nonsense." Her mother tucked a hand beneath her elbow. "If he came this far to see you, the least you can do is say hello."

"Mother, no, please!" Jacquie protested anxiously.

Maureen Grey stopped, frowning. "Why on earth are you so afraid to see the man?"

"I'm not afraid." The denial was an outright lie. "It's just that" — she began helplessly, then realized it was no use. She couldn't make her mother understand without explaining in detail — "I guess I have time," she sighed in defeat.

"That's more like it," her mother nodded. "He's in the living room waiting to see you."

Choya was standing in front of the sofa when Jacquie entered the living room with her mother. Tall and even more masculine than she remembered, he wore new-looking jeans and a chambray shirt — and that same ancient concho belt.

She tensed all over as the tawny cat eyes held her gaze with ease. Not for the first time Jacquie had the sensation that she was looking at a predator who'd sighted its prey. The taut alertness was etched in every muscled inch of him. She felt weak at the knees.

"How are you, Jacquie?" The rich timbre of his voice tugged painfully at her heart.

"Fine." She swallowed convulsively. "And you?"

"Doing all right." He paused. "I promised Robbie I would see you while I was here."

So that was why he had to come, Jacquie thought silently — to fulfill a promise to his son. The tiny hope that he might have wanted to see her for himself was dashed instantly.

"How nice." Her mother's blue eyes sparkled. "Thank you for being so nice to our daughter when she ended up in Tombstone. You know how it is. Parents always worry, and Cam and I are no exception."

"Ah — yes, ma'am. I did my best. And she certainly worked hard." His gaze narrowed slightly on Jacquie and the faintest possible smile flickered over his lips. "She's a little headstrong but she's a fast learner."

"Thanks," Jacquie said stiffly.

"That's our girl," Maureen beamed.

"I'd recommend her to anyone, in fact. But I don't think she wants to make a career out of cooking and cleaning," Choya added. "She's too smart for that."

"How nice of you to say so," her mother replied.

Jacquie cleared her throat. "Well, thanks for stopping by, Choya. I'm sorry I can't ask you to stay, but I have a ton of work to do. I was on my way to the library when Mom told me you were here."

"I see." Choya's friendly cheerfulness diminished visibly.

"If you'd known Jacquie before she went to Arizona," her mother spoke up, "you wouldn't believe the way she's changed since she came back. It used to be her evenings were taken up with parties and socializing. Now, it's studying. She doesn't even want to go out."

"Mother, please!" Jacquie murmured angrily, turned away from Choya's piercing gaze.

"Would you mind, Mrs. Grey, if I spoke to your daughter alone for a few minutes?" he asked with annoying deference.

"Of course not." She smiled, missing Jacquie's beseeching look for her to stay. "I have to start dinner anyway."

An electric silence filled the room when her mother left. The charged undercurrents made her feel slightly unsteady. Jacquie walked shakily to the large picture window.

"How did you know where I was?"

"I contacted your insurance company and they gave me your parents' name and address here in Dallas," Choya answered. Jacquie had forgotten all about giving him the name of her insurance company back when she'd collided with his jeep. "I phoned the other night to see if they knew where you were. I found out you were here."

Jacquie tipped her head back, looking at the ceiling, then around the room — anywhere but at him. She felt like a fool. Vaguely she remembered her mother mentioning that some man had phoned the other evening and asked for her, but hadn't left a name. It hadn't meant anything at the time. Although she hadn't gone out at night since she'd come back, that hadn't stopped a couple of former dates from contacting her. She'd spoken to them and brushed them off. Just his luck that he'd gotten her mother, who wouldn't have recognized Choya's voice.

"Unfortunately, I didn't know you were coming or I would have arranged to be somewhere else," she said with bitter truthfulness.

"That's what I thought." His comment was clipped and harsh. At the sound of his approach, she turned warily to face him. "Well, I didn't come here just to chat. You left this behind."

Her gaze flicked briefly to the dull green of folded bills in his hand. She guessed it was the money she'd left on the nightstand.

"It's yours. I always pay my debts in full!" she flashed.

A muscle leaped in his jaw. "I deserved that." Choya breathed in slowly, glancing at the money in his hand.

"You've explained how you found me. Now tell me why you're really here," Jacquie challenged, reeling at his intoxicating closeness yet unable to walk away from him.

Like a magnet, his tawny eyes seemed to draw her toward him. The enigmatic light in their depths tightened her ribs until she could hardly breathe.

"Changed my mind. I want you back," he stated. "I thought it might be easier to persuade you in person."

Her eyes widened. "No. We ended it — let's leave it that way."

"I did some more thinking. I don't think it's over yet. That was just Round One."

There was a twinkle in his eye, but Jacquie deliberately ignored it. "I don't want to fight with you, Choya. We did too much of that."

"That wasn't all we did." His low tone

was gentle. "We had good times too. And Robbie misses you."

A wavering laugh broke from her throat. She had a strong feeling that his concern for his son was mostly the reason why Choya wanted her back. But as much as she loved the boy, that would never be enough. She turned back to the window, cradling her arms around her middle to ward off the sudden chill.

"What exactly are you saying, Choya? That you want me back as an employee or your girlfriend?"

"You tell me. I'm ready for Round Two. On your terms," Choya said firmly, leaving her in no doubt that he meant it.

"I miss Robbie too," she murmured in a choked voice. "Walking away from him was about the hardest thing I ever did. But what if I go back and it doesn't work out and then" — she broke up, looking at him — "I can't do that twice," she whispered. "It would hurt him too much."

Choya took a little while to respond. "He learned something worthwhile from it, Jacquie."

"Like what?" she asked in an agonized voice.

Choya sighed deeply. "He learned that you lose people you love and you still survive.

Life goes on."

His voice was calm but she knew instinctively how much he himself had been hurt. No matter what, she would always respect his hard-won strength of character.

"Oh, Choya. I just wish he hadn't had to learn that from me," she answered, racked with guilt.

"Well, now — I take some responsibility for the way things turned out. I was too tired to think straight by the time I found you the day you wandered off. All I could think of that night, watching you sleep, was how damn young you are."

She hadn't known he'd watched over her. The thought filled her with renewed tenderness for him.

"Jacquie, I was angry because you made a dangerous mistake by heading out alone. Too angry. You didn't know any better."

He hesitated and she took the chance. A question about something he'd said to her had stayed with her.

"You said you had gone through something like it before," she said softly. "What?"

"I owe you an explanation on that — and some other things. But that can wait. Just seeing you again is making me so damn happy."

She could feel herself sway toward him.

Jacquie stiffened her spine.

"But that night, whatever we were doing just seemed to come apart. I really didn't see how you and I could ever make it work. I wasn't lying to your mother when I said you were headstrong."

Leave it to Choya to put it so bluntly. She searched his face, hoping her feelings didn't show on hers. "So why on earth would you want me to come back?"

"I don't think I gave you a chance to prove yourself. And I never did tell you that I love you, Jacquie."

"You do?"

His hands settled onto her shoulders and she found she didn't have the strength to move away. She closed her eyes, reveling in the almost painful sensation of his touch.

"Yes. I do. And I was wrong when I said you were trouble." His low whisper was like a caress. "The trouble has been living without you, Jacqueline."

Exerting the slightest pressure, he turned her into his arms. Her turquoise eyes were riveted on his mouth, watching it form more words she wanted to hear more than she'd ever wanted anything in her life.

"I've wanted to do this ever since you walked into the room," he murmured.

His fingers tangled themselves in the

silken length of her silver blond hair. His mouth covered hers in a searching, possessive kiss, and Jacquie responded to it with all the pent-up longing in her heart.

Then he was tearing his mouth away from her lips. The iron band of his arms held her so tightly she didn't think she could breathe, but she didn't care. She felt him shudder against her and the joy seared her veins.

"Lord knows I never intended to fall in love with you," Choya muttered thickly against her hair. "After what I've done to you, it would be poetic justice if you hated me."

"So you missed me too," Jacquie breathed, letting go of the anguished thought that he only wanted her back for his son.

"Not in the same way Robbie does, but maybe more. I can't sleep without remembering what it was like to have you in my arms and cuddling you against me like a kitten," he said. "I told myself I was only coming to see you to make sure you were all right. But the minute I saw you, I knew I had to do what I could to get you to come back."

"I'm not sure it was fair to mention Robbie."

Choya took the hit and stood. "Maybe it wasn't. But I knew you loved him."

"Not as much as I love his father," she whispered.

He lifted his head to gaze doubtingly into her eyes. "Do you?"

"Y-yes." Her voice quaked with the depth of her feelings — and a measure of uncertainty. "I think I have from the beginning. But that doesn't mean you and I are going to get along. Love doesn't guarantee anything."

"I know that," he groaned, raining kisses over her face and throat as if trying to make up for all the hurt they'd both been through. "And I think we could do better. Just give me a second chance."

"Why did you let me go? Why didn't you make me stay?" Jacquie quivered in his passionate embrace.

"Maybe I wasn't man enough. I've been thinking about that since you went away."

"Uh-oh," she laughed, but this time without pain. "You're more than enough man for me."

"Are you going to come back?" It was barely a question. She had to smile at his commanding tone.

"Yes —"

Jacquie never had a chance to complete her answer as his mouth came down on hers, demanding an answer that wasn't verbal. Her arms slid around his shoulders, clinging to him.

The front door opened and Cameron Grey walked in. He glanced at the embracing couple and halted in shock. It was several seconds before Choya bothered to lift his lips from Jacquie's.

Tawny eyes danced to the older man standing just inside the door. The kiss ended by silent mutual agreement. Choya was the first to speak.

"You must be Jacquie's dad." He removed one arm from around Jacquie, still holding her firmly against his chest with the other. He offered his hand to her stunned father. "I'm Choya Barnett. Your daughter's going back with me to Arizona."

Cameron blinked. "But she just came home!"

"Dad, it's my decision," Jacquie assured him.

He glared at Choya and turned to walk out of the room. "Maureen!" they heard him yell down the hall. "Did you know about this?"

"Know about what?" her mother answered distantly.

They couldn't hear the rest of the heated discussion that ensued because Jacquie's mother had closed a door somewhere.

"They've had you all to themselves for twenty-one years." Choya smiled into her upturned face. "Now it's my turn. And I have a feeling that a lifetime together isn't going to be enough."

"Whoa." She looked at him with wide, startled eyes. "Where did that come from?"

"My heart."

Jacquie felt thrown. "But we barely know each other."

"I know what I want."

"Good for you — I don't. And I didn't say anything about a lifetime, Choya. I just said I'd come back, that's all. When I do, we can take it from there."

If he was fazed, he didn't show it. "All right. Have it your way. I'm not going to push you. How about we go with the original plan?"

She nuzzled the smooth warmth of the chambray shirt front as she went into his arms. "What was it again? Refresh my memory."

"You were going to stay through Christmas." He stroked her hair and held her close. With quiet pleasure she heard the words rumbling in his chest.

"Oh, right. Okay, we can start with that. But if this is going to be on my terms, I have to have a car or truck that can handle those back roads."

"You know, I meant it when I told you I was planning to buy a new car. I looked at a used SUV on the way here. It's almost new, still on the warranty. A friend of mine owns it — he'll give me a good deal."

She didn't feel the least bit guilty about asking for her own wheels. She wouldn't last a week on the ranch if she was stuck there day in and day out again. "And there's one other thing I want under the tree," she said boldly.

"Only one? Name it."

"A new stove," she said. "Buy a lot of wrapping paper."

"Done. And you don't have to do all the cooking. Or any of the cooking. Now, how fast can you pack?"

Jacquie tilted her head to listen. The discussion her parents were having was somewhat less heated but far from over, by the sound of it. "It won't take me long to pack, but I'm not going to run away again. This time I'm going to wrap things up here, say a proper good-bye to my parents before I leave. After I take care of everything here, I'll fly to Tucson and you can meet me." She looked up at him and he kissed the tip of her nose. "But first, are you ready to be interrogated by my dad? He's going to have a lot of questions and he'll expect answers."

"I don't doubt it. I'll do the best I can."

Jacquie laughed. "My mom's probably in your corner already. Except for me not going to Galveston with them."

"Excuse me?"

"Relatives with a beach house invited us all for Christmas. I don't want to go, period."

"And you won't. You'll be spending Christmas with us on the ranch."

"That's a deal then."

"Jacquie, do you know how much I love you?"

"Show me."

He bent her over backward for an amazing kiss, then brought her up gently. "How's that?"

"Whew," she laughed dizzily. "It's a start."

She still couldn't specify if, or how, or when what they had would all work out. But she hoped like hell it would. She did love Choya. She'd made a whole lot of mistakes and so had he. Jacquie suspected they both had a whole lot more to learn. The ranch would be the proving ground.

Chapter 11

Choya sat behind the wheel. Jacquie was happy to have him drive for the return journey from the Tucson airport to Tombstone and on to the Barnett ranch. His meeting with her parents in Dallas had gone well, and it had been worth the plane fare to take the time she needed to get her college transcript and explain her plans to her mom and dad.

Robbie had been thrilled by the news that she was returning and his excited greeting at the airport still warmed her heart. Now, he was in the rear seat of the jeep, resting his blond head on a pillow atop Jacquie's college textbooks. His limp fingers almost reached the handles of her padded laptop case, tucked in the back footwell and out of the way.

She'd brought most of her clothes from Dallas, filling a couple of suitcases, mostly with jeans and tops. She'd thrown in a low-cut dress in scarlet knit that flared at the hem, in case she and Choya ever went dancing.

"How's he doing?" Choya asked her. "Asleep yet?"

She cast an amused glance backward at him. "Hard to tell. His eyes are closed. But if he can't help smiling when we talk about him, then he's awake." She studied his peaceful expression and tightly shut eyes. "Robbie," she cooed, "are you sleeping?"

Robbie didn't answer or smile. The deep indentation in the pillow cradled his blond head and his relaxed little body was motionless.

"He's out cold," she said to Choya, turning back. "All that excitement finally caught up with him."

"He's just so happy to have you back again." He grinned at Jacquie, adding wryly, "And he's not the only one."

"I'm glad to be going back." Contentedly, she looked out of the window at the desert scenery. "You're still driving the old jeep," she noted.

"Don't remind me," Choya growled apologetically. "I called Fred about that SUV. He's taking it in for a tuneup and you'll have it by Monday. You need a vehicle with four-wheel drive."

Jacquie nodded. By mutual agreement, they'd left her small foreign car back in Dallas. Her father had volunteered to list it online and send her a check when he sold it. It really wasn't suitable for the ranch.

"Sounds good." She glanced back at the sound of a childish snore. "Okay. He really is asleep. Now you can tell me what my dad said to you. I never got a chance to ask."

"Do you really want to know?" Choya said wryly.

"Yes. Unless it falls into the category of absolutely none of my business."

"Well, the conversation was all about you. He wanted to know my intentions, quote unquote."

"So what did you say?"

Choya shifted his ungloved hands on the wheel. "I said I was serious about you. And that I loved you. He's getting used to that idea, but he was worried about other things — like you not returning to the university right away."

"Taking time off isn't something he understands. He never did." She paused for a fraction of a second. "I bet he wanted to know where you went to college. That was always the first question he asked my dates —"

Jacquie stopped midsentence, realizing

that she honestly didn't know if Choya had or not. The subject had never come up and it wasn't like she'd checked his house for framed diplomas. But she didn't care whether he had a degree.

Choya only shrugged. "I didn't go to college. I thought about it, sure, but I never applied."

"Did you tell my father that?"

Choya nodded. "He didn't look too happy about it but he didn't ask for details."

Jacquie fumed. Her father had some nerve. "It's none of his business."

"He doesn't know much about me and he doesn't know Sam at all. I didn't get into the whole story." He glanced her way, then looked back at the endless road ahead. "Can't remember if I told you that he was over seventy when I graduated high school."

"No, you didn't."

"It was clear he needed me to help him run the ranch and that's why I stuck around. And then I got married and we had Robbie — okay, you know the rest." He seemed to feel the look she shot at him. "I mean, almost all the rest. I did promise you an explanation." Choya pointed a thumb backward at Robbie to tell her silently that it would have to wait a little longer.

"Got it." His laconic explanation of his

upbringing fit what she'd learned about him. For all his bull-headedness, Choya put the people he loved first and didn't think twice.

"Getting back to your dad — he only wants what's best for you, Jacquie. I just wasn't going to argue with him."

She knew Choya's sense of what was right wouldn't allow him to criticize Cameron Grey, but it still made her mad that her father had been so patronizing. "No one ever does."

"You did, honey. And you may be out of his house, but he wanted me to know he's still watching over you and always will. Just in case I slip up."

"Did he say that in so many words?" she asked indignantly.

"No. But he made himself real clear."

That sounded like her dear old dad all over. She couldn't exactly take him to task when Choya seemed to be on his side.

"Well, I told him I intend to keep up on the course reading and switch majors," she huffed. "I'm surprised he didn't take me aside when he was done with you to give me the usual lecture on my grade-point average and career potential. He doesn't know when to let up."

Choya answered in a level voice. "He paid

every penny of your tuition and expenses for, what, two years? Two and a half? Give him credit for that."

"It doesn't give him the right to control my life," she said heatedly. "Anyway, I'm going to apply for financial aid and scholarships when I transfer." She didn't want to be dependent on Choya either.

"Where to?"

"I have to think about that," she admitted. "The university in Tucson, I guess. It's closest." She spoke with assurance, but she knew that going there wasn't necessarily a sure thing. What if she wasn't accepted?

"When you decide, tell him. My guess is that he feels left out."

"He is. That's intentional," she snapped. "He needs to stop hovering. And he really could have talked to me."

"You were busy with your mother most of the time."

Jacquie nodded, remembering the mother-daughter conversation they'd had. "She didn't say a word about anything like that. We were concentrating on girl talk." In retrospect, she was even more grateful than before for her mother's instinctive understanding of the situation. Maureen hadn't felt compelled to ask Choya a lot of nosy questions and she hadn't badgered Jacquie about her future plans. She seemed to trust her daughter's judgment — and she'd been impressed by Choya.

But Jacquie had to admit, if only to herself, that she wasn't as confident. She didn't quite know how to define her relationship with Choya at this point.

She rolled down the window an inch or two to get a breath of bracingly cold air. The day was clear and it wasn't long before she caught a glimpse of Tombstone, though they were several miles outside the town limits. They fell silent until they were nearly there. Choya slowed the car and bumped along the shoulder.

"Do you have a flat?" she asked anxiously.

"No," he laughed, "I just want to show you something."

He pulled the jeep over and parked underneath the WELCOME TO TOMBSTONE sign she'd seen when she first entered the old town. That seemed like a lifetime ago.

"Do I have to get out?" she asked in a teasing tone. The car was deliciously warm and she knew it wasn't outside. In fact, there was visible frost on the low, gnarled shrubs that dotted the rock-strewn land.

Choya nodded. "Yes. You can't see it from here."

"See what?" she protested. But he was

already out and shutting his door with a quiet click so as not to wake his son. Jacquie followed suit. She walked to where he was standing in front of the sign, pointing to a faint scrawl that sparkled in the sun.

"Robbie added you to the town's population," he said.

Jacquie peered up. The blowing desert dust had stuck to the crayon marks and made them glitter. She read aloud, "Population, one thousand and sixty . . . one."

"You're the one." Choya pulled her into a hug and dropped a kiss on the top of her head. She smiled and looked at Robbie's addition to the sign again, reading her misspelled name in his little-boy handwriting.

"J-A-K-K-Y. That is so sweet," she said softly. "He never told me. When did he do this?"

"The day you decided to be our housekeeper. He was hoping you would see it."

Jacquie was touched. "I wish I had." She looked up again at Robbie's crayon addition to the town sign and sighed. "He's such a funny kid. He expected me to stay put from the start."

"Yes, he did. I wasn't so sure," Choya said. He didn't seem to be teasing.

"Thanks a lot."

He put an arm around her shoulders and

drew her close. "Jacquie, you still have to really think about whether living out here with us is what you want."

She burrowed into the warmth of his big jacket, slipping her hands around his middle. "I have. It is."

"Give it time, girl. Don't answer too quickly. You've got to be sure. For your sake and Robbie's."

"What about you?"

"Don't worry about me."

"Oh, right. I almost forgot. You're tougher than tough."

"I try to be." His chin rested on top of her head as he turned to glance toward the car and check on his son. "Good. He's still snoozing." He hesitated, as though he was about to say something more, but he didn't.

She looked up at him. "What's on your mind? Tell me now. He's going to wake up sooner or later."

Choya's mouth turned downward in a slight frown. "Well, it is important — we haven't discussed the sleeping situation from here on in. You can't move into my bedroom just yet."

"I hadn't planned on it." By mutual agreement, they hadn't told Robbie anything yet, deciding it was better to let him get used to having her around again.

He gave her a warmly possessive hug. "You know you belong there, don't you? I want to wake up with you and I want to fall asleep with you and . . ." He whispered the rest of his want-to's in her ear and Jacquie smiled with pleasure.

"Yes to everything. When we can."

Choya dropped his head and rubbed his cheek against hers. "Grrr. I can't wait," he growled playfully. The reply and the tickle of his light stubble made her laugh. Then he held her close again and she sobered.

"We will have to, though. I don't like sneaking around either. But until you and I have definite plans" — she hesitated, reminding herself that they weren't even engaged, just on Round Two — "he doesn't have to know everything."

"I think he understands that things have changed for the better," Choya mused. "But not exactly how or why."

"Let's keep it simple and leave it at that." She unwrapped her arms from around him and moved out of his embrace, shivering at the coldness of the air. "Brrr. And let's go. Mind if I drive the rest of the way?"

"Not at all."

She wanted to do something besides think.

Robbie wasn't the only one who knew that

things had changed. Of course Sam didn't have to guess at the reasons why. In fact, he'd told Jacquie that he'd encouraged Choya to head for Dallas, lasso her, and bring her back — and added with a wink that his son hadn't needed or asked for his old man's approval because Choya was just as damned headstrong as she was.

Jacquie closed the sociology textbook she'd been reading and looked around the tidy kitchen. Sam had taken over most of the cooking, freeing her, as he said cheerfully, to do something besides scorch food and scrub pans.

Since her return, she'd felt less isolated. Choya had caved to Robbie's insistence — he wanted what his friends had, like any other kid — and he'd put up a satellite dish during her absence. Having an internet connection helped, though it wasn't that consistent way out here, more like old-fashioned dial-up than the high-speed service she'd taken for granted in Dallas. In the afternoons, when schoolkids for miles around were hogging the available bandwidth with assignments and games, it took a while to connect. The evenings were worse, when everybody and their cat checked their e-mail and went online. Late morning was her preferred time.

Jacquie went into the living room and picked up the laptop she'd left on a side table, settling down on the couch and flipping it open. She got online in just a few minutes — and didn't fight the temptation to waste a little time and see what everyone she used to know was up to these days. A couple of clicks and she was looking at posted photos of girls she knew from class or study groups or had hung out with at Dallas clubs. Jacquie didn't leave any messages on their walls, just moved on to check out a few of the guys she'd dated casually, hoisting mugs of beer in some crowded joint or jostling each other in the bleachers at sports events. They looked younger to her now and not in an appealing way.

They didn't have anything on Choya, that was for sure. The rugged rancher made them look like a bunch of loud punks.

He'd undoubtedly heard of social-media sites but she'd bet anything he didn't give a hoot about them or post photos — feeling guilty, she checked to make sure of that. Nope. Nothing.

She looked at her own page. There were no new comments on her wall from friends or acquaintances and no pokes. The photos were a couple months old. Jacquie honestly didn't remember wearing that much makeup or being in half those places. But, she thought wistfully, it had been fun sometimes.

Jacquie caught up on the news, scrolling through her favorite sites and a couple of blogs, then clicked out and went to the Tucson university site, checking out the new buildings and landscaped campus filled with smiling students before she looked at the left bar and the list of choices.

Admissions. She let the little arrow hover over it for a second and clicked, downloading the form. It wasn't that complicated but Jacquie wanted to deal with something else first: *Financial Aid.*

That form ran to more than twenty pages, she saw with dismay. Loan packages. Scholarships. Matching grants, state and federal. The amount of information was bewildering. The cost of tuition made her cringe.

That much?

She wouldn't be able to pay back loans, if she could get them, for years. That left scholarships and grants. Her GPA was high, but she had withdrawn for a term. That didn't put her in the top, gradewise. She skimmed through the form, filling in a blank here and there. Her current income and other assets — zero. Her projected income for the school year — also zero. Choya had paid her in cash and it hadn't added up to anything that would interest the IRS.

The next page asked questions about her parents' income and Jacquie blew out a frustrated breath. She had some idea of what it was but nothing concrete. She was going to have to forward the form to her father.

Cameron Grey had covered all of her college expenses, just as Choya had said — she'd known that from the day the acceptance letter had arrived in their mailbox. Now she wondered how she ever could have taken that commitment totally for granted.

With a sigh, Jacquie saved all the forms in a new folder on the desktop screen.

She couldn't even check them off her to-do list, because they weren't done. Jacquie shut down the laptop and set it aside on another one of her textbooks. Then she reached around and rubbed her lower back with one hand, feeling cranky and tired from sitting in one place.

What she really wanted to do was get out into the wide open space of the desert and just ride. But there was no one to ride with and she was afraid of getting lost again. She put the thought aside and got up, looking at the clock on the mantel.

More than two hours had gone by without

her knowing it. It was probably a good thing that internet access out here was hit-or-miss sometimes. It would keep her from constantly checking it throughout the day and into the evening, a bad habit she'd let go of during her first days at the ranch.

Robbie would be home from school soon and he was sure to follow her around. She would have to think of something they could do together before he settled down to his homework. Jacquie was a little worried about him.

The boy had been on his best behavior ever since her return, anxious to please and overly concerned with whether he was doing right. That was the last thing she'd ever wanted Robbie to think — that she'd left after the dust-up with Choya because of something he'd done.

The silence in the house bothered her, but it wasn't like she could play loud music and dance away her momentary blues. Not with Sam around. As for Choya, he had gone into Tombstone on business, taking the jeep.

Which left her with the new SUV but nowhere to go. There really wasn't time to run errands or anything like that. Jacquie thought again how right Choya had been when he'd told her to think about what she wanted. Yet, despite the loneliness of the high desert, she was beginning to feel at home on the Barnett ranch.

Jacquie forced herself to get up and stretch. Then she paced, going down the hall and back again into the living room, where she plunked herself onto the sofa.

She didn't even want to look out of the window. The time she'd spent on the internet had made her irritable and presented her with problems she didn't know how to solve.

Independence was harder than she'd thought. Her parents would have to be in on her plans to go back to college. She dreaded the questions she'd be peppered with when they got the financial aid form.

Jacquie decided not to send it just yet. There was time — not much, but some. She would just as soon postpone thinking about all that until after Christmas.

As agreed, she wasn't going home to visit her parents in Dallas until after New Year's. The Greys had accepted the invitation to visit their relatives in Galveston, and they planned to have a grand time with good old Gale and Dudley. Jacquie had begged off.

Trimming the tree with her mom and dad was a tradition she was going to miss. But that couldn't be helped. It was time, she thought with a flash of pleasure, to make new traditions of her own. With Choya.

CHAPTER 12

Choya sat next to Robbie in the barbershop, leaning back in his chair as they waited and looking around idly. His son was leafing through a magazine from a stack of them, swinging his legs because his feet didn't touch the floor.

The barber, Floyd Simmons, gestured toward the old-fashioned chair with a large comb. "Who wants to be first?"

Choya glanced toward his son. "I will. Unless you want to be first."

"No," Robbie replied absently. "I want to read."

Choya rose and settled into the barber chair, putting up his weathered boots on the footrest and relaxing. The barber whipped a protective white cloth around the upper part of his body and fastened it at the neck.

"The usual?" Floyd asked.

"Yup."

The older man got to work with a pair of sharp scissors, holding the clippers in readiness in his other hand. Choya bent his head, casting a sideways look now and again at his son. Robbie seemed completely engrossed in the magazine, even though it wasn't about animals or geography, but carpentry. Choya smiled to himself.

"So what do you want for Christmas, Robbie?" the barber asked, glancing his way. "A workbench?"

"I have one. My grandpa made it for me."

"Does Sam still do his own carpentry, Choya?"

Choya answered without nodding, trying to keep his head still against the clippers. "Sometimes. Robbie's in and out of his workshop all the time. When I was a kid I used to love to hang around and watch Sam cut lumber and build things."

"My boy used to watch me cut hair," Floyd said amiably. "But I couldn't say he was interested in it — he went into the army. Now he's a medic."

"What's that?" Robbie asked.

"They take care of the hurt soldiers, son."

The boy looked up, interested, and the barber chuckled. "The army ain't ready for you yet, Robbie. Stick with the carpentry." He took a brush to whisk the back of

Choya's neck and finish up. "You're done."

The white cloth removed, Choya sat up and looked toward his son. "Robbie, your turn."

The boy was perusing the ads in the back of the magazine and didn't reply for a moment.

"You can take that home with you," the barber told him. "Just hand it to your dad. Up you go."

"Thanks, Mr. Simmons," Robbie said. He quickly turned down a corner of a page and rolled up the magazine, giving it to his father before he clambered into the barber chair. His haircut was over with in a few minutes because he sat so still, staring straight ahead with a serious expression.

The boy was growing up fast, Choya thought, standing to one side to watch. Floyd whisked the back of Robbie's neck more gently, but Robbie wrinkled his nose, fighting the tickling sensation. "Almost finished," the barber said. "There."

Choya reached for his wallet to pay, adding a healthy tip and tucking the bills under a tall jar of blue disinfectant in front of the mirror. Their monthly haircuts were a father-son ritual that both Barnetts enjoyed.

"Thanks, Floyd," he said. He tapped Robbie on his newly shorn head with the rolled-up magazine. "Your ears are going to freeze if you don't put your hood up before we go outside."

Robbie slipped on his down jacket and obeyed. The hood came down nearly over his brown eyes, but he didn't seem to mind. "When can I get a hat like yours, Dad?" he asked. It wasn't a complaint, just a request.

"When you're old enough not to lose it," Choya replied with a laugh. He took his Stetson from the hat rack and put it on, then unhooked his own jacket, an old one of battered denim lined with striped wool material. One of its metal buttons caught on a tinsel garland hung along the wainscoting. Choya carefully disentangled it. "Oops. There go the decorations," he said.

The barber only laughed. "Don't worry. I can always get more. What are you doing for the holidays, by the way?" The question was routine.

"Nothing much. We're just going to celebrate at home."

"Yeah. Jacquie and Gramps got the ornaments and lights out already," Robbie said eagerly. "But we don't have a tree yet."

"Oh. Well, that's something to look forward to then," Floyd replied. They left with a wave to the barber, making the old-fashioned bell hanging above the door jingle loudly on their way out.

"Is that what sleigh bells sound like?" Robbie wanted to know when they were outside on the board sidewalk. "There was a picture of a sleigh on that Christmas card from your friend in Michigan. It had bells. Can we go on a sleigh ride?"

Choya smiled with a shake of his head. "We don't get snow that deep around here, son. You know that."

"I was thinking we could go to where he lives."

"Not this year. Maybe the next."

Robbie nodded, satisfied with that answer. "We could take Jacquie too."

Choya looked down at his son's face as they walked toward the jeep. He seemed convinced that Jacquie would be around next year. There was nothing Choya wanted more. He was feeling optimistic about that, and a lot of things, as he opened the door on Robbie's side and let his son scramble in. He handed him the carpentry magazine and closed the door.

When he got in on the driver's side, Robbie had unrolled it to the page he'd turned down. "Dad, look at this," he said, pointing to an ad. "I didn't know houses came in kits."

Choya put the key into the ignition but he

didn't start the engine. He looked at the ad for prefabricated structures from sheds to Southwest-style cottages. "So that's what caught your eye," he said, adding indulgently, "nothing doing. We have a house. Your great-grandpa built it."

"I didn't know that. By himself?"

"I expect he had help. But we don't need to build another one."

"But it would be a really great Christmas present for Jacquie," his son said enthusiastically. "She's still stuck in that little back room."

"Ah" — Choya wasn't expecting his son to say that. He collected himself — "she told me she likes that room just fine, Robbie."

His son didn't seem convinced.

"But you know, I bet she'd like to redecorate. You and I could take her to a mall and let her pick out new curtains and a rug and a matching bedspread and some pretty knickknacks — anything she wanted."

Robbie pondered the idea. "I think she'd like this little house a lot better," he argued, studying the ad again and reading it aloud. "Model shown has one bedroom and a kitch-en-ette." He sounded out the unfamiliar word.

"Hmm," Choya said. "Let me see that."

He made a show of looking it over.

Robbie leaned into him and pointed again. "Look. It even has a living room that opens into a screen porch. She could watch the sunset and stuff."

"Well, now," Choya hedged, "she probably would like that. But don't you think we should ask her?"

The boy shook his head. "It oughta be a surprise. Surprises are more fun."

"Not when they're that size," his father said dryly.

"I bet it comes in a giant box."

"Nope. It comes on a flatbed truck. Kind of hard to sneak that under a Christmas tree."

"We could do it, if the tree was outside," Robbie reasoned.

Choya rolled up the magazine and stuck it in the cup holder. "I like the way you think, son. But we wouldn't have time to build it before Christmas."

"We could so, if Gramps was in on it," Robbie insisted. "And I'd help too. We have plenty of land."

"That's true. But your grandpa isn't strong enough to be raising walls," Choya answered.

Robbie looked a little disappointed as he sat back.

"We'll think of something for Jacquie, don't worry. I know you want to give her something special."

The boy wasn't sulking, just thinking hard. "We don't have to have it done by Christmas. We could build it for her birthday." He looked around the side of his down hood at his dad. "When is her birthday?"

"I don't know," Choya said after a beat. He started the engine. "I never asked her that."

Robbie wriggled as he pulled out his seat belt and clipped it. "I can ask her if you want."

"Okay." Choya's gaze was on the rearview mirror as he pulled out. The cold weather meant there were practically no tourists in Tombstone, but there were still local people out, crossing the streets without looking. "If she wants to move out of the back bedroom" — something he very much wanted to happen, for reasons he couldn't share with a seven-year-old — "we probably should plan in advance."

"You mean we're going to buy the house kit?" The boy's eyes shone.

"I didn't say yes to that."

Robbie slumped inside his jacket, grumbling almost inaudibly.

"And I didn't say no either," Choya

responded. “Now sit up. Let’s not argue over nothing.”

“Sorry.” The boy straightened and both of them fell silent, Choya driving at a steady speed and Robbie looking absently at the road unrolling in front of them.

Choya thought of the present he had in mind for Jacquie — it was a whole lot smaller than a prefab house kit but just about as expensive in the model he wanted, complete with a little velvet box. He hadn’t picked it up yet. But he was going to, soon as he could get away to Tucson. By himself.

The other day, when he’d come home late, the three of them — his son, his father, and Jacquie — had been sitting around the kitchen table, laughing and talking. Robbie’s homework was done and set aside, and Jacquie’s textbook was closed. They’d all finished eating and the dishes were in the sink. There was a plate in the stove filled with plain, good food prepared by Sam, kept warm for his return.

No sight in the world was ever more welcome to Choya. He’d paused to savor it, when Jacquie heard him come in and turned to look his way. The thoughtful look she’d given him made him uneasy for a moment — a feeling that was instantly erased by her warm smile and the quickness with which she rose from her chair and came to greet him.

She'd almost kissed him on the cheek, but Choya gave an infinitesimal shake of his head, looking toward Robbie, and she'd understood.

The day would come when it was all settled. Jacquie Barnett — the name had a fine ring to it. But he couldn't rush her until she knew her own mind. This would be her first Christmas away from her parents and she had to have mixed emotions about that. Emotions that might get the better of her. He wasn't going to take advantage of the situation.

He glanced over at Robbie, who had dozed off, lulled by the unvarying sameness of the scenery and the warmth of the jeep's interior. It was kind of funny that his son assumed Jacquie needed her own little house to be happy. As far as Choya could tell, Robbie had picked up on the difference in the relationship between himself and Jacquie, but still had no clue as to the details. He knew that she wasn't a paid housekeeper but that was about it. He hoped that his son thought of her as a family friend. Just in case. But she sure as hell wasn't obsessing over floorwax and feather dusters.

Not that she'd ever been good at cooking and cleaning anyway. Choya wouldn't let Sam do it all either — his father was too creaky to keep the ranch house in order, no matter how willing he was to do it. Lately he and Robbie rotated the household chores with Jacquie doing some too, keeping to a schedule marked on a calendar, and Sam did most of the cooking again.

The arrangement seemed to agree with everyone. Of course, they'd soon be able to hire a real housekeeper — someone in sensible shoes and a permanent apron, who could take care of everything in half the time it took for Jacquie to burn dinner and clean up afterward. The business deals he'd been working on were being wrapped up in a Tucson lawyer's office, and there would be plenty of money when the contracts were signed.

They needed an influx of cash. Sam was frugal by nature and smart about money — he'd managed to hang onto the ranch and live on the investment income from the land near Tucson he'd sold more than twenty years ago for a record price. It was worth triple that now, Choya thought with a frown. Couldn't be helped. Lately they'd taken financial hits like everyone else. Stocks were down, taxes were up, funds kept fluctuating. But the copper the mining company expected to find on the Barnett ranch was worth a fortune. Leasing mineral rights was a fine way to make money off land that wasn't much good for grazing livestock.

He thought about that back bedroom. Choya had been good about not going into it. But Robbie was right — she deserved better.

He didn't want to tell Jacquie about the pending deal until every last clause in the mining lease and contracts was nailed down. He didn't want to give her a false picture of what she could expect with him. Choya drummed his fingers on the steering wheel. New Year's Eve didn't seem too soon to ask her to marry him. Choya began to whistle, then realized it was a carol.

The sound woke up Robbie, who rubbed his eyes. "Are we home yet?" he asked drowsily.

"There's the ranch." Choya raised one finger from the wheel and pointed into the near distance. A slender figure in jacket, gloves, and a wide-brimmed hat was riding in the corral. "And there's Jacquie on Johnnycake. I guess he talked her into taking him out of the barn."

"Horses can't talk, Dad," Robbie remonstrated. He leaned forward to see better. "She's riding good now. You taught her a lot."

"She learns fast."

Robbie's hand rested on the seat belt clasp. Choya knew he was ready to unclip it the second they stopped in the ranch yard so he could get out fast and run to see Jacquie.

He swung the jeep into the rutted track that led to his home. No, he thought to himself. Our home. His and hers. He had a whole different feeling about it lately.

That afternoon, Choya was in the barn, cleaning tack and inspecting it for worn spots and ripped stitching. He'd liked doing it as a youngster in the winter months and he still did. The familiar, slightly spicy smell of saddle soap brought back pleasant memories of working beside his dad as a boy, just the two of them, killing time and being together. Sam had instructed him in basic repairs to bridles and reins, and when they were done with that, taught him a bit of fancy leathercraft. Choya had worked for weeks on a bookmark for his dad, gussied up with curlicues and leaves. Sam probably still had it somewhere.

He set aside the piece of tack he was soaping when Jacquie opened the door to the barn. "Choya? You in here?"

He grinned at her wide-eyed expression, knowing it would take her several seconds to adjust to the dim light. He wasn't going to sneak up on her, though it was tempting. She was wearing a sleeveless, tightly fitting ski vest over a turtleneck that showed off her curves.

"Over here," he called. She spotted him and came over, closing the wide door behind her. It groaned in protest, dried out in the winter winds. Brilliant sunlight speared through cracks in the walls he hadn't gotten around to chinking, making her pale hair glow like a halo. She turned to latch the door so the wind wouldn't blow it open and walked toward him, smiling.

"Is Robbie with you?" she asked.

"Nope. He's with his grandfather in town. Sam's buddy Garth gave them a ride in and he's bringing them back."

"Oh. What are they doing in Tombstone?" She leaned against a beam and smiled at him.

"Buying woodworking tools, for one thing. Robbie wants to make you a Christmas present."

"Oh my. I won't ask what it is. But I

haven't bought anything for him. Have you?"

Choya shook his head. "He usually gives me a list. A long list. I pick two or three things from the top. But I don't think he's made it out yet. He's concentrating on you."

Jacquie straightened away from the pole. "I know. He hardly lets me out of his sight when he's home from school."

"Can't blame him. You're worth looking at." He gave her a wink. "Of course, Robbie and I see you very differently."

"Oh, hush."

He was close enough to encircle her and quick enough to do it before she could step back. "The best way to do that is to let me kiss you."

Her smile agreed with that statement. She relaxed in his close hold and bent her head back. He moved a hand into her flowing hair and cupped her head, then just touched his lips to hers. Jacquie responded eagerly, and he kissed her with passion, stopping only to nip the sensitive skin of her neck, producing tiny gasps of pleasure from Jacquie. "Like that?" he growled.

"Whew." Her face was rosy and not from the cold air inside the barn when he let go. "Yes I do. It's been a while."

"You'd be surprised how much fun you

can have with your clothes on. After you, girl." He gestured to the ladder that led to the hayloft and Jacquie climbed it, laughing with anticipation.

He was right behind her. When she stopped and turned around, he swept her up in his arms and they tumbled down together.

His jeans-clad leg slid between hers, the hard muscle of his thigh pressing sensually as he settled above her, resting his upper body on his forearms so as not to crush her while they kissed again and again. Jacquie curled her hands around his biceps, testing their strength with gentle caresses, then sinking her nails into his shirtsleeves as he moved against her. Their closeness kept them from noticing the cold in the barn, and the heat between them intensified to a fever that threatened to consume them both. A cascade of sensation rushed through her, ending with a final, tender kiss that left her wanting nothing more.

They lay for a long time in each other's arms, not hearing a car on the road and so close to being dressed it would take only a few buttons to restore them to respectability when Sam and Robbie did return.

Her hand drifted lazily over the warm flannel of his open shirt, moving into his springy chest hair. "Bet this keeps you warm in the winter," she said with lazy amusement.

"You do a much better job," he answered.

"I guess we should get up," she said after another minute. It was bliss to lie with him and think about nothing but how good it felt. Dust motes danced in the shafts of sunlight that crisscrossed the barn. She took a deep breath, inhaling the delicious scent of dry hay mixed with warm man.

"Not yet." He was stroking her hair with slow warmth. "This is heaven. Just stay with me."

"For how long?" she asked playfully.

"Forever. Unless you have other plans."

"Not at the moment."

He rolled over and kissed her again.

They were in the kitchen and he was broiling a steak on top of the stove in a cast-iron frying pan, and heating a second pan. The windows were wide open.

"There's method in my madness," he assured her. "Sorry about the smoke." He waved it away.

"It's okay," she coughed. "It smells great. Can't wait."

"Another minute on both sides." Choya took the frying pan off the flame and used a spatula to free the steak, then flipped the meat over into the second pan. It sizzled wildly when it hit the hot iron surface and more smoke rose up.

"How come you don't call it a burnt offering when you do that?" she demanded.

"Because it's still rare inside."

The smoke detector began to shriek a warning.

"Okay. It's done," he said confidently. He took a platter from the warm oven and served up the steak in all its juicy glory, setting the platter in the middle of the table.

"Thanks, caveman." Her eyes were watering but it did look good. They were still alone. Robbie and Sam had been invited to Garth's house to have dinner with him and his wife.

She got out the butter and set it next to the baked potatoes. The breeze kicked up and soon cleared the smoke and the detector shut off. Jacquie closed the window when it did.

He cut the steak expertly into thin slices with a carving knife and speared a potato for her, proffering it on the end of the matching fork. "Care for a cave-spud?"

"I'd love one."

They ate the simple meal with gusto and skipped the small talk. She sipped the good red wine he'd uncorked — the second of the evening — and poured into glasses for both of them.

He pushed back from the table, finishing after she did. "I needed that."

"It was excellent. Thank you."

In sync, they cleared the table and put away what was left over, forgoing dessert in favor of coffee, which they took into the living room.

The fire he'd made earlier was doing well. They didn't want to do anything but stare into it for a while, cuddled up.

"Choya," she said, letting her fingers take a walk up his shirt buttons. She tapped him on the chin.

"Huh? What?"

"Can I ask you a question?"

He groaned softly. "Is this a we-have-to-talk type of question? What'd I do?"

"Nothing," she laughed softly. "I just thought since we were alone, I should ask it."

"Go ahead." He adjusted his position so that both of them were more comfortable.

She raised her head. "Sam told me about adopting you." At his frown, Jacquie took a deep breath. "I wanted to know more about that story of how he found you."

Choya gave an impatient sigh. "You mean

in the cholla patch — I'm never going to live that down. Too bad it's true."

His flip response had an edge to it. She got the message: *Proceed with caution.* And ignored it. "Sam doesn't lie."

"No. He exaggerates sometimes. But not about that. What do you want to know?" His tone was suddenly flat. "I was abandoned. Someone wanted him to find me."

"That's basically what he said."

Choya sighed. "Sounds like you got the unabridged version. He told me everything he knew when he thought I was old enough."

"When was that?"

"I was seven. Robbie's age now. Though he'd let me know I was adopted before that. But not the rest of it."

"How did you —"

"React?" he finished her sentence. "Not quite the way he'd expected. I think he regretted telling me so much. I guess he didn't want me to hear it from some other kid, who'd heard his parents talk about it. After that I stuck to him like a burr for about a year."

He straightened away from her, not looking at her.

"I'm sorry, Choya."

"Well, I guess we should talk about it."

"Maybe now isn't the right time."

He shifted uneasily. "It's as good as any other. If it's on your mind, we might as well get it out of the way before Sam gets back with Robbie. I don't want him to brood about things he overhears and doesn't understand. He's more sensitive than I was at his age."

"Sounds like you were afraid," Jacquie said tentatively.

"Does that surprise you? Yeah, I was sometimes when I was a kid. I imagined that my mother or father or both of them might show up someday to take me away. And I was angry."

Jacquie hesitated. She hadn't expected him to say that.

"If you're adopted, you generally want to know where you came from — or you don't. In my case, there were absolutely no clues and no one ever came forward to claim me or give information about my parents." His voice was shaded with bitterness. "I never wanted to look for them. I know Sam tried to find my mother, but he gave up long ago."

Jacquie only nodded.

"She didn't even leave a damn note, let alone a birth certificate. Officially, I didn't exist until the court ruled that he could adopt me. Do you know what that feels like?" he asked coldly. "When I look in the mirror I see a face that doesn't resemble anyone I know. I can't explain it better than that."

He got up and stood in front of the fire, then moved away as if it was too warm for him, even though it was dying down.

"Sam thought he might have seen your mother once," she whispered.

"He told me that too, but he waited until I was a teenager. I didn't care then. I still don't."

She looked at him with questioning eyes and he shook his head.

"Sam raised me. He's my only parent. Period. Maybe he didn't do it by the book, but he did right by me."

"Choya, you don't have to explain —" she began, then broke off, biting her lip to keep back tears. She hadn't been hurt. But she had hurt him, simply from her desire to know more about the enigmatic man who had aroused so much passion in her. "I'm just so very sorry."

"For what? Being curious? You have a right to ask a few questions. I wish I could answer them."

"I won't mention it again."

Choya shook his head. "I just don't want Robbie to hear all the details."

"You mean he doesn't know?" She looked at him with genuine shock.

"He's been told I was adopted by Sam when I was a baby. But don't forget that he lost his mother when he was too young to remember her — he doesn't need to know that mine abandoned me. Not until he's a whole lot older."

"I understand."

"Hell." He raked his hands through his hair and then let them drop. "I guess it's time I told you what happened to Rosemary."

"Only if you want to." His expression made her shrink back into the sofa. He seemed suddenly like a very different man.

"I said I would, didn't I? It won't take long. She and I — well, we got married too young. She felt trapped by the time Robbie came along. We started to fight and we were both too stubborn to stop. She used to get away from me by going into town and having a good time. It was like she was running away and looking behind her at the same time, making sure I would take care of everything. She didn't want to be bothered with a toddler. She wouldn't listen to me or Sam or her own parents. She did what she pleased."

Jacquie swallowed hard. *Running away and*

looking behind her at the same time. She had done the same thing. Not on purpose, though.

"I'm not saying she hit the bottle, Jacquie — or that she cheated. But I heard that she flirted. Danced with anyone she wanted. Came home at all hours. One night she ran that damn car off the road and went through the windshield. She wasn't wearing a seat belt. An hour after the deputies stopped by to tell me she'd been taken by helicopter to a trauma center in Tucson, I didn't have a wife and Robbie didn't have a mother."

There was nothing she could say. Platitudes weren't made for tragedy.

"I don't let myself think about it. I put our photo album away. Robbie can look through it when he's older — he can have it, in fact. Right now he doesn't seem to be asking questions about her. And he does have that one photo." His eyes held a dark fire of remembered anger over his terrible loss. "I don't have a damn thing."

"You have me," she whispered.

Choya looked at her without replying. His golden eyes gave nothing away.

Chapter 13

A high wind had roared around the corners of the house all night, scouring the barren land with dust and dry, blowing weeds. Jacquie hadn't slept well, troubled by the angry sound, and she'd woken up with a headache.

The intense discussion with Choya had stayed with her. Admittedly, they'd both had too much wine and she had caught him off guard with some very personal questions. But she'd never meant to press on a sore point. And it wasn't as though the story of how he'd been found was classified information — it was more like a local legend.

What had happened to Rosemary was not something people talked about. The tragedy of her accidental death still cast a shadow down the years — a shadow that might come between them eventually.

Done with the explanation, Choya had turned away from her and said nothing more, until she'd gotten up from the sofa and simply left the room. He'd kept his distance ever since, speaking to her courteously but unemotionally.

The sudden ring of the phone made her jump in her seat at the breakfast table where she was sipping coffee. Choya rose to get it. She looked at Robbie over the rim of her coffee cup, watching him scoop up the last of his milky cereal. Absently, she listened to Choya's brief, low-voiced reply to whomever was on the other end of the line without making much sense of it.

"The wind took down some power lines," he announced when he came back to the table. "Robbie, you're in luck. The elementary school is going to be closed today."

Robbie had grabbed his down jacket in anticipation of the school bus's arrival and had the hood over his head. But it didn't prevent him from hearing the good news.

"Yay!" He took off the jacket and flung it in a corner. Choya shot him a disapproving look, and he picked it up again, returning it to the coat rack.

"Jacquie, did you have plans for today?" Choya asked.

"Um, no." She finished the last of her coffee. "Are you saying that you do?" Choya wasn't usually indirect about anything.

"I was going to drive to Tucson and I wanted to get an early start."

He could have told her that last night, she thought with a flash of irritation. But he'd turned in right after Sam and Robbie came home, she reminded herself, not seeming bothered by the relentless wind. He'd grown up listening to it.

Choya added quickly, "I'll be back around suppertime. Maybe a little later."

"No problem. I could take Robbie into Tombstone." There wasn't really anywhere else to go. "We can amuse ourselves, can't we, Robbie?"

The little boy bobbed his head eagerly. "Yeah. We can walk around town and later we can finish sorting out the ornaments. Dad, can you bring a Christmas tree back from Tucson?"

Choya shook his head. "I think we should pick it out together, son. You and me and Jacquie and Sam."

His father walked slowly into the kitchen. "A tree is a tree. Y'all can choose one without me. My knees are aching today." He eased into a chair. "That means a change in the weather," he told Robbie.

"Really? Why?"

"Knees don't lie when you're my age," his grandfather said solemnly. "Winter is officially here."

"Robbie, we'll get the Christmas tree on Saturday," his father inserted. "The feed store ordered a truckload from Colorado. I drove by there yesterday. They looked nice and fresh."

"Okay." The boy didn't seem terribly disappointed.

"You going to be okay with this bundle of energy?" He half-turned to nod toward his son.

"Of course."

Robbie picked up his cereal bowl and put it in the sink. Jacquie rose and added her cup to the breakfast dishes.

Sam got up too and shuffled out. "I'm going back to bed," he announced.

Choya took down his jacket and Stetson, turning to give Jacquie one last look. "Do you want anything from Tucson?" he asked.

She shook her head. "No. Thanks, though. Drive safely."

Choya did no more than nod in reply. Jacquie lifted a hand in farewell. She could have used a hug — a big hug. The physical contact would have told her instantly whether the rift between them was something to worry about. She told herself not to be such a baby as he tipped his Stetson to her and left.

Jacquie heard the TV go on. Robbie quickly lowered the volume on a silly show and made a flying jump onto the sofa. Not the end of the world, she thought idly. His father was gone — she could see the dust cloud behind the jeep, though not the jeep itself. She'd let Robbie watch TV for twenty minutes or so while she showered and took extra time to do her hair, something that always soothed her. The wind picked up again and she frowned. Her hair would be in tangles the second she went outside. She decided to braid it and wear a baseball cap.

Two hours later, she and Robbie were strolling the board sidewalks of Tombstone. There wasn't a storefront without Christmas decorations and merchandise. Red bandannas were everywhere and the gaudy displays cheered her up. Stopping in front of the souvenir store, she eyed a gorgeous gingerbread house atop a box. It was a perfect replica of the photo on the front, covered with candy in a riot of colors and set in sculpted white icing that was supposed to be snow.

"Look at that," she said to Robbie, enchanted. "It's a kit. You put it together yourself."

"Really? That's so cool," he breathed.

"You know, I saw this other kit in a magazine —"

"Not now." Jacquie took his hand and swung open the door. "Let's find out how much this one costs."

The friendly saleswoman at the counter greeted Robbie by name. "And you must be Jacquie Grey." She beamed at both of them. "What can I do for you today?"

"How much is the gingerbread house kit in the window?"

"Isn't that something? A customer made that one." The saleswoman named the price. It was inexpensive for such a spectacular confection. "That's a very popular item. We only have one left." She smiled down at Robbie. "Would you like to look at it, honey?"

He nodded with interested eagerness.

She moved toward a back shelf and took the boxed kit down. Then she set it on the counter. "The instructions are inside. I understand you just slap it together," she said to Jacquie. "The gingerbread's already baked."

"What holds it up?" Jacquie wanted to know. The illustration showed piped frosting along the edges. Somehow she didn't think the Barnett kitchen had a squeeze-type frosting bag. If it did, Sam had probably used it for barbecue sauce.

"The frosting, I believe. I know there's a recipe for it included. Or you can use the tub kind. I stocked some when I got the kits in. Who wants to fuss with homemade frosting when you can buy it?"

Jacquie peered at the small print on the box. "Not me. I see the candy's not included either." No wonder the kit was inexpensive.

"We have both right over here." The store owner pointed to a stack of icing tubs — chocolate, strawberry, lemon, and plain white — and a basket filled with small bags of hard candy in different shapes. "Take your pick."

Jacquie let Robbie choose the candy he wanted, but she insisted on white icing. One way or another, she was going to get some snow this Christmas.

"Can we build it before Dad gets home?" he wanted to know as they got into the car.

"We can try. But I've never made a gingerbread house before, have you?"

"Nope." He held the box to his chest to protect it. The ride back to the ranch seemed longer than ever but at least they had a project to occupy their time when they returned. That was something to look forward to. It was late afternoon by the time they pulled into the yard and Sam had turned on a few lights. The red-shaded lamp that he liked to read by glowed a welcome in the front window.

Robbie went ahead of her, waiting on the front slab step for Jacquie to open the door for him, still cradling the box in his arms. "Wait 'til I show Gramps," he said in a whisper, "he knows how to build stuff."

"Okay," she whispered back, turning the doorknob and swinging it open, "but you don't use hammer and nails for gingerbread."

Robbie marched in and headed for the living room. His grandfather sat by the red-shaded lamp, reading an old shoot-'em-up with a cowboy on the cover. The well-thumbed pages told Jacquie he'd read it before, several times. There was a shelf devoted to them.

"There you are," he said, looking over his half-glasses. "It's gettin' dark. I was just beginning to worry."

"Jacquie knows the way to Tombstone and back by now," Robbie defended her. "Look what we got!"

Sam's gnarled hands steadied the large box that his grandson plopped onto his lap. "A gingerbread house!"

"We want to put it together right now so it's ready before Dad comes home," Robbie said, taking the box back and handing it to Jacquie. "Want to help?"

Sam held up the old book. "Nope. Things are heating up at the Oh-No Corral. I gotta find out what happens. You two go ahead and have fun."

"Okay!" Robbie headed toward the kitchen, followed by Jacquie.

He struggled out of his down jacket and took hers to hang up, then scampered back. She had already slit one side of the box and was pulling on the packaging inside.

"Wow," Robbie said, studying the color brochure taped over the slabs of hard gingerbread. Whoever had made the house in the shop window had followed the instructions to the last lemon drop — it was identical. They didn't have the same candy, Jacquie realized. But Robbie wouldn't care if their house wasn't exactly like the other two. "I feel hungry."

"Well, you're not eating this," she said firmly. Then she smiled. "You can fix some cheese and crackers if you like."

Robbie made a plate of both and they munched as they studied the simple instructions. Jacquie got down a cutting board and set it on the table, along with a butter knife. "Here goes."

She opened the tub of frosting and used

the knife to smear some on the sides of a gingerbread slab, then did the same to another slab, setting them together at a right angles on the board. Two more slabs and the walls were up.

"Can I put candy on it now?" Robbie asked through a mouthful of cracker.

"No. We have to wait for the frosting to get hard. Then we put on the roof, piece by piece."

"How long do we have to wait?"

She looked at the instructions again. "It doesn't say."

He shrugged and finished his snack. Jacquie poked the frosting with a fingertip — it still seemed soft to her. She looked up at the clock. Five minutes had passed. She thought about the few times she'd helped her mother with holiday baking and remembered that tub frosting never did get all that hard. But a gingerbread house didn't have to pass a building inspection. They could take a few shortcuts.

"Okay," she said. "Now for the roof." She followed the same procedure, pleased when the thin slabs of gingerbread stayed in position on top of the walls.

"Now can I put candy on it?" he begged.

"Let's do the snow on the ground first," she replied. Jacquie gave him the butter knife and let him spread oodles of white goo around the little brown house, licking his fingers afterward. He handed the tub and the knife to her so she could cover the roof with more frosting.

Robbie was already undoing the wire ties that closed the bags of candy. One by one he tipped them over and ribbon candy, red hots, lemon drops, and peppermints rolled out onto the table.

"Go for it," she told him.

With surprising patience, he stuck every single piece of candy onto the house in a totally random way. It took him an hour. Then Robbie sat back and admired his handiwork. The end result was a glorious, colorful hodgepodge that looked nothing like the illustration on the box. Just as she'd thought, he didn't care.

Then he shook his head.

"What's the matter?"

"There's no Christmas tree," he said. He looked at her hopefully.

"Hmm." Jacquie's gaze moved around the kitchen and stopped above the sink, on a new green sponge still in its cellophane wrapper. She got up to get it, found some scissors and cut the wrapper, then cut the sponge into two triangles, sticking both upright in the frosting snow. "How's that?"

"Awesome," he said happily. "Now it's perfect."

"Yes, it is," they heard Choya's deep voice say. Both Jacquie and Robbie turned around to see him standing in the doorway between the kitchen and living room, looking weary but glad to be home. "Hello, you two."

"Daddy!" Robbie scrambled out of his chair and raced toward him. The chair wobbled, then fell hard against the edge of the kitchen table, knocking the kit box to the floor.

The thin slab walls shook. The frosting parted. The gingerbread house collapsed.

Jacquie looked at it in shock, then at Robbie and Choya. The little boy hadn't seen what just happened — his face was buried in Choya's shirt and his father was patting him on the back, laughing.

Then Choya saw too. Jacquie reached for the fallen house as she nodded toward the living room. Choya understood. "I'll just start cleaning up, Robbie," she said quickly. "You pick out a book and your dad will read to you."

"But I want to show the house to Gramps," Robbie said, his voice growing slightly distant as Choya carried him away.

"Shh," she heard Choya say to his son, "he dozed off. You can show him later. How about I read you a chapter book?"

"A whole chapter?"

"Sure."

"Bet you won't finish, Dad. You drove all the way to Tucson and back. You were gone for hours and hours."

"Not that long. And I'm not that tired. Now hush and listen."

There were vague sounds of the two of them settling in on the sofa and then Choya began to read. It was nice to have backup, Jacquie thought as she examined the gingerbread catastrophe. By no stretch of the imagination could it be called a house. And it wasn't going to be easy to take it apart and start over.

She used the butter knife to lift a wall up but it wobbled in the gooey white frosting and fell. So did the next, and the next. The last wall stood, then fell too. The green sponge trees were buried in white. Jacquie sighed. The roof tiles lay in the middle of the mess, heavily weighted with candy. She would have to pick it off piece by piece and start over.

"Jacquie, what are you doing in there?" Robbie called.

"Oh — just putting things away."

Choya admonished Robbie to sit back and listen again.

"Okay," he said reluctantly. "But can you do the voices, Dad? Please?"

"Sure."

Choya became one character in the book, then another. He was buying her time. Jacquie used her fingernails to get up the candy, then lifted the roof tiles with a spatula and set them aside.

She heard Sam's awakening cough and bit her lip, looking worriedly toward the living room.

"Gramps, go look at the gingerbread house! Me and Jacquie built it while you were sleeping!"

There was a pause. "How about that," Sam yawned, making slow progress toward the kitchen. "Be right back. You stay with your dad."

Choya must have given him some kind of sign, because he didn't seem shocked when he saw the wreck. He lifted an acknowledging hand to Jacquie, who gave him a sticky-fingered wave back, clutching the spatula.

"Robbie, that is the finest gingerbread house I ever did see," he called to the living room.

Robbie's mumbled thank-you told them he was engrossed in the chapter book his dad was reading to him. For the moment.

Sam walked more quickly, though the effort made his knees creak. He went to the pantry and found a box of baking soda.

"This might do it," he said in a low voice. Jacquie wasn't sure what he meant until he held the box over the center of the fallen house. It would fit. "Yep," he said. "Exactly right."

"That's cheating," she whispered, smiling at him.

"No, it ain't," he whispered back.

She used globs of frosting to stick the walls to the box and then Sam added tightly crumpled wads of paper towels to help hold up the roof pieces. She positioned them carefully, using the last of the icing, and she and Sam decorated the whole thing with candy again in the same random way. She hoped Robbie wouldn't notice.

"I think we did it," she said in a low voice when she heard Robbie laugh at a funny part of the story. "Except for the trees." She fished them out from under the snow frosting and set them upright again.

"Hey, I was saving that sponge," Sam murmured with mock indignation.

"And now you know why."

Choya finished the chapter and Robbie's feet hit the living room floor. He came running into the kitchen, followed by his father. "Do you like it, Gramps? It was really fun to make — I don't even want to eat it! Not yet, anyway," he amended.

"It's wonderful," Sam said with a wink at Choya and his grandson. "And built right." He thumped the table and Jacquie threw him a shocked look, then held her breath.

The patch job had worked. The candy-laden roof didn't fall in.

"They don't make gingerbread houses like that anymore," the old man said with satisfaction.

Robbie got close to it and studied it with wide eyes. "It looks different," he stated.

"Not to me," his father said.

"You didn't see it enough because I was hugging you, Dad," the little boy said patiently. "But it is different. There's snow on the trees now. Did you do that, Jacquie?"

"Um — yes, I did," she answered quickly. "I thought they looked better that way. More like real Christmas trees."

The two older Barnetts grinned at her over Robbie's head, amused by her instantaneous alibi. The little boy touched one of the trees with a fingertip and savored the dab of frosting. "Yeah. Can we make another house?"

She stiffened for a second, then breathed a sigh of relief. "No, we can't. We bought the last kit in the store, remember?"

He nodded, admiring his creation a little longer. "Can we put the house on the mantel for a decoration, Dad?" he asked.

"Of course. That'll keep you from nibbling at it."

"I was just tasting the frosting," Robbie protested. He slid his small hands under the board that held the house, but his father moved swiftly to intercept it.

"Let me help," Choya said.

Robbie didn't argue and the four of them went into the living room together.

"Good save." Choya was still amused by the incident. He had her tucked under his arm and gave her a squeeze that warmed her through and through. They were in the living room, cuddled up on the sofa and watching the fire.

"I had to try," she murmured. "And I had help."

"Sam's quick on the draw," he laughed. "But that has to be the first gingerbread house he ever built or fixed. And I'll tell you a secret." His gaze rested on the mantel a little longer and she lifted her head to follow it.

"Go ahead."

"It's another hard-luck story," he warned her. "I promise not to get maudlin."

"Stop it. Just tell me."

"I always wanted one of those when I was a kid. And I'm sure Sam would've obliged if he'd known that. But I never asked." The jumbled candy on the little roof gleamed and sparkled in the firelight, casting specks of color on the white icing. "Worth waiting for," he chuckled.

He rubbed her upper arm with his big hand, and Jacquie settled back down. The fire blazed up, warming them both. Choya had used desert wood, sinewy and hard, that burned hot. The scarlet flames danced with twists of blue and green.

"Okay," he said in a low voice. "I did some thinking about the way I acted last night — I mean overreacted. I'm sorry. It was the wine, I guess."

She felt a wave of relief. "We both had too much. And I asked one too many questions."

"Can we let it go? I want the past to stay in the past."

"I understand. And thank you for explaining. I know it was hard for you but I — I needed to know."

They were quiet together for a minute or more.

"Thank you for doing that for Robbie." He nodded toward the gingerbread house.

"He loved making it," she said. "Putting it together really was fun."

"Where'd you get the kit? I forgot to ask."

She nestled closer. "In the souvenir shop, of all places. It was an impulse buy. I saw it and I had to have it. But Robbie thinks I bought it for him."

He stroked her blond hair in a deliberate way. "So we both went shopping today, huh? I'm glad you did. You seemed kind of blue this morning."

"I was," she admitted honestly. "No big deal. It's over."

The sound of slow footsteps came into the living room, and she felt Choya half-turn to acknowledge his father's presence. "Dad — come on in and relax. We got a great fire going."

"So I see. I'll look at it from here, thanks. If I get too comfortable, I won't get up until morning. I don't want to fall asleep in the armchair."

The old man stood for a minute, looking into the fire and not at them.

Choya thought of something he'd forgotten. "Don't go to bed yet. I stopped by the lawyer's office in Tucson. There's some new developments."

Choya shifted to one side, then rose, letting Jacquie adjust her position so she was upright without him. The empty space where he'd been felt suddenly chilly. She reached for an afghan and drew it around her, looking at the Barnett men, old Sam leaning on his cane and Choya, tall and strong. He rested a hand on his father's shoulder.

"New developments, eh?" Sam asked. There was a sharp twinkle in his eyes. "Fill me in."

"The lawyer gave me some documents you need to look over. They're in my study. Be right back," Choya said to her.

Jacquie smiled politely, though she felt a little out of sorts at being left to herself while the men went off to talk. The Barnetts traveled the short distance to the study at Sam's slow pace and Choya closed the door behind them.

She leaned back into the sofa cushions, trying not to listen in. But Choya's deep voice carried, even through walls. Still, the occasional words she could hear didn't connect. He was saying something about specified share and assigned rights . . . legal terms that didn't make much sense to her. It all had something to do with Barnett land and minerals.

Jacquie dozed off.

▪ ▪ ▪ ▪

Behind the study door, Sam set the legal documents and geological surveys his son had given him back on Choya's desk.

"Well, things are moving right along," he said. "I just hope they won't tear up the land too much."

Choya shook his head. "The deal and the survey both specify vertical drilling, straight as a plumb line. Which means minimal impact on the surface."

"What about the groundwater?"

"That won't be affected."

Sam crossed his arms over his chest and leaned against the desk. "My father always thought those mines weren't played out, but he couldn't get anyone to believe him." He straightened with a sigh. "I guess we oughta sign on the dotted line and get the rest of that bonus."

"It's substantial. More than we were expecting at first. They upped it by a lot." Choya flipped through the pages of documents and named the new figure he'd negotiated.

Sam whistled under his breath. "Good work. Now you can go ahead and marry Jacquie."

Choya's mouth quirked in an odd smile.

Sam studied him. "Did I say something wrong? I thought that was why you went to Dallas to get her. Has there been a change in plans?"

"No."

"Choya," his father wagged a finger at him, "I was glad to see you two all hugged up on the sofa just now, but you two were giving each other odd looks this morning, not to mention all that circling around and polite talk. I wasn't going to say anything but — what happened?"

"You told her where I came from. We started talking about it and it got intense. That's all," he added firmly.

"She asked me. Everyone knows that story."

"Not all of it."

"Son, why wouldn't you want her to know? She's curious as a cat, that's all."

"Then I told her what happened to Rosemary."

"I see," Sam said after a long pause. "It was right that you did. Jacquie should know."

Choya shook his head and sighed. "She shouldn't feel like she has to stay and be Robbie's mama because she feels sorry for him and me."

"I very much doubt she'd do that."

"How do you know?" Choya shot back.

"I know a few things about women. She has strong feelings for you, and pity ain't the uppermost one."

Choya didn't reply to that. He changed the subject. "Let's get back to spending the money we haven't made yet. Should I mention that when I propose?"

"Might as well." Sam gave him a scornful look, but the corners of his eyes crinkled with humor. "Why wouldn't you let her know what your prospects are? A woman needs to know she'll be taken care of. In every way," he added.

The last three words seemed to rankle Choya, but he didn't respond specifically to them. "You're old-fashioned," was all he said.

"I'm experienced," Sam snapped. "Mind if I ask what the hell you're waiting for?"

Choya leaned back in his swivel chair, gripping the arms and looking thoughtful. "I have to know if she's going to be happy here. Life on a ranch like this is very different from Dallas."

"She does all right for a city girl," Sam pointed out. "Jacquie has a lot of spunk. Nothing fazes her. And Robbie just about worships the ground she walks on."

Choya gave an agreeing nod. "I almost wish he didn't. If she changes her mind and leaves again, he'll be heartbroken."

"She won't. Listen to what I'm tellin' ya. Besides, no matter what happens, he'll still have us," Sam insisted. "He always has. And weren't you the one to tell her it was over that first time? That was a damn fool thing to do."

His son glared at him. "She's just so young and inexperienced. And after Rosemary" — he shook his head — "I apologized."

"Damn straight. She didn't mean no harm and you know it."

Choya softened his tone but only a little. "It still worries me that she went off like that. I can't raise her and Robbie. I have to protect him."

"Hmph. You ain't protecting Robbie. You're protecting yourself. Jacquie won't cut and run if you ease up some. Anyone can see that she loves the boy. She even loves you," he added tartly.

"Yeah, well, she told me on the way back from Dallas that love didn't guarantee anything," Choya said quietly.

"What's that supposed to mean?"

"You oughta know, Sam." He gave the old man a wry look. "How come you never married when you were raising me?"

"I put you first."

"Same goes for Robbie."

His father scowled. "Son, I never found anyone that had what it took to keep me in line and bring up a boy at the same time. But Jacquie's different. Don't let her get away."

"I can't stand in her way either. She wants to go back to college and her father will tar-and-feather me if she doesn't."

"That's a fine old remedy for many things. He sounds like a man after my own heart," Sam pronounced.

"Would you be serious? We live way the hell out in the back of beyond."

"So?" Sam shot him a look of disbelief. "You just bought an SUV with automatic everything and cruise control," he said. "Tucson is less than two hours away. She can go to college there."

"If she wants to. I can't force her to make that choice. Besides, you've done that drive and so have I, more times than either of us can count. It wears you out."

Sam leveled a fierce look at his son. "Why don't you let her try?"

That blunt question hit home. Choya got up and paced the room without answering for a couple of minutes.

Sam took the chance to sit down gingerly in the swivel chair his son had vacated, and examined the documents again, just for something to do. "Looks like the shaft buildings won't be visible from the house. They're proposing to drill way out there in the north section." He propped up the geologist's survey. "That's good. I don't want anything to get in the way of the sunset."

Choya muttered something noncommittal in reply. His father stretched out his long legs under the desk and folded his arms across his chest again.

"Of course, I may not be living on this ranch forever," the older man said idly.

Choya turned to him. "What are you talking about?"

"I'm gettin' old — really old. And I've been thinkin' it could be time for me to move closer to town."

"Nothing doing." Choya was genuinely surprised. "This is your home."

"I know that. But it's going to be yours. And if you two are goin' to marry, Jacquie oughta feel that it's hers too. She won't want to dust around me while I nap."

Choya gave a snort. "In case you haven't noticed, she doesn't think dusting is a big thrill."

Sam made a wry face. "Mebbe so. But I think you understand me, son."

Choya held up a hand like a stop sign. "You're not moving anywhere. With all this money about to come in, we could add a whole new wing if we wanted to."

His father shook his head. "My grandfather built this house right the first time. Let's not mess with it."

"So what's the solution?" Choya asked with evident annoyance. "Either we move out or you do?"

"Don't you think you oughta marry her before anyone does any moving?" Sam asked sagely. "The way I see it, you gotta take charge of the situation. Let her know you'd do anything for her, but be a man about it. If you want her to stay on the ranch, you'd damn well better make it worth her while."

"I just told you" — Choya broke off abruptly — "this conversation is going in circles."

Sam only laughed. "So it is. Meeting adjourned," he declared. "I'm turning in." He picked up the cane from near the desk and walked slowly to the door, opening it. "See you in the morning."

Jacquie heard the study door and then the

slow thump of the cane. She closed her eyes, not quite ready to wake up all the way. Sam went his way to his bedroom and Choya came in, standing in front of her and looking down.

"You asleep, Jacquie?"

She gave him a drowsy smile as she opened her eyes again. "Not anymore. I was, though."

"Sorry to take so long. My dad and I needed to talk," he said quietly, sitting down again. "I wanted to go over the Tucson meeting with him while it was still fresh in my mind."

Jacquie kept the afghan drawn tightly around her and didn't reply.

Choya studied her for a long minute. "You cold?" She nodded. "Stay here. I'll fix the fire."

He stood up and strode to the fireplace, going down on one knee to get the blaze roaring again, wielding the iron poker with practiced skill and blowing where it counted. A black shadow against the upward rush of sparks and flame, his broad-shouldered body looked powerful and mysterious. If only they had a bed to themselves, she thought naughtily, and he was bending over her just like that . . . the thought scorched her soul with remembered pleasure.

He straightened, getting to his feet but standing where he was, facing the fireplace to warm his outstretched hands.

"That'll do it," he said softly as he turned to her. His rugged features were in shadow but she could see the golden gleam in his eyes. Jacquie kept the afghan draped over herself as he crossed to her and sat.

Choya didn't waste any time. She felt his lips brush her hair and then his hands slipped under the afghan and around her waist, drawing her close to him. His caress held all the heat of the fire, and her instinctive response was to arch against him.

He seized his chance, and his mouth covered hers, gently opening her lips to taste her sweetness, triggering ardent desire. She half-yielded and half-struggled. "We can't," she whispered when he let her go.

"I know. But I want to," was his growled answer.

"Choya — stop. We're not really alone."

He made no answer, just moved his mouth to the side of her neck, nipping the silky, heated skin of her neck and moving lower still as he tugged her shirt out of her jeans. Urgently, his exploring hand moved beneath it and up over her ribs, stopping — but only for a second — when he touched her bra.

Front clasp. He flicked it open.

Jacquie's fingers reached into his thick, dark hair and held his head. He kissed her as he cupped one bare breast, then the other, caressing her with sensual expertise until he made her arch against him again.

A sound outside the living room put an end to the heated embrace. He raised his head and listened, then smiled slightly. "It's just the wind." But the momentary pause gave her a chance to collect her wits, even though she didn't want to.

Jacquie sat up straight and wriggled away, pulling down her shirt and yanking the afghan around her like soft armor. Her arms were crossed underneath it when he reached for her again. "Nothing doing," she murmured. "We can't get caught."

"Don't you want to —"

"You know the answer to that," she said almost fiercely. Jacquie rose, tossed the afghan at him to keep his hands busy and made it out of the living room, not looking back. She entered the bedroom and firmly closed the door. A deal was a deal — even though the terms of theirs seemed to change every time she turned around. She leaned her back against the solid wood. She didn't hear him following her.

The problem was, she wanted him to. Desperately.

Breakfast the next morning was as wholesome as a TV ad for frozen waffles, only there weren't any waffles. The winter sun streamed in, brightening the table, set with a pitcher of orange juice and another of milk, and plates that replaced Robbie's unfinished bowl of cereal. Choya sat on his side of the table, freshly shaved in a clean shirt, and she sat on hers, already dressed and buttoned up in more ways than one. Silence prevailed, broken only by a polite request for the buttered toast and scrambled eggs she'd prepared and the salt shaker. They both had excellent appetites, as if they had spent the night doing exactly what they'd wanted to do instead of sleeping apart.

Sam was still asleep and Robbie had been escorted to the bus. It was the last day of school remaining before the Christmas break, and the kids were restless, bouncing in their seats as the bus pulled away, despite the driver's shout to sit down and shut up.

"So," he said in a level voice as he took his plate to the sink, "I was wondering if you'd like to ride out with me today. I have to look over the land to the north — it has to do with the business deal that Sam and I are working on," he added.

"Oh." She was somewhat taken aback by the offer, but nodded her agreement. Anything to get out of working on her college application forms. She still hadn't worked up the nerve to send the financial aid questionnaire to her father. "All right. Why not?"

Her tepid response actually seemed to encourage him. "Meet you at the barn in a half hour then," he said briskly. He walked to the front door, grabbing his denim jacket and Stetson on the way.

Jacquie finished up in the kitchen and put on warmer clothes. She was getting used to the sudden changes in desert weather — in minutes, the brilliant morning sunlight had faded away, covered by fast-rolling clouds that formed a gray ceiling over the land.

But the clouds were high and there was no moisture in the air. Choya wouldn't head out if he thought rain was imminent — he didn't take chances like that. He'd instructed her on the dangers of flash floods and other unexpected things that happened in the desert.

She was grateful for the opportunity to ride with him. She hadn't ventured out alone on horseback since her unintentional expedition into the mountains, although she had more confidence in her ability now. All three of the Barnetts, each in his own way, had taught her everything they knew about horses and riding.

When she got to the barn, Choya was coming out, leading both horses, saddled and ready. He didn't say anything about the weather, just looped the buckskin's reins around a fence post and led Apache to her. So she would be on the palomino, she thought nervously. Apache was a beautiful horse but that didn't mean he would tolerate a rider he didn't know.

"You'll be fine," Choya said. Had he read her mind?

Without further comment, he helped her mount, sliding a strong hand around her waist and half-lifting her with no effort. Her bottom slid over the curved leather and her boot toes moved into the stirrups as if she'd been riding all her life. Choya nodded approval and walked to Johnnycake, swinging up and into his saddle as she waited for him, patting Apache's arched neck.

The wind lifted his pale mane, blowing it straight to one side over her hand. She lifted it, trying to control her own flyaway locks, and looped the reins over the saddle horn to search in her pocket for a scrunchie.

Jacquie quickly whipped her hair into a ponytail and sat up straight again.

Choya was watching her with a faint smile.

Embarrassed, she wheeled Apache around so she wouldn't have to look at him. He went ahead.

The horses lifted their velvet noses, inhaling the crisp tang of the desert in winter, glad to be out and going somewhere even though clouds had covered the sun. Choya led the way, down a previously invisible trail she'd never noticed — but then it could only be seen by someone on a horse.

Johnnycake and Apache moved at a brisk trot over the low rises and shallow valleys of the ranch land. She surveyed it with renewed interest, wondering exactly how big the ranch was. Then she remembered being lost in it and how she'd not even known that she was lost until the mountains seemed to swallow her up.

She urged Apache forward, catching up with the man on horseback ahead of her. He rode as though he'd been in the saddle from babyhood — which was undoubtedly the case. But Choya radiated physical confidence no matter what he was doing.

"How far are we going?" she called to him. The cold wind snatched the words from her mouth and conveyed them to Choya. Her cheeks were flushed from the brisk ride — the open air was exhilarating.

"Another mile or so," he called back, barely turning his head to answer.

She settled down again, letting the horse make his way, relaxing into the rhythm of Apache's easygoing gait. After a while, she saw a handful of ramshackle structures in the near distance. They turned out to be several shacks of various sizes, not as close together as they'd seemed from afar but bigger, with large holes in their slanted roofs and missing planks from the sides, lying on the hard ground exactly where'd they fallen.

Clearly, the shacks had never been meant for living in or storage. Drawing closer, she noticed unfamiliar pieces of rusty machinery left out in the open and guessed that the tumbledown shacks covered tunnels into the earth. Choya had reined in Johnnycake and was circling the shacks when she and Apache reached him.

"Mineshafts," he said. The curt explanation was offered as if she already knew all about them. "Drilled and abandoned. The pure copper deposits didn't reach this far, or so it was believed back then."

Jacquie looked curiously at the shacks as her horse stamped and whickered softly to Choya's mount. "Oh. And now?" He had obviously brought her out here for a reason — he'd wanted to tell her that much. There was something going on that had to do with this godforsaken area, unspecified business that he'd discussed with his father last night.

She didn't really care. The shacks were depressing to look at and the rusted machinery was almost scary. It spoke of long ago, and vanished men whose efforts to wrest treasure from the earth had failed.

Dallas had never felt farther away than at that moment — the desolate landscape was utterly devoid of other structures. Jacquie felt her horse shift uneasily beneath her. Apache was spooked by the place too.

"But a mining company is negotiating a long-term lease on the land."

She nodded and tried to look interested. "I take it they pay for the privilege."

"Yup. You got that right. A couple of the ranchers with spreads next to ours are negotiating too. We'll all get a better deal that way."

"Why is that?"

Choya warmed to his subject. "Because mineral deposits don't respect boundaries. They can run for miles underground or stop short."

"How many acres do you own?" She was curious about that. It occurred to her that she'd never once seen a fence on her occasional journeys through his land. It seemed to go on and on.

"About five thousand."

"Oh. That sounds like a lot." She looked around at the endless vista of scrub and rocks. "At least you don't have to mow, right?"

"That's one way of looking at it."

"So what stage are you at with this?"

"Me and Sam — and the other ranchers I mentioned — are on the verge of signing contracts. We've been meeting with the company representatives for a while."

Jacquie hadn't paid that much attention to his comings and goings. It was a little strange to think of so much hidden wealth beneath this unforgiving land.

"Anyway, I just wanted you to see this so you know what's going on," he said.

She actually was interested by now. "Thanks. Keep me posted. As you can see, I know zip about the subject."

"You'll learn. Things are happening fast. The company reps play it close to the vest, but we all know there's serious interest in this area for miles around. A couple of played-out mines closer to the Dragoons just got opened up and yielded high-grade copper."

"Oh. I guess when I think of Arizona mines, I think of gold."

Choya laughed. "I don't think we'll get that lucky. There hasn't been a major gold find in the state for decades. No, they're looking for copper."

Geology wasn't something she'd studied, but she did know copper was valuable.

He soothed his horse with a few soft words. Johnnycake was growing restless and stamped a hoof. "Want to go inside?"

Jacquie looked dubiously at the holes in the walls and roofs of the shacks. "No thanks. I can see inside from here."

Choya was grinning at her. "I meant the tunnels."

Jacquie flushed for reasons that had nothing to do with the nip in the air. "Oh — yeah. Where it's nice and dark, and I'll be scared and — are you kidding? You're not getting me to go down an abandoned shaft." The thought made her shudder.

He laughed out loud. "Don't worry. Sam had them sealed up decades ago."

Jacquie looked at the shacks again and frowned with distaste — and a measure of disbelief. "Do you really think you're going to strike it rich?"

"It happens. And when it does, I'll be ready. How about you?"

Without waiting for an answer, he spurred his horse and galloped away to the south, leaving her gaping after him for a startled second.

"Choya!"

Much to her annoyance, he kept going.

"Wait for me!" she screamed.

He didn't.

Jacquie put her knees into Apache's sides and rode for dear life, into the wind. Choya disappeared over a rise and she went that way, following the little puffs of dust that hung in the air. It wasn't easy. The damned wind made them disappear too.

She got to the top of a rise and looked around and down, seeing a dry streambed. There were hoofprints in the earth that led around a bend. In another few seconds, Choya and Johnnycake ambled back the way they'd gone. He laughed up at her. "Good work. You didn't get lost."

Jacquie picked her way down the other side of the rise and pulled up next to him. Furious, she gave his arm a hard thump that didn't seem to register with him at all.

"Did you want me to? Is that what that was all about?" she demanded.

"Just wanted to see if you could keep up and if you could find me." He kept on riding at a slower pace. "We'll make a ranchwoman out of you yet."

"Oh. So it was a test," Jacquie snapped out the words. "Did I pass?"

"I was only having some fun with you," he said in a mild voice.

"I'm not in the mood," she retorted.

He turned and gave her an inquisitive look that made her squirm in the saddle. She wanted to bite her tongue.

"Let me know when you are," he said wickedly.

She shut up. She wasn't going to give him any more straight lines that he could interpret the wrong way.

She was right behind him as they entered the yard and went to dismount first, clumsily, getting one hand tangled in Apache's reins. The palomino turned his head and snorted softly at her. She freed her hand and flung the reins at Choya, who barely managed to catch them.

But he did. And he used them to pull her nearer. The horses' sides brushed as he got her close enough to kiss. She put a hand on the reins that Choya controlled and did her damnedest to stay where she was, enjoying the softness of his lips, pressing her thighs against the smooth saddle to rise up and kiss him back.

Johnnycake snorted and sidestepped, and

that ended it. The horse rolled his eyes as if he couldn't believe what humans got up to. Choya laughed and tossed the reins back at her.

Her restlessness increased by the hour. She tried to work on the application essay, but was put off by the helpful hints: *Write about a moment that changed your life. Be personal and concise.* She couldn't remember a word of the essay that had gotten her into college the first time. What had she found to write about then? She'd been so sheltered, a little spoiled, never on her own — and now, none of the above applied to her life at all.

She set pen and paper aside and went online instead, researching financial aid packages until her head ached. No one was going to hand her the money to go to college. She would either have to earn it, or qualify for aid. The first option was impossible. The second was quickly turning into Plan D. As in Dad.

Jacquie spent an hour composing an e-mail that ended up being only three sentences long. She wasn't going to whine or beg, but she still felt she was humbling herself. She kept deleting drafts until she got it right, then summoned up her courage and clicked SEND.

■ ■ ■ ■

By evening, she'd left Robbie to his homework in the living room, and the men to another conversation in the study. Jacquie bundled up and went outside, staying near the house. Its glowing, unshaded windows were the only spots of light in the dark landscape. She wandered over to the corral and found a bucket she could sit on, flipping it upside down. The clank of the handle reached the ears of a horse inside the barn, who gave a brief whinny, as if expecting a delivery of oats.

Jacquie set the bucket in the dry dirt by a fence post and sat down, leaning her back against the post and looking up at the stars that filled the sky, clear but dark. The last traces of cloud cover were being dragged away by the wind, a constant presence in the winter months.

Over to the east, the lights of a large jet high above seemed to push the stars aside, flying steadily on through the night. It was heading west, she thought. Probably to Los Angeles. Her plans to settle there and start a whole new life seemed so strange now, as if some other person had that notion and started down that road.

Jacquie shivered as she watched the jet fly away.

Chapter 14

"Let's go to Tucson," Choya said a couple days later. "Just you and me."

Jacquie looked up, startled, from behind her laptop and around a stack of textbooks and papers. She couldn't fathom why he was asking, but she really wanted to take him up on it. She was thoroughly sick of what she was doing. Christmas vacation had begun for the local school system and Robbie was underfoot every minute of the day.

"Tucson? You mean civilization? Sign me up." She regretted her sarcastic remark when she looked at all three of the Barnett males. They were in cahoots, she realized. In a nice way.

"I mean shopping," Choya said calmly.

"Yeah," Robbie chimed in. "You need some new stuff for your bedroom."

"I do? Like what?"

It dawned on her that Choya was trying to make up for galloping away from her the other day. The kiss, interrupted, had been more frustrating than not. She hadn't been particularly friendly to him since. Of course, there were other reasons her mood hadn't improved. She hadn't heard from her father. She couldn't request that an official copy of her university transcript be sent to Tucson until her application was filed. And she hadn't finished the essay for that.

The little boy shrugged. "You know, like inferior decorating stuff."

Choya burst out laughing. "That's interior decorating, son. And Jacquie gets to buy the best. Nothing inferior for her."

"No arguments, Jacquie," Sam said with rough friendliness. "You're going to the biggest mall in Tucson. That room needs something." He pondered for a few seconds. "It doesn't have any curtains. You get some of them ruffled ones and a comforter to match. And anything else your heart desires. Consider it a Christmas present in advance from me and Robbie."

"Yeah, and we want you to get a nice picture for the wall too." Robbie slid a look toward his father. "Can I tell her?"

"Go right ahead."

"I was going to loan you my snakes-and-reptiles poster but Dad said you wouldn't like it."

Jacquie smiled at him. "It looks great in your bedroom, Robbie. But I don't need anything new for mine. It's okay like it is."

Choya shook his head. "No, it isn't. Let me know when you're ready to go."

Jacquie began to shut down her laptop but Robbie squeezed in next to her and peered into the screen. "Can I look up stuff while you're gone?"

He was allowed to use the new computer in his father's study and he was careful with it. Jacquie agreed with a nod. She'd activated the child-safe software program as soon as she'd come back from Dallas and he couldn't stumble across anything inappropriate. "Okay. But you have to keep it right here on the kitchen table," she told him. "Don't download anything and don't change the settings."

"I'll watch him," Sam offered. "Maybe he can teach me a few new tricks."

Robbie took Jacquie's place when she got up. "It's easy, Gramps. But you have to sit next to me."

"Can I check my e-mail?" Sam asked, changing chairs.

Choya gave him a surprised look. "I didn't know you had e-mail."

"Like the kid says, it's easy." Sam's wrinkled face creased into a smile.

■ ■ ■ ■

The drive from the ranch to the highway was made in silence, but the mood was relaxed.

"Seemed to me you might be getting cabin fever," Choya finally remarked.

"Not really. I'm just — oh, I don't know. Out of sorts."

"Robbie never leaves you alone."

"You noticed. But he's still a great kid. Just a little clingy." She looked out the window.

"That's not your fault, Jacquie. Tell me if he bothers you." Choya's profile was stern. He didn't turn to glance at her.

"I can handle him."

"Disciplining him is my responsibility."

She didn't want to argue with that. But she didn't want to get Robbie in trouble either. "It's not that big of a problem. Don't worry about it, okay?"

He nodded, keeping his eyes on the road ahead. They had it to themselves. Absently, she studied the unvarying landscape. It seemed the same, unlike the Arizona sky above, which changed constantly, different every time she lifted her head.

She lowered her seat back to look up now,

trying to spot a golden eagle. She'd seen them fly over the mostly wild land of the ranch, soaring high above the scrub. She was getting better at spotting the prey they hunted when she was out — jackrabbits with pricked ears and smaller furry critters that scuffled and hid. The desert was nowhere near as empty as she'd thought. But nothing in it was cuddly or cute. Still, she'd come to understand it to some degree and even admire the toughness of its inhabitants.

Like Choya. He'd been on his best behavior since she'd come back, but he was still Choya. Lean and strong and wild himself. She couldn't rationalize away his powerful sensual attraction or resist it. Jacquie closed her eyes after a while. She drifted off without knowing it.

"Hey, sleeping beauty," she heard his low voice say. He reached out a hand and stroked her jeans-clad thigh. The sensation of his touch brought her back to full consciousness. She clasped his hand to make him stop, then, impulsively, lifted it to her lips to brush a kiss on the back of it.

He looked at her, startled, and put both hands on the wheel again. "Don't make me swerve."

Jacquie had to laugh. "Pay attention, please."

"You don't make it easy."

"Want me to drive?" She raised her seat back up and leaned over the dashboard to see that they were well away from the ranch.

"Nope. I like driving. It helps me think."

She teased him by running a fingertip around his ear and tugging on the lobe. "What were you thinking while I was asleep?"

"That you're beautiful and that I'm lucky." He didn't say anything else. They'd come to the highway on-ramp and a semi roared by where it joined the main road, followed by several cars. He merged the jeep into the flow of traffic.

In another half hour, they were getting close to Tucson. He pointed to a low ridge that was home to an expensive-looking subdivision. "That used to be Barnett land," he said. "Sam sold it when I was in high school."

Jacquie's eyes widened. The handsome stucco houses were surrounded by native plantings and many had pools. It was hard to imagine that the ridge had ever been the lonely place Sam had told her about. She looked her fill until they'd whizzed by, then sat back, keeping her mouth shut. What had happened to Choya was in the past. Let it stay there.

He drove several more miles into Tucson and made a left on a wide street that led into a very large parking lot. All the way Jacquie had fought the odd feeling of being closed in. Weird, she thought, considering how often she'd shopped in downtown Dallas and at the huge malls near it. Living on the ranch had imperceptibly changed her and she hadn't known it.

Walking through the parking lot, which was filled with Christmas shoppers, felt even more odd. The smooth asphalt under her boot soles had no give and no grit. The circling drivers searching for places to park seemed rushed and harassed, jockeying madly for spaces as they opened up. A red-faced man yelled soundlessly through his windshield at another driver, then pulled ahead of him, zooming out of the lot.

It was nothing out of the ordinary. But it felt all wrong to her. Choya seemed to know it. He took her elbow and guided her quickly to the wide glass portals of the mall.

Inside they encountered a full-blast festival of good cheer. Giant garlands and outsized decorations hung everywhere. The swarming crowds didn't seem to hear the piped-in carols, but Jacquie wanted to cover her ears. If this was civilization, she'd changed her mind about it.

Choya didn't seem too comfortable with the noise level either. He stopped only to consult the mall map on the kiosk and led the way to an escalator, striding off at the top and heading into a department store.

"Whew." Jacquie blew out her breath. "Where are we?"

Choya looked around. "In the right place. How did I do that?"

A display of fake windows glowed with opaque light, showing off the different types of curtains. Beyond it was the bed-and-bath area.

"Let's look around." She took his arm and glanced at the curtains without stopping at any of the displays as they walked. The puffy, perfectly made-up beds looked a lot more enticing.

Choya grinned at an extravagant model covered in fake spotted fur and heaped with satin pillows. "Look at that. We should try to get locked in the store overnight."

Jacquie rested her head on his arm. "We could use a little privacy."

"I'm working on that," he said seriously.

She patted another comforter, liking its velvety softness and subtle color. "This is pretty."

"You want it, buy it. One way or another, that bedroom needs a do-over. I can't wait until you move in to mine."

An elderly lady overheard and shot Choya a beady-eyed look of disapproval, but that wasn't why the casual remark gave Jacquie pause. She hadn't wanted to discuss that subject with him until they had reached agreement on a lot of other things. And she certainly didn't want to get into it on the sales floor of a busy department store.

"Right," she said, just as casually. "Well, this other comforter is just as nice. And it's cheaper." She didn't really look at her choice, just pulled a packaged one in twin size from the shelves, and handed it to him.

They completed their purchases, including curtains with no ruffles, without saying much more. After picking out Jacquie's gifts for Robbie and Sam, they threaded through the mall crowds to get back to the parking lot and the jeep. Choya tossed the bags into the back and slid behind the wheel. "Want to get something to eat?"

She shook her head. "It's so crowded here. Let's just go, okay?" she coaxed him. "I've had enough. I just want to get home."

He liked the sound of that. She'd said the word as though it was the most natural thing in the world to call his ranch her home. They were getting somewhere. Choya turned the key in the ignition and put the car in gear, backing out fast.

"Want to pick a tree?"

Jacquie looked at Choya, then his son, who'd asked the eager question. She hadn't planned to go into Tombstone after the trip to Tucson, but there was no reason they couldn't. Its small-town friendliness might be the antidote she needed right now. "Choya?"

He set the department store bags onto one of the kitchen chairs. "We might as well. It's not dark yet."

Robbie grabbed her hand and tugged on it. "Jacquie, say yes!"

Choya shook his head in reproof, and the little boy stepped back. "I mean, if you're not tired or anything," he added.

"No. Your dad did all the driving. But what about your grandfather?"

"He told me to pick the biggest one," Robbie said importantly.

"All right. Let's go."

The ride to town seemed to take no time, what with Robbie's excitement. As soon as they were parked in front of the feed store, he clambered out and ran in.

"He's going straight through to the back," Choya said. "That's where they keep the trees."

He got out and so did Jacquie, brushing her windblown hair out of her face. "Where are you going?"

Choya was walking around the side of the wood-shingled building. "Follow me."

She took a hairbrush from her purse and drew it quickly through her blond locks, then walked quickly to catch up with him. There was an animal pen at the side of the feed store and in it was a rotund, black-faced sheep, calmly chewing a wisp of hay while a teenaged girl combed burrs and bits of twigs out of its thick white wool. Jacquie, no expert on barnyard animals, guessed from the absence of horns that the sheep was a ewe.

"Jacquie, meet Ashley. And this is Old Nelly." Choya scratched the sheep's knobby head. The black ears twitched. Nelly's eyes closed halfway as she stood, blissed out and motionless.

"Looks like she likes that," Jacquie said to Choya. "Hello, Ashley."

"Hi." The teenager smiled and waved the grooming comb. "You can watch if you want. Nothing bothers her."

"I thought Nelly might be here," he told Jacquie. "Did your uncle bring her in from the ranch, Ashley?"

The girl nodded. "Yeah. She always likes

the ride. I'm getting her ready to rehearse with the Sunday school kids for the Christmas show," she told Jacquie. "Nelly's in the manger scene."

"Does she really need to rehearse?" Choya asked teasingly. "She does the same thing every year."

"That's what my mom says," Ashley laughed. "Nelly was born to just stand there. That's all she ever does."

The placid sheep lived up to her reputation while they chatted a bit more.

"Is Robbie in the show?" Jacquie asked. Choya hadn't mentioned it before now.

"No. But we always go. He likes to watch his pals onstage."

Robbie came running around the back side of the feed store and around to them, crashing into his father's leg on purpose. "Dad, they have a super-huge tree! Can we buy it?"

"Whoa, son. Let's look at it first." He waved good-bye to Ashley. "See you at the church. When is the show, by the way?"

"Eight o'clock. The night before Christmas Eve. Same as always."

Nelly blinked and stood in place, watching the three of them walk away.

Robbie ran ahead, stopping in front of the tallest tree on the lot. The feed store clerk came over to them. “Hi, Choya. And you must be Jacquie. I’m Nate.”

“Hello.” She was still a little surprised by the way the locals all seemed to know her name, even ones she’d never met. But their interest suddenly felt like a warm welcome, especially after the impersonal bustle of the city.

“So,” Nate said, “Robbie told me you all want to buy a tree.”

“This one, this one!”

“Robbie, pipe down.” Choya steered him toward the feed store’s back door. “Go count the cowbells behind the counter and stay out of trouble.”

“Aw, Dad —”

“I’ll go in with him,” Jacquie said quickly. Robbie took her hand to drag her away, but not before Choya caught her eye. She read his silent question and nodded. The giant tree was definitely okay with her.

The interior of the store was dim by comparison with the clear winter sunlight outside. She let her eyes adjust, then spotted Robbie, who’d let go of her hand to chat with the woman at the counter. Sure enough, a collection of antique, hand-hammered cowbells adorned the wall behind her.

“My dad says I have to count the bells,”

Robbie told her.

"Does he?" the woman asked kindly. Jacquie guessed at a family relationship between her and the girl grooming the sheep. Despite the intervening years, there was a definite resemblance between them.

"You go right ahead and count," the woman was saying to Robbie. "I don't even know how many there are myself."

The boy began, getting as far as seventeen, when Choya came back and ruffled Robbie's hair. "We did the deal. You got your tree."

"Thanks, Dad!" He forgot all about the cowbells and dashed outside again.

"Is that going to fit on top of the jeep?" Jacquie asked.

"Most of it will." Choya put an arm around her shoulders to lead her out. The woman looked at them with avid interest and said good-bye with a smile, which Jacquie returned. She wondered how long it would take before all of Tombstone heard about who just bought the biggest tree on the lot.

Sam had the ornament boxes ready and waiting when they got home. Choya held the massive tree by the trunk, carrying most of its weight as Jacquie steered the top through the door.

"Where's the stand?" Choya asked his father.

"I found that too," Sam assured him. "It's in the living room."

Getting the tree set up straight took a while but the four of them managed it. Small enough to crawl underneath, Robbie filled the stand with water from a big plastic bottle and crawled back out.

Jacquie stepped back to admire it. Undecorated, the tree was a deep, dark green that emanated the fragrance of pine. Its branches were still pointing up, fresh and sharp-needled.

"So how do you usually do the decorating?" she asked.

"I get the bottom, Gramps does the middle, and Dad takes care of everything on the top. But he holds me up so I can put on the star," Robbie explained.

"Count me out," his grandfather said. "This year I'm going to be the consultant. Jacquie can do the middle."

"What's a consultant?" Robbie wanted to know.

"They tell everyone else what to do. And they get to sit down." Sam dragged over a chair and eased himself into it. "You can begin, people."

Choya made quick work of putting on the

colored lights but it took two hours to decorate the whole tree. The weight of the ornaments leveled the branches, making the tree seem even larger. It filled the whole corner where it had been placed.

Robbie tired himself out with running back and forth, and he was rubbing his eyes when it was time to put on the star.

Choya hoisted the little boy up onto his shoulder and Jacquie handed him the star.

"Ready?" his father asked.

He nodded, and stretched out, sticking it on the topmost branch. It tipped and caught on the needles, crooked but not about to fall. Choya didn't straighten it.

"We don't light up the star until Christmas Eve," Robbie explained to Jacquie. "So it doesn't have to be perfect yet." He slid down from his perch, aided by Choya, and took her hand and then his father's, standing between them.

Sam, who hadn't budged from the chair or said a word, put his hands together and applauded loudly. "That's a fine sight," his grandfather said to one and all. "Not one broken ornament this year. And that has to be the biggest damn tree in Arizona. Good work, everyone."

Chapter 15

Christmas Eve was just days away and Robbie had the sniffles. Jacquie dreaded the prospect of coming down with a cold — they all might. So far she was feeling fine, and Sam and Choya didn't seem to have caught it. She prayed for their luck to hold. And in the meantime, Robbie was making the most of being sick.

He'd taken over the sofa, dragging blankets to it to make a cocoon and piling the cushions with picture books he never got around to reading. His father wouldn't let him watch TV all day and he complained about that. She took back her laptop and Robbie burrowed into the blankets, feeling sorry for himself.

Sam and Choya weren't big on coddling children and it wasn't like he'd come down with something serious. Both men had retreated and left her to deal with a kid who wasn't well enough to go outside and run around, and wasn't sick enough to go to the doctor.

There seemed to be a tacit agreement among the three adults to just let him have the sofa. They all had things to do.

Jacquie still hadn't coordinated everything she needed to support her transfer application to the university in Tucson. It would be a good idea, she thought, to figure out the scheduling of the classes she wanted to take, now that she had a better idea of how long the drive there and back would be.

She rested her head in her hands, wishing she'd had the nerve to talk it over with Choya when they'd had time to themselves. She knew it was childish to keep postponing the difficult discussion. Their relationship was still new — and at the moment, seesawing between passion and distance. Living in the same house wasn't helping with either. They couldn't be lovers, not openly, until they'd decided to make a serious commitment. But they saw each other constantly, which didn't give either of them a lot of breathing room.

The arrangement wasn't anything like dating. And they had yet to talk about marriage, let alone an engagement. It had been kind of funny the way Choya had shown off those old shacks and hinted that he'd soon be rolling in money. She wanted to believe he was telling the truth, but she wondered now if he'd been teasing her, the way he had when he'd galloped out of sight to see if she could find him. The shopping trip to the mall to buy a twin-size comforter wasn't a step in the right direction.

She sat up, and tapped the button that turned on her laptop, looking absently at the white screen and the tiny spinning wheel in the center of it. The connection was slow today.

Jacquie leaned back, her arms in the air, and stretched out her shoulders. The wheel spun. She mulled over the situation as she waited.

Was he going to be upset if she went off to classes in Tucson? She would be living here on the ranch — just not all the time. Choya couldn't leave his family the way she had. He had no one to take care of Robbie besides Sam, and it was clear enough that his father would soon need some help with that.

She snapped out of her reverie when the screen filled with color and the usual icons appeared. Then a cartoon candy bar floated across the screen. What the . . . oh no, she said to herself. Robbie had downloaded something, despite her specifically telling him not to. It was a game or an interactive ad. She clicked on the candy bar when it stopped for a second and CandyDandy opened up.

Before the colorful graphics really got going, she clicked out to follow his trail. Jacquie sighed with irritation. He'd downloaded the whole game, not just the cute little introductory app, and installed it on her hard drive.

"Robbie!" she called, exasperated.

She heard a mumbled "What?" from the living room.

"You get in here right now."

She waited a few minutes until he appeared, wearing pajamas and dragging a blanket. His sullen expression and flushed face told her he'd been cocooned too long.

"I told you not to download anything onto my laptop." She clicked a button and pointed at the screen. More floating candy bars appeared.

"It's only a game," he said in a small voice.

"Did your grandpa know you did that?"

"No," he muttered. "He was making me lunch."

She couldn't fault Sam. But she was really annoyed with Robbie. "That's it. You just lost your laptop privileges. Sit down. I want to talk to you."

"I don't feel good." Robbie stood there.

"You're not that sick. Do what I told you and sit down. It's going to take me a while to get that game off my hard drive and make sure you didn't put it in a folder or someplace else."

"I don't know how to do that. It downloaded itself anyway."

Jacquie's fingers clicked firmly over the keys. "No, it didn't, Robbie. Don't lie."

He took two steps back and suddenly yelled, "I don't like you anymore! You're not my mother!"

She opened her mouth in surprise but he was gone. The corner of the blanket he dragged caught on the door frame until he yanked it loose and disappeared.

Jacquie stopped typing and listened. No sound came from the living room, not even a muffled sob. He had to be expecting her to come in there and yell back.

She wasn't going to. Jacquie rubbed her pounding temples. Arguing with a seven-year-old was an exercise in futility. And he was right about her not being his mother. Right at the moment, she wished his father would step in, but Choya, as far as she knew, was out in the barn doing something that was more important. To him.

The screen flickered as the delete commands took effect and the game was removed from her hard drive. It *was* only a game, she reminded herself. Not some great big deal. But she still felt angry about Robbie's disobedience.

She considered going out to the barn to find Choya but decided against it. She could tell him later, when she was calmer. Jacquie really didn't want to sound more childish than Robbie, even though right was on her side. And she had no idea how Choya would take it. If he came down hard on his son, with Christmas so close, the whole holiday could be ruined.

She set the laptop to standby mode, leaving aside the task of scheduling her classes. Jacquie was inclined to call in an expert. She picked up the phone and dialed her parents' number, relieved when her mother answered.

"Hi, honey! I was just packing for Galveston — it's so nice to hear from you."

Jacquie knew her mother meant "we" and not "I." She could imagine the two suitcases on the bed, one for her father and one for her mother, carefully filled with folded, ironed clothes.

"I'm ready to take a break," her mother was saying. "So what's up? Are you ready for Christmas?"

"We got the tree up and decorated it," Jacquie began.

"That's wonderful. Did you take pictures?"

"Not yet, Mom. I will."

Maureen's charming laugh filled the air. "You left your digital camera here, you know. Do you mind if I take it to Galveston?"

"Go ahead. I can always get one of those tourist cameras at a Tombstone store." She fell silent.

"Okay," her mother said soothingly. "What's wrong? I hope you're not homesick."

Thoughts of the Dallas house at Christmastime had crossed her mind, but only fleetingly. "No," she answered honestly.

"Well, good. I have to tell you, your dad and I are pretty happy to be going to Galveston for a change. The holidays can be overwhelming."

"It's not that. It's Robbie," Jacquie said quietly.

"Oh, Choya's little boy," her mother said. "Is he all right?"

"Basically, yes — I mean, he has a not-too-serious case of the sniffles. No biggie. But he just got angry with me and stormed off."

"Why?"

"I told him not to download a game or anything else on my laptop and he did, when I was in Tucson with Choya. Then he lied about it."

Her mother's disembodied voice hesitated. "That wasn't right and I'm sure you were upset. But kids will do things like that. He admires you so much and I bet he was thrilled that you let him use your laptop. He just didn't think about the consequences."

Jacquie cradled the phone between her ear and her shoulder, listening and looking into the living room. There was only silence. A small foot twitched at the edge of the blanket. Shaking her head, she went back to the kitchen. "Well, he's thinking about them now."

"What did Choya say?"

"He doesn't know yet. It just happened."

"I see." Jacquie heard vague sounds on the other end of the call. A closet door being opened, a muffled flop of more clothes landing on the bed — she'd watched her mother pack so many times, she felt she was observing the process now. "Honey, did you say Robbie had sniffles?"

"Yes. Nothing dire. He doesn't have a fever."

"Well, you'd still better keep an eye on

him. Colds and flu can start slowly. And by the way, either one will make a child very irritable at first. They can behave so differently you almost don't recognize them."

Jacquie could vouch for that. In one afternoon, Robbie had gone from her biggest fan to being a total brat. She was glad to hear confirmation of that — but her mother still didn't know everything. She took a deep breath and got to the point. "Mom, it wasn't the game or that he disobeyed me or even that he could be coming down with something worse than sniffles."

"Let's hear it."

"I made it clear that I was annoyed, and he yelled that he didn't like me anymore. And that I wasn't his mother."

"Oh dear." Maureen stopped what she was doing and sat down with a sigh. "The honeymoon is over. That was bound to happen."

"What?" For a second, Jacquie misunderstood.

"I didn't mean you and Choya, dear. Goodness, your father would hit the roof if he heard you'd gotten married. He and I sincerely hope you'll take your time before you take that step. No, I was talking about Choya's little boy and you."

Jacquie sat down herself. "I'm listening."

"Honey, it's only natural that he thinks of you as his mother. You told me how attached he was to you. And vice versa." Maureen stopped for a few moments to think. "He's been trying so hard to be good — almost too good. Sounds to me like he's having an awful day and he did something wrong and he said the worst thing he could think of. In a funny way, it's not that bad. He trusted you enough to yell at you."

"Food for thought," Jacquie said wryly.

"Of course there should be consequences for what he did, but you can figure that out with his father. How is Choya, by the way?"

"He's fine."

"Not in the room with you, I take it."

Jacquie smiled. Her mother was a smart cookie. "Not even in the house."

"So you're coping with a cranky kid who decided to be naughty, and you're on your own."

"That about sums it up. I'm not sure if I should tell Choya, though. I don't want this to ruin Christmas."

"Tell him," her mother said firmly. "Just do it when you aren't upset." She paused for a second. "You know, I never did get the whole story on his family and we haven't talked much since you went back to Arizona with him. Does Choya's mother live near you?"

"Ah" — Jacquie didn't want to get into all the complicated details — "Choya doesn't know her at all. Sam Barnett adopted him as a single parent when he was a baby."

"Oh my." Maureen gave a heartfelt sigh. "That's a sad story. But hooray for Sam. It's not easy raising a child alone. I'm sure Choya doesn't want to."

Jacquie felt tears well suddenly at the back of her eyes. She blinked them fiercely away.

"Honey? You still on?"

"Yes," she answered in a choked voice. "I know he wants more for Robbie than Sam was able to give him. But what if I'm not sure I want to be a stepmother?"

"Oh . . . I feel so badly that I'm not there to hug you and sit with you — do you want to come home?" Maureen asked. "We could cancel the Galveston trip."

Amazed that she didn't want that, not at all, Jacquie whispered, "No. I want to stay here."

"Are you sure?"

She scrubbed away the stinging wetness. "Actually . . . yes. Talking to you helped. I'm sorry I got emotional." She heard the front door open and close. "I have to go."

"You hang in there, honey. Just remember,

you can call me anytime, day or night."
"I know."
Maureen seemed about to end the call, then rushed to add a little more. "Oh, and check Robbie for fever. If his forehead is cool to the touch, he probably doesn't have one, but if he feels hot, you should use a thermometer — those digital ones work pretty well."
"I'll check. And I'll call you back. Thanks, Mom. I love you."
"I love you too, baby. Bye for now."
Choya came into the kitchen. His jacket was off but he radiated the coldness of outdoors. The fresh smell of hay clung to his clothes. "All right. Did the walkthrough. Two stalls — didn't take me long," he said in a joking tone. "How's your mother?"
"She's fine. Packing for their trip. I didn't talk to my dad."
He leaned into the refrigerator and took out an empty aluminum pie plate that had held a store-bought pie. "Fee-fie-fo-fum. Someone else ate every crumb," he said with amused annoyance. "I wish Robbie wouldn't put empty containers back."
"He hasn't been behaving too well. My mother said to check his temperature."
"Good idea. I'm glad you called her. Want me to do it?"

"No, I can. You eat." Jacquie got up as he put together a half-sandwich from leftovers and brought it to the table, pulling out a chair.

"I assume your mother gave you detailed instructions."

She managed a smile. "More or less. Be right back."

The living room was still dark and the boy under the blankets didn't seem to have moved. She lifted the blanket and saw his peaceful, sleeping face, feeling a rush of tenderness as she placed a hand on his forehead. It was cool. His breathing was no longer congested and he hadn't broken out in a sweat.

Jacquie felt a deep relief. He was okay. She and Choya could take turns checking on him. And they could talk about the laptop some other time. The brief storm had passed for now.

She heard the phone ring as she walked back to the kitchen. Choya was quick to answer it. "Hello, Mrs. Grey. It's nice to talk to you. Okay, Maureen it is — just trying to be respectful," he laughed. "I assume you want Jacquie. She's right here." He handed the receiver to her.

"I knew you wouldn't wait for me to call you back," Jacquie said with faint amusement. "I did what you said. He doesn't have a fever and he's sound asleep. Yes. I'll call you if anything changes. Thanks, Mom."

"Tell her I said thank you too," Choya demanded in a low voice.

Jacquie relayed the message and listened with surprise to her mother's next words.

"Honey, I forgot to tell you that your father received the financial aid application. He's filling it out — you know how he is with dotting each 'i' and crossing every 't.' "

"Yes I do."

"Cam said to tell you he'll have it back to you before the first of January. He's very pleased you want to go back to college, Jacquie. That was about the best Christmas present you could have given him."

"Glad to hear it, Mom. Okay, talk to you soon. Have a great time in Galveston." They exchanged a little more small talk and then said good-bye. Jacquie slowly hung up the receiver. "I sent my father the financial aid form for the Tucson tuition. Apparently he's filling it out."

Choya finished the last of his sandwich. "I sort of gathered that you've been working on that and the application. How come you never talk about it?"

She sat down and slouched over her folded arms, resting her head on them but looking at him. "I don't want to. Choya, I'd forgotten how complicated they were. The personal information, the reasons I want to transfer, the essay — I haven't even started writing that."

"Got a topic?"

She smiled slightly but didn't raise her head. "As of today, yes. How One Peanut-Butter-and-Jelly Sandwich Can Change Your Life."

He raised a dark eyebrow. "Come again?"

"I was thinking of writing about what it was like the first time I made one for Robbie. And why."

"Because he was hungry?"

"No, Choya. Because I came out here to live with you and your son and that totally changed my life in a hundred ways and — and I'm not sure I even know what I'm doing most of the time."

He was taken aback and reached out a hand, which she gently pushed away. Choya studied her face. "You're doing great. I should tell you that more often."

She didn't answer.

"Let me fill in the blanks. Long day. Crabby kid. No one to spell you. I'm sorry, Jacquie. I shouldn't have left you with him for hours. I got busy — but that's no excuse."

"He was a handful."

Choya gave a curt nod. "He can be sometimes. I know exactly what you're talking about."

She heaved a rueful sigh. "I just want to get through Christmas and not yell at anyone or break anything. That's my goal."

"Just don't break my heart — I'd appreciate that. You're not going back to Dallas, are you?" He seemed to be speaking only half in jest.

"No. Why do you ask?"

"Just making sure, babe." A long look passed between them, filled with feeling neither could express in words. Then he leaned over and pressed a kiss to her forehead. Jacquie lifted her face to his and he kissed her lips, slowly, breaking it off to take her hand and help her out of her chair. Then he lifted her into his arms. "I can't stand it another second. To hell with being a gentleman. But I will let you choose. Big bed or twin bed?"

"You're too much. Either will do. But I'm sleeping alone." She wrapped her arms around his neck and kissed him again, cradled in strong arms that held her as if she weighed nothing.

They both heard Robbie stir and call fretfully. “Dad,” he said faintly. “Dad? Are you home?”

Choya set her down with obvious reluctance. “Yes, Robbie. Stay there. I’ll be out in a minute.”

Jacquie smiled wickedly at him. “Your turn.”

Choya left her to see to his son, then came back into the kitchen to heat up a can of chicken noodle soup and carry the bowl to the living room on a tray.

Jacquie distracted herself by looking up on-campus living arrangements and class schedules. She created a calendar grid and filled it in, studying it with a frown.

Choya wasn’t going to like it. Neither did she. She lifted her head when he went by in the hall, his son in his arms, on the way to his real bed. Jacquie didn’t offer to help and Robbie, who was awake, didn’t look at her. She hid a smile, remembering her father getting her to bed when she’d been an uncooperative little girl. She’d mastered the art of going limp and maximizing her slight weight, not to mention plaintive requests for “just one more.” As in one more glass of water, one more hug, one more fairytale — she wondered how her parents had managed to raise her and keep on smiling through it all.

She heard the sound of a storybook being read aloud from the little boy's bedroom, and concentrated again on what she was doing. Jacquie hardly heard Choya come back downstairs again and she jumped when he put a hand on her shoulder.

"Relax. He's so restless I don't have a chance in hell of sneaking away. I only got him to stay in bed by telling him he couldn't ride Apache if he was really sick."

"Do you think we should take him to the doctor?"

Choya gave a dismissive shake of his head. "No. He bounces back from this kind of thing really fast. For some reason, he's decided to make the most of it this time."

"Oh?" she asked, not willing to tell him about Robbie's misbehavior. "Why is that?"

"Probably because he has a sympathetic audience. You."

Jacquie smiled weakly. "Oh, I can be tough."

"Nothing wrong with that. He's never been spoiled and I don't want to start now."

She gave an acknowledging nod and glanced into her laptop, clicking out of the web pages she'd pulled up one by one. The screen was a blank again. If only her mind was.

"So what are you up to? If you don't mind my asking, that is."

Jacquie leaned back in her chair. Now or never. She would have to tell him.

"I'm putting together a tentative schedule for the spring term in Tucson," she told him.

"Great. Glad to hear it."

"Um — taking the classes I want will mean being in Tucson four days a week. Almost five, actually, if I figure in the driving time."

"That's more than half the week." He studied her face as she bit her lower lip, worrying it thoughtfully. "Are you sure that's what you want to do?"

"No way around it." She took a deep breath and looked into his concerned eyes. "I was thinking of sharing an apartment with someone in the middle of the week — I really don't think I could stand a dorm. Otherwise it will be too much driving and I'll be too tired to study."

"I see." His voice was flat. "Sharing, huh? Anyone particular in mind?"

Jacquie knew instantly that she had crossed an invisible line.

"I don't know anyone in Tucson. I'll contact campus housing, see if they have any listings for someone looking for a roommate."

"So it's a done deal."

"No, not at all. I still haven't finished my application or the rest of the paperwork — it all has to go in together, though."

His expression was controlled and so was his voice. "Why not just move to Tucson and get it over with?"

"Choya, it's not like that —"

The soft sound of footed pajamas reached them at the same time. Choya turned first. "Robbie, get back to bed. And stay there."

The little boy looked beseechingly at Jacquie. How much had he heard? He was likely to get the wrong idea, given how abruptly she'd left the first time.

"Do what your dad says." She had to back up Choya on that point, even though the look in his son's eyes made her feel unnecessarily guilty. "Get under the covers. Then I'll come up and read you another story so you can fall asleep."

Choya's level look moved from Robbie to her for a beat. Then he spoke. "I'd rather you didn't," he said crisply.

She wasn't going to argue with him. Not in front of Robbie. When the little boy ran back upstairs, Choya leveled a look at her from his superior height. "I know I'm not going to win this one, Jacquie. Do what you have to do. If I stand in the way of you getting an education, you'll walk out that door and never come back. I want you here."

"Gee whiz," she said sarcastically. "You sound like a man in love."

He only shrugged and turned to go to his son. "I'm a realist. That's all."

The kids waiting to see the Christmas play were squirming in their folding chairs or turning around to look at each other. They were shushed by the grown-ups, not very effectively. Jacquie looked around the small church, recognizing a lot of the people she'd met in town over the last several weeks. The old frame church was drafty. The audience members held the program in gloved and mittened hands, not bothering to look at it.

It didn't matter, Jacquie told herself. It wasn't like the Christmas story changed from year to year, even if the young actors did. She had tucked an extra program into her pocket for Sam, who'd decided to stay home but insisted on knowing who this year's players were.

A home-sewn curtain with an uneven hem had been rigged over the raised altar, where the nativity tableau would be set, its two halves held in place with a clothespin. Now and then, the curtain bumped out as an adult or child crossed from one side to the other, getting ready for the annual show.

The lady from the feed store was two rows back, with a couple of younger children that Jacquie guessed were nieces and nephews, probably Ashley's siblings. Floyd Simmons, the barber, was only a few seats away, and she saw Robbie lean forward to wave at him. The boy was sitting on the other side of Choya, almost concealed by his dad's brawn. Jacquie had to wonder if he was keeping away from her deliberately, then told herself not to read anything into what was either chance or an innocent choice. But Robbie didn't look her way very often and when he did, his expression was guarded. She missed the little boy's open-hearted happiness.

It wasn't what he had happened to overhear — which really wasn't anything much — but how he interpreted it that worried her. Jacquie looked at Choya's impassive profile and wished she could know his thoughts. As though he sensed her gaze on him, he turned and looked into her eyes, pinning her with that golden gaze she still could not read very well.

Jacquie smiled reflexively, and sat back. Two rows in front, the salesclerk from the souvenir store recognized her and raised a hand, waggling gloved fingers in a hello.

Jacquie only waved back, glad the woman was far enough away to keep them from engaging in a discussion of the gingerbread house.

An older man parted the curtain and stepped in front of it, while an unseen hand dimmed the overhead lights.

"Good evening, ladies and gentlemen. I'm Deacon Knowles, and I'd like to thank you all for coming out tonight. Hope you're ready for the pageant. I know these youngsters behind the curtain are eager to get on with it."

The sounds of scuffling and giggling reached the waiting audience. Two boys in shepherd garb came out from the sides and pulled the curtains open, revealing a rough-hewn manger filled with hay, covered by a sheltering roof made of ocotillo branches. Slowly the players in the pageant filed out from left and right, trying hard not to look out at the audience without always succeeding.

Cameras flashed and some proud parents held up small video recorders as more shepherds appeared, dressed in burlap tied with rope over their jeans and sneakers. Then came three Wise Men, who were no more than five or six years old, in brocade robes and improvised turbans. The Bethlehem villagers were made up of the remaining kids, younger still, who bumped into each other now and then.

The ragtag group was joined by Joseph, a sturdy third-grader, who led Nelly by a rope. The ewe seemed to know exactly what was expected of her and took her place by the manger and stood there, greeted by name by her loyal fans. Old Nelly took her chance to get into the hay and chewed a piece calmly as little Mary entered, clad in blue, solemnly smiling as the deacon narrated the Christmas story. The children played their parts and remembered their brief lines without a hitch or stumble. The brief pageant concluded with the appearance of a star high in the painted sky — it was a camping lantern, by Jacquie's guess — and a carol sung in high, sweet voices.

There was a burst of heartfelt applause, and the audience gathered in the foyer for cocoa and cookies.

"Weren't they darling?" the souvenir shop clerk asked Jacquie. "I come every year. It just doesn't seem like Christmas until this happens. This is your first time, isn't it?"

Jacquie agreed with a nod. "Yes, it is. The kids were wonderful." She looked around for Choya and Robbie. The rugged rancher was chatting with another older woman, gray-haired and friendly-looking, who glanced toward Jacquie with eager interest.

She smiled in their general direction, hoping to catch Robbie's eye. The boy kept his gaze firmly fixed on the woman who was talking to his father, to Jacquie's dismay.

There wasn't anything she could do about it, she reasoned, only half-listening to the clerk's chatter. "Yes, it was easy," she responded to a question about the gingerbread house, still looking at the two Barnetts.

She felt . . . closed out.

"I'm glad to hear that. You have a happy holiday now." The clerk moved on to someone else, a friend, perhaps.

Jacquie had no way of knowing. She walked over to Choya, who put his arm around her shoulders and introduced her to the woman he'd been talking to, a family friend. Robbie let go of his father's hand and moved away through the small crowd. Jacquie shrugged off Choya's embrace to look in the direction the boy had gone, worried about him.

Choya seemed to understand. "He just wants to talk to his friends," he reassured her. The little shepherds were gathering around the sheep, who'd been led away by the teenaged Ashley and was now standing just outside the church.

Jacquie turned her head, smiling at the woman, whose name she didn't catch. She forced herself to relax in Choya's casual embrace, fighting her uneasiness.

On the way home, Robbie took the back seat, resting his head against the side of the car by the window.

"Sleepy, son?" Choya asked.

"No. I was just looking at the stars."

There seemed to be thousands, twinkling sharply in the cold night air. Jacquie glanced up at them. "I never saw so many," she said softly.

"They're always there," Choya replied.

"Not in Dallas," she said in a teasing voice.

Robbie hummed the carol the children had sung, and the familiar melody made Jacquie feel a little sad. Then he stopped. "Dad — is that the Star of Bethlehem?"

"No," Choya replied. "That star appeared a long, long time ago. Hasn't been seen since."

"That could be it," Robbie insisted. "It sure is a big one."

"True enough," was his father's indulgent answer.

"Well, if it's only a regular star, then I can make a wish on it," Robbie reasoned.

"You go right ahead."

Jacquie didn't interrupt, amused by the discussion. The little boy made his wish in silence and neither she nor Choya questioned him as to what he had wished for.

The house was quiet when they went in, with no sign of Sam.

"Gramps must be in bed," Robbie said in a low voice.

"Which is where you're headed," Choya reminded him. "Go get ready. Then you can come down and I'll read to you."

The little boy didn't look at Jacquie as he requested his story to be read in his bedroom. It wasn't her imagination. He was keeping away from her. She couldn't bring herself to ask him why and she didn't want to ask Choya later.

Let it go, she told herself. The holidays were stressful for everyone and it was common sense to expect a sensitive boy like Robbie to react accordingly. She wandered around the lower floor of the house when Choya went upstairs, hearing his voice, faint but deep, from above. It seemed to her when the story was done that Choya was answering questions from Robbie and the last thing she wanted to do was listen in.

She went into the living room and switched on the tree lights. The candy-laden gingerbread house on the mantel sparkled in their glow. She saw cracks in the hard frosting. It didn't matter. The box inside would keep it together a while longer. She had a feeling Robbie would fight the house's inevitable demolition — or offer to do it himself, by eating it, stale frosting and all.

Jacquie sighed and headed for the sofa to curl up and try to relax. Hugging a pillow to her chest to keep warm and to stave off a growing feeling of loneliness, she couldn't help but remember what Christmas was like at her parents' house in Dallas — they'd always invited their friends and relatives, even the most distant, serving punch and eggnog, and slicing an enormous Christmas ham into sandwiches for all comers. Her mother made cakes and pie and frosted cookies. No one went hungry.

The stairs creaked as Choya came downstairs again.

"In here," she called.

"Sorry that took so long. I seem to be popular with him again."

"Yes. I guess you noticed he's barely talking to me," she said as his long strides brought him into the room.

"I hadn't noticed that. Why, did he misbehave?"

"Only a little," she quickly covered. "Nothing I couldn't handle."

Choya shot her a curious look from where he'd stopped, then shrugged. "I wouldn't worry about it," he said. "Let him sulk."

Jacquie nodded, not feeling like she had any choice. Choya's gaze moved to the tree as though he was checking it for burned-out lights — there weren't any — then to her. "Not too cheerful in here. Want me to build a fire?" he asked.

"No," she replied. "I don't want to stay up late. Christmas Eve is tomorrow. I can't think of what I should be doing, but I feel like I should be doing something."

He came to sit by her, stretching out an arm along the back of the sofa cushions until his fingertips grazed her folded elbow. She didn't make a move toward him, just rested her head on her upper arm and looked at him wistfully.

"The freezer and fridge are stocked," he reminded her. "You don't have to do a thing."

"My mother always went all out and cooked like crazy and invited a hundred people — okay, not that many. I guess I should be glad I don't have to, right?"

He studied her for a long moment. "If you want to throw a party, I'm game. Can't think of anyone to invite, though."

"Never mind. It's just that it's my first

Christmas away from home. I'm being a big baby, aren't I?"

"I couldn't say," he answered thoughtfully, "not having ever spent a Christmas away from the ranch. I don't know what it would feel like. But judging by the look in your eyes — oh, come here," he said. "Be my baby."

She shook her head and he gave her a sideways look, then dropped the subject. They chatted, but his thoughts seemed to be elsewhere. The warmth and magic of the show at the church seemed to have vanished on the ride home. And it bothered her.

She told herself not to succumb to self-pity. The Barnetts had their own quiet way of celebrating, that was all. And it wasn't as if Maureen and Cameron Grey were going to any trouble this year. They'd escaped, figuring that the Galveston branch of the family could throw a party this Christmas. If there was one. Jacquie had spoken briefly to both of her parents that afternoon — they'd been walking on the beach barefoot and watching seagulls fly. That seemed even odder to her than being here in the rugged high desert, where Christmas trees had to be imported.

"Did you like the pageant?" he asked.

"Oh — yes, I really did," she answered,

startled out of her reverie. "The kids were so cute." She hesitated. "There was something I wanted to ask you, though. Why doesn't Robbie participate?"

Choya gave her a half-smile. "He never did want to. I was thinking this year would be different, especially since you started living here. But he didn't seem to ever mention it when he got home after Sunday school and I didn't feel like pushing it — besides, there doesn't seem to be any shortage of shepherds in the cast. I know he will someday. Maybe next Christmas." He looked her way and the returned warmth in his golden eyes captured her.

Jacquie wriggled closer, irresistibly drawn to him despite her moodiness, and ended up under his encircling arm, her head resting against his chest. Choya rubbed her shoulder and kissed her silky hair, lifting it away from her neck with the other hand so as not to trap it.

The tenderness he'd had to hold back began to surface, and she was the willing recipient, craving his attention and listening with growing joy to loving murmurs that promised her everything she wanted. Maybe she was foolish to want so much from him, but it was impossible to believe he didn't mean every word.

"You know something?" he whispered in her ear when she'd finally relaxed against him.

"What?" she asked dreamily, feeling caressed and comforted. "Don't bring me back to reality. Even if you are a realist."

His low laugh at himself warmed her. "Am I forgiven?"

"I think so."

"Can I say what I was going to say to you?"

"Go ahead."

He stroked her hair and wound its length around his hand. "With this hair and those beautiful dreamy eyes, you'd make a perfect angel."

"Oh, Choya," she whispered with a trace of dismay. "I'm not."

"Good," he said with satisfaction. Then he went back to kissing her. Jacquie arched with renewed desire, giving in to the pleasure of his very masculine company and forgetting all about being homesick.

CHAPTER 16

The morning dawned clear but very cold. The mountains in the near distance were dusted with snow, to her amazement. Choya grinned when he saw her marveling at the sight, as proud as if he'd personally arranged for the rugged Dragoons to look like a Christmas card.

"You picked the right year. That doesn't happen every December."

Then the three Barnetts ate completely different breakfasts and none of them sat down, managing only a few bites of food as they rushed off to do last-minute errands.

Choya was starting his day with chores.

Jacquie waved good-bye to Robbie and his grandfather as they waited in the yard for Sam's old friend Garth. Hesitantly, Robbie lifted a hand to wave back and managed a smile. Good enough. That was progress. She turned away again, surveying the kitchen. She had half a mind to bake cookies and astonish them all. But she needed to find a foolproof, unburnable recipe first.

If nothing else got done, she'd earn points for Christmas baking.

She'd overheard Sam and Robbie whispering together about how to finish her presents when they were putting on their jackets, but she had no idea what those presents might be. She had picked up gifts for both of them when she'd been in Tucson with Choya — small trucks for Robbie's collection and a new robe for Sam in a bold buffalo plaid. As far as Choya, she'd had no idea what to give him. Just buying any old thing so that he had a box to open didn't seem right. But the stores within driving distance would start closing by early afternoon, and she'd already decided she would rather do that than give him nothing at all.

Looking out the window again when she heard a car pull up, she felt a little dispirited by the sight of Sam and Robbie leaving. Choya was going into town later, in the jeep. Right now he was in the barn, chinking the cracks between its planks before the horses froze their tails off, as he put it.

He always had something to do and he did everything on his own and did it well. With a wry smile, Jacquie remembered her mother's frustration with her father's interfering ways after he took early retirement. The mild-mannered Maureen would have given anything to have Cameron out of the house and out of her hair. Eventually they'd settled down, he took on work as a consultant, and they figured out how to get along again — and now, with Jacquie grown and gone, they probably were enjoying their first vacation without a worry in the world for their darling daughter.

She considered wandering out to the barn to see if Choya needed help, but decided against it. The love nest in the hayloft was probably still there, but it was much too cold for fooling around, even fully dressed, and they'd never get anything else done if that got started.

Jacquie went looking for her laptop and found it in the living room. She brought it back to the kitchen, turned it on and waited only two minutes before she was able to go online. A recipe site provided easy cookie recipes and she picked the easiest of all: plain sugar dough that was chilled and then rolled out. She would have to use a glass to cut out the cookies and she didn't have any icing, but there were chocolate chips, a whole bag of them, inside a container in the pantry marked BAKING SODA.

Sam was no fool.

Jacquie pinned her hair up, then found an apron. She assembled the ingredients and mixed up a big sticky lump of dough that she wrapped up in plastic and stuck in the fridge. That and the washing up killed an hour. She looked at the clock, another idea taking shape in her mind. She hadn't caught up with any of her friends in months and she'd better do it before Christmas Eve. Starting with Tammy in Bisbee.

She checked her e-mail, then fired off one to Tammy. Within five minutes she had an answer — and in ten, they were chatting on video, catching up on everything and happily interrupting each other.

"It's been way too long," Tammy said eagerly. "How are you? You look great — so healthy and bright-eyed. So how are things with the rugged rancher?"

Jacquie grinned. "My mother told you about him, I see."

"She sure did. I called to get your new address in Los Angeles and I got an earful. She seemed sure you were okay up there in Tombstone, so I didn't worry. Long story, huh?"

"I wouldn't even know where to start by now. But yes, I'm living with Choya."

"Your mom thinks he's a good guy and a great dad."

Jacquie nodded, pleased by hearing that.

"So," Tammy said casually. "Where is he right now?"

"Out in the barn."

"Too bad," Tammy pouted. "I wanted to get a look at the man who stole your heart. I hear he's tall and handsome — yes, your mom told me that too. What if," she added with a mischievous look in her eyes, "he heard us talking like this and sneaked up on you?"

"That's not going to happen. He wears cowboy boots."

A large hand dropped onto her shoulder. Jacquie jumped halfway out of her chair and shrieked. Then she turned to see Choya standing right behind her, in socks, his boots in his other hand.

"Sorry," he laughed. "I saw you two online when I came in the door and your friend saw me. I couldn't resist."

"You scared me half to death!"

He only laughed again as she pummeled him, not really angry. Then she turned back to the screen, settling down again. He really had startled her. "Tammy, meet Choya."

He bent down to look into the screen. "Hello."

Tammy waved madly and cracked up, all at the same time. Choya spent only a few minutes more with both of them, then excused himself to go back to the barn.

"Wow," her friend said as she eyed the rear view of Choya in jeans slipping his jacket back on.

Jacquie felt a flash of something she'd rarely experienced and recognized it as jealousy. She turned the laptop around, following a feminine instinct to guard what was hers. "You can look at my kitchen," she instructed her friend. "The stove is new — check it out. I'm just going to walk him to the door. Be right back."

"I don't care about your stove. Besides, he's already at the door," she heard Tammy protest.

Jacquie got up to run to Choya.

"You're so happy," he said in a dry tone. "I think I've been keeping you to myself for too long." He chucked her under the chin and pressed a quick kiss to her forehead. "Your friend seems nice."

"She is." Jacquie hesitated, feeling that unfamiliar sensation again. "And she's pretty. Don't you think so?"

He scoffed at that idea. "Not compared to you. Don't be ridiculous." He set his Stetson on his head and tipped it to her with a wink. "Enjoy the girl talk."

He left. Tammy and Jacquie talked for at

least an hour more, covering every subject under the sun and eventually getting around to what they were doing for Christmas. Like her, Tammy was at home doing not much of anything. Unlike Jacquie, she seemed perfectly content.

But a few minutes later, half-listening but happy just to see her friend's face, Jacquie realized that video chats were the best cure ever invented for being lonely and wondered why she'd waited so long. She wouldn't make that mistake again. The conversation wound down naturally and then Jacquie remembered one more thing she'd wanted to ask.

"Tammy — do you know anyone in Tucson who might be interested in subletting an apartment or studio? I'm putting together my application for the university there, and I'd rather not commute from here if I don't have to."

"Um, yes. Tell me more."

Jacquie explained the situation, including her finances, and added, "So I need something cheap."

"Got a pencil? I'll give you Hannah's e-mail. Her parents actually own several apartment buildings in the Tucson area — I'm sure they'd help you out. But are you sure you want to leave that gorgeous hunk of burning mesquite on his own for four days a week?"

"Shut up," Jacquie giggled. "Even if you are my best friend."

"It's a good thing I'm happily married," Tammy said primly. They wrapped up the call with promises to see each other soon and Jacquie clicked out of the video app. She felt warm all over, and it wasn't from the coziness of the kitchen — she was at peace with her decision to be here now that she'd reconnected with a friend who was no more than a click away.

Thinking of the cookie dough, Jacquie got up to take a look at it. She opened the refrigerator door and gave the plastic-wrapped lump a poke. It hadn't changed. Maybe it needed to be colder. Whatever. It could wait and she could e-mail Hannah in the meantime.

Tammy's friend was online and answered in seconds. She was as nice as Tammy, from what Jacquie could tell, and instantly offered to help, telling Jacquie to send her the date she needed to move by and how much rent she could realistically afford to pay. She promised to get back to Jacquie right after the first of January.

Thanking Hannah several times, Jacquie signed off, grateful to have a friend like

Tammy and very pleased with the information she now had. Everything was coming together. Jacquie didn't shut down the laptop, trying to think of someone else she could video-chat with. No one came to mind.

Jacquie got the dough and patted it out on the flour-covered table. So what if the cookies were a little bumpy? It wouldn't affect how they tasted and she swore a solemn oath not to let them burn. The neat circles of dough came easily out of the water glass she used for a cookie cutter and the first batch went in.

She made herself sit down in sight of the clock, knowing that if she left the kitchen, she would get involved in something else and ruin the cookies. Wiping her floury fingers on her jeans first, she touched a key and reread the e-mail exchange. For once in her life, she was going to be thoroughly prepared and not just go running off somewhere.

The clock ticked away the minutes as she prepared the second sheet of cookies and daydreamed simultaneously about driving down to Bisbee with Choya and showing him off — there was nothing more attractive than a shy guy in a Stetson, she decided. Make that a shy but rugged guy with a wild streak and gentleman's manners. All mine, she thought.

No wonder Tammy had shown such avid interest. And yes, it was a good thing that she was married. Jacquie looked down at her hands and wondered how the left one would look with a ring on the fourth finger. Then she caught the very faint whiff of sugary smoke and grabbed a pot holder, pulling down the oven door. Just in time. They were dark brown around the edges, but not burnt.

She had the hang of it.

Jacquie had baked three dozen cookies by the time Robbie and Sam came back. With practiced skill, she removed a freshly baked batch and slipped in the next one.

"What smells so darned good?" she heard Sam call.

"Christmas cookies!"

Robbie beat his grandfather into the kitchen and looked at the pile on the platter. "Can I have one right now?" he asked breathlessly.

"You bet. They taste best right out of the oven." She'd added chocolate chips to some, simply by pressing them down into the unbaked tops. He selected one of those and sat down to eat it.

Sam came into the kitchen and took a

plain sugar cookie for himself.

"Okay," she said, "if one of you would watch the clock for me, I can take a break. My hair's falling down."

"You go right ahead and pin it up again," Sam assured her. "Take your time. Robbie and I will do random quality checks on these here cookies while you're gone."

"Don't eat them all," she called over her shoulder, heading for the bathroom.

Sam had the sheet in the oven out and cooling when she got back. But Robbie's bright smile seemed to have faded. He sat at the table, nibbling at another one he'd taken from the platter, looking unhappy.

"He ate too fast, I think," Sam said. "Robbie, I told you fresh-baked goods fill you up fast. You gotta pace yourself."

"Yeah," he said in a dull voice.

"Why don't you go lie down on your bed for a bit?" she asked him. "You two must have done a lot of running around. Did you get everything you needed, Sam?"

The old man nodded. "Yep. And you should get going if you intend to do last-minute shopping."

Jacquie untied her apron. "Good idea. There's dough left but I made enough for an army. It'll keep, right?"

"Yes indeedy."

"Okay, then off I go. Be good, you two." She ruffled Robbie's hair on her way to get her jacket and the car keys, and ran out the door without closing it. The last thing she saw was his pale face and mournful eyes.

Could he really have that bad a stomach ache after only a few cookies? Maybe his grandfather had let him have treats while they were out. Jacquie felt bad for the boy but she was positive he'd improve by tonight. Christmas Eve! She was finally beginning to get the holiday feeling.

Jacquie pulled into the ranch yard as the sun was beginning its afternoon descent. It hadn't warmed up the desert any, or dispelled the heavy clouds that didn't seem to want to cross over the mountains. They hung in the sky, heavy and gray, a contrast to its blue. The radio weather forecast had predicted rain in scattered locales for northern Arizona but not here, which was fine with her. The dusting of snow on the Dragoons might even stick around for another day.

She reached onto the seat next to her for a rectangular package, wishing she could unwrap it for a final look. She had finally found something to give Choya — a hand-tooled belt of supple dark leather with real silver, hand-hammered conchos. Jacquie had spotted it in a Tombstone store she'd never been into, on the top shelf in a glass case. Quickly, she'd checked her balance on an ATM before she'd even asked the price, hoping and praying her father had put some money into her account for Christmas. He hadn't said he would and her pride had kept from asking — but her daughterly instincts told her that he might have done it all the same. She was overjoyed to find out that she was right.

The belt was in a flat presentation box that was half its length. Wrapped, it wasn't easy to guess what was inside. But she was glad she'd been able to afford something really nice that didn't look last-minute at all.

Jacquie got out and crossed the ranch yard, not seeing the red glow of Sam's favorite lamp. She wondered what she would do if he hadn't started supper yet. Even if there was a Christmas turkey or ham in the freezer, she didn't have time to thaw it.

Which left the menu choices to hamburgers or chicken, both of which Robbie loved. She had to assume his tummyache was gone. Jacquie shed her jacket and breezed into the kitchen, hearing Sam moving about in there from the hall.

"I got something really nice for Choya," she announced, waving the wrapped package at the older man. "Is he here?"

"Yup. He never did leave. But he's still in the barn," Sam reported. "I told him he could use your cookie dough for chinkin' if he had to."

"You didn't," she said with mock indignation.

Sam chuckled and shook his head. "I wrapped it up and put it back in the fridge. Choya took a bunch of them cookies out to the barn. To keep up his strength, he said."

"Oh, good. I guess I should go out and say hello."

Sam bent down to open the oven door and a heavenly smell of baking ham wafted out.

"Where did that come from?" she asked, distracted by the sight — and the size — of it. "Not the freezer."

"Hell no. This is country ham — the real thing, smoked right. Garth's son lives in Virginia and air-ships him two every Christmas. So he gave me one. I set it aside in the hall but you were rushing around and then you dashed out."

"Wow. We are going to have a delicious dinner and I didn't have to do a thing."

Sam basted the ham with its juices, using a long spoon, and then plastered brown sugar mixed with spices over the glossy surface. Straightening up with an effort, he closed the oven door again and adjusted the heat. "Won't be too long from now," he declared. "An hour, mebbe."

"I'll go ahead and make a salad."

"I can do that," Sam volunteered. "You go put your feet up."

Jacquie didn't want to argue with that pleasant scenario and headed for her bedroom, then decided to double back and put Choya's present under the tree. There were a few others underneath it that had been placed there in her absence. She bent down and investigated. There was a strangely shaped one from Robbie to her, wrapped and double-wrapped with a lot of tape, and a soft, not very thick present from Sam, that was wrapped in a new bandanna and tied with thin cotton rope in a cowboy hitch.

Jacquie ran a hand over the gift from Robbie, unable even to take a guess as to what it was. But she remembered Choya saying that Robbie was making something for her — tomorrow morning, all would be revealed. Glancing toward the kitchen, where Sam still was, she held the bandanna-wrapped present and guessed gloves. Feeling a little childish, she put it back and added hers.

She backed out and stood up, brushing pine needles from her knees.

"How'd you make out?" a deep voice asked.

Jacquie turned to see Choya standing in the doorway, his hands in the pockets of his jeans. He surveyed her with lazy amusement. She looked and listened for Robbie, heard nothing, and went to him, slipping her arms around his waist. "Looks interesting," she said pertly. "I got you something very nice."

"Well, thank you. I haven't wrapped yours yet."

"There's extra paper in my room."

"I thought I was supposed to stay out of there," he teased her.

Jacquie was enjoying being so close to him, stretching up on tiptoe to rub her cheek against his. "That's right," she whispered in his ear. "But we can always improvise."

"Hmm. That won't do." He pulled her tightly to him. "Things are going to change, Jacquie."

"When?" she asked, daring him with her eyes.

"Soon. Very soon."

She stayed in his embrace for several more minutes and they made the most of the time they had to be alone.

Then Sam called from the kitchen, discreet enough to stay there until someone answered. Jacquie broke away from the sensual heat of Choya's body, but still held his hand. "What is it?"

"I need someone to heave this ham up and out of the oven," he answered when they both came into the kitchen. "I think the glaze might be turning black. I want to add some water to the pan and —"

"And put out the fire?" Jacquie asked sweetly.

"It ain't that bad," Sam said. "Not yet, anyway."

Choya took over and she watched, waving away the faint haze in the air and trying not to cough. "Smells good," she said diplomatically.

"Robbie oughta come down here and taste this," Choya said. "Some of it is already well-done. He loves ham."

"Is his stomach ache better?" Jacquie asked Sam.

"I don't rightly know. Haven't seen him since I told him to go lie down."

"I'll get him. Probably no worse than that case of sniffles." Choya straightened and tossed the pot holders onto the kitchen table. They landed on Jacquie's open laptop and skidded across the keys. "Sorry. Didn't mean to do that."

"I'll take care of it," Jacquie said.

The screen flickered to life as Choya left the kitchen. Jacquie frowned, annoyed at her carelessness at leaving it on the table in the first place. "That shouldn't be there." She went over to it just as Choya came down the stairs, more quickly than he'd gone up.

"He isn't in his room."

The other two turned to him, picking up on the worry in his voice. "He must be around here somewhere," Sam said. "It's freezing out. He wouldn't just run off."

Jacquie looked down at her laptop screen and saw the e-mail she'd left pulled up. She'd forgotten all about it. With a sinking heart, she reread the information she'd given to Tammy's friend. It was to the point with no explanations. A move-to-Tucson date. The amount of rent she could afford. Even her thank-you for the unexpected help.

He wouldn't have deliberately snooped, not after the brief confrontation they'd had over the downloaded game. Robbie was fundamentally a good kid who was afraid of doing wrong. He must have touched a key or bumped against the laptop's shell when he'd reached for a cookie. He had to have seen the e-mail — and misinterpreted it to mean that she was leaving again. For good.

"Oh my God," she said, her voice breaking with fear. "He might have done just that. And it's my fault."

Choya's intent gaze narrowed on her stricken face. "What the hell are you talking about?"

CHAPTER 17

He cut her explanation short, racing out to check the barn, the stalls and even Robbie's hiding place for treasures. Jacquie concentrated on the house, checking every corner and closet where a boy could hide. They found no trace of Robbie. Choya came back at a run to where Sam stood in the open doorway, waiting for him with Jacquie clattering down the stairs. "He's not inside," she called to Choya.

"His jacket ain't here," the old man said grimly. "At least he's got that. It's damn cold and it's only gonna get colder."

Choya brushed past him to grab his own jacket. "I'm calling the sheriff. We need help." He flipped open his cell and placed the call, talking rapidly. "Gil — Choya here. Listen, we have an emergency. Robbie got upset about something and took off. No, I don't know how long he's been gone or which way he went. Can you —" He stopped talking to listen as Sam and Jacquie watched him intently.

She slid on her jacket too, finding the car keys in one pocket, watching his face anxiously.

"Okay. Will do," Choya said abruptly. He turned to her and his waiting father. "They're sending a couple of cars but they're twenty miles away. He suggested you and I stick to the same road and start searching but in opposite directions. Slowly. Use your high beams. Look hard. There's a lot of ground to cover and it's getting dark."

Sam nodded, tension in his gaunt frame. The knuckles around the head of his cane tightened as he thumped it on the floor, heading for the old landline in the study. "I'll stay by this phone. Either of you see anything or find him, call in," he said.

Choya jabbed at the keypad on his phone and Jacquie was startled when hers rang in her other pocket. "Why are you —" she began.

"I'm forwarding you the sheriff's personal number. I know you don't have it," he snapped. "Gil Levi is county, not local. We need that kind of reach."

They scrambled out the door, running toward their respective vehicles. Choya paused for only a second to look at the sky.

The heavy clouds had moved closer. He swore at the sky, a vicious oath that shocked her.

"If it rains" — he broke off and she stared at him mutely — "we could get a flash flood. No telling where it would happen."

"But the clouds aren't that close," she pointed out in a small voice.

"Didn't I explain this to you?" The question was laced with anger. "It could be pouring miles away and not rain here at all. But dry land like this doesn't soak up floodwater. It channels it."

Choya reached into the back of the jeep and found a flashlight, tossing it at her. Jacquie barely caught it, wincing when it hit her hand.

"Get going." He started the jeep and roared away, turning left and north in less than a minute. She went south only seconds after that.

The road was empty. That was nothing new but now it seemed haunted. The heavy clouds really were closer, edged with drifting mist that stole over the desert and trapped the bright light of her high beams, bouncing it back toward her. Alarmed by the low visibility, Jacquie crept along, her gaze sweeping from one side of the road to the other, looking for the smallest possible clue.

A broken branch. An overturned rock. Anything. The sameness and spareness of the desert landscape ought to make it somewhat easier to spot things like that, but the mist didn't help.

She saw nothing. How far could he have gone on foot? Guilt racked her and she forced her mind to ignore it. She needed to stay calm.

The slowly moving car went over a low, almost imperceptible rise in the road that barely registered with her until she had gone another half mile. Then she remembered what it was. The rise covered a culvert. Choya had gone over it at top speed on one of their drives to town, just to give her a bump.

She drove onto the shoulder, turning the car around, hearing the rocks crunch under her tires. Then she headed back the way she'd come at the same agonizingly slow pace, still looking carefully to each side before she felt the subtle rise in the road and pulled over.

Jacquie grabbed the flashlight and put her cell phone into a front pocket where she could grab it easily. Before she got out, she switched on the flashlight and opened the window to follow its powerful beam with her eyes, letting it sweep over the area directly in front of her.

Another pair of eyes, wild ones, gleamed back from a few feet away and disappeared just as suddenly. She sucked in a breath, fighting an uncanny feeling that the mist would swallow her voice if she called Robbie's name, just as it swallowed her high beams, but she did it anyway.

"Robbie! Robbie, answer me! Are you here? Robbie!"

Her voice died away but not before she heard a faint, very faint scuffle. Where it was coming from, she didn't know. She strained to listen. The surrounding darkness hid critters that hunted at night. But what she'd heard wasn't an animal noise. Newly awakened instinct told her that much.

She left the engine running and the lights on, pushing the emergency blinker. Its steady tick was not reassuring. She got out and closed the door quietly.

Jacquie stepped carefully to the edge, realizing that the culvert was directly beneath her. She would need to move to the side and scramble down from there to see into it. The faint scuffling sound came again. "Robbie, please answer me if you're there," she said softly.

Then she cursed her own stupidity. He could be hurt, unable to answer. She moved quickly, stooping and twisting her body to get down to ground level, praying she wouldn't get hurt herself. Jacquie jumped the last several inches, landing in the dust of a dry wash, choking as the fine particles rose around her. She coughed and moved toward the culvert, not seeing footprints. But then, he could have gone in from the other side.

She pulled her cell phone from her pocket, intending to call Choya to let him know that she'd stopped on the road. But it slipped from her fingers when she fumbled to flip it open and disappeared. Her flashlight beam didn't pick up the gleam of metal or a glowing screen. She swore. The phone was as good as gone, and she wasn't going to look for it.

She pointed the beam into the concrete cavern — it was longer and wider than she'd thought, with a jumble of dry pebbles and white sticks down its center. She realized those were bones. Animals brought their kills here and gnawed the flesh in solitude. She pointed the flashlight right down the middle and toward the walls — and then she saw him.

Robbie cowered at the far end, pressing

himself against the curved wall of the culvert. Jacquie realized that he couldn't see her behind the flashlight beam. In the echoing culvert, perhaps he hadn't recognized her voice either.

"Oh my God — it's you." She bent to go toward him, not able to stand up. "Come with me, honey. No one's mad at you. We just want to get you home. The car's waiting."

His face was grimy and she knew he'd been crying here in the dark. "Let's go," she insisted gently, reaching out. He slipped his hand into hers, and she felt the grit on his palm. He must have crawled in here for shelter when dark fell, going on hands and knees over the rocks and small bones, not realizing at first that he could stand up in the confined space.

She stayed bent, leading him back to where she'd come in. A sound began — at first she thought it was their footsteps, nothing more. Then she realized the rocks were rattling, swept forward by water that seeped into her shoes. Robbie didn't seem to notice it — the soles of his sneakers were thick and there was less than an inch of water by her frightened guess.

In seconds it got higher. Two inches. Then three.

Jacquie scooped him up under her arm and sloshed on at a run, going as fast as she could, toward the other end of the culvert. A light blazed over the round walls. Not hers. Someone was waiting there. The rocks rattled and she stumbled in water over her ankles that rushed on.

They were out — she didn't have time to straighten before she was half-shoved and half-dragged out of danger. Choya had them both in his strong grip and pulled them to safety.

Jacquie broke away, taking heaving breaths that made her throat raw. Disoriented, she stared at the nearly silent flood that gushed from the culvert. In seconds it had risen to just under the top of the concrete and spread far and wide out over the wash. She turned her face to the sky, expecting pelting rain and finding only the chilly mist. Feeling sick to her stomach, she used the fender of her SUV to pull herself up and stand unsteadily. Choya's jeep was on the other side of the road, parked with the engine running and the lights on. He held his son, cradling the boy's head in one large hand, soothing him.

"You're okay. Shh. You're okay," he repeated in a whisper.

Robbie hid his face in his dad's jacket for

a moment. Then he lifted it and looked around, peering into the misty darkness. "Where's Jacquie? She found me."

"I figured that." Choya nodded to her to come closer. "I tried to call her. When I didn't get an answer, I drove the way she'd gone. And here you both were, safe and sound."

Robbie clung to his father with one arm but reached out a hand to her. "I was scared — that you were going to leave again."

"I'm not," Jacquie assured. "I think I know what happened" — she broke off at Choya's warning look — "maybe I don't. But I'm not going anywhere."

"Never mind that," Choya said quietly. "There's a lot to talk about, but we're not going to do it here. Let's get home," he said to Robbie when the boy murmured in protest. He turned to cross the road to his jeep but Robbie shook his head.

"I want to ride with Jacquie," he insisted.

Choya almost said something, but then bit back the words. She was shaking, suddenly feeling the effects of her narrow escape. The torrent of water had slowed, as if a faucet had been turned on full blast and then shut off little by little. She peered out into the mist, then noticed bright lights in a row, haloed by the mist, coming closer. The deputies had found them.

It turned out to be one deputy. The car ground over the rocky shoulder to a full stop, and a young officer scrambled out. "You all okay? I just radioed in that I thought I found you — do we need an ambulance out here?"

Choya looked at Jacquie and lifted Robbie up to hand him to her. "I don't think so. He didn't break anything. But I'm not so sure she's ready to drive."

"I'm okay," she said, rallying. The little boy in her arms nestled against her. She bit her lip to keep from crying. "Just give me another minute or two." Exhausted, she leaned against her car, still holding him.

The deputy turned his head and looked out at the wash. Pebbles still rattled in the mud, but the floodwater had spread out over an area too vast to see in the headlights. He gave a low whistle. "Look at that. We got reports of others tonight, but nothing that big."

Jacquie shook her head at him and put a hand over Robbie's ear — the one that wasn't pressed against her.

"Tell you what," the young officer said. "I'll follow you all home, make sure you get there okay. Just let me radio in that I found you in good shape and we'll go." He walked over to Jacquie to look her over and patted Robbie on the back. "Glad you're all right, pal. You're awful young to be out on your own at night."

"I went for a walk," Robbie mumbled. "Then I forgot to go home."

The deputy nodded as though he'd heard similar stories from other lost kids. "Well," he said kindly, "your mom and dad can talk to you about that later."

"I'm not his —" She didn't finish the sentence, because the deputy turned to respond to a sudden squawk on the police radio, going back to his car. Jacquie became aware of the way Choya was looking at her. Jacquie didn't quite know what to make of the expression in his eyes but one thing was for sure, he'd never looked at her like that before. Respect and admiration mixed with love — she blew out a breath and turned her head to the side, overwhelmed.

Robbie buried his face in her neck. "I love you, Jacquie," he whispered.

"I love you too, sweetie," she answered with a catch in her voice. "And everything's going to be all right. Let's go home. Your gramps is waiting. Choya, did you call him?"

He nodded impassively, standing there and still looking at them in the same way. She told herself to get a grip on her emotions and even managed to give him a small smile.

Robbie gave a huge sigh. "Did I ruin Christmas?"

"No," she said firmly. "The tree's right there and so are the presents under it and we can set out cookies for Santa before you go to bed."

"I don't want to be alone. I didn't like being way out here." He heaved a wrenching sigh and added, "I'm sorry I ran away. I'm really sorry."

"We know you are," Choya said.

She struggled to get him into a more comfortable position. "You don't have to be alone tonight. We'll figure something out. And don't worry. We're closer to home than you think."

Choya came over to lift his son from her arms and get him settled in the front seat of her SUV. Jacquie went around to her side and got in, rolling down the window. She let Choya swing out and lead the way. The deputy followed her.

The mist didn't lift. They drove just as slowly. The young officer honked as they turned off on the track that led to the ranch house, and headed north on another call.

Jacquie saw a welcoming red glow ahead in a window of the house. Sam's lamp. A beacon in the darkness. As they pulled into the ranch yard, she saw him standing in the open doorway, silhouetted by the light from inside, patiently waiting.

The next hours passed by in a blur. No one went to bed. The sofa was where Jacquie wanted to be — she and Robbie snuggled up together, watching Choya build a fire. He'd explained to Robbie in a serious voice that Santa would see the smoke rising from the chimney and know to come in another way. They'd leave the front door unlocked.

Sam settled into his armchair, making small talk as he sipped at a glass of whiskey Choya had set on a folding table beside him. She suspected he needed one himself, for all his outward calm. But Choya had poured the shot for his father and capped the bottle, and that was that. The Barnett men really were tough — and they didn't seem to dwell on life's misfortunes. Robbie had been found and that was all that counted.

Of course he'd get a talking-to. But not now. Christmas wasn't going to be postponed. At some point the low male voices and the warmth of the little boy who dozed in her lap were too much for Jacquie. She drifted off to sleep.

Dawn was breaking when she opened her eyes and looked through her lashes at the uncurtained windows. She was covered up and stretched out on the sofa by herself. Groggy, she tried to focus on the colorful lights on the tree and noticed that someone had straightened the crooked star. It glowed brightest of all.

She rubbed her eyes, wondering where everyone was. Then she heard a clatter in the kitchen and smelled something good. Robbie appeared bearing a tray.

"Merry Christmas, Jacquie," he said proudly. "I made coffee and pancakes."

"It's all good, too," Sam added, following his grandson into the living room. "Me and Choya never did fall asleep, and neither did he. So we had a pancake breakfast in the wee hours and played poker at the kitchen table. I think we should do that every Christmas Eve from now on, don't you, Choya?"

"Sure. Why not?"

He entered last.

Jacquie sat up halfway, feeling stiff all over. She knew he was looking at her disheveled hair and flushed face. He didn't seem to mind either. His gaze moved over like she was the most beautiful woman on earth.

"Thanks, Robbie," she said as he set the tray across her lap. "This looks great." She took a knife and fork to the syrupy pancakes, and cut herself a bite, then sipped at the coffee. “Mmm. Wonderful. Did you open any presents yet?”

Robbie looked longingly at the pile, which had grown since she’d last seen it.

“Nope. Dad said we had to wait for you.” He looked hopefully at his father.

“Pick one,” Choya said.

Robbie scrambled off the sofa and dragged out the lumpy object swaddled in paper and tape. “For you,” he said with even more pride. “Me and Gramps made it, but it’s from me.”

“Oh my.” She set aside the tray and took it from him. “I was so curious about this one.”

“Go ahead and open it!” the little boy said eagerly.

Jacquie pulled at the paper and got it off with some difficulty. An object made of wood appeared, nailed together at odd angles with more enthusiasm than skill. She smiled at him and turned it around in her hand, belatedly realizing that it looked something like the ranch house. “It’s wonderful, Robbie. You made that?”

He nodded with pride.

“It’s our house.” She touched a finger to a bottle cap mounted on a wire. “And this is the satellite dish. Am I right?”

"Told you she'd know," he said, turning to his father. "Next I'm going to make you a barn. Gramps said he'd teach me to whittle, so I can make a whole herd of horses for it."

"That's great. Thank you both." She set the wooden house aside and reached out to hug him.

The rest of the presents got unwrapped with blinding speed. Robbie brought the crumpled wrapping paper over and piled it in Jacquie's lap. She played with a tag that had been taped to a plate of Christmas cookies left for Santa, absently wrapping its ribbon tie around her finger as she watched the happy frenzy.

Santa had done right by everyone. She looked down at the tag, noticing Robbie's handwriting on it.

To Santa With Love. And Thanks for Everything.

She smiled to herself. Santa might as well take credit for this much happiness — they couldn't have coordinated it all on their own.

The robe for Sam and the belt for Choya were both big hits, and so were the new additions to Robbie's collection of vehicles, including the biggest, which was a radio-operated, battery-powered patrol car with real roof lights and a noisy siren.

Choya, who'd bought it, set his foot in front of it on its fourth trip around the living room, making the little wheels spin. He picked it up and switched it off.

"Set that under the tree, son." Robbie nodded and obeyed.

The little boy felt around under the tree to make sure he hadn't missed anything, picking up a few scraps of discarded paper. "Dad — how come you didn't give Jacquie anything?"

"Ah — I haven't wrapped it yet."

Sam rose from his chair and told Robbie to get the tray. "Let's clean up in the kitchen. You don't want to leave a mess like that for Jacquie, do you?"

He and his grandson headed out, talking about whether Santa had come in the back door or the front. She heard the kitchen door click shut. Puzzled, she cast a look at Choya. "What's going on?"

He came over to the sofa and she pushed aside the blanket, folding up her legs to make room for him. "It doesn't need wrapping. I just wanted to be alone with you and I arranged that in advance with Sam." He clasped his hands behind his head and leaned back.

"Oh." She looked him up and down. Whatever the present was, it was small. Then she noticed the boxy bulge in his shirt pocket. "Is that it?"

Choya looked down and unclasped his hands. "Why, I believe it is. Hang on — I need to be on one knee to do this right."

Jacquie opened her mouth to say something, but he had taken out the little velvet box and was presenting it to her on bended knee in one swift motion.

"Be mine, Jacquie."

It wasn't a question. As usual, Choya was direct. She blinked at the closed box and then at him. His golden eyes hid nothing — his gaze was warm with joy and love. Slowly, she took it from him and opened it. The white satin lining cradled an engagement ring set with a diamond solitaire. It was simple — and spectacular. Jacquie gulped.

"Do you mean it?"

He nodded. "I love you and I want you, Jacquie. Every which way and forever. I know it's much too soon and it's crazy even to ask, but — marry me."

She looked at him, then at the ring, not knowing what to do or say next. Choya shook his head and smiled at her, taking the ring out and then taking her hand.

He slipped it on her finger and looked steadily at her. "Your turn. To say something, I mean."

It dawned on her that he was waiting for an answer and he wasn't going to go away or stop looking at her until he got one. A single beautiful word came to mind. "Yes!"

Chapter 18

Several minutes later, Robbie and Sam peeked in to make sure everything had gone according to plan. They admired the ring, but it was clear the little boy had something much more important on his mind. "Now can I show her, Dad? Please?"

"All right. It won't last much longer." He separated from her and rose to his feet, extending a hand to help her up.

"What won't last?" She was walking right behind him and bumped into him, laughing, when he stopped short by the front door.

"Boots on, girl. It's freezing cold out there."

"You mean I have to go outside?"

Choya reached down to get her boots and handed them to her by the side tabs. "You won't regret it."

"Jacquie, go and see!" Robbie said excitedly. His grandfather was barely able to hold on to the boy's hand. "You won't believe it!"

"Close your eyes," Choya commanded. His hand rested on the doorknob.

She obeyed without argument and let him lead her through the door as he opened it. Once they were outside, he put an arm around her shoulder and drew her close to his warmth.

"Now look," he said softly.

She did — and gasped. The drifting mist of the night before had left the desert plants sheathed in glittering ice. The landscape was a spun-glass wonderland, its dusty greens and grays magically transformed overnight.

"You're right," she whispered. "I don't believe it." She took a few steps to the cactus nearest to her, a prickly pear. Each and every one of its spines was covered in thin, clear ice.

"Just for you," he said.

"It's incredible." She smiled at him and came back to his side, an awed look in her eyes.

"The desert will always surprise you."

"Not as much as you did." She held up her left hand and the diamond ring he'd given her, the symbol of their love, caught the sun's fire.

"You're the one, Jacquie," he said, pulling her into his arms. "And you always will be."

ABOUT THE AUTHOR

Janet Dailey's first book was published in 1976. In the years since, she has written over one hundred more novels and become the third largest-selling female author in the world, with 325 million copies of her books sold in nineteen languages in ninety-eight countries. She is known for her strong, decisive characters, her extraordinary ability to recreate a time and a place, and her unerring courage to confront important, controversial issues in her stories. She lives in Branson, Missouri.

The employees of Thorndike Press hope you have enjoyed this Large Print book. All our Thorndike, Wheeler, and Kennebec Large Print titles are designed for easy reading, and all our books are made to last. Other Thorndike Press Large Print books are available at your library, through selected bookstores, or directly from us.

For information about titles, please call:
(800) 223-1244

or visit our Web site at:
http://gale.cengage.com/thorndike

To share your comments, please write:

Publisher
Thorndike Press
10 Water St., Suite 310
Waterville, ME 04901